A Publication Distributed by Heron Books

THE ASPERN PAPERS

THE TURN OF THE SCREW
and
THE SPOILS OF POYNTON

HENRY JAMES

1843–1916

THE ASPERN PAPERS

THE TURN OF THE SCREW
and
THE SPOILS OF POYNTON

BY

HENRY JAMES

DISTRIBUTED BY HERON BOOKS

CONTENTS

THE ASPERN PAPERS

I

I HAD taken Mrs. Prest into my confidence; without
her in truth I should have made but little advance,
for the fruitful idea in the whole business dropped
from her friendly lips. It was she who found the
short cut and loosed the Gordian knot. It is not
supposed easy for women to rise to the large free
view of anything, anything to be done; but they
sometimes throw off a bold conception—such as a
man wouldn't have risen to—with singular serenity.
" Simply make them take you in on the footing of a
lodger "—I don't think that unaided I should have
risen to that. I was beating about the bush, trying
to be ingenious, wondering by what combination of
arts I might become an acquaintance, when she
offered this happy suggestion that the way to become
an acquaintance was first to become an intimate.
Her actual knowledge of the Misses Bordereau was
scarcely larger than mine, and indeed I had brought
with me from England some definite facts that were
new to her. Their name had been mixed up ages
before with one of the greatest names of the century,
and they now lived obscurely in Venice, lived on very
small means, unvisited, unapproachable, in a sequestered and dilapidated old palace: this was the substance of my friend's impression of them. She herself
had been established in Venice some fifteen years and

had done a great deal of good there ; but the circle of
her benevolence had never embraced the two shy,
mysterious and, as was somehow supposed, scarcely
respectable Americans—they were believed to have
lost in their long exile all national quality, besides
being as their name implied of some remoter French
affiliation—who asked no favours and desired no
attention.   In the early years of her residence she
had made an attempt to see them, but this had been
successful only as regards the little one, as Mrs. Prest
called the niece ; though in fact I afterwards found
her the bigger of the two in inches.   She had heard
Miss Bordereau was ill and had a suspicion she was
in want, and had gone to the house to offer aid, so
that if there were suffering, American suffering in
particular, she shouldn't have it on her conscience.
The " little one " had received her in the great cold
tarnished Venetian *sala*, the central hall of the house,
paved with marble and roofed with dim cross-beams,
and hadn't even asked her to sit down.   This was
not encouraging for me, who wished to sit so fast,
and I remarked as much to Mrs. Prest.   She replied,
however, with profundity, " Ah, but there's all the
difference : I went to confer a favour and you'll go
to ask one.   If they're proud you'll be on the right
side."   And she offered to show me their house to
begin with—to row me thither in her gondola.   I
let her know I had already been to look at it half a
dozen times ; but I accepted her invitation, for it
charmed me to hover about the place.   I had made
my way to it the day after my arrival in Venice—it
had been described to me in advance by the friend
in England to whom I owed definite information as
to their possession of the papers—laying siege to it
with my eyes while I considered my plan of campaign.   Jeffrey Aspern had never been in it that I
knew of, but some note of his voice seemed to abide

there by a roundabout implication and in a " dying fall."

Mrs. Prest knew nothing about the papers, but was interested in my curiosity, as always in the joys and sorrows of her friends. As we went, however, in her gondola, gliding there under the sociable hood with the bright Venetian picture framed on either side by the movable window, I saw how my eagerness amused her and that she found my interest in my possible spoil a fine case of monomania. " One would think you expected from it the answer to the riddle of the universe," she said ; and I denied the impeachment only by replying that if I had to choose between that precious solution and a bundle of Jeffrey Aspern's letters I knew indeed which would appear to me the greater boon. She pretended to make light of his genius and I took no pains to defend him. One doesn't defend one's god : one's god is in himself a defence. Besides, to-day, after his long comparative obscuration, he hangs high in the heaven of our literature for all the world to see ; he's a part of the light by which we walk. The most I said was that he was no doubt not a woman's poet ; to which she rejoined aptly enough that he had been at least Miss Bordereau's. The strange thing had been for me to discover in England that she was still alive : it was as if I had been told Mrs. Siddons was, or Queen Caroline, or the famous Lady Hamilton, for it seemed to me that she belonged to a generation as extinct. " Why she must be tremendously old—at least a hundred," I had said ; but on coming to consider dates I saw it not strictly involved that she should have far exceeded the common span. None the less she was of venerable age and her relations with Jeffrey Aspern had occurred in her early womanhood. " That's her excuse," said Mrs. Prest half-sententiously and yet also somewhat as if she were ashamed of making

5

a speech so little in the real tone of Venice. As if a woman needed an excuse for having loved the divine poet ! He had been not only one of the most brilliant minds of his day — and in those years, when the century was young, there were, as every one knows, many—but one of the most genial men and one of the handsomest.

The niece, according to Mrs. Prest, was of minor antiquity, and the conjecture was risked that she was only a grand-niece. This was possible ; I had nothing but my share in the very limited knowledge of my English fellow worshipper John Cumnor, who had never seen the couple. The world, as I say, had recognised Jeffrey Aspern, but Cumnor and I had recognised him most. The multitude to-day flocked to his temple, but of that temple he and I regarded ourselves as the appointed ministers. We held, justly, as I think, that we had done more for his memory than any one else, and had done it simply by opening lights into his life. He had nothing to fear from us because he had nothing to fear from the truth, which alone at such a distance of time we could be interested in establishing. His early death had been the only dark spot, as it were, on his fame, unless the papers in Miss Bordereau's hands should perversely bring out others. There had been an impression about 1825 that he had " treated her badly," just as there had been an impression that he had " served," as the London populace says, several other ladies in the same masterful way. Each of these cases Cumnor and I had been able to investigate, and we had never failed to acquit him conscientiously of any grossness. I judged him perhaps more indulgently than my friend ; certainly, at any rate, it appeared to me that no man could have walked straighter in the given circumstances. These had been almost always diffi- cult and dangerous. Half the women of his time, to

6

speak liberally, had flung themselves at his head, and while the fury raged—the more that it was very catching—accidents, some of them grave, had not failed to occur. He was not a woman's poet, as I had said to Mrs. Prest, in the modern phase of his reputation ; but the situation had been different when the man's own voice was mingled with his song. That voice, by every testimony, was one of the most charming ever heard. " Orpheus and the Mænads ! " had been of course my foreseen judgement when first I turned over his correspondence. Almost all the Mænads were unreasonable and many of them unbearable ; it struck me that he had been kinder and more considerate than in his place — if I could imagine myself in any such box — I should have found the trick of.

It was certainly strange beyond all strangeness, and I shall not take up space with attempting to explain it, that whereas among all these other relations and in these other directions of research we had to deal with phantoms and dust, the mere echoes of echoes, the one living source of information that had lingered on into our time had been unheeded by us. Every one of Aspern's contemporaries had, according to our belief, passed away ; we had not been able to look into a single pair of eyes into which his had looked or to feel a transmitted contact in any aged hand that his had touched. Most dead of all did poor Miss Bordereau appear, and yet she alone had survived. We exhausted in the course of months our wonder that we had not found her out sooner, and the substance of our explanation was that she had kept so quiet. The poor lady on the whole had had reason for doing so. But it was a revelation to us that self-effacement on such a scale had been possible in the latter half of the nineteenth century—the age of newspapers and telegrams and photographs and interviewers. She had taken no great trouble for it either — hadn't hidden herself away in an undiscoverable hole, had boldly settled down in a city of exhibition. The one apparent secret of her safety had been that Venice contained so many much greater curiosities. And then accident had somehow favoured her, as was shown for example in the fact that Mrs. Prest had never happened to name her to me, though I had spent three weeks in Venice—under her nose, as it were — five years before. My friend indeed had not named her much to any one ; she appeared almost to have forgotten the fact of her continuance. Of course Mrs. Prest hadn't the nerves of an editor. It was meanwhile no explanation of the old woman's having eluded us to say that she lived abroad, for our researches had again and again taken us—not only by correspondence but by personal inquiry— to France, to Germany, to Italy, in which countries, not counting his important stay in England, so many of the too few years of Aspern's career had been spent. We were glad to think at least that in all our promulgations — some people now consider I believe that we have overdone them—we had only touched in passing and in the most discreet manner on Miss Bordereau's connexion. Oddly enough, even if we had had the material — and we had often wondered what could have become of it—this would have been the most difficult episode to handle.

The gondola stopped, the old palace was there ; it was a house of the class which in Venice carries even in extreme dilapidation the dignified name. " How charming ! It's grey and pink ! " my companion exclaimed ; and that is the most comprehensive description of it. It was not particularly old, only two or three centuries ; and it had an air not so much of decay as of quiet discouragement, as if it had rather missed its career. But its wide front, with a stone balcony from end to end of the *piano nobile* or most important floor, was architectural enough, with the aid of various pilasters and arches ; and the stucco with which in the intervals it had long ago been endued was rosy in the April afternoon. It overlooked a clean melancholy rather lonely canal, which had a narrow *riva* or convenient footway on either side. " I don't know why — there are no brick gables," said Mrs. Prest, " but this corner has seemed to me before more Dutch than Italian, more like Amsterdam than like Venice. It's eccentrically neat, for reasons of its own ; and though you may pass on foot scarcely any one ever thinks of doing so. It's as negative—considering *where* it is—as a Protestant Sunday. Perhaps the people are afraid of the Misses Bordereau. I daresay they have the reputation of witches."

I forget what answer I made to this—I was given up to two other reflexions. The first of these was that if the old lady lived in such a big and imposing house she couldn't be in any sort of misery and therefore wouldn't be tempted by a chance to let a couple of rooms. I expressed this fear to Mrs. Prest, who gave me a very straight answer. " If she didn't live in a big house how could it be a question of her having rooms to spare ? If she were not amply lodged you'd lack ground to approach her. Besides, a big house here, and especially in this *quartier perdu*, proves nothing at all : it's perfectly consistent with a state of penury. Dilapidated old palazzi, if you'll go out of the way for them, are to be had for five shillings a year. And as for the people who live in them—no, until you've explored Venice socially as much as I have, you can form no idea of their domestic desolation. They live on nothing, for they've nothing to live on." The other idea that had come into my head was connected with a high blank wall which appeared

9

to confine an expanse of ground on one side of the house. Blank I call it, but it was figured over with the patches that please a painter, repaired breaches, crumblings of plaster, extrusions of brick that had turned pink with time ; while a few thin trees, with the poles of certain rickety trellises, were visible over the top. The place was a garden and apparently attached to the house. I suddenly felt that so attached it gave me my pretext.

I sat looking out on all this with Mrs. Prest (it was covered with the golden glow of Venice) from the shade of our *felze*, and she asked me if I would go in then, while she waited for me, or come back another time. At first I couldn't decide—it was doubtless very weak of me. I wanted still to think I *might* get a footing, and was afraid to meet failure, for it would leave me, as I remarked to my companion, without another arrow for my bow. " Why not another ? " she inquired as I sat there hesitating and thinking it over ; and she wished to know why even now and before taking the trouble of becoming an inmate—which might be wretchedly uncomfortable after all, even if it succeeded—I hadn't the resource of simply offering them a sum of money down. In that way I might get what I wanted without bad nights.

" Dearest lady," I exclaimed, " excuse the impatience of my tone when I suggest that you must have forgotten the very fact—surely I communicated it to you—which threw me on your ingenuity. The old woman won't have her relics and tokens so much as spoken of ; they're personal, delicate, intimate, and she hasn't the feelings of the day, God bless her ! If I should sound that note first I should certainly spoil the game. I can arrive at my spoils only by putting her off her guard, and I can put her off her guard only by ingratiating diplomatic arts. Hypo-

crisy, duplicity are my only chance. I'm sorry for
it, but there's no baseness I wouldn't commit for
Jeffrey Aspern's sake. First I must take tea with her
—then tackle the main job." And I told over what
had happened to John Cumnor on his respectfully
writing to her. No notice whatever had been taken
of his first letter, and the second had been answered
very sharply, in six lines, by the niece. " Miss Bordereau requested her to say that she couldn't imagine
what he meant by troubling them. They had none
of Mr. Aspern's ' literary remains,' and if they *had*
had wouldn't have dreamed of showing them to
any one on any account whatever. She couldn't
imagine what he was talking about and begged he
would let her alone." I certainly didn't want to be
met that way.

" Well," said Mrs. Prest after a moment and all
provokingly, " perhaps they really haven't anything.
If they deny it flat how are you sure ? "

" John Cumnor's sure, and it would take me long
to tell you how his conviction, or his very strong
presumption—strong enough to stand against the old
lady's not unnatural fib—has built itself up. Besides, he makes much of the internal evidence of the
niece's letter."

" The internal evidence ? "

" Her calling him ' Mr. Aspern.' "

" I don't see what that proves."

" It proves familiarity, and familiarity implies the
possession of mementoes, of tangible objects. I can't
tell you how that ' Mr.' affects me—how it bridges
over the gulf of time and brings our hero near to me—
nor what an edge it gives to my desire to see Juliana.
You don't say ' Mr.' Shakespeare."

" Would I, any more, if I had a box full of
his letters ? "

" Yes, if he had been your lover and some one

wanted them." And I added that John Cumnor was so convinced, and so all the more convinced by Miss Bordereau's tone, that he would have come himself to Venice on the undertaking were it not for the obstacle of his having, for any confidence, to disprove his identity with the person who had written to them, which the old ladies would be sure to suspect in spite of dissimulation and a change of name. If they were to ask him point-blank if he were not their snubbed correspondent it would be too awkward for him to lie ; whereas I was fortunately not tied in that way. I was a fresh hand—I could protest without lying.

" But you'll have to take a false name," said Mrs. Prest. " Juliana lives out of the world as much as it is possible to live, but she has none the less probably heard of Mr. Aspern's editors. She perhaps possesses what you've published."

" I've thought of that," I returned ; and I drew out of my pocket-book a visiting-card neatly engraved with a well-chosen *nom de guerre*.

" You're very extravagant—it adds to your immorality. You might have done it in pencil or ink," said my companion.

" This looks more genuine."

" Certainly you've the courage of your curiosity. But it will be awkward about your letters ; they won't come to you in that mask."

" My banker will take them in and I shall go every day to get them. It will give me a little walk."

" Shall you depend all on that ? " asked Mrs. Prest. " Aren't you coming to see me ? "

" Oh you'll have left Venice for the hot months long before there are any results. I'm prepared to roast all summer—as well as through the long hereafter perhaps you'll say ! Meanwhile John Cumnor will bombard me with letters addressed, in my feigned name, to the care of the padrona."

"She'll recognise his hand," my companion suggested.

"On the envelope he can disguise it."

"Well, you're a precious pair! Doesn't it occur to you that even if you're able to say you're not Mr. Cumnor in person they may still suspect you of being his emissary?"

"Certainly, and I see only one way to parry that."

"And what may that be?"

I hesitated a moment. "To make love to the niece."

"Ah," cried my friend, "wait till you see her!"

II

" I MUST work the garden—I must work the garden,"
I said to myself five minutes later and while I waited,
upstairs, in the long, dusky sala, where the bare
scagliola floor gleamed vaguely in a chink of the
closed shutters. The place was impressive, yet looked
somehow cold and cautious. Mrs. Prest had floated
away, giving me a rendezvous at the end of half an
hour by some neighbouring water-steps ; and I had
been let into the house, after pulling the rusty bell-
wire, by a small red-headed and white-faced maid-
servant, who was very young and not ugly and wore
clicking pattens and a shawl in the fashion of a hood.
She had not contented herself with opening the door
from above by the usual arrangement of a creaking
pulley, though she had looked down at me first from
an upper window, dropping the cautious challenge
which in Italy precedes the act of admission. I was
irritated as a general thing by this survival of medi-
eval manners, though as so fond, if yet so special, an
antiquarian I suppose I ought to have liked it ; but,
with my resolve to be genial from the threshold at
any price, I took my false card out of my pocket and
held it up to her, smiling as if it were a magic token.
It had the effect of one indeed, for it brought her, as I
say, all the way down. I begged her to hand it to
her mistress, having first written on it in Italian the
words : " Could you very kindly see a gentleman,

14

a travelling American, for a moment ? " The little maid wasn't hostile—even that was perhaps something gained. She coloured, she smiled and looked both frightened and pleased. I could see that my arrival was a great affair, that visits in such a house were rare and that she was a person who would have liked a bustling place. When she pushed forward the heavy door behind me I felt my foot in the citadel and promised myself ever so firmly to keep it there. She pattered across the damp stony lower hall and I followed her up the high staircase—stonier still, as it seemed—without an invitation. I think she had meant I should wait for her below, but such was not my idea, and I took up my station in the sala. She flitted, at the far end of it, into impenetrable regions, and I looked at the place with my heart beating as I had known it to do in dentists' parlours. It had a gloomy grandeur, but owed its character almost all to its noble shape and to the fine architectural doors, as high as those of grand frontages, which, leading into the various rooms, repeated themselves on either side at intervals. They were surmounted with old faded painted escutcheons, and here and there in the spaces between them hung brown pictures, which I noted as speciously bad, in battered and tarnished frames that were yet more desirable than the canvases themselves. With the exception of several straw-bottomed chairs that kept their backs to the wall the grand obscure vista contained little else to minister to effect. It was evidently never used save as a passage, and scantly even as that. I may add that by the time the door through which the maid-servant had escaped opened again my eyes had grown used to the want of light.

I hadn't meanwhile meant by my private ejaculation that I must myself cultivate the soil of the tangled enclosure which lay beneath the windows, but the lady who came toward me from the distance over the hard shining floor might have supposed as much from the way in which, as I went rapidly to meet her, I exclaimed, taking care to speak Italian : " The garden, the garden — do me the pleasure to tell me if it's yours ! "

She stopped short, looking at me with wonder ; and then, " Nothing here is mine," she answered in English, coldly and sadly.

" Oh you're English ; how delightful ! " I ingenuously cried. " But surely the garden belongs to the house ? "

" Yes, but the house doesn't belong to me." She was a long lean pale person, habited apparently in a dull-coloured dressing-gown, and she spoke very simply and mildly. She didn't ask me to sit down, any more than years before—if she were the niece— she had asked Mrs. Prest, and we stood face to face in the empty pompous hall.

" Well then, would you kindly tell me to whom I must address myself ? I'm afraid you'll think me horribly intrusive, but you know I *must* have a garden—upon my honour I must ! "

Her face was not young, but it was candid ; it was not fresh, but it was clear. She had large eyes which were not bright, and a great deal of hair which was not " dressed," and long fine hands which were— possibly—not clean. She clasped these members almost convulsively as, with a confused alarmed look, she broke out : " Oh don't take it away from us ; we like it ourselves ! "

" You have the use of it then ? "

" Oh yes. If it wasn't for that——! " And she gave a wan vague smile.

" Isn't it a luxury, precisely ? That's why, intending to be in Venice some weeks, possibly all summer, and having some literary work, some reading and writing to do, so that I must be quiet and yet if possible a great deal in the open air—that's why I've felt a garden to be really indispensable. I appeal to your own experience," I went on with as sociable a smile as I could risk. " Now can't I look at yours ? "

" I don't know, I don't understand," the poor woman murmured, planted there and letting her weak wonder deal—helplessly enough, as I felt—with my strangeness.

" I mean only from one of those windows—such grand ones as you have here—if you'll let me open the shutters." And I walked toward the back of the house. When I had advanced halfway I stopped and waited as in the belief she would accompany me. I had been of necessity quite abrupt, but I strove at the same time to give her the impression of extreme courtesy. " I've looked at furnished rooms all over the place, and it seems impossible to find any with a garden attached. Naturally in a place like Venice gardens are rare. It's absurd if you like, for a man, but I can't live without flowers."

" There are none to speak of down there." She came nearer, as if, though she mistrusted me, I had drawn her by an invisible thread. I went on again, and she continued as she followed me : " We've a few, but they're very common. It costs too much to cultivate them ; one has to have a man."

" Why shouldn't I be the man ? " I asked. " I'll work without wages ; or rather I'll put in a gardener. You shall have the sweetest flowers in Venice."

She protested against this with a small quaver of sound that might have been at the same time a gush of rapture for my free sketch. Then she gasped : " We don't know you—we don't know you."

" You know me as much as I know you ; or rather much more, because you know my name. And if you're English I'm almost a countryman."

" We're not English," said my companion, watching me in practical submission while I threw open the shutters of one of the divisions of the wide high window.

" You speak the language so beautifully : might I ask what you are ? " Seen from above the garden was in truth shabby, yet I felt at a glance that it had great capabilities. She made no rejoinder, she was so lost in her blankness and gentleness, and I exclaimed : " You don't mean to say you're also by chance American ? "

" I don't know. We used to be."

" Used to be ? Surely you haven't changed ? "

" It's so many years ago. We don't seem to be anything now."

" So many years that you've been living here ? Well, I don't wonder at that ; it's a grand old house. I suppose you all use the garden," I went on, " but I assure you I shouldn't be in your way. I'd be very quiet and stay quite in one corner."

" We all use it ? " she repeated after me vaguely, not coming close to the window but looking at my shoes. She appeared to think me capable of throwing her out.

" I mean all your family—as many as you are."

" There's only one other than me. She's very old. She never goes down."

I feel again my thrill at this close identification of Juliana ; in spite of which, however, I kept my head. " Only one other in all this great house ! " I feigned to be not only amazed but almost scandalised. " Dear lady, you must have space then to spare ! "

" To spare ? " she repeated—almost as for the rich unwonted joy to her of spoken words.

" Why you surely don't live (two quiet women— I see *you* are quiet, at any rate) in fifty rooms ! " Then with a burst of hope and cheer I put the question straight. " Couldn't you for a good rent *let* me two or three ? That would set me up ! "

I had now struck the note that translated my purpose, and I needn't reproduce the whole of the tune I played. I ended by making my entertainer believe me an undesigning person, though of course I didn't even attempt to persuade her I was not an eccentric one. I repeated that I had studies to pursue ; that I wanted quiet ; that I delighted in a garden and had vainly sought one up and down the city : that I would undertake that before another month was over the dear old house should be smothered in flowers. I think it was the flowers that won my suit, for I afterwards found that Miss Tina — for such the name of this high tremulous spinster proved somewhat incongruously to be— had an insatiable appetite for them. When I speak of my suit as won I mean that before I left her she had promised me she would refer the question to her aunt. I invited information as to who her aunt might be and she answered, " Why Miss Bordereau ! " with an air of surprise, as if I might have been expected to know. There were contradictions like this in Miss Tina which, as I observed later, contributed to make her rather pleasingly incalculable and interesting. It was the study of the two ladies to live so that the world shouldn't talk of them or touch them, and yet they had never altogether accepted the idea that it didn't hear of them. In Miss Tina at any rate a grateful susceptibility to human contact had not died out, and contact of a limited order there would be if I should come to live in the house.

" We've never done anything of the sort ; we've never had a lodger or any kind of inmate." So much as this she made a point of saying to me. " We're very poor, we live very badly—almost on nothing. The rooms are very bare—those you might take ;

they've nothing at all in them. I don't know how you'd sleep, how you'd eat."

"With your permission I could easily put in a bed and a few tables and chairs. *C'est la moindre des choses* and the affair of an hour or two. I know a little man from whom I can hire for a trifle what I should so briefly want, what I should use ; my gondolier can bring the things round in his boat. Of course in this great house you must have a second kitchen, and my servant, who's a wonderfully handy fellow "—this personage was an evocation of the moment—" can easily cook me a chop there. My tastes and habits are of the simplest : I live on flowers ! " And then I ventured to add that if they were very poor it was all the more reason they should let their rooms. They were bad economists—I had never heard of such a waste of material.

I saw in a moment my good lady had never before been spoken to in any such fashion—with a humorous firmness that didn't exclude sympathy, that was quite founded on it. She might easily have told me that my sympathy was impertinent, but this by good fortune didn't occur to her. I left her with the understanding that she would submit the question to her aunt and that I might come back the next day for their decision.

"The aunt will refuse ; she'll think the whole proceeding very *louche* ! " Mrs. Prest declared shortly after this, when I had resumed my place in her gondola. She had put the idea into my head and now—so little are women to be counted on—she appeared to take a despondent view of it. Her pessimism provoked me and I pretended to have the best hopes ; I went so far as to boast of a distinct prevision of success. Upon this Mrs. Prest broke out : " Oh I see what's in your head ! You fancy you've made such an impression in five minutes that she's dying for you to come and can be depended on to bring the old one round. If you do get in you'll count it as a triumph."

I did count it as a triumph, but only for the commentator—in the last analysis—not for the man, who had not the tradition of personal conquest. When I went back on the morrow the little maid-servant conducted me straight through the long sala—it opened there as before in large perspective and was lighter now, which I thought a good omen—into the apartment from which the recipient of my former visit had emerged on that occasion. It was a spacious shabby parlour with a fine old painted ceiling under which a strange figure sat alone at one of the windows. They come back to me now almost with the palpitation they caused, the successive states. marking my consciousness that as the door of the room closed behind me I was really face to face with the Juliana of some of Aspern's most exquisite and most renowned lyrics. I grew used to her afterwards, though never completely ; but as she sat there before me my heart beat as fast as if the miracle of resurrection had taken place for my benefit. Her presence seemed somehow to contain and express his own, and I felt nearer to him at that first moment of seeing her than I ever had been before or ever have been since. Yes, I remember my emotions in their order, even including a curious little tremor that took me when I saw the niece not to be there. With her, the day before, I had become sufficiently familiar, but it almost exceeded my courage—much as I had longed for the event—to be left alone with so terrible a relic as the aunt. She was too strange, too literally resurgent. Then came a check from the perception that we weren't really face to face, inasmuch as she had over her eyes a horrible green shade which served for her almost as a mask. I believed for the instant that she had put it on expressly, so that from underneath it she might take me all in without my getting at herself. At the same time it created a presumption of some ghastly death's-head lurking behind it. The divine Juliana as a grinning skull—the vision hung there until it passed. Then it came to me that she *was* tremendously old—so old that death might take her at any moment, before I should have time to compass my end. The next thought was a correction to that ; it lighted up the situation. She would die next week, she would die to-morrow —then I could pounce on her possessions and ransack her drawers. Meanwhile she sat there neither moving nor speaking. She was very small and shrunken, bent forward with her hands in her lap. She was dressed in black and her head was wrapped in a piece of old black lace which showed no hair.

My emotion keeping me silent she spoke first, and the remark she made was exactly the most unexpected.

III

" Our house is very far from the centre, but the little canal is very *comme il faut*."

" It's the sweetest corner of Venice and I can imagine nothing more charming," I hastened to reply. The old lady's voice was very thin and weak, but it had an agreeable, cultivated murmur and there was wonder in the thought that that individual note had been in Jeffrey Aspern's ear.

" Please to sit down there. I hear very well," she said quietly, as if perhaps I had been shouting ; and the chair she pointed to was at a certain distance. I took possession of it, assuring her I was perfectly aware of my intrusion and of my not having been properly introduced, and that I could but throw myself on her indulgence. Perhaps the other lady, the one I had had the honour of seeing the day before, would have explained to her about the garden. That was literally what had given me courage to take a step so unconventional. I had fallen in love at sight with the whole place—she herself was probably so used to it that she didn't know the impression it was capable of making on a stranger—and I had felt it really a case to risk something. Was her own kindness in receiving me a sign that I was not wholly out in my calculation ? It would make me extremely happy to think so. I could give her my word of honour that I was a most respectable inoffensive

23

person and that as a co-tenant of the palace, so to speak, they would be barely conscious of my existence. I would conform to any regulations, any restrictions, if they would only let me enjoy the garden. Moreover I should be delighted to give her references, guarantees ; they would be of the very best, both in Venice and in England, as well as in America.

She listened to me in perfect stillness and I felt her look at me with great penetration, though I could see only the lower part of her bleached and shrivelled face. Independently of the refining process of old age it had a delicacy which once must have been great. She had been very fair, she had had a wonderful complexion. She was silent a little after I had ceased speaking ; then she began : " If you're so fond of a garden why don't you go to *terra firma*, where there are so many far better than this ? "

" Oh it's the combination ! " I answered, smiling ; and then with rather a flight of fancy : " It's the idea of a garden in the middle of the sea."

" This isn't the middle of the sea ; you can't so much as see the water."

I stared a moment, wondering if she wished to convict me of fraud. " Can't see the water ? Why, dear madam, I can come up to the very gate in my boat."

She appeared inconsequent, for she said vaguely in reply to this : " Yes, if you've got a boat. I haven't any ; it's many years since I've been in one of the *gondole*." She uttered these words as if they designed a curious far-away craft known to her only by hearsay.

" Let me assure you of the pleasure with which I would put mine at your service ! " I returned. I had scarcely said this, however, before I became aware that the speech was in questionable taste and might also do me the injury of making me appear too eager, too possessed of a hidden motive. But the old woman remained impenetrable and her attitude worried me by suggesting that she had a fuller vision of me than I had of her. She gave me no thanks for my somewhat extravagant offer, but remarked that the lady I had seen the day before was her niece ; she would presently come in. She had asked her to stay away a little on purpose—had had her reasons for seeing me first alone. She relapsed into silence and I turned over the fact of these unmentioned reasons and the question of what might come yet ; also that of whether I might venture on some judicious remark in praise of her companion. I went so far as to say I should be delighted to see our absent friend again : she had been so very patient with me, considering how odd she must have thought me—a declaration which drew from Miss Bordereau another of her whimsical speeches.

"She has very good manners ; I bred her up myself ! " I was on the point of saying that that accounted for the easy grace of the niece, but I arrested myself in time, and the next moment the old woman went on : " I don't care who you may be—I don't want to know : it signifies very little to-day." This had all the air of being a formula of dismissal, as if her next words would be that I might take myself off now that she had had the amusement of looking on the face of such a monster of indiscretion. Therefore I was all the more surprised when she added in her soft venerable quaver : " You may have as many rooms as you like—if you'll pay me a good deal of money."

I hesitated but an instant, long enough to measure what she meant in particular by this condition. First it struck me that she must have really a large sum in her mind ; then I reasoned quickly that her idea of a

25

large sum would probably not correspond to my own. My deliberation, I think, was not so visible as to diminish the promptitude with which I replied : " I will pay with pleasure and of course in advance whatever you may think it proper to ask me."

" Well then, a thousand francs a month," she said instantly, while her baffling green shade continued to cover her attitude.

The figure, as they say, was startling and my logic had been at fault. The sum she had mentioned was, by the Venetian measure of such matters, exceedingly large ; there was many an old palace in an out-of-the-way corner that I might on such terms have enjoyed the whole of by the year. But so far as my resources allowed I was prepared to spend money, and my decision was quickly taken. I would pay her with a smiling face what she asked, but in that case I would make it up by getting hold of my " spoils " for nothing. Moreover if she had asked five times as much I should have risen to the occasion, so odious would it have seemed to me to stand chaffering with Aspern's Juliana. It was queer enough to have a question of money with her at all. I assured her that her views perfectly met my own and that on the morrow I should have the pleasure of putting three months' rent into her hand. She received this announcement with apparent complacency and with no discoverable sense that after all it would become her to say that I ought to see the rooms first. This didn't occur to her, and indeed her serenity was mainly what I wanted. Our little agreement was just concluded when the door opened and the younger lady appeared on the threshold. As soon as Miss Bordereau saw her niece she cried out almost gaily : " He'll give three thousand — three thousand tomorrow ! "

Miss Tina stood still, her patient eyes turning

from one of us to the other ; then she brought out, scarcely above her breath : " Do you mean francs ? "

" Did you mean francs or dollars ? " the old woman asked of me at this.

" I think francs were what you said," I sturdily smiled.

" That's very good," said Miss Tina, as if she had felt how overreaching her own question might have looked.

" What do *you* know ? You're ignorant," Miss Bordereau remarked ; not with acerbity but with a strange soft coldness.

" Yes, of money — certainly of money ! " Miss Tina hastened to concede.

" I'm sure you've your own fine branches of knowledge," I took the liberty of saying genially. There was something painful to me, somehow, in the turn the conversation had taken, in the discussion of dollars and francs.

" She had a very good education when she was young. I looked into that myself," said Miss Bordereau. Then she added : " But she has learned nothing since."

" I've always been with *you*," Miss Tina rejoined very mildly, and of a certainty with no intention of an epigram.

" Yes, but for that——! " her aunt declared with more satirical force. She evidently meant that but for this her niece would never have got on at all ; the point of the observation, however, being lost on Miss Tina, though she blushed at hearing her history revealed to a stranger. Miss Bordereau went on, addressing herself to me : " And what time will you come to-morrow with the money ? "

" The sooner the better. If it suits you I'll come at noon."

" I'm always here, but I have my hours," said the

old woman as if her convenience were not to be taken for granted.

" You mean the times when you receive ? "

" I never receive. But I'll see you at noon, when you come with the money."

" Very good, I shall be punctual." To which I added : " May I shake hands with you on our contract ? " I thought there ought to be some little form ; it would make me really feel easier, for I was sure there would be no other. Besides, though Miss Bordereau couldn't to-day be called personally attractive and there was something even in her wasted antiquity that bade one stand at one's distance, I felt an irresistible desire to hold in my own for a moment the hand Jeffrey Aspern had pressed.

For a minute she made no answer, and I saw that my proposal failed to meet with her approbation. She indulged in no movement of withdrawal, which I half-expected ; she only said coldly : " I belong to a time when that was not the custom."

I felt rather snubbed but I exclaimed good-humouredly to Miss Tina, " Oh you'll do as well ! " I shook hands with her while she assented with a small flutter. " Yes, yes, to show it's all arranged ! "

" Shall you bring the money in gold ? " Miss Bordereau demanded as I was turning to the door.

I looked at her a moment. " Aren't you a little afraid, after all, of keeping such a sum as that in the house ? " It was not that I was annoyed at her avidity, but was truly struck with the disparity between such a treasure and such scanty means of guarding it.

" Whom should I be afraid of if I'm not afraid of you ? " she asked with her shrunken grimness.

" Ah well," I laughed, " I shall be in point of fact a protector and I'll bring gold if you prefer."

"Thank you," the old woman returned with dignity and with an inclination of her head which evidently signified my dismissal. I passed out of the room, thinking how hard it would be to circumvent her. As I stood in the sala again I saw that Miss Tina had followed me, and I supposed that as her aunt had neglected to suggest I should take a look at my quarters it was her purpose to repair the omission. But she made no such overture ; she only stood there with a dim, though not a languid smile, and with an effect of irresponsible incompetent youth almost comically at variance with the faded facts of her person. She was not infirm, like her aunt, but she struck me as more deeply futile, because her inefficiency was inward, which was not the case with Miss Bordereau's. I waited to see if she would offer to show me the rest of the house, but I didn't precipitate the question, inasmuch as my plan was from this moment to spend as much of my time as possible in her society. A minute indeed elapsed before I committed myself.

"I've had better fortune than I hoped. It was very kind of her to see me. Perhaps you said a good word for me."

"It was the idea of the money," said Miss Tina.

"And did you suggest that ? "

"I told her you'd perhaps pay largely."

"What made you think that ? "

"I told her I thought you were rich."

"And what put that into your head ? "

"I don't know ; the way you talked."

"Dear me, I must talk differently now," I returned. "I'm sorry to say it's not the case."

"Well," said Miss Tina, "I think that in Venice the *forestieri* in general often give a great deal for something that after all isn't much." She appeared to make this remark with a comforting intention, to wish to remind me that if I had been extravagant I wasn't foolishly singular. We walked together along the sala, and as I took its magnificent measure I observed that I was afraid it wouldn't form a part of my *quartiere*. Were my rooms by chance to be among those that opened into it ? " Not if you go above—to the second floor," she answered as if she had rather taken for granted I would know my proper place.

" And I infer that that's where your aunt would like me to be."

" She said your apartments ought to be very distinct."

" That certainly would be best." And I listened with respect while she told me that above I should be free to take whatever I might like ; that there was another staircase, but only from the floor on which we stood, and that to pass from it to the garden-level or to come up to my lodging I should have in effect to cross the great hall. This was an immense point gained ; I foresaw that it would constitute my whole leverage in my relations with the two ladies. When I asked Miss Tina how I was to manage at present to find my way up she replied with an access of that sociable shyness which constantly marked her manner :

" Perhaps you can't. I don't see—unless I should go with you." She evidently hadn't thought of this before.

We ascended to the upper floor and visited a long succession of empty rooms. The best of them looked over the garden ; some of the others had above the opposite rough-tiled house-tops a view of the blue lagoon. They were all dusty and even a little disfigured with long neglect, but I saw that by spending a few hundred francs I should be able to make three or four of them habitable enough. My experiment was turning out costly, yet now that I had all but taken possession I ceased to allow this to trouble me. I mentioned to my companion a few of the things I should put in, but she replied rather more precipitately than usual that I might do exactly what I liked : she seemed to wish to notify me that the Misses Bordereau would take none but the most veiled interest in my proceedings. I guessed that her aunt had instructed her to adopt this tone, and I may as well say now that I came afterwards to distinguish perfectly (as I believed) between the speeches she made on her own responsibility and those the old woman imposed upon her. She took no notice of the unswept condition of the rooms and indulged neither in explanations nor in apologies. I said to myself that this was a sign Juliana and her niece—disenchanting idea !—were untidy persons with a low Italian standard ; but I afterwards recognised that a lodger who had forced an entrance had no *locus standi* as a critic. We looked out of a good many windows, for there was nothing within the rooms to look at, and still I wanted to linger. I asked her what several different objects in the prospect might be, but in no case did she appear to know. She was evidently not familiar with the view—it was as if she had not looked at it for years—and I presently saw that she was too preoccupied with something else to pretend to care for it. Suddenly she said — the remark was not suggested :

"I don't know whether it will make any difference to you, but the money is for me."

"The money —— ? "

"The money you're going to bring."

"Why you'll make me wish to stay here two or three years ! " I spoke as benevolently as possible, though it had begun to act on my nerves that these women so associated with Aspern should so constantly bring the pecuniary question back.

" That would be very good for me," she answered almost gaily.

" You put me on my honour ! "

She looked as if she failed to understand this, but went on : " She wants me to have more. She thinks she's going to die."

" Ah not soon I hope ! " I cried with genuine feeling. I had perfectly considered the possibility of her destroying her documents on the day she should feel her end at hand. I believed that she would cling to them till then, and I was as convinced of her reading Aspern's letters over every night or at least pressing them to her withered lips. I would have given a good deal for some view of those solemnities. I asked Miss Tina if her venerable relative were seriously ill, and she replied that she was only very tired—she had lived so extraordinarily long. That was what she said herself—she wanted to die for a change. Besides, all her friends had been dead for ages ; either they ought to have remained or she ought to have gone. That was another thing her aunt often said : she was not at all resigned—resigned, that is, to life.

" But people don't die when they like, do they ? " Miss Tina inquired. I took the liberty of asking why, if there was actually enough money to maintain both of them, there would not be more than enough in case of her being left alone. She considered this difficult problem a moment and then said : " Oh well, you know, she takes care of me. She thinks that when I'm alone I shall be a great fool and shan't know how to manage."

" I should have supposed rather that you took care of *her*. I'm afraid she's very proud."

" Why, have you discovered that already ? " Miss Tina cried with a dimness of glad surprise.

" I was shut up with her there for a considerable

time and she struck me, she interested me extremely. It didn't take me long to make my discovery. She won't have much to say to me while I'm here."

"No, I don't think she will," my companion averred.

"Do you suppose she has some suspicion of me?"

Miss Tina's honest eyes gave me no sign I had touched a mark. "I shouldn't think so—letting you in after all so easily."

"You call it easily? She has covered her risk," I said. "But where is it one could take an advantage of her?"

"I oughtn't to tell you if I knew, ought I?" And Miss Tina added, before I had time to reply to this, smiling dolefully: "Do you think we've any weak points?"

"That's exactly what I'm asking. You'd only have to mention them for me to respect them religiously."

She looked at me hereupon with that air of timid but candid and even gratified curiosity with which she had confronted me from the first; after which she said: "There's nothing to tell. We're terribly quiet. I don't know how the days pass. We've no life."

"I wish I might think I should bring you a little."

"Oh, we know what we want," she went on. "It's all right."

There were twenty things I desired to ask her: how in the world they did live; whether they had any friends or visitors, any relations in America or in other countries. But I judged such probings premature; I must leave it to a later chance. "Well, don't *you* be proud," I contented myself with saying. "Don't hide from me altogether."

"Oh I must stay with my aunt," she returned without looking at me. And at the same moment, abruptly, without any ceremony of parting, she quitted me and disappeared, leaving me to make my own way downstairs. I stayed a while longer, wandering about the bright desert—the sun was pouring in—of the old house, thinking the situation over on the spot. Not even the pattering little *serva* came to look after me, and I reflected that after all this treatment showed confidence.

IV

PERHAPS it did, but all the same, six weeks later, towards the middle of June, the moment when Mrs. Prest undertook her annual migration, I had made no measurable advance. I was obliged to confess to her that I had no results to speak of. My first step had been unexpectedly rapid, but there was no appearance it would be followed by a second. I was a thousand miles from taking tea with my hostesses —that privilege of which, as I reminded my good friend, we both had had a vision. She reproached me with lacking boldness and I answered that even to be bold you must have an opportunity : you may push on through a breach, but you can't batter down a dead wall. She returned that the breach I had already made was big enough to admit an army, and accused me of wasting precious hours in whimpering in her salon when I ought to have been carrying on the struggle in the field. It is true that I went to see her very often—all on the theory that it would console me (I freely expressed my discouragement) for my want of success on my own premises. But I began to feel that it didn't console me to be perpetually chaffed for my scruples, especially since I was really so vigilant ; and I was rather glad when my ironic friend closed her house for the summer. She had expected to draw amusement from the drama of my inter- course with the Misses Bordereau, and was disappointed that the intercourse, and consequently the drama, had not come off. "They'll lead you on to your ruin," she said before she left Venice. "They'll get all your money without showing you a scrap." I think I settled down to my business with more concentration after her departure.

It was a fact that up to that time I had not, save on a single brief occasion, had even a moment's contact with my queer hostesses. The exception had occurred when I carried them according to my promise the terrible three thousand francs. Then I found Miss Tina awaiting me in the hall, and she took the money from my hand with a promptitude that prevented my seeing her aunt. The old lady had promised to receive me, yet apparently thought nothing of breaking that vow. The money was contained in a bag of chamois leather, of respectable dimensions, which my banker had given me, and Miss Tina had to make a big fist to receive it. This she did with extreme solemnity, though I tried to treat the affair a little as a joke. It was in no jocular strain, yet it was with a clearness akin to a brightness that she inquired, weighing the money in her two palms : " Don't you think it's too much ? " To which I replied that this would depend on the amount of pleasure I should get for it. Hereupon she turned away from me quickly, as she had done the day before, murmuring in a tone different from any she had used hitherto : " Oh pleasure, pleasure—there's no pleasure in this house ! "

After that, for a long time, I never saw her, and I wondered the common chances of the day shouldn't have helped us to meet. It could only be evident that she was immensely on her guard against them ; and in addition to this the house was so big that for each other we were lost in it. I used to look out for her hopefully as I crossed the sala in my comings and

goings, but I was not rewarded with a glimpse of the
tail of her dress. It was as if she never peeped out of
her aunt's apartment. I used to wonder what she
did there week after week and year after year. I had
never met so stiff a policy of seclusion ; it was more
than keeping quiet — it was like hunted creatures
feigning death. The two ladies appeared to have no
visitors whatever and no sort of contact with the
world. I judged at least that people couldn't have
come to the house and that Miss Tina couldn't have
gone out without my catching some view of it. I
did what I disliked myself for doing—considering
it but as once in a way : I questioned my servant
about their habits and let him infer that I should be
interested in any information he might glean. But
he gleaned amazingly little for a knowing Venetian :
it must be added that where there is a perpetual fast
there are very few crumbs on the floor. His ability
in other ways was sufficient, if not quite all I had
attributed to him on the occasion of my first interview with Miss Tina. He had helped my gondolier
to bring me round a boat-load of furniture ; and when
these articles had been carried to the top of the palace
and distributed according to our associated wisdom
he organised my household with such dignity as
answered to its being composed exclusively of himself. He made me in short as comfortable as I could
be with my indifferent prospects. I should have been
glad if he had fallen in love with Miss Bordereau's
maid, or, failing this, had taken her in aversion : either
event might have brought about some catastrophe,
and a catastrophe might have led to some parley. It
was my idea that she would have been sociable, and
I myself on various occasions saw her flit to and fro
on domestic errands, so that I was sure she was
accessible. But I tasted of no gossip from that
fountain, and I afterwards learned that Pasquale's

affections were fixed upon an object that made him heedless of other women. This was a young lady with a powdered face, a yellow cotton gown and much leisure, who used often to come to see him. She practised, at her convenience, the art of a stringer of beads—these ornaments are made in Venice to profusion ; she had her pocket full of them and I used to find them on the floor of my apartment—and kept an eye on the possible rival in the house. It was not for me of course to make the domestics tattle, and I never said a word to Miss Bordereau's cook.

It struck me as a proof of the old woman's resolve to have nothing to do with me that she should never have sent me a receipt for my three months' rent. For some days I looked out for it and then, when I had given it up, wasted a good deal of time in wondering what her reason had been for neglecting so indispensable and familiar a form. At first I was tempted to send her a reminder ; after which I put by the idea—against my judgement as to what was right in the particular case—on the general ground of wishing to keep quiet. If Miss Bordereau suspected me of ulterior aims she would suspect me less if I should be businesslike, and yet I consented not to be. It was possible she intended her omission as an impertinence, a visible irony, to show how she could overreach people who attempted to overreach her. On that hypothesis it was well to let her see that one didn't notice her little tricks. The real reading of the matter, I afterwards gathered, was simply the poor lady's desire to emphasise the fact that I was in the enjoyment of a favour as rigidly limited as it had been liberally bestowed. She had given me part of her house, but she wouldn't add to that so much as a morsel of paper with her name on it. Let me say that even at first this didn't make me too miserable, for the whole situation had the charm of its oddity. I foresaw that I should have a summer after my own literary heart, and the sense of playing with my opportunity was much greater after all than any sense of being played with. There could be no Venetian business without patience, and since I adored the place I was much more in the spirit of it for having laid in a large provision. That spirit kept me perpetual company and seemed to look out at me from the revived immortal face—in which all his genius shone—of the great poet who was my prompter. I had invoked him and he had come ; he hovered before me half the time ; it was as if his bright ghost had returned to earth to assure me he regarded the affair as his own no less than as mine and that we should see it fraternally and fondly to a conclusion. It was as if he had said : " Poor dear, be easy with her ; she has some natural prejudices ; only give her time. Strange as it may appear to you she was very attractive in 1820. Meanwhile, aren't we in Venice together, and what better place is there for the meeting of dear friends ? See how it glows with the advancing summer ; how the sky and the sea and the rosy air and the marble of the palaces all shimmer and melt together." My eccentric private errand became a part of the general romance and the general glory—I felt even a mystic companionship, a moral fraternity with all those who in the past had been in the service of art. They had worked for beauty, for a devotion ; and what else was I doing ? That element was in everything that Jeffrey Aspern had written, and I was only bringing it to light.

I lingered in the sala when I went to and fro ; I used to watch—as long as I thought decent—the door that led to Miss Bordereau's part of the house. A person observing me might have supposed I was trying to cast a spell on it or attempting some odd experiment in hypnotism. But I was only praying it might open or thinking what treasure probably lurked behind it. I hold it singular, as I look back, that I should never have doubted for a moment that the sacred relics were there ; never have failed to know the joy of being beneath the same roof with them. After all they were under my hand—they had not escaped me yet ; and they made my life continuous, in a fashion, with the illustrious life they had touched at the other end. I lost myself in this satisfaction to the point of assuming—in my quiet extravagance— that poor Miss Tina also went back, and still went back, as I used to phrase it. She did indeed, the gentle spinster, but not quite so far as Jeffrey Aspern, who was simple hearsay to her quite as he was to me. Only she had lived for years with Juliana, she had seen and handled all mementoes and—even though she was stupid—some esoteric knowledge had rubbed off on her. That was what the old woman repre- sented—esoteric knowledge ; and this was the idea with which my critical heart used to thrill. It liter- ally beat faster often of an evening when I had been out, as I stopped with my candle in the re-echoing hall on my way up to bed. It was as if at such a moment as that, in the stillness and after the long contradiction of ·the day, Miss Bordereau's secrets were in the aïr, the wonder of her survival more vivid. These were the acute impressions. I had them in another form, with more of a certain shade of reci- procity, during the hours I sat in the garden looking up over the top of my book at the closed windows of my hostess. In these windows no sign of life ever appeared · it was as if, for fear of my catching a glimpse of them, the two ladies passed their days in the dark. But this only emphasised their having matters to conceal ; which was what I had wished to prove. Their motionless shutters became as expres- sive as eyes consciously closed, and I took comfort in the probability that, though invisible themselves, they kept me in view between the lashes.

I made a point of spending as much time as possible in the garden, to justify the picture I had originally given of my horticultural passion. And I not only spent time, but (hang it! as I said) spent precious money. As soon as I had got my rooms arranged and could give the question proper thought I surveyed the place with a clever expert and made terms for having it put in order. I was sorry to do this, for personally I liked it better as it was, with its weeds and its wild rich tangle, its sweet characteristic Venetian shabbiness. I had to be consistent, to keep my promise that I would smother the house in flowers. Moreover I clung to the fond fancy that by flowers I should make my way—I should succeed by big nosegays. I would batter the old women with lilies—I would bombard their citadel with roses. Their door would have to yield to the pressure when a mound of fragrance should be heaped against it. The place in truth had been brutally neglected. The Venetian capacity for dawdling is of the largest, and for a good many days unlimited litter was all my gardener had to show for his ministrations. There was a great digging of holes and carting about of earth, and after a while I grew so impatient that I had thoughts of sending for my " results " to the nearest stand. But I felt sure my friends would see through the chinks of their shutters where such tribute *couldn't* have been gathered, and might so make up their minds against my veracity. I possessed my soul, and finally, though the delay was long, perceived some appearances of bloom. This encouraged me, and I waited serenely enough till they multiplied. Meanwhile the real summer days arrived and began to pass, and as I look back upon them they seem to me almost the happiest of my life. I took more and more care to be in the garden whenever it was not too hot. I had an arbour arranged and a low table and an armchair put into it ; and I carried out books and portfolios—I had always some business of writing in hand—and worked and waited and mused and hoped, while the golden hours elapsed and the plants drank in the light and the inscrutable old palace turned pale and then, as the day waned, began to recover and flush and my papers rustled in the wandering breeze of the Adriatic.

Considering how little satisfaction I got from it at first it is wonderful I shouldn't have grown more tired of trying to guess what mystic rites of ennui the Misses Bordereau celebrated in their darkened rooms ; whether this had always been the tenor of their life and how in previous years they had escaped elbowing their neighbours. It was supposable they had then had other habits, forms and resources ; that they must once have been young or at least middle-aged. There was no end to the questions it was possible to ask about them and no end to the answers it was not possible to frame. I had known many of my country-people in Europe and was familiar with the strange ways they were liable to take up there ; but the Misses Bordereau formed altogether a new type of the American absentee. Indeed it was clear the American name had ceased to have any application to them—I had seen this in the ten minutes I spent in the old woman's room. You could never have said whence they came from the appearance of either of them ; wherever it was they had long ago shed and unlearned all native marks and notes. There was nothing in them one recognised or fitted, and, putting the ques-tion of speech aside, they might have been Norwegians or Spaniards. Miss Bordereau, after all, had been in Europe nearly three-quarters of a century ; it appeared by some verses addressed to her by Aspern on the occasion of his own second absence from America—

verses of which Cumnor and I had after infinite conjecture established solidly enough the date—that she
was even then, as a girl of twenty, on the foreign side
of the sea. There was a profession in the poem—I
hope not just for the phrase—that he had come back
for her sake. We had no real light on her circumstances at that moment, any more than we had upon
her origin, which we believed to be of the sort usually
spoken of as modest. Cumnor had a theory that she
had been a governess in some family in which the poet
visited and that, in consequence of her position, there
was from the first something unavowed, or rather
something quite clandestine, in their relations. I on
the other hand had hatched a little romance according to which she was the daughter of an artist, a
painter or a sculptor, who had left the Western world,
when the century was fresh, to study in the ancient
schools. It was essential to my hypothesis that this
amiable man should have lost his wife, should have
been poor and unsuccessful and should have had
a second daughter of a disposition quite different
from Juliana's. It was also indispensable that he
should have been accompanied to Europe by these
young ladies and should have established himself
there for the remainder of a struggling saddened life.
There was a further implication that Miss Bordereau
had had in her youth a perverse and reckless, albeit
a generous and fascinating character, and that she
had braved some wondrous chances. By what
passions had she been ravaged, by what adventures
and sufferings had she been blanched, what store of
memories had she laid away for the monotonous
future ?

I asked myself these things as I sat spinning
theories about her in my arbour and the bees
droned in the flowers. It was incontestable that,
whether for right or for wrong, most readers of certain

of Aspern's poems (poems not as ambiguous as the sonnets—scarcely more divine, I think—of Shakespeare) had taken for granted that Juliana had not always adhered to the steep footway of renunciation. There hovered about her name a perfume of impenitent passion, an intimation that she had not been exactly as the respectable young person in general. Was this a sign that her singer had betrayed her, had given her away, as we say nowadays, to posterity ? Certain it is that it would have been difficult to put one's finger on the passage in which her fair fame suffered injury. Moreover was not any fame fair enough that was so sure of duration and was associated with works immortal through their beauty ? It was a part of my idea that the young lady had had a foreign lover—and say an unedifying tragical rupture—before her meeting with Jeffrey Aspern. She had lived with her father and sister in a queer old-fashioned expatriated artistic Bohemia of the days when the esthetic was only the academic and the painters who knew the best models for *contadina* and *pifferaro* wore peaked hats and long hair. It was a society less awake than the coteries of to-day— in its ignorance of the wonderful chances, the opportunities of the early bird, with which its path was strewn—to tatters of old stuff and fragments of old crockery ; so that Miss Bordereau appeared not to have picked up or have inherited many objects of importance. There was no enviable *bric-à-brac*, with its provoking legend of cheapness, in the room in which I had seen her. Such a fact as that suggested bareness, but none the less it worked happily into the sentimental interest I had always taken in the early movements of my countrymen as visitors to Europe. When Americans went abroad in 1820 there was something romantic, almost heroic in it, as compared with the perpetual ferryings of the present hour, the hour at which photography and other conveniences have annihilated surprise. Miss Bordereau had sailed with her family on a tossing brig in the days of long voyages and sharp differences ; she had had her emotions on the top of yellow diligences, passed the night at inns where she dreamed of travellers' tales, and was most struck, on reaching the Eternal City, with the elegance of Roman pearls and scarfs and mosaic brooches. There was something touching to me in all that, and my imagination frequently went back to the period. If Miss Bordereau carried it there of course Jeffrey Aspern had at other times done so with greater force. It was a much more important fact, if one was looking at his genius critically, that he had lived in the days before the general transfusion. It had happened to me to regret that he had known Europe at all ; I should have liked to see what he would have written without that experience, by which he had incontestably been enriched. But as his fate had ruled otherwise I went with him—I tried to judge how the general old order would have struck him. It was not only there, however, I watched him ; the relations he had entertained with the special new had even a livelier interest. His own country after all had had most of his life, and his muse, as they said at that time, was essentially American. That was originally what I had prized him for : that at a period when our native land was nude and crude and provincial, when the famous " atmosphere " it is supposed to lack was not even missed, when literature was lonely there and art and form almost impossible, he had found means to live and write like one of the first ; to be free and general and not at all afraid ; to feel, understand and express everything.

V

I was seldom at home in the evening, for when I attempted to occupy myself in my apartments the lamplight brought in a swarm of noxious insects, and it was too hot for closed windows. Accordingly I spent the late hours either on the water—the moon-lights of Venice are famous — or in the splendid square which serves as a vast forecourt to the strange old church of Saint Mark. I sat in front of Florian's café eating ices, listening to music, talking with acquaintances : the traveller will remember how the immense cluster of tables and little chairs stretches like a promontory into the smooth lake of the Piazza. The whole place, of a summer's evening, under the stars and with all the lamps, all the voices and light footsteps on marble—the only sounds of the immense arcade that encloses it—is an open-air saloon dedicated to cooling drinks and to a still finer degustation, that of the splendid impressions received during the day. When I didn't prefer to keep mine to myself there was always a stray tourist, disencumbered of his Bädeker, to discuss them with, or some domesticated painter rejoicing in the return of the season of strong effects. The great basilica, with its low domes and bristling embroideries, the mystery of its mosaic and sculpture, looked ghostly in the tempered gloom, and the sea-breeze passed between the twin columns of the Piazzetta, the lintels of a door no longer

46

guarded, as gently as if a rich curtain swayed there.
I used sometimes on these occasions to think of the
Misses Bordereau and of the pity of their being shut
up in apartments which in the Venetian July even
Venetian vastness couldn't relieve of some stuffiness.
Their life seemed miles away from the life of the
Piazza, and no doubt it was really too late to make
the austere Juliana change her habits. But poor
Miss Tina would have enjoyed one of Florian's ices,
I was sure ; sometimes I even had thoughts of carry-
ing one home to her. Fortunately my patience
bore fruit and I was not obliged to do anything so
ridiculous.

One evening about the middle of July I came in
earlier than usual—I forget what chance had led to
this—and instead of going up to my quarters made
my way into the garden. The temperature was very
high ; it was such a night as one would gladly have
spent in the open air, and I was in no hurry to go to
bed. I had floated home in my gondola, listening to
the slow splash of the oar in the dark narrow canals,
and now the only thought that occupied me was that
it would be good to recline at one's length in the
fragrant darkness on a garden-bench. The odour
of the canal was doubtless at the bottom of that
aspiration, and the breath of the garden, as I entered
it, gave consistency to my purpose. It was delicious
—just such an air as must have trembled with Romeo's
vows when he stood among the thick flowers and
raised his arms to his mistress's balcony. I looked
at the windows of the palace to see if by chance the
example of Verona—Verona being not far off—had
been followed ; but everything was dim, as usual,
and everything was still. Juliana might on the
summer nights of her youth have murmured down
from open windows at Jeffrey Aspern, but Miss Tina
was not a poet's mistress any more than I was a

poet. This, however, didn't prevent my gratification from being great as I became aware on reaching the end of the garden that my younger padrona was seated in one of the bowers: At first I made out but an indistinct figure, not in the least counting on such an overture from one of my hostesses; it even occurred to me that some enamoured maid-servant had stolen in to keep a tryst with her sweetheart. I was going to turn away, not to frighten her, when the figure rose to its height and I recognised Miss Bordereau's niece. I must do myself the justice that I didn't wish to frighten her either, and much as I had longed for some such accident I should have been capable of retreating. It was as if I had laid a trap for her by coming home earlier than usual and by adding to that oddity my invasion of the garden. As she rose she spoke to me, and then I guessed that perhaps, secure in my almost inveterate absence, it was her nightly practice to take a lonely airing. There was no trap in truth, because I had had no suspicion. At first I took the words she uttered for an impatience of my arrival; but as she repeated them—I hadn't caught them clearly—I had the surprise of hearing her say : " Oh dear, I'm so glad you've come ! " She and her aunt had in common the property of unexpected speeches. She came out of the arbour almost as if to throw herself in my arms.

I hasten to add that I escaped this ordeal and that she didn't even then shake hands with me. It was an ease to her to see me and presently she told me why—because she was nervous when out-of-doors at night alone. The plants and shrubs looked so strange in the dark, and there were all sorts of queer sounds—she couldn't tell me what they were—like the noises of animals. She stood close to me, looking about her with an air of greater security but without any demonstration of interest in me as an individual. Then I felt how little nocturnal prowlings could have been her habit, and I was also reminded—I had been afflicted by the same in talking with her before I took possession—that it was impossible to allow too much for her simplicity.

" You speak as if you were lost in the backwoods," I cheeringly laughed. " How you manage to keep out of this charming place when you've only three steps to take to get into it is more than I've yet been able to discover. You hide away amazingly so long as I'm on the premises, I know ; but I had a hope you peeped out a little at other times. You and your poor aunt are worse off than Carmelite nuns in their cells. Should you mind telling me how you exist without air, without exercise, without any sort of human contact ? I don't see how you carry on the common business of life."

She looked at me as if I had spoken a strange tongue, and her answer was so little of one that I felt it make for irritation. " We go to bed very early— earlier than you'd believe." I was on the point of saying that this only deepened the mystery, but she gave me some relief by adding : " Before you came we weren't so private. But I've never been out at night."

" Never in these fragrant alleys, blooming here under your nose ? "

" Ah," said Miss Tina, " they were never nice till now ! " There was a finer sense in this and a flattering comparison, so that it seemed to me I had gained some advantage. As I might follow that further by establishing a good grievance I asked her why, since she thought my garden nice, she had never thanked me in any way for the flowers I had been sending up in such quantities for the previous three weeks. I had not been discouraged—there had been, as she would have observed, a daily armful ; but I had been brought up in the common forms and a word of recognition now and then would have touched me in the right place.

" Why, I didn't know they were for me ! "

" They were for both of you. Why should I make a difference ? "

Miss Tina reflected as if she might be thinking of a reason for that, but she failed to produce one. Instead of this she asked abruptly : " Why in the world do you want so much to know us ? "

" I ought after all to make a difference," I replied. " That question's your aunt's ; it isn't yours. You wouldn't ask it if you hadn't been put up to it."

" She didn't tell me to ask you," Miss Tina replied without confusion. She was indeed the oddest mixture of shyness and straightness.

" Well, she has often wondered about it herself and expressed her wonder to you. She has insisted on it, so that she has put the idea into your head that I'm insufferably pushing. Upon my word I think I've been very discreet. And how completely your aunt must have lost every tradition of sociability, to see anything out of the way in the idea that respectable intelligent people, living as we do under the same roof, should occasionally exchange a remark ! What could be more natural ? We're of the same country and have at least some of the same tastes, since, like you, I'm intensely fond of Venice."

My friend seemed incapable of grasping more than one clause in any proposition, and she now spoke quickly, eagerly, as if she were answering my whole speech. " I'm not in the least fond of Venice. I should like to go far away ! "

" Has she always kept you back so ? " I went on, to show her I could be as irrelevant as herself.

" She told me to come out to-night ; she has told

me very often," said Miss Tina. " It is I who wouldn't come. I don't like to leave her."

" Is she too weak, is she really failing ? " I demanded, with more emotion, I think, than I meant to betray. I measured this by the way her eyes rested on me in the darkness. It embarrassed me a little, and to turn the matter off I continued genially : " Do let us sit down together comfortably somewhere —while you tell me all about her."

Miss Tina made no resistance to this. We found a bench less secluded, less confidential, as it were, than the one in the arbour ; and we were still sitting there when I heard midnight ring out from those clear bells of Venice which vibrate with a solemnity of their own over the lagoon and hold the air so much more than the chimes of other places. We were together more than an hour, and our interview gave, as it struck me, a great lift to my undertaking. Miss Tina accepted the situation without a protest ; she had avoided me for three months, yet now she treated me almost as if these three months had made me an old friend. If I had chosen I might have gathered from this that though she had avoided me she had given a good deal of consideration to doing so. She paid no attention to the flight of time—never worried at my keeping her so long away from her aunt. She talked freely, answering questions and asking them and not even taking advantage of certain longish pauses by which they were naturally broken to say she thought she had better go in. It was almost as if she were waiting for something—something I might say to her—and intended to give me my opportunity. I was the more struck by this as she told me how much less well her aunt had been for a good many days, and in a way that was rather new. She was markedly weaker ; at moments she showed no strength at all ; yet more than ever before she

51

wished to be left alone. That was why she had told her to come out—not even to remain in her own room, which was alongside ; she pronounced poor Miss Tina " a worry, a bore and a source of aggravation." She sat still for hours together, as if for long sleep ; she had always done that, musing and dozing ; but at such times formerly she gave, in breaks, some small sign of life, of interest, liking her companion to be near her with her work. This sad personage confided to me that at present her aunt was so motionless as to create the fear she was dead ; moreover she scarce ate or drank—one couldn't see what she lived on. The great thing was that she still on most days got up ; the serious job was to dress her, to wheel her out of her bedroom. She clung to as many of her old habits as possible and had always, little company as they had received for years, made a point of sitting in the great parlour.

I scarce knew what to think of all this—of Miss Tina's sudden conversion to sociability and of the strange fact that the more the old woman appeared to decline to her end the less she should desire to be looked after. The story hung indifferently together, and I even asked myself if it mightn't be a trap laid for me, the result of a design to make me show my hand. I couldn't have told why my companions (as they could only by courtesy be called) should have this purpose—why they should try to trip up so lucrative a lodger. But at any hazard I kept on my guard, so that Miss Tina shouldn't have occasion again to ask me what I might really be "up to." Poor woman, before we parted for the night my mind was at rest as to what *she* might be. She was up to nothing at all.

She told me more about their affairs than I had hoped ; there was no need to be prying, for it evidently drew her out simply to feel me listen and care. She ceased wondering why I *should*, and at last, while describing the brilliant life they had led years before, she almost chattered. It was Miss Tina who judged it brilliant ; she said that when they first came to live in Venice, years and years back—I found her essentially vague about dates and the order in which events had occurred—there was never a week they hadn't some visitor or didn't make some pleasant *passeggio* in the town. They had seen all the curiosities ; they had even been to the Lido in a boat—she spoke as if I might think there was a way on foot ; they had had a collation there, brought in three baskets and spread out on the grass. I asked her what people they had known and she said, Oh very nice ones—the Cavaliere Bombicci and the Contessa Altemura, with whom they had had a great friendship ! Also English people—the Churtons and the Goldies and Mrs. Stock-Stock, whom they had loved dearly ; she was dead and gone, poor dear. That was the case with most of their kind circle—this expression was Miss Tina's own ; though a few were left, which was a wonder considering how they had neglected them. She mentioned the names of two or three Venetian old women ; of a certain doctor, very clever, who was so attentive—he came as a friend, he had really given up practice ; of the *avvocato* Pochintesta, who wrote beautiful poems and had addressed one to her aunt. These people came to see them without fail every year, usually at the *capo d' anno*, and of old her aunt used to make them some little present—her aunt and she together : small things that she, Miss Tina, turned out with her own hand, paper lamp-shades, or mats for the decanters of wine at dinner, or those woollen things that in cold weather are worn on the wrists. The last few years there hadn't been many presents ; she couldn't think what to make and her aunt had lost interest and never suggested. But the people came all the same ; if the good Venetians liked you once they liked you for ever.

There was affecting matter enough in the good faith of this sketch of former social glories ; the picnic at the Lido had remained vivid through the ages and poor Miss Tina evidently was of the impression that she had had a dashing youth. She had in fact had a glimpse of the Venetian world in its gossiping home-keeping parsimonious professional walks ; for I noted for the first time how nearly she had acquired by contact the trick of the familiar soft-sounding almost infantile prattle of the place. I judged her to have imbibed this invertebrate dialect from the natural way the names of things and people—mostly purely local—rose to her lips. If she knew little of what they represented she knew still less of anything else. Her aunt had drawn in—the failure of interest in the table-mats and lamp-shades was a sign of that —and she hadn't been able to mingle in society or to entertain it alone ; so that her range of reminiscence struck one as an old world altogether. Her tone, hadn't it been so decent, would have seemed to carry one back to the queer rococo Venice of Goldoni and Casanova. I found myself mistakenly think of her too as one of Jeffrey Aspern's contemporaries ; this came from her having so little in common with my own. It was possible, I indeed reasoned, that she hadn't even heard of him ; it might very well be that Juliana had forborne to lift for innocent eyes the veil that covered the temple of her glory. In this case she perhaps wouldn't know of the existence of the papers, and I welcomed that presumption—it made me feel more safe with her —till I remembered we had believed the letter of disavowal received by Cumnor to be in the hand-writing of the niece. If it had been dictated to her

she had of course to know what it was about; though
the effect of it withal was to repudiate the idea of
any connexion with the poet. I held it probable at
all events that Miss Tina hadn't read a word of his
poetry. Moreover if, with her companion, she had
always escaped invasion and research, there was little
occasion for her having got it into her head that
people were "after" the letters. People had not
been after them, for people hadn't heard of them.
Cumnor's fruitless feeler would have been a solitary
accident.

When midnight sounded Miss Tina got up; but
she stopped at the door of the house only after she
had wandered two or three times with me round the
garden. "When shall I see you again?" I asked
before she went in; to which she replied with prompt-
ness that she should like to come out the next night.
She added, however, that she shouldn't come—she
was so far from doing everything she liked.

"You might do a few things *I* like," I quite
sincerely sighed.

"Oh you—I don't believe you!" she murmured
at this, facing me with her simple solemnity.

"Why don't you believe me?"

"Because I don't understand you."

"That's just the sort of occasion to have faith."
I couldn't say more, though I should have liked to,
as I saw I only mystified her; for I had no wish to
have it on my conscience that I might pass for having
made love to her. Nothing less should I have seemed
to do had I continued to beg a lady to "believe in
me" in an Italian garden on a midsummer night.
There was some merit in my scruples, for Miss Tina
lingered and lingered: I made out in her the conviction that she shouldn't really soon come down again
and the wish therefore to protract the present. She
insisted, too, on making the talk between us personal

to ourselves; and altogether her behaviour was such as would have been possible only to a perfectly artless and a considerably witless woman.

"I shall like the flowers better now that I know them also meant for me."

"How could you have doubted it? If you'll tell me the kind you like best I'll send a double lot."

"Oh I like them all best!" Then she went on familiarly: "Shall you study—shall you read and write—when you go up to your rooms?"

"I don't do that at night—at this season. The lamplight brings in the animals."

"You might have known that when you came."

"I did know it!"

"And in winter do you work at night?"

"I read a good deal, but I don't often write." She listened as if these details had a rare interest, and suddenly a temptation quite at odds with all the prudence I had been teaching myself glimmered at me in her plain mild face. Ah yes, she was safe and I could make her safer! It seemed to me from one moment to another that I couldn't wait longer—that I really must take a sounding. So I went on: "In general before I go to sleep (very often in bed; it's a bad habit, but I confess to it) I read some great poet. In nine cases out of ten it's a volume of Jeffrey Aspern."

I watched her well as I pronounced that name, but I saw nothing wonderful. Why should I indeed? Wasn't Jeffrey Aspern the property of the human race?

"Oh *we* read him—we *have* read him," she quietly replied.

"He's my poet of poets—I know him almost by heart."

For an instant Miss Tina hesitated; then her sociability was too much for her. "Oh by heart—

56

that's nothing ; " and, though dimly, she quite lighted.
" My aunt used to know him, to know him "—she
paused an instant and I wondered what she was going
to say—" to know him as a visitor."

" As a visitor ? " I guarded my tone.

" He used to call on her and take her out."

I continued to stare. " My dear lady, he died a
hundred years ago ! "

" Well," she said amusingly, " my aunt's a hundred
and fifty."

" Mercy on us ! " I cried ; " why didn't you tell
me before ? I should like so to ask her about him."

" She wouldn't care for that—she wouldn't tell
you," Miss Tina returned.

" I don't care what she cares for ! She *must* tell
me—it's not a chance to be lost."

" Oh you should have come twenty years ago.
Then she still talked about him."

" And what did she say ? " I eagerly asked.

" I don't know—that he liked her immensely."

" And she—didn't she like *him* ? "

" She said he was a god." Miss Tina gave me this
information flatly, without expression ; her tone
might have made it a piece of trivial gossip. But it
stirred me deeply as she dropped the words into the
summer night ; their sound might have been the light
rustle of an old unfolded love-letter.

" Fancy, fancy ! " I murmured. And then : " Tell
me this, please—has she got a portrait of him ?
They're distressingly rare."

" A portrait ? I don't know," said Miss Tina ; and
now there was discomfiture in her face. " Well, good-
night ! " she added ; and she turned into the house.

I accompanied her into the wide dusky stone-paved
passage that corresponded on the ground floor with
our great sala. It opened at one end into the garden,
at the other upon the canal, and was lighted now only

by the small lamp always left for me to take up as I
went to bed. An extinguished candle which Miss Tina
apparently had brought down with her stood on the
same table with it. " Good-night, good-night ! " I
replied, keeping beside her as she went to get her
light. " Surely you'd know, shouldn't you, if she
had one ? "

" If she had what ? " the poor lady asked, looking
at me queerly over the flame of her candle.

" A portrait of the god. I don't know what I
wouldn't give to see it."

" I don't know what she has got. She keeps her
things locked up." And Miss Tina went away toward
the staircase with the sense evidently of having said
too much.

I let her go—I wished not to frighten her—and I
contented myself with remarking that Miss Bordereau
wouldn't have locked up such a glorious possession
as that : a thing a person would be proud of and
hang up in a prominent place on the parlour-wall.
Therefore of course she hadn't any portrait. Miss
Tina made no direct answer to this and, candle in
hand, with her back to me, mounted two or three
degrees. Then she stopped short and turned round,
looking at me across the dusky space.

" Do you write—do you write ? " There was a
shake in her voice—she could scarcely bring it out.

" Do I write ? Oh don't speak of my writing on
the same day with Aspern's ! "

" Do you write about *him*—do you pry into his
life ? "

" Ah that's your aunt's question ; it can't be
yours ! " I said in a tone of slightly wounded
sensibility.

" All the more reason then that you should answer
it. Do you, please ? "

I thought I had allowed for the falsehoods I should

have to tell, but I found that in fact when it came to the point I hadn't. Besides, now that I had an opening there was a kind of relief in being frank. Lastly—it was perhaps fanciful, even fatuous—I guessed that Miss Tina personally wouldn't in the last resort be less my friend. So after a moment's hesitation I answered : " Yes, I've written about him and I'm looking for more material. In heaven's name have you got any ? "

" *Santo Dio !* " she exclaimed without heeding my question ; and she hurried upstairs and out of sight. I might count upon her in the last resort, but for the present she was visibly alarmed. The proof of it was that she began to hide again, so that for a fortnight I kept missing her. I found my patience ebbing, and after four or five days of this I told the gardener to stop the " floral tributes."

VI

One afternoon, at last, however, as I came down from my quarters to go out, I found her in the sala : it was our first encounter on that ground since I had come to the house. She put on no air of being there by accident ; there was an ignorance of such arts in her honest angular diffidence. That I might be quite sure she was waiting for me she mentioned it at once, but telling me with it that Miss Bordereau wished to see me : she would take me into the room at that moment if I had time. If I had been late for a love-tryst I would have stayed for this, and I quickly signified that I should be delighted to wait on my benefactress. " She wants to talk with you—to know you," Miss Tina said, smiling as if she herself appreciated that idea ; and she led me to the door of her aunt's apartment. I stopped her a moment before she had opened it, looking at her with some curiosity. I told her that this was a great satisfaction to me and a great honour ; but all the same I should like to ask what had made Miss Bordereau so markedly and suddenly change. It had been only the other day that she wouldn't suffer me near her. Miss Tina was not embarrassed by my question ; she had as many little unexpected serenities, plausibilities almost, as if she told fibs, but the odd part of them was that they had on the contrary their source in her truthfulness.

" Oh my aunt varies," she answered ; " it's so terribly dull—I suppose she's tired."

" But you told me she wanted more and more to be alone."

Poor Miss Tina coloured as if she found me too pushing. " Well, if you don't believe she wants to see you, I haven't invented it ! I think people often are capricious when they're very old."

" That's perfectly true. I only wanted to be clear as to whether you've repeated to her what I told you the other night."

" What you told me ? "

" About Jeffrey Aspern—that I'm looking for materials."

" If I had told her do you think she'd have sent for you ? "

" That's exactly what I want to know. If she wants to keep him to herself she might have sent for me to tell me so."

" She won't speak of him," said Miss Tina. Then as she opened the door she added in a lower tone : " I told her nothing."

The old woman was sitting in the same place in which I had seen her last, in the same position, with the same mystifying bandage over her eyes. Her welcome was to turn her almost invisible face to me and show me that while she sat silent she saw me clearly. I made no motion to shake hands with her ; I now felt too well that this was out of place for ever. It had been sufficiently enjoined on me that she was too sacred for trivial modernisms—too venerable to touch. There was something so grim in her aspect— it was partly the accident of her green shade—as I stood there to be measured, that I ceased on the spot to doubt her suspecting me, though I didn't in the least myself suspect that Miss Tina hadn't just spoken the truth. She hadn't betrayed me, but the old woman's brooding instinct had served her ; she had turned me over and over in the long still hours and had guessed. The worst of it was that she looked terribly like an old woman who at a pinch would, even like Sardanapalus, burn her treasure. Miss Tina pushed a chair forward, saying to me, " This will be a good place for you to sit." As I took possession of it I asked after Miss Bordereau's health ; expressed the hope that in spite of the very hot weather it was satisfactory. She answered that it was good enough—good enough ; that it was a great thing to be alive.

" Oh as to that, it depends upon what you compare it with ! " I returned with a laugh.

" I don't compare—I don't compare. If I did that I should have given everything up long ago."

I liked to take this for a subtle allusion to the rapture she had known in the society of Jeffrey Aspern —though it was true that such an allusion would have accorded ill with the wish I imputed to her to keep him buried in her soul. What it accorded with was my constant conviction that no human being had ever had a happier social gift than his, and what it seemed to convey was that nothing in the world was worth speaking of if one pretended to speak of that. But one didn't pretend ! Miss Tina sat down beside her aunt, looking as if she had reason to believe some wonderful talk would come off between us.

" It's about the beautiful flowers," said the old lady ; " you sent us so many — I ought to have thanked you for them before. But I don't write letters and I receive company but at long intervals."

She hadn't thanked me while the flowers continued to come, but she departed from her custom so far as to send for me as soon as she began to fear they wouldn't come any more. I noted this ; I remembered what an acquisitive propensity she had shown when it was a question of extracting gold from me, and I privately rejoiced at the happy thought I had had in suspending my tribute. She had missed it and was willing to make a concession to bring it back. At the first sign of this concession I could only go to meet her. " I'm afraid you haven't had many, of late, but they shall begin again immediately— to-morrow, to-night."

" Oh do send us some to-night ! " Miss Tina cried as if it were a great affair.

" What else should you do with them ? It isn't a manly taste to make a bower of your room," the old woman remarked.

" I don't make a bower of my room, but I'm exceedingly fond of growing flowers, of watching their ways. There's nothing unmanly in that ; it has been the amusement of philosophers, of statesmen in re- tirement ; even, I think, of great captains."

" I suppose you know you can sell them—those you don't use," Miss Bordereau went on. " I daresay they wouldn't give you much for them ; still, you could make a bargain."

" Oh I've never in my life made a bargain, as you ought pretty well to have gathered. My gardener disposes of them and I ask no questions."

" I'd ask a few, I can promise you ! " said Miss Bordereau ; and it was so I first heard the strange sound of her laugh, which was as if the faint " walk- ing " ghost of her old-time tone had suddenly cut a caper. I couldn't get used to the idea that this vision of pecuniary profit was most what drew out the divine Juliana.

" Come into the garden yourself and pick them ; come as often as you like ; come every day. The flowers are all for you," I pursued, addressing Miss Tina and carrying off this veracious statement by treating it as an innocent joke. " I can't imagine

63

why she doesn't come down," I added for Miss Bordereau's benefit.

" You must make her come ; you must come up and fetch her," the old woman said to my stupefaction. " That odd thing you've made in the corner will do very well for her to sit in."

The allusion to the most elaborate of my shady coverts, a sketchy " summer-house," was irreverent ; it confirmed the impression I had already received that there was a flicker of impertinence in Miss Bordereau's talk, a vague echo of the boldness or the archness of her adventurous youth and which had somehow automatically outlived passions and faculties. None the less I asked : " Wouldn't it be possible for you to come down there yourself ? Wouldn't it do you good to sit there in the shade and the sweet air ? "

" Oh sir, when I move out of this it won't be to sit in the air, and I'm afraid that any that may be stirring around me won't be particularly sweet ! It will be a very dark shade indeed. But that won't be just yet," Miss Bordereau continued cannily, as if to correct any hopes this free glance at the last receptacle of her mortality might lead me to entertain. " I've sat here many a day and have had enough of arbours in my time. But I'm not afraid to wait till I'm called."

Miss Tina had expected, as I felt, rare conversation, but perhaps she found it less gracious on her aunt's side—considering I had been sent for with a civil intention—than she had hoped. As to give the position a turn that would put our companion in a light more favourable she said to me : " Didn't I tell you the other night that she had sent me out ? You see I can do what I like ! "

" Do you pity her—do you teach her to pity herself ? " Miss Bordereau demanded, before I had time to answer this appeal. "She has a much easier life than I had at her age."

"You must remember it has been quite open to me," I said, "to think you rather inhuman."

"Inhuman? That's what the poets used to call the women a hundred years ago. Don't try that; you won't do as well as they!" Juliana went on. "There's no more poetry in the world—that *I* know of at least. But I won't bandy words with you," she said, and I well remember the old-fashioned artificial sound she gave the speech. "You make me talk, talk, talk! It isn't good for me at all." I got up at this and told her I would take no more of her time; but she detained me to put a question. "Do you remember, the day I saw you about the rooms, that you offered us the use of your gondola?" And when I assented promptly, struck again with her disposition to make a "good thing" of my being there and wondering what she now had in her eye, she produced: "Why don't you take that girl out in it and show her the place?"

"Oh dear aunt, what do you want to do with me?" cried the "girl" with a piteous quaver. "I know all about the place!"

"Well then go with him and explain!" said Miss Bordereau, who gave an effect of cruelty to her implacable power of retort. This showed her as a sarcastic profane cynical old woman. "Haven't we heard that there have been all sorts of changes in all these years? You ought to see them, and at your age—I don't mean because you're so young—you ought to take the chances that come. You're old enough, my dear, and this gentleman won't hurt you. He'll show you the famous sunsets, if they still go on—*do* they go on? The sun set for me so long ago. But that's not a reason. Besides, I shall never miss you; you think you're too important.

Take her to the Piazza ; it used to be very pretty,"
Miss Bordereau continued, addressing herself to me.
" What have they done with the funny old church ?
I hope it hasn't tumbled down. Let her look at the
shops ; she may take some money, she may buy
what she likes."

Poor Miss Tina had got up, discountenanced and
helpless, and as we stood there before her aunt it
would certainly have struck a spectator of the scene
that our venerable friend was making rare sport of
us. Miss Tina protested in a confusion of exclama-
tions and murmurs ; but I lost no time in saying that
if she would do me the honour to accept the hospi-
tality of my boat I would engage she really shouldn't
be bored. Or if she didn't want so much of my
company the boat itself, with the gondolier, was at
her service ; he was a capital oar and she might have
every confidence. Miss Tina, without definitely
answering this speech, looked away from me and
out of the window, quite as if about to weep, and I
remarked that once we had Miss Bordereau's approval we could easily come to an understanding.
We would take an hour, whichever she liked, one of
the very next days. As I made my obeisance to the
old lady I asked her if she would kindly permit me
to see her again.

For a moment she kept me ; then she said : " Is it
very necessary to your happiness ? "

" It diverts me more than I can say."

" You're wonderfully civil. Don't you know it
almost kills *me* ? "

" How can I believe that when I see you more
animated, more brilliant than when I came in ? "

" That's very true, aunt," said Miss Tina. " I
think it does you good."

" Isn't it touching, the solicitude we each have
that the other shall enjoy herself ? " sneered Miss

Bordereau. "If you think me brilliant to-day you don't know what you're talking about ; you've never seen an agreeable woman. What do you people know about good society ? " she cried ; but before I could tell her, "Don't try to pay me a compliment ; I've been spoiled," she went on. "My door's shut, but you may sometimes knock."

With this she dismissed me and I left the room. The latch closed behind me, but Miss Tina, contrary to my hope, had remained within. I passed slowly across the hall and before taking my way downstairs waited a little. My hope was answered ; after a minute my conductress followed me. "That's a delightful idea about the Piazza," I said. "When will you go—to-night, to-morrow ? "

She had been disconcerted, as I have mentioned, but I had already perceived, and I was to observe again, that when Miss Tina was embarrassed she didn't—as most women would have in like case—turn away, floundering and hedging, but came closer, as it were, with a deprecating, a clinging appeal to be spared, to be protected. Her attitude was a constant prayer for aid and explanation, and yet no woman in the world could have been less of a comedian. From the moment you were kind to her she depended on you absolutely ; her self-consciousness dropped and she took the greatest intimacy, the innocent intimacy that was all she could conceive, for granted. She didn't know, she now declared, what possessed her aunt, who had changed so quickly, who had got some idea. I replied that she must catch the idea and let me have it : we would go and take an ice together at Florian's and she should report while we listened to the band.

" Oh it will take me a long time to be able to ' report ' ! " she said rather ruefully ; and she could promise me this satisfaction neither for that night nor for the next. I was patient now, however, for I felt I had only to wait ; and in fact at the end of the week, one lovely evening after dinner, she stepped into my gondola, to which in honour of the occasion I had attached a second oar.

We swept in the course of five minutes into the Grand Canal ; whereupon she uttered a murmur of ecstasy as fresh as if she had been a tourist just arrived. She had forgotten the splendour of the great water-way on a clear summer evening, and how the sense of floating between marble palaces and reflected lights disposed the mind to freedom and ease. We floated long and far, and though my friend gave no high-pitched voice to her glee I was sure of her full surrender. She was more than pleased, she was transported ; the whole thing was an immense liberation. The gondola moved with slow strokes, to give her time to enjoy it, and she listened to the plash of the oars, which grew louder and more music-ally liquid as we passed into narrow canals, as if it were a revelation of Venice. When I asked her how long it was since she had thus floated she answered : " Oh I don't know ; a long time—not since my aunt began to be ill." This was not the only show of her extreme vagueness about the previous years and the line marking off the period of Miss Bordereau's eminence. I was not at liberty to keep her out long, but we took a considerable *giro* before going to the Piazza. I asked her no questions, holding off by design from her life at home and the things I wanted to know ; I poured, rather, treasures of information about the objects before and around us into her ears, describing also Florence and Rome, discoursing on the charms and advantages of travel. She reclined, receptive, on the deep leather cushions, turned her eyes conscientiously to everything I noted and never mentioned to me till some time afterwards that she might be supposed to know Florence better than I, as she had lived there for years with her kinswoman. At last she said with the shy impatience of a child : " Are we not really going to the Piazza ? That's what I want to see ! " I immediately gave the order that we should go straight, after which we sat silent with the expectation of arrival. As some time still passed, however, she broke out of her own movement : " I've found out what's the matter with my aunt : she's afraid you'll go ! "

I quite gasped. " What has put that into her head ? "

" She has had an idea you've not been happy. That's why she's different now."

" You mean she wants to make me happier ? "

" Well, she wants you not to go. She wants you to stay."

" I suppose you mean on account of the rent," I remarked candidly.

Miss Tina's candour but profited. " Yes, you know ; so that I shall have more."

" How much does she want you to have ? " I asked with all the gaiety I now felt. " She ought to fix the sum, so that I may stay till it's made up."

" Oh that wouldn't please me," said Miss Tina. " It would be unheard of, your taking that trouble."

" But suppose I should have my own reasons for staying in Venice ? "

" Then it would be better for you to stay in some other house."

" And what would your aunt say to that ? "

" She wouldn't like it at all. But I should think you'd do well to give up your reasons and go away altogether."

" Dear Miss Tina," I said, " it's not so easy to give up my reasons ! "

She made no immediate answer to this, but after a

moment broke out afresh : " I think I know what your reasons are ! "

" I daresay, because the other night I almost told you how I wished you'd help me to make them good."

" I can't do that without being false to my aunt."

" What do you mean by being false to her ? "

" Why, she would never consent to what you want. She has been asked, she has been written to. It makes her fearfully angry."

" Then she *has* papers of value ? " I precipitately cried.

" Oh she has everything ! " sighed Miss Tina with a curious weariness, a sudden lapse into gloom.

These words caused all my pulses to throb, for I regarded them as precious evidence. I felt them too deeply to speak, and in the interval the gondola approached the Piazzetta. After we had disembarked I asked my companion if she would rather walk round the square or go and sit before the great café ; to which she replied that she would do whichever I liked best—I must only remember again how little time she had. I assured her there was plenty to do both, and we made the circuit of the long arcades. Her spirits revived at the sight of the bright shop-windows, and she lingered and stopped, admiring or disapproving of their contents, asking me what I thought of things, theorising about prices. My attention wandered from her; her words of a while before, "Oh she has everything ! " echoed so in my consciousness. We sat down at last in the crowded circle at Florian's, finding an unoccupied table among those that were ranged in the square. It was a splendid night and all the world out-of-doors ; Miss Tina couldn't have wished the elements more auspicious for her return to society. I saw she felt it all even more than she told, but her impressions were well-nigh too many for her. She had forgotten the attraction of the world and was learning that she had for the best years of her life been rather mercilessly cheated of it. This didn't make her angry ; but as she took in the charming scene her face had, in spite of its smile of appreciation, the flush of a wounded surprise. She didn't speak, sunk in the sense of opportunities, for ever lost, that ought to have been easy; and this gave me a chance to say to her : " Did you mean a while ago that your aunt has a plan of keeping me on by admitting me occasionally to her presence ? "

" She thinks it will make a difference with you if you sometimes see her. She wants you so much to stay that she's willing to make that concession."

" And what good does she consider I think it will do me to see her ? "

" I don't know ; it must be interesting," said Miss Tina simply. " You told her you found it so."

" So I did ; but every one doesn't think that."

" No, of course not, or more people would try."

" Well, if she's capable of making that reflexion she's capable also of making this further one," I went on : " that I must have a particular reason for not doing as others do, in spite of the interest she offers—for not leaving her alone." Miss Tina looked as if she failed to grasp this rather complicated proposition ; so I continued : " If you've not told her what I said to you the other night may she not at least have guessed it ? "

" I don't know—she's very suspicious."

" But she hasn't been made so by indiscreet curiosity, by persecution ? "

" No, no ; it isn't that," said Miss Tina, turning on me a troubled face. " I don't know how to say it : it's on account of something—ages ago, before I was born—in her life."

" Something ? What sort of thing ? "—and I asked it as if I could have no idea.

" Oh she has never told me." And I was sure my friend spoke the truth.

Her extreme limpidity was almost provoking, and I felt for the moment that she would have been more satisfactory if she had been less ingenuous. " Do you suppose it's something to which Jeffrey Aspern's letters and papers—I mean the things in her possession—have reference ? "

" I daresay it is ! " my companion exclaimed as if this were a very happy suggestion. " I've never looked at any of those things."

" None of them ? Then how do you know what they are ? "

" I don't," said Miss Tina placidly. " I've never had them in my hands. But I've seen them when she has had them out."

" Does she have them out often ? "

" Not now, but she used to. She's very fond of them."

" In spite of their being compromising ? "

" Compromising ? " Miss Tina repeated as if vague as to what that meant. I felt almost as one who corrupts the innocence of youth.

" I allude to their containing painful memories."

" Oh I don't think anything's painful."

" You mean there's nothing to affect her reputation ? "

An odder look even than usual came at this into the face of Miss Bordereau's niece—a confession, it seemed, of helplessness, an appeal to me to deal fairly, generously with her. I had brought her to the Piazza, placed her among charming influences, paid her an attention she appreciated, and now I appeared to show it all as a bribe—a bribe to make her turn in some way against her aunt. She was of a yielding nature and capable of doing almost anything to please a person markedly kind to her ; but the greatest kindness of all would be not to presume too much on this. It was strange enough, as I afterwards thought, that she had not the least air of resenting my want of consideration for her aunt's character, which would have been in the worst possible taste if anything less vital —from my point of view—had been at stake. I don't think she really measured it. " Do you mean she ever did something bad ? " she asked in a moment.

" Heaven forbid I should say so, and it's none of my business. Besides, if she did," I agreeably put it, " that was in other ages, in another world. But why shouldn't she destroy her papers ? "

" Oh she loves them too much."

" Even now, when she may be near her end ? "

" Perhaps when she's sure of that she will."

" Well, Miss Tina," I said, " that's just what I should like you to prevent."

" How can I prevent it ? "

" Couldn't you get them away from her ? "

" And give them to you ? "

This put the case, superficially, with sharp irony, but I was sure of her not intending that. " Oh I mean that you might let me see them and look them over. It isn't for myself, or that I should want them at any cost to any one else. It's simply that they would be of such immense interest to the public, such immeasurable importance as a contribution to Jeffrey Aspern's history."

She listened to me in her usual way, as if I abounded in matters she had never heard of, and I felt almost as base as the reporter of a newspaper who forces his way into a house of mourning. This was marked when she presently said : " There was a gentleman who some time ago wrote to her in very much those words. He also wanted her papers."

" And did she answer him ? " I asked, rather ashamed of not having my friend's rectitude.

" Only when he had written two or three times. He made her very angry."

" And what did she say ? "

" She said he was a devil," Miss Tina replied categorically.

" She used that expression in her letter ? "

" Oh no ; she said it to me. She made me write to him."

" And what did you say ? "

" I told him there were no papers at all."

" Ah poor gentleman ! " I groaned.

"I knew there were, but I wrote what she bade me."

" Of course you had to do that. But I hope I shan't pass for a devil."

" It will depend upon what you ask me to do for you," my companion smiled.

" Oh if there's a chance of *your* thinking so my affair's in a bad way ! I shan't ask you to steal for me, nor even to fib—for you *can't* fib, unless on paper. But the principal thing is this — to prevent her destroying the papers."

" Why, I've no control of her," said Miss Tina. " It's she who controls me."

" But she doesn't control her own arms and legs, does she ? The way she would naturally destroy her letters would be to burn them. Now she can't burn them without fire, and she can't get fire unless you give it her."

" I've always done everything she has asked," my poor friend pleaded. " Besides, there's Olimpia."

I was on the point of saying that Olimpia was probably corruptible, but I thought it best not to sound that note. So I simply put it that this frail creature might perhaps be managed.

" Every one can be managed by my aunt," said Miss Tina. And then she remembered that her holiday was over ; she must go home.

I laid my hand on her arm, across the table, to stay her a moment. " What I want of you is a general promise to help me."

" Oh how *can* I, how *can* I ? " she asked, wondering and troubled. She was half-surprised, half-frightened at my attaching that importance to her, at my calling on her for action.

" This is the main thing : to watch our friend carefully and warn me in time, before she commits that dreadful sacrilege."

" I can't watch her when she makes me go out."

" That's very true."

" And when you do too."

" Mercy on us—do you think she'll have done anything to-night ? "

" I don't know. She's very cunning."

" Are you trying to frighten me ? " I asked.

I felt this question sufficiently answered when my companion murmured in a musing, almost envious way : " Oh but she loves them—she loves them ! "

This reflexion, repeated with such emphasis, gave me great comfort ; but to obtain more of that balm I said : " If she shouldn't intend to destroy the objects we speak of before her death she'll probably have made some disposition by will."

" By will ? "

" Hasn't she made a will for your benefit ? "

" Ah she has so little to leave. That's why she likes money," said Miss Tina.

" Might I ask, since we're really talking things over, what you and she live on ? "

" On some money that comes from America, from a gentleman—I think a lawyer—in New York. He sends it every quarter. It isn't much ! "

" And won't she have disposed of that ? "

My companion hesitated—I saw she was blushing. " I believe it's mine," she said ; and the look and tone which accompanied these words betrayed so the absence of the habit of thinking of herself that I almost thought her charming. The next instant she added : " But she had in an *avvocato* here once, ever so long ago. And some people came and signed something."

" They were probably witnesses. And you weren't asked to sign ? Well then," I argued, rapidly and hopefully, " it's because you're the legatee. She must have left all her documents to you ! "

" If she has it's with very strict conditions," Miss Tina responded, rising quickly, while the movement gave the words a small character of decision. They seemed to imply that the bequest would be accompanied with a proviso that the articles bequeathed should remain concealed from every inquisitive eye, and that I was very much mistaken if I thought her the person to depart from an injunction so absolute.

" Oh of course you'll have to abide by the terms," I said ; and she uttered nothing to mitigate the rigour of this conclusion. None the less, later on, just before we disembarked at her own door after a return which had taken place almost in silence, she said to me abruptly : " I'll do what I can to help you." I was grateful for this—it was very well so far as it went ; but it didn't keep me from remembering that night in a worried waking hour that I now had her word for it to re-enforce my own impression that the old woman was full of craft.

VII

THE fear of what this side of her character might have led her to do made me nervous for days afterwards. I waited for an intimation from Miss Tina ; I almost read it as her duty to keep me informed, to let me know definitely whether or no Miss Bordereau had sacrificed her treasures. But as she gave no sign I lost patience and determined to put the case to the very touch of my own senses. I sent late one afternoon to ask if I might pay the ladies a visit, and my servant came back with surprising news. Miss Bordereau could be approached without the least difficulty ; she had been moved out into the sala and was sitting by the window that overlooked the garden. I descended and found this picture correct ; the old lady had been wheeled forth into the world and had a certain air, which came mainly perhaps from some brighter element in her dress, of being prepared again to have converse with it. It had not yet, however, begun to flock about her ; she was perfectly alone and, though the door leading to her own quarters stood open, I had at first no glimpse of Miss Tina. The window at which she sat had the afternoon shade and, one of the shutters having been pushed back, she could see the pleasant garden, where the summer sun had by this time dried up too many of the plants —she could see the yellow light and the long shadows.

" Have you come to tell me you'll take the rooms

for six months more ? " she asked as I approached her, startling me by something coarse in her cupidity almost as much as if she hadn't already given me a specimen of it. Juliana's desire to make our acquaintance lucrative had been, as I have sufficiently indicated, a false note in my image of the woman who had inspired a great poet with immortal lines ; but I may say here definitely that I after all recognised large allowance to be made for her. It was I who had kindled the unholy flame ; it was I who had put into her head that she had the means of making money. She appeared never to have thought of that ; she had been living wastefully for years, in a house five times too big for her, on a footing that I could explain only by the presumption that, excessive as it was, the space she enjoyed cost her next to nothing and that, small as were her revenues, they left her, for Venice, an appreciable margin. I had descended on her one day and taught her to calculate, and my almost extravagant comedy on the subject of the garden had presented me irresistibly in the light of a victim. Like all persons who achieve the miracle of changing their point of view late in life, she had been intensely converted : she had seized my hint with a desperate tremulous clutch.

I invited myself to go and get one of the chairs that stood, at a distance, against the wall—she had given herself no concern as to whether I should sit or stand ; and while I placed it near her I began gaily : " Oh dear madam, what an imagination you have, what an intellectual sweep ! I'm a poor devil of a man of letters who lives from day to day. How can I take palaces by the year ? My existence is precarious. I don't know whether six months hence I shall have bread to put in my mouth. I've treated myself for once ; it has been an immense luxury. But when it comes to going on—— ! "

" Are your rooms too dear ? if they are you can have more for the same money," Juliana responded. " We can arrange, we can *combinare*, as they say here."

" Well yes, since you ask me, they're too dear, much too dear," I said. " Evidently you suppose me richer than I am."

She looked at me as from the mouth of her cave. " If you write books don't you sell them ? "

" Do you mean don't people buy them ? A little, a very little—not so much as I could wish. Writing books, unless one be a great genius—and even then ! —is the last road to fortune. I think there's no more money to be made by good letters."

" Perhaps you don't choose nice subjects. What do you write about ? " Miss Bordereau implacably pursued.

" About the books of other people. I'm a critic, a commentator, an historian, in a small way." I wondered what she was coming to.

" And what other people now ? "

" Oh better ones than myself : the great writers mainly—the great philosophers and poets of the past ; those who are dead and gone and can't, poor darlings, speak for themselves."

" And what do you say about them ? "

" I say they sometimes attached themselves to very clever women ! " I replied as for pleasantness. I had measured, as I thought, my risk, but as my words fell upon the air they were to strike me as imprudent. However, I had launched them and I wasn't sorry, for perhaps after all the old woman would be willing to treat. It seemed tolerably obvious that she knew my secret : why therefore drag the process out ? But she didn't take what I had said as a confession ; she only asked :

" Do you think it's right to rake up the past ? "

" I don't feel that I know what you mean by raking it up. How can we get at it unless we dig a little ? The present has such a rough way of treading it down."

" Oh I like the past, but I don't like critics," my hostess declared with her hard complacency.

" Neither do I, but I like their discoveries."

·" Aren't they mostly lies ? "

" The lies are what they sometimes discover," I said, smiling at the quiet impertinence of this. " They often lay bare the truth."

" The truth is God's, it isn't man's : we had better leave it alone. Who can judge of it ?—who can say ? "

" We're terribly in the dark, I know," I admitted ; " but if we give up trying what becomes of all the fine things ? What becomes of the work I just mentioned, that of the great philosophers and poets ? It's all vain words if there's nothing to measure it by."

" You talk as if you were a tailor," said Miss Bordereau whimsically ; and then she added quickly and in a different manner : " This house is very fine ; the proportions are magnificent. To-day I wanted to look at this part again. I made them bring me out here. When your man came just now to learn if I would see you I was on the point of sending for you to ask if you didn't mean to go on. I wanted to judge what I'm letting you have. This sala is very grand," she pursued like an auctioneer, moving a little, as I guessed, her invisible eyes. " I don't believe you often have lived in such a house, eh ? "

" I can't often afford to ! " I said.

" Well then how much will you give me for six months ? "

I was on the point of exclaiming—and the air of excruciation in my face would have denoted a moral fact—" Don't, Juliana ; for *his* sake, don't ! " But

I controlled myself and asked less passionately : " Why should I remain so long as that ? "

" I thought you liked it," said Miss Bordereau with her shrivelled dignity.

" So I thought I should."

For a moment she said nothing more, and I left my own words to suggest to her what they might. I half-expected her to say, coldly enough, that if I had been disappointed we needn't continue the discussion, and this in spite of the fact that I believed her now to have in her mind—however it had come there—what would have told her that my disappointment was natural. But to my extreme surprise she ended by observing : " If you don't think we've treated you well enough perhaps we can discover some way of treating you better." This speech was somehow so incongruous that it made me laugh again, and I excused myself by saying that she talked as if I were a sulky boy pouting in the corner and having to be " brought round." I hadn't a grain of complaint to make ; and could anything have exceeded Miss Tina's graciousness in accompanying me a few nights before to the Piazza ? At this the old woman went on : " Well, you brought it on yourself ! " And then in a different tone : " She's a very fine girl." I assented cordially to this proposition, and she expressed the hope that I did so not merely to be obliging, but that I really liked her. Meanwhile I wondered still more what Miss Bordereau was coming to. " Except for me, to-day," she said, " she hasn't a relation in the world." Did she by describing her niece as amiable and unencumbered wish to represent her as a *parti* ?

It was perfectly true that I couldn't afford to go on with my rooms at a fancy price and that I had already devoted to my undertaking almost all the hard cash I had set apart for it. My patience and my time were by no means exhausted, but I should be able to draw upon them only on a more usual Venetian basis. I was willing to pay the precious personage with whom my pecuniary dealings were such a discord twice as much as any other *padrona di casa* would have asked, but I wasn't willing to pay her twenty times as much. I told her so plainly, and my plainness appeared to have some success, for she exclaimed : " Very good ; you've done what I asked—you've made an offer ! "

" Yes, but not for half a year. Only by the month."

" Oh I must think of that then." She seemed disappointed that I wouldn't tie myself to a period, and I guessed that she wished both to secure me and to discourage me ; to say severely : " Do you dream that you can get off with less than six months ? Do you dream that even by the end of that time you'll be appreciably nearer your victory ? " What was most in my mind was that she had a fancy to play me the trick of making me engage myself when in fact she had sacrificed her treasure. There was a moment when my suspense on this point was so acute that I all but broke out with the question, and what kept it back was but an instinctive recoil—lest it should be a mistake—from the last violence of self-exposure. She was such a subtle old witch that one could never tell where one stood with her. You may imagine whether it cleared up the puzzle when, just after she had said she would think of my proposal and without any formal transition, she drew out of her pocket with an embarrassed hand a small object wrapped in crumpled white paper. She held it there a moment and then resumed : " Do you know much about curiosities ? "

" About curiosities ? "

" About antiquities, the old gimcracks that people

pay so much for to-day. Do you know the kind of price they bring ? "

I thought I saw what was coming, but I said ingenuously : " Do you want to buy something ? "

" No, I want to sell. What would an amateur give me for that ? " She unfolded the white paper and made a motion for me to take from her a small oval portrait. I possessed myself of it with fingers of which I could only hope that they didn't betray the intensity of their clutch, and she added : " I would part with it only for a good price."

At the first glance I recognised Jeffrey Aspern, and was well aware that I flushed with the act. As she was watching me, however, I had the consistency to exclaim : " What a striking face ! Do tell me who he is."

" He's an old friend of mine, a very distinguished man in his day. He gave it me himself, but I'm afraid to mention his name, lest you never should have heard of him, critic and historian as you are. I know the world goes fast and one generation forgets another. He was all the fashion when I was young."

She was perhaps amazed at my assurance, but I was surprised at hers ; at her having the energy, in her state of health and at her time of life, to wish to sport with me to that tune simply for her private entertainment—the humour to test me and practise on me and befool me. This at least was the interpretation that I put upon her production of the relic, for I couldn't believe she really desired to sell it or cared for any information I might give her. What she wished was to dangle it before my eyes and put a prohibitive price on it. " The face comes back to me, it torments me," I said, turning the object this way and that and looking at it very critically. It was a careful but not a supreme work of art, larger than the ordinary miniature and representing a young man with a remarkably handsome face, in a high-collared green coat and a buff waistcoat. I felt in the little work a virtue of likeness and judged it to have been painted when the model was about twenty-five. There are, as all the world knows, three other portraits of the poet in existence, but none of so early a date as this elegant image. " I've never seen the original, clearly a man of a past age, but I've seen other reproductions of this face," I went on. " You expressed doubt of this generation's having heard of the gentleman, but he strikes me for all the world as a celebrity. Now who is he? I can't put my finger on him—I can't give him a label. Wasn't he a writer? Surely he's a poet." I was determined that it should be she, not I, who should first pronounce Jeffrey Aspern's name.

My resolution was taken in ignorance of Miss Bordereau's extremely resolute character, and her lips never formed in my hearing the syllables that meant so much for her. She neglected to answer my question, but raised her hand to take back the picture, using a gesture which though impotent was in a high degree peremptory. " It's only a person who should know for himself that would give me my price," she said with a certain dryness.

" Oh then you have a price? " I didn't restore the charming thing ; not from any vindictive purpose, but because I instinctively clung to it. We looked at each other hard while I retained it.

" I know the least I would take. What it occurred to me to ask you about is the most I shall be able to get."

She made a movement, drawing herself together as if, in a spasm of dread at having lost her prize, she had been impelled to the immense effort of rising to snatch it from me. I instantly placed it in her hand again, saying as I did so : " I should like to have it myself, but with your ideas it would be quite beyond my mark."

She turned the small oval plate over in her lap, with its face down, and I heard her catch her breath as after a strain or an escape. This, however, did not prevent her saying in a moment : " You'd buy a likeness of a person you don't know by an artist who has no reputation ? "

" The artist may have no reputation, but that thing's wonderfully well painted," I replied, to give myself a reason.

" It's lucky you thought of saying that, because the painter was my father."

" That makes the picture indeed precious ! " I returned with gaiety ; and I may add that a part of my cheer came from this proof I had been right in my theory of Miss Bordereau's origin. Aspern had of course met the young lady on his going to her father's studio as a sitter. I observed to Miss Bordereau that if she would entrust me with her property for twenty-four hours I should be happy to take advice on it ; but she made no other reply than to slip it in silence into her pocket. This convinced me still more that she had no sincere intention of selling it during her lifetime, though she may have desired to satisfy herself as to the sum her niece, should she leave it to her, might expect eventually to obtain for it. " Well, at any rate, I hope you won't offer it without giving me notice," I said as she remained irresponsive. " Remember me as a possible purchaser."

" I should want your money first ! " she returned with unexpected rudeness ; and then, as if she bethought herself that I might well complain of such a tone and wished to turn the matter off, asked abruptly what I talked about with her niece when I went out with her that way of an evening.

" You speak as if we had set up the habit," I

replied. " Certainly I should be very glad if it were to become our pleasant custom. But in that case I should feel a still greater scruple at betraying a lady's confidence."

" Her confidence ? Has my niece confidence ? "

" Here she is—she can tell you herself," I said ; for Miss Tina now appeared on the threshold of the old woman's parlour. " Have you confidence, Miss Tina ? Your aunt wants very much to know."

" Not in her, not in her ! " the younger lady declared, shaking her head with a dolefulness that was neither jocular nor affected. " I don't know what to do with her ; she has fits of horrid imprudence. She's so easily tired—and yet she has begun to roam, to drag herself about the house." And she looked down at her yoke-fellow of long years with a vacancy of wonder, as if all their contact and custom hadn't made her perversities, on occasion, any more easy to follow.

" I know what I'm about. I'm not losing my mind. I daresay you'd like to think so," said Miss Bordereau with a crudity of cynicism.

" I don't suppose you came out here yourself. Miss Tina must have had to lend you a hand," I interposed for conciliation.

" Oh she insisted we should push her ; and when she insists ! " said Miss Tina, in the same tone of apprehension : as if there were no knowing what service she disapproved of her aunt might force her next to render.

" I've always got most things done I wanted, thank God ! The people I've lived with have humoured me," the old woman continued, speaking out of the white ashes of her vanity.

I took it pleasantly up. " I suppose you mean they've obeyed you."

" Well, whatever it is—when they like one."

" It's just because I like you that I want to resist," said Miss Tina with a nervous laugh.

" Oh I suspect you'll bring Miss Bordereau upstairs next to pay me a visit," I went on ; to which the old lady replied :

" Oh no ; I can keep an eye on you from here ! "

" You're very tired ; you'll certainly be ill to-night ! " cried Miss Tina.

" Nonsense, dear ; I feel better at this moment than I've done for a month. To-morrow I shall come out again. I want to be where I can see this clever gentleman."

" Shouldn't you perhaps see me better in your sitting-room ? " I asked.

" Don't you mean shouldn't you have a better chance at *me* ? " she returned, fixing me a moment with her green shade.

" Ah I haven't that anywhere ! I look at you but don't see you."

" You agitate her dreadfully — and that's not good," said Miss Tina, giving me a reproachful deterrent headshake.

" I want to watch you—I want to watch you ! " Miss Bordereau went on.

" Well then let us spend as much of our time together as possible—I don't care where. That will give you every facility."

" Oh I've seen you enough for to-day. I'm satisfied. Now I'll go home," Juliana said. Miss Tina laid her hands on the back of the wheeled chair and began to push, but I begged her to let me take her place. " Oh yes, you may move me this way—you shan't in any other ! " the old woman cried as she felt herself propelled firmly and easily over the smooth hard floor. Before we reached the door of her own apartment she bade me stop, and she took a long last look up and down the noble sala. " Oh it's a prodigious house!" she murmured; after which I pushed her forward. When we had entered the parlour Miss Tina let me know she should now be able to manage, and at the same moment the little red-haired *donna* came to meet her mistress. Miss Tina's idea was evidently to get her aunt immediately back to bed. I confess that in spite of this urgency I was guilty of the indiscretion of lingering; it held me there to feel myself so close to the objects I coveted—which would be probably put away somewhere in the faded unsociable room. The place had indeed a bareness that suggested no hidden values; there were neither dusky nooks nor curtained corners, neither massive cabinets nor chests with iron bands. Moreover it was possible, it was perhaps even likely, that the old lady had consigned her relics to her bedroom, to some battered box that was shoved under the bed, to the drawer of some lame dressing-table, where they would be in the range of vision by the dim night-lamp. None the less I turned an eye on every article of furniture, on every conceivable cover for a hoard, and noticed that there were half a dozen things with drawers, and in particular a tall old secretary with brass ornaments of the style of the Empire—a receptacle somewhat infirm but still capable of keeping rare secrets. I don't know why this article so engaged me, small purpose as I had of breaking into it; but I stared at it so hard that Miss Tina noticed me and changed colour. Her doing this made me think I was right and that, wherever they might have been before, the Aspern papers at that moment languished behind the peevish little lock of the secretary. It was hard to turn my attention from the dull mahogany front when I reflected that a plain panel divided me from the goal of my hopes; but I gathered up my slightly scattered prudence and with an effort took leave of my hostess. To make the effort graceful I said to her that I should **certainly** bring her an opinion about the little picture.

" The little picture ? " Miss Tina asked in surprise.

" What do *you* know about it, my dear ? " the old woman demanded. " You needn't mind. I've fixed my price."

" And what may that be ? "

" A thousand pounds."

" Oh Lord ! " cried poor Miss Tina irrepressibly.

" Is that what she talks to you about ? " said Miss Bordereau.

" Imagine your aunt's wanting to know ! " I had to separate from my younger friend with only those words, though I should have liked immensely to add : " For heaven's sake meet me to-night in the garden ! "

VIII

As it turned out the precaution had not been needed,
for three hours later, just as I had finished my dinner,
Miss Tina appeared, unannounced, in the open doorway of the room in which my simple repasts were
served. I remember well that I felt no surprise at
seeing her; which is not a proof of my not believing
in her timidity. It was immense, but in a case in
which there was a particular reason for boldness it
never would have prevented her from running up to
my floor. I saw that she was now quite full of a
particular reason; it threw her forward—made her
seize me, as I rose to meet her, by the arm.

"My aunt's very ill; I think she's dying!"

"Never in the world," I answered bitterly. "Don't
you be afraid!"

"Do go for a doctor—do, do! Olimpia's gone
for the one we always have, but she doesn't come
back; I don't know what has happened to her. I
told her that if he wasn't at home she was to follow
him where he had gone; but apparently she's following him all over Venice. I don't know what to do—
she looks so as if she were sinking."

"May I see her, may I judge?" I asked. "Of
course I shall be delighted to bring some one; but
hadn't we better send my man instead, so that I may
stay with you?"

Miss Tina assented to this and I despatched my servant for the best doctor in the neighbourhood. I hurried downstairs with her, and on the way she told me that an hour after I quitted them in the afternoon Miss Bordereau had had an attack of " oppression," a terrible difficulty in breathing. This had subsided, but had left her so exhausted that she didn't come up ; she seemed all spent and gone. I repeated that she wasn't gone, that she wouldn't go yet ; whereupon Miss Tina gave me a sharper sidelong glance than she had ever favoured me withal and said : " Really, what do you mean ? I suppose you don't accuse her of making-believe ! " I forget what reply I made to this, but I fear that in my heart I thought the old woman capable of any weird manœuvre. Miss Tina wanted to know what I had done to her ; her aunt had told her I had made her so angry. I declared I had done nothing whatever—I had been exceedingly careful ; to which my companion rejoined that our friend had assured her she had had a scene with me—a scene that had upset her. I answered with some resentment that the scene had been of *her* making—that I couldn't think what she was angry with me for unless for not seeing my way to give a thousand pounds for the portrait of Jeffrey Aspern. " And did she show you that ? Oh gracious —oh deary me ! " groaned Miss Tina, who seemed to feel the situation pass out of her control and the elements of her fate thicken round her. I answered her I'd give anything to possess it, yet that I had no thousand pounds ; but I stopped when we came to the door of Miss Bordereau's room. I had an immense curiosity to pass it, but I thought it my duty to represent to Miss Tina that if I made the invalid angry she ought perhaps to be spared the sight of me. " The sight of you ? Do you think she can *see* ? " my companion demanded almost with indignation. I did think so but forebore to say it, and I softly followed my conductress.

I remember that what I said to her as I stood for a moment beside the old woman's bed was : " Does she never show you her eyes then ? Have you never seen them ? " Miss Bordereau had been divested of her green shade, but—it was not my fortune to behold Juliana in her nightcap—the upper half of her face was covered by the fall of a piece of dingy lace-like muslin, a sort of extemporised hood which, wound round her head, descended to the end of her nose, leaving nothing visible but her white withered cheeks and puckered mouth, closed tightly and, as it were, consciously. Miss Tina gave me a glance of surprise, evidently not seeing a reason for my impatience. " You mean she always wears something ? She does it to preserve them."

" Because they're so fine ? "

" Oh to-day, to-day ! " And Miss Tina shook her head speaking very low. " But they used to be magnificent ! "

" Yes indeed — we've Aspern's word for that." And as I looked again at the old woman's wrappings I could imagine her not having wished to allow any supposition that the great poet had overdone it. But I didn't waste my time in considering Juliana, in whom the appearance of respiration was so slight as to suggest that no human attention could ever help her more. I turned my eyes once more all over the room, rummaging with them the closets, the chests of drawers, the tables. Miss Tina at once noted their direction and read, I think, what was in them ; but she didn't answer it, turning away restlessly, anxiously, so that I felt rebuked, with reason, for an appetite well-nigh indecent in the presence of our dying companion. All the same I took another view, endeavouring to pick out mentally the receptacle to try first, for a person who should wish to put his hand on Miss Bordereau's papers directly after her death. The place was a dire confusion ; it looked like the dressing-room of an old actress. There were clothes hanging over chairs, odd-looking shabby bundles here and there, and various pasteboard boxes piled together, battered, bulging and discoloured, which might have been fifty years old. Miss Tina after a moment noticed the direction of my eyes again, and, as if she guessed how I judged such appearances—forgetting I had no business to judge them at all—said, perhaps to defend herself from the imputation of complicity in the disorder :

" She likes it this way ; we can't move things. There are old bandboxes she has had most of her life." Then she added, half-taking pity on my real thought : " Those things were *there*." And she pointed to a small low trunk which stood under a sofa that just allowed room for it. It struck me as a queer super-annuated coffer, of painted wood, with elaborate handles and shrivelled straps and with the colour— it had last been endued with a coat of light green— much rubbed off. It evidently had travelled with Juliana in the olden time — in the days of adventures, which it had shared. It would have made a strange figure arriving at a modern hotel.

" *Were* there — they aren't now ? " I asked, startled by Miss Tina's implication.

She was going to answer, but at that moment the doctor came in—the doctor whom the little maid had been sent to fetch and whom she had at last over-taken. My servant, going on his own errand, had met her with her companion in tow, and in the sociable Venetian spirit, retracing his steps with them, had also come up to the threshold of the padrona's room, where I saw him peep over the doctor's shoulder. I motioned him away the more instantly that the sight of his prying face reminded me how little I myself had to do there—an admonition confirmed by the sharp way the little doctor eyed me, his air of taking me for a rival who had the field before him. He was a short fat brisk gentleman who wore the tall hat of his profession and seemed to look at everything but his patient. He kept me still in range, as if it struck him I too should be better for a dose, so that I bowed to him and left him with the women, going down to smoke a cigar in the garden. I was nervous ; I couldn't go further ; I couldn't leave the place. I don't know exactly what I thought might happen, but I felt it important to be there. I wandered about the alleys—the warm night had come on—smoking cigar after cigar and studying the light in Miss Bordereau's windows. They were open now, I could see ; the situation was different. Sometimes the light moved, but not quickly ; it didn't suggest the hurry of a crisis. Was the old woman dying or was she already dead ? Had the doctor said that there was nothing to be done at her tremendous age but to let her quietly pass away ? or had he simply announced with a look a little more conventional that the end of the end had come ? Were the other two women just going and coming over the offices that follow in such a case ? It made me uneasy not to be nearer, as if I thought the doctor himself might carry away the papers with him. I bit my cigar hard while it assailed me again that perhaps there were now no papers to carry !

I wandered about an hour and more. I looked out for Miss Tina at one of the windows, having a vague idea that she might come there to give me some sign. Wouldn't she see the red tip of my cigar in the dark and feel sure I was hanging on to know what the doctor had said ? I'm afraid it's a proof of the grossness of my anxieties that I should have taken in some degree for granted at such an hour, in the midst of the greatest change that could fall on her, poor Miss Tina's having also a free mind for them. My servant came down and spoke to me; he knew nothing save that the doctor had gone after a visit of half an hour. If he had stayed half an hour then Miss Bordereau was still alive : it couldn't have taken so long to attest her decease. I sent the man out of the house; there were moments when the sense of his curiosity annoyed me, and this was one of them. *He* had been watching my cigar-tip from an upper window, if Miss Tina hadn't ; he couldn't know what I was after and I couldn't tell him, though I suspected in him fantastic private theories about me which he thought fine and which, had I more exactly known them, I should have thought offensive.

I went upstairs at last, but I mounted no higher than the sala. The door of Miss Bordereau's apartment was open, showing from the parlour the dimness of a poor candle. I went toward it with a light tread, and at the same moment Miss Tina appeared and stood looking at me as I approached. "She's better, she's better," she said even before I had asked. "The doctor has given her something ; she woke up, came back to life while he was there. He says there's no immediate danger."

"No immediate danger? Surely he thinks her condition serious."

"Yes, because she had been excited. That affects her dreadfully."

"It will do so again then, because she works herself up. She did so this afternoon."

"Yes, she mustn't come out any more," said Miss Tina with one of her lapses into a deeper detachment.

"What's the use of making such a remark as that," I permitted myself to ask, "if you begin to rattle her about again the first time she bids you ? "

" I won't—I won't do it any more."

" You must learn to resist her," I went on.

" Oh yes, I shall ; I shall do so better if you tell me it's right."

" You mustn't do it for me—you must do it for yourself. It all comes back to you, if you're scared and upset."

" Well, I'm not upset now," said Miss Tina placidly enough. " She's very quiet."

" Is she conscious again—does she speak ? "

" No, she doesn't speak, but she takes my hand. She holds it fast."

" Yes," I returned, " I can see what force she still has by the way she grabbed that picture this afternoon. But if she holds you fast how comes it that you're here ? "

Miss Tina waited a little ; though her face was in deep shadow—she had her back to the light in the parlour and I had put down my own candle far off, near the door of the sala—I thought I saw her smile ingenuously. " I came on purpose—I had heard your step."

" Why, I came on tiptoe, as soundlessly as possible."

" Well, I had heard you," said Miss Tina.

" And is your aunt alone now ? "

" Oh no—Olimpia sits there."

On my side I debated. " Shall we then pass in there ? " And I nodded at the parlour ; I wanted more and more to be on the spot.

" We can't talk there—she'll hear us."

I was on the point of replying that in that case we'd sit silent, but I felt too much this wouldn't do, there was something I desired so immensely to ask her. Thus I hinted we might walk a little in the sala, keeping more at the other end, where we shouldn't disturb our friend. Miss Tina assented unconditionally ; the doctor was coming again, she said, and she would be there to meet him at the door. We strolled through the fine superfluous hall, where on the marble floor—particularly as at first we said nothing—our footsteps were more audible than I had expected. When we reached the other end— the wide window, inveterately closed, connecting with the balcony that overhung the canal—I submitted that we had best remain there, as she would see the doctor arrive the sooner. I opened the window and we passed out on the balcony. The air of the canal seemed even heavier, hotter than that of the sala. The place was hushed and void ; the quiet neighbourhood had gone to sleep. A lamp, here and there, over the narrow black water, glimmered in double ; the voice of a man going homeward singing, his jacket on his shoulder and his hat on his ear, came to us from a distance. This didn't prevent the scene from being very *comme il faut*, as Miss Bordereau had called it the first time I saw her. Presently a gondola passed along the canal with its slow rhythmical plash, and as we listened we watched it in silence. It didn't stop, it didn't carry the doctor ; and after it had gone on I said to Miss Tina :

" And where are they now—the things that were in the trunk ? "

" In the trunk ? "

" That green box you pointed out to me in her room. You said her papers had been there ; you seemed to mean she had transferred them."

" Oh yes ; they're not in the trunk," said Miss Tina.

" May I ask if you've looked ? "

" Yes, I've looked—for you."

" How for me, dear Miss Tina ? Do you mean you'd have given them to me if you had found them ? " —and I fairly trembled with the question.

She delayed to reply and I waited. Suddenly she

broke out : " I don't know what I'd do—what I wouldn't ! "

" Would you look again—somewhere else ? "

She had spoken with a strange unexpected emotion, and she went on in the same tone : " I can't—I can't —while she lies there. It isn't decent."

" No, it isn't decent," I replied gravely. " Let the poor lady rest in peace." And the words, on my lips, were not hypocritical, for I felt reprimanded and shamed.

Miss Tina added in a moment, as if she had guessed this and were sorry for me, but at the same time wished to explain that I did push her, or at least harp on the chord, too much : " I can't deceive her that way. I can't deceive her— perhaps on her deathbed."

" Heaven forbid I should ask you, though I've been guilty myself ! "

" You've been guilty ? "

" I've sailed under false colours." I felt now I must make a clean breast of it, must tell her I had given her an invented name on account of my fear her aunt would have heard of me and so refuse to take me in. I explained this as well as that I had really been a party to the letter addressed them by John Cumnor months before.

She listened with great attention, almost in fact gaping for wonder, and when I had made my confession she said : " Then your real name—what is it ? " She repeated it over twice when I had told her, accompanying it with the exclamation, " Gracious, gracious ! " Then she added : " I like your own best."

" So do I "—and I felt my laugh rueful. " Ouf ! it's a relief to get rid of the other."

" So it was a regular plot—a kind of conspiracy ? "

" Oh a conspiracy—we were only two," I replied, leaving out of course Mrs. Prest.

She considered ; I thought she was perhaps going to pronounce us very base. But this was not her way, and she remarked after a moment, as in candid impartial contemplation : " How much you must want them ! "

" Oh I do, passionately ! " I grinned, I fear, to admit. And this chance made me go on, forgetting my compunction of a moment before. " How can she possibly have changed their place herself ? How can she walk ? How can she arrive at that sort of muscular exertion ? How can she lift and carry things ? "

" Oh when one wants and when one has so much will ! " said Miss Tina as if she had thought over my question already herself and had simply had no choice but that answer—the idea that in the dead of night, or at some moment when the coast was clear, the old woman had been capable of a miraculous effort.

" Have you questioned Olimpia ? Hasn't she helped her—hasn't she done it for her ? " I asked ; to which my friend replied promptly and positively that their servant had had nothing to do with the matter, though without admitting definitely that she had spoken to her. It was as if she were a little shy, a little ashamed now, of letting me see how much she had entered into my uneasiness and had me on her mind. Suddenly she said to me without any immediate relevance :

" I rather feel you a new person, you know, now that you've a new name."

" It isn't a new one ; it's a very good old one, thank fortune ! "

She looked at me a moment. " Well, I do like it better."

99

"Oh if you didn't I would almost go on with the other!"

"Would you really?"

I laughed again, but I returned for all answer: "Of course if she can rummage about that way she can perfectly have burnt them."

"You must wait—you must wait," Miss Tina mournfully moralised; and her tone ministered little to my patience, for it seemed after all to accept that wretched possibility. I would teach myself to wait, I declared nevertheless; because in the first place I couldn't do otherwise and in the second I had her promise, given me the other night, that she would help me.

"Of course if the papers are gone that's no use," she said; not as if she wished to recede, but only to be conscientious.

"Naturally. But if you could only find out!" I groaned, quivering again.

"I thought you promised you'd wait."

"Oh you mean wait even for that?"

"For what then?"

"Ah nothing," I answered rather foolishly, being ashamed to tell her what had been implied in my acceptance of delay—the idea that she would perhaps do more for me than merely find out.

I know not if she guessed this; at all events she seemed to bethink herself of some propriety of showing me more rigour. "I didn't promise to deceive, did I? I don't think I did."

"It doesn't much matter whether you did or **not,** for you couldn't!"

Nothing is more possible than that she wouldn't have contested this even hadn't she been diverted by our seeing the doctor's gondola shoot into the little canal and approach the house. I noted that he came as fast as if he believed our proprietress still in danger. We looked down at him while he disembarked and then went back into the sala to meet him. When he came up, however, I naturally left Miss Tina to go off with him alone, only asking her leave to come back later for news.

I went out of the house and walked far, as far as the Piazza, where my restlessness declined to quit me. I was unable to sit down ; it was very late now though there were people still at the little tables in front of the cafés : I could but uneasily revolve, and I did so half a dozen times. The only comfort, none the less, was in my having told Miss Tina who I really was. At last I took my way home again, getting gradually and all but inextricably lost, as I did whenever I went out in Venice : so that it was considerably past midnight when I reached my door. The sala, upstairs, was as dark as usual, and my lamp as I crossed it found nothing satisfactory to show me. I was disappointed, for I had notified Miss Tina that I would come back for a report, and I thought she might have left a light there as a sign. The door of the ladies' apartment was closed ; which seemed a hint that my faltering friend had gone to bed in impatience of waiting for me. I stood in the middle of the place, considering, hoping she would hear me and perhaps peep out, saying to myself too that she would never go to bed with her aunt in a state so critical ; she would sit up and watch—she would be in a chair, in her dressing-gown. I went nearer the door ; I stopped there and listened. I heard nothing at all and at last I tapped gently. No answer came, and after another minute I turned the handle. There was no light in the room ; this ought to have prevented my entrance, but it had no such effect. If I have frankly stated the importunities, the indelicacies, of which my desire to possess myself of Jeffrey Aspern's papers had made me capable I needn't shrink, it seems to me, from confessing this last in-discretion. I regard it as the worst thing I did, yet there were extenuating circumstances. I was deeply though doubtless not disinterestedly anxious for more news of Juliana, and Miss Tina had accepted from me, as it were, a rendezvous which it might have been a point of honour with me to keep. It may be objected that her leaving the place dark was a positive sign that she released me, and to this I can only reply that I wished not to be released.

The door of Miss Bordereau's room was open and I could see beyond it the faintness of a taper. There was no sound—my footstep caused no one to stir. I came farther into the room ; I lingered there lamp in hand. I wanted to give Miss Tina a chance to come to me if, as I couldn't doubt, she were still with her aunt. I made no noise to call her ; I only waited to see if she wouldn't notice my light. She didn't, and I explained this—I found afterwards I was right —by the idea that she had fallen asleep. If she had fallen asleep her aunt was not on her mind, and my explanation ought to have led me to go out as I had come. I must repeat again that it didn't, for I found myself at the same moment given up to something else. I had no definite purpose, no bad intention, but felt myself held to the spot by an acute, though absurd, sense of opportunity. Opportunity for what I couldn't have said, inasmuch as it wasn't in my mind that I might proceed to thievery. Even had this tempted me I was confronted with the evident fact that Miss Bordereau didn't leave her secretary, her cupboard and the drawers of her tables gaping. I had no keys, no tools and no ambition to smash her furniture. None the less it came to me that I was now, perhaps, alone, unmolested, at the hour of free-dom and safety, nearer to the source of my hopes than I had ever been. I held up my lamp, let the light play on the different objects as if it could tell me something. Still there came no movement from the other room. If Miss Tina was sleeping she was sleeping sound. Was she doing so—generous creature —on purpose to leave me the field? Did she know I was there and was she just keeping quiet to see what I would do—what I *could* do? Yet might I, when it came to that? She herself knew even better than I how little.

I stopped in front of the secretary, gaping at it vainly and no doubt grotesquely; for what had it to say to me after all? In the first place it was locked, and in the second it almost surely contained nothing in which I was interested. Ten to one the papers had been destroyed, and even if they hadn't the keen old woman wouldn't have put them in such a place as that after removing them from the green trunk—wouldn't have transferred them, with the idea of their safety on her brain, from the better hiding-place to the worse. The secretary was more conspicuous, more exposed in a room in which she could no longer mount guard. It opened with a key, but there was a small brass handle, like a button, as well: I saw this as I played my lamp over it. I did something more, for the climax of my crisis; I caught a glimpse of the possibility that Miss Tina wished me really to understand. If she didn't so wish me, if she wished me to keep away, why hadn't she locked the door of communication between the sitting-room and the sala? That would have been a definite sign that I was to leave them alone. If I didn't leave them alone she meant me to come for a purpose—a purpose now represented by the super-subtle inference that to oblige me she had unlocked the secretary. She hadn't left the key, but the lid would probably move if I touched the button. This possibility pressed me hard and I bent very close to judge. I didn't propose to do anything, not even—not in the least—to let down the lid ; I only wanted to test my theory, to see if the cover *would* move. I touched the button with my hand—a mere touch would tell me ; and as I did so—it is embarrassing for me to relate it —I looked over my shoulder. It was a chance, an instinct, for I had really heard nothing. I almost let my luminary drop and certainly I stepped back, straightening myself up at what I saw. Juliana stood there in her night-dress, by the doorway of her room, watching me ; her hands were raised, she had lifted the everlasting curtain that covered half her face, and for the first, the last, the only time I beheld her extraordinary eyes. They glared at me ; they were like the sudden drench, for a caught burglar, of a flood of gaslight ; they made me horribly ashamed. I never shall forget her strange little bent white tottering figure, with its lifted head, her attitude, her expression ; neither shall I forget the tone in which as I turned, looking at her, she hissed out passionately, furiously :

"Ah you publishing scoundrel ! "

I can't now say what I stammered to excuse myself, to explain ; but I went toward her to tell her I meant no harm. She waved me off with her old hands, retreating before me in horror ; and the next thing I knew she had fallen back with a quick spasm, as if death had descended on her, into Miss Tina's arms.

IX

I LEFT Venice the next morning, directly on learning that my hostess had not succumbed, as I feared at the moment, to the shock I had given her——the shock I may also say she had given me. How in the world could I have supposed her capable of getting out of bed by herself ? I failed to see Miss Tina before going ; I only saw the *donna*, whom I entrusted with a note for her younger mistress. In this note I mentioned that I should be absent but a few days. I went to Treviso, to Bassano, to Castelfranco ; I took walks and drives and looked at musty old churches with ill-lighted pictures ; I spent hours seated smoking at the doors of cafés, where there were flies and yellow curtains, on the shady side of sleepy little squares. In spite of these pastimes, which were mechanical and perfunctory, I scantly enjoyed my travels : I had had to gulp down a bitter draught and couldn't get rid of the taste. It had been devilish awkward, as the young men say, to be found by Juliana in the dead of night examining the attachment of her bureau ; and it had not been less so to have to believe for a good many hours after that it was highly probable I had killed her. My humiliation galled me, but I had to make the best of it, had, in writing to Miss Tina, to minimise it, as well as account for the posture in which I had been discovered. As she gave me no word of answer I couldn't know what impression I made on her. It rankled for me that I had been called a publishing scoundrel, since certainly I did publish and no less certainly hadn't been very delicate. There was a moment when I stood convinced that the only way to purge my dishonour was to take myself straight away on the instant; to sacrifice my hopes and relieve the two poor women for ever of the oppression of my intercourse. Then I reflected that I had better try a short absence first, for I must already have had a sense (unexpressed and dim) that in disappearing completely it wouldn't be merely my own hopes I should condemn to extinction. It would perhaps answer if I kept dark long enough to give the elder lady time to believe herself rid of me. That she would wish to be rid of me after this—if I wasn't rid of her—was now not to be doubted : that midnight monstrosity would have cured her of the disposition to put up with my company for the sake of my dollars. I said to myself that after all I couldn't abandon Miss Tina, and I continued to say this even while I noted that she quite ignored my earnest request—I had given her two or three addresses, at little towns, *poste restante*—for some sign of her actual state. I would have made my servant write me news but that he was unable to manage a pen. Couldn't I measure the scorn of Miss Tina's silence—little disdainful as she had ever been ? Really the soreness pressed ; yet if I had scruples about going back I had others about not doing so, and I wanted to put myself on a better footing. The end of it was that I did return to Venice on the twelfth day ; and as my gondola gently bumped against our palace steps a fine palpitation of suspense showed me the violence my absence had done me.

I had faced about so abruptly that I hadn't even telegraphed to my servant. He was therefore not at the station to meet me, but he poked out his head from an upper window when I reached the house. " They have put her into earth, *quella vecchia*," he said to me in the lower hall while he shouldered my valise ; and he grinned and almost winked as if he knew I should be pleased with his news.

" She's dead ! " I cried, giving him a very different look.

" So it appears, since they've buried her."

" It's all over then ?   When was the funeral ? "

" The other yesterday.   But a funeral you could scarcely call it, signore : *roba da niente—un piccolo passeggio brutto* of two gondolas.   *Poveretta !* " the man continued, referring apparently to Miss Tina. His conception of funerals was that they were mainly to amuse the living.

I wanted to know about Miss Tina, how she might be and generally where ; but I asked him no more questions till we had got upstairs.   Now that the fact had met me I took a bad view of it, especially of the idea that poor Miss Tina had had to manage by herself after the end.   What did she know about arrangements, about the steps to take in such a case ? Poveretta indeed !   I could only hope the doctor had given her support and that she hadn't been neglected by the old friends of whom she had told me, the little band of the faithful whose fidelity consisted in coming to the house once a year.   I elicited from my servant that two old ladies and an old gentleman had in fact rallied round Miss Tina and had supported her— they had come for her in a gondola of their own— during the journey to the cemetery, the little red-walled island of tombs which lies to the north of the town and on the way to Murano.   It appeared from these signs that the Misses Bordereau were Catholics, a discovery I had never made, as the old woman couldn't go to church and her niece, so far as I perceived, either didn't, or went only to early mass in the parish before I was stirring. Certainly even the priests respected their seclusion ; I had never caught the whisk of the curato's skirt. That evening, an hour later, I sent my servant down with five words on a card to ask if Miss Tina would see me a few moments. She was not in the house, where he had sought her, he told me when he came back, but in the garden walking about to refresh herself and picking the flowers quite as if they belonged to her. He had found her there and she would be happy to see me.

I went down and passed half an hour with poor Miss Tina. She had always had a look of musty mourning, as if she were wearing out old robes of sorrow that wouldn't come to an end ; and in this particular she made no different show. But she clearly had been crying, crying a great deal—simply, satis-fyingly, refreshingly, with a primitive retarded sense of solitude and violence. But she had none of the airs or graces of grief, and I was almost surprised to see her stand there in the first dusk with her hands full of admirable roses and smile at me with reddened eyes. Her white face, in the frame of her mantilla, looked longer, leaner than usual. I hadn't doubted her being irreconcilably disgusted with me, her con-sidering I ought to have been on the spot to advise her, to help her ; and, though I believed there was no rancour in her composition and no great conviction of the importance of her affairs, I had prepared myself for a change in her manner, for some air of injury and estrangement, which should say to my conscience : "Well, you're a nice person to have professed things !" But historic truth compels me to declare that this poor lady's dull face ceased to be dull, almost ceased to be plain, as she turned it gladly to her late aunt's lodger. That touched him extremely, and he thought it simplified his situation until he found it didn't. I was as kind to her that evening as I knew how to be, and I walked about the garden with her as long as seemed good. There was no explanation of any sort between us ; I didn't ask her why she hadn't answered my letter. Still less did I repeat what I had said to her in that communication ; if she chose to let me suppose she had forgotten the position in which Miss Bordereau had surprised me and the effect of the discovery on the old woman, I was quite willing to take it that way : I was grateful to her for not treating me as if I had killed her aunt.

We strolled and strolled, though really not much passed between us save the recognition of her bereavement, conveyed in my manner and in the expression she had of depending on me now, since I let her see I still took an interest in her. Miss Tina's was no breast for the pride or the pretence of independence ; she didn't in the least suggest that she knew at present what would become of her. I forbore to press on that question, however, for I certainly was not prepared to say that I would take charge of her. I was cautious ; not ignobly, I think, for I felt her knowledge of life to be so small that in her unsophisticated vision there would be no reason why— since I seemed to pity her—I shouldn't somehow look after her. She told me how her aunt had died, very peacefully at the last, and how everything had been done afterwards by the care of her good friends— fortunately, thanks to me, she said, smiling, there was money in the house. She repeated that when once the " nice " Italians like you they are your friends for life, and when we had gone into this she asked me about my *giro*, my impressions, my adventures, the places I had seen. I told her what I could, making it up partly, I'm afraid, as in my disconcerted state I had taken little in ; and after she had heard me she exclaimed, quite as if she had forgotten her aunt and her sorrow, " Dear, dear, how much I should like to do such things—to take an amusing little journey ! " It came over me for the moment that I ought to propose some enterprise, say I would accompany her anywhere she liked ; and I remarked at any rate that a pleasant excursion—to give her a change— might be managed : we would think of it, talk it over. I spoke never a word of the Aspern documents, asked no question as to what she had ascertained or what had otherwise happened with regard to them before Juliana's death. It wasn't that I wasn't on pins and needles to know, but that I thought it more decent not to show greed again so soon after the catastrophe. I hoped she herself would say something, but she never glanced that way, and I thought this natural at the time. Later on, however, that night, it oc- curred to me that her silence was matter for suspicion ; since if she had talked of my movements, of anything so detached as the Giorgione at Castelfranco, she might have alluded to what she could easily remember was in my mind. It was not to be supposed the emotion produced by her aunt's death had blotted out the recollection that I was interested in that lady's relics, and I fidgeted afterwards as it came to me that her reticence might very possibly just mean that no relics survived. We separated in the garden—it was she who said she must go in ; now that she was alone on the *piano nobile* I felt that (judged at any rate by Venetian ideas) I was on rather a different footing in regard to the invasion of it. As I shook hands with her for good-night I asked if she had some general plan, had thought over what she had best do. " Oh yes, oh yes, but I haven't settled anything yet," she replied quite cheerfully. Was her cheerfulness ex- plained by the impression that I would settle for her ?

I was glad the next morning that we had neglected

practical questions, as this gave me a pretext for seeing her again immediately. There was a practical enough question now to be touched on. I owed it to her to let her know formally that of course I didn't expect her to keep me on as a lodger, as also to show some interest in her own tenure, what she might have on her hands in the way of a lease. But I was not destined, as befell, to converse with her for more than an instant on either of these points. I sent her no message ; I simply went down to the sala and walked to and fro there. I knew she would come out ; she would promptly see me accessible. Somehow I preferred not to be shut up with her ; gardens and big halls seemed better places to talk. It was a splendid morning, with something in the air that told of the waning of the long Venetian summer ; a freshness from the sea that stirred the flowers in the garden and made a pleasant draught in the house, less shuttered and darkened now than when the old woman was alive. It was the beginning of autumn, of the end of the golden months. With this it was the end of my experiment—or would be in the course of half an hour, when I should really have learned that my dream had been reduced to ashes. After that there would be nothing left for me but to go to the station ; for seriously—and as it struck me in the morning light—I couldn't linger there to act as guardian to a piece of middle-aged female helplessness. If she hadn't saved the papers wherein should I be indebted to her ? I think I winced a little as I asked myself how much, if she *had* saved them, I should have to recognise and, as it were, reward such a courtesy. Mightn't that service after all saddle me with a guardianship ? If this idea didn't make me more uncomfortable as I walked up and down it was because I was convinced I had nothing to look to. If the old woman hadn't destroyed everything before she pounced on me in the parlour she had done so the next day.

It took Miss Tina rather longer than I had expected to act on my calculation ; but when at last she came out she looked at me without surprise. I mentioned I had been waiting for her and she asked why I hadn't let her know. I was glad a few hours later on that I had checked myself before remarking that a friendly intuition might have told her : it turned to comfort for me that I hadn't played even to that mild extent on her sensibility. What I did say was virtually the truth—that I was too nervous, since I expected her now to settle my fate.

" Your fate ? " said Miss Tina, giving me a queer look ; and as she spoke I noticed a rare change in her. Yes, she was other than she had been the evening before—less natural and less easy. She had been crying the day before and was not crying now, yet she struck me as less confident. It was as if something had happened to her during the night, or at least as if she had thought of something that troubled her— something in particular that affected her relations with me, made them more embarrassing and more complicated. Had she simply begun to feel that her aunt's not being there now altered my position ?

" I mean about our papers. *Are* there any ? You must know now."

" Yes, there are a great many ; more than I sup- posed." I was struck with the way her voice trembled as she told me this.

" Do you mean you've got them in there—and that I may see them ? "

" I don't think you can see them," said Miss Tina with an extraordinary expression of entreaty in her eyes, as if the dearest hope she had in the world now was that I wouldn't take them from her. But how could she expect me to make such a sacrifice as that after all that had passed between us ? What had I come back to Venice for but to see them, to take them ? My joy at learning they were still in existence was such that if the poor woman had gone down on her knees to beseech me never to mention them again I would have treated the proceeding as a bad joke. " I've got them but I can't show them," she lamentably added.

" Not even to me ? Ah Miss Tina ! " I broke into a tone of infinite remonstrance and reproach.

She coloured and the tears came back to her eyes ; I measured the anguish it cost her to take such a stand, which a dreadful sense of duty had imposed on her. It made me quite sick to find myself confronted with that particular obstacle; all the more that it seemed to me I had been distinctly encouraged to leave it out of account. I quite held Miss Tina to have assured me that if she had no greater hindrance than that——! " You don't mean to say you made her a deathbed promise ? It was precisely against your doing anything of that sort that I thought I was safe. Oh I would rather she had burnt the papers outright than have to reckon with such a treachery as that."

" No, it isn't a promise," said Miss Tina.

" Pray what is it then ? "

She hung fire, but finally said : " She tried to burn them, but I prevented it. She had hid them in her bed."

" In her bed——? "

" Between the mattresses. That's where she put them when she took them out of the trunk. I can't understand how she did it, because Olimpia didn't help her. She tells me so and I believe her. My aunt only told her afterwards, so that she shouldn't undo the bed—anything but the sheets. So it was very badly made," added Miss Tina simply.

" I should think so ! And how did she try to burn them ? "

" She didn't try much ; she was too weak those last days. But she told me—she charged me. Oh it was terrible ! She couldn't speak after that night. She could only make signs."

" And what did you do ? "

" I took them away. I locked them up."

" In the secretary ? "

" Yes, in the secretary," said Miss Tina, reddening again.

" Did you tell her you'd burn them ? "

" No, I didn't—on purpose."

" On purpose to gratify me ? "

" Yes, only for that."

" And what good will you have done me if after all you won't show them ? "

" Oh none. I know that—I know that," she dismally sounded.

" And did she believe you had destroyed them ? "

" I don't know what she believed at the last. I couldn't tell—she was too far gone."

" Then if there was no promise and no assurance I can't see what ties you."

" Oh she hated it so—she hated it so ! She was so jealous. But here's the portrait—you may have that," the poor woman announced, taking the little picture, wrapped up in the same manner in which her aunt had wrapped it, out of her pocket.

" I may have it—do you mean you give it to me ? " I gasped as it passed into my hand.

" Oh yes."

" But it's worth money—a large sum."

" Well ! " said Miss Tina, still with her strange look.

I didn't know what to make of it, for it could scarcely mean that she wanted to bargain like her aunt. She spoke as for making me a present. " I can't take it from you as a gift," I said, " and yet I can't afford to pay you for it according to the idea Miss Bordereau had of its value. She rated it at a thousand pounds."

" Couldn't we sell it ? " my friend threw off.

" God forbid ! I prefer the picture to the money."

" Well then keep it."

" You're very generous."

" So are you."

" I don't know why you should think so," I returned ; and this was true enough, for the good creature appeared to have in her mind some rich reference that I didn't in the least seize.

" Well, you've made a great différence for me," she said.

I looked at Jeffrey Aspern's face in the little picture, partly in order not to look at that of my companion, which had begun to trouble me, even to frighten me a little—it had taken so very odd, so strained and unnatural a cast. I made no answer to this last declaration ; I but privately consulted Jeffrey Aspern's delightful eyes with my own—they were so young and brilliant and yet so wise and so deep : I asked him what on earth was the matter with Miss Tina. He seemed to smile at me with mild mockery ; he might have been amused at my case. I had got into a pickle for him—as if he needed it ! He was unsatisfactory for the only moment since I had known him. Nevertheless, now that I held the little picture in my hand I felt it would be a precious possession. " Is this a bribe to make me give up the papers ? " I presently and all perversely asked. " Much as I value this, you know, if I were to be obliged to choose, the papers are what I should prefer. Ah but ever so much ! "

" How can you choose—how can you choose ? " Miss Tina returned slowly and woefully.

"I see ! Of course there's nothing to be said if you regard the interdiction that rests on you as quite insurmountable. In this case it must seem to you that to part with them would be an impiety of the worst kind, a simple sacrilege ! "

She shook her head, only lost in the queerness of her case. "You'd understand if you had known her. I'm afraid," she quavered suddenly—"I'm afraid ! She was terrible when she was angry."

"Yes, I saw something of that, that night. She was terrible. Then I saw her eyes. Lord, they were fine ! "

"I see them—they stare at me in the dark ! " said Miss Tina.

"You've grown nervous with all you've been through.

"Oh yes, very—very ! "

"You mustn't mind ; that will pass away," I said kindly. Then I added resignedly, for it really seemed to me that I must accept the situation : "Well, so it is, and it can't be helped. I must renounce." My friend, at this, with her eyes on me, gave a low soft moan, and I went on : "I only wish to goodness she had destroyed them : then there would be nothing more to say. And I can't understand why, with her ideas, she didn't."

"Oh she lived on them ! " said Miss Tina.

"You can imagine whether that makes me want less to see them," I returned not quite so desperately. "But don't let me stand here as if I had it in my soul to tempt you to anything base. Naturally, you understand, I give up my rooms. I leave Venice immediately." And I took up my hat, which I had placed on a chair. We were still rather awkwardly on our feet in the middle of the sala. She had left the door of the apartments open behind her, but had not led me that way.

A strange spasm came into her face as she saw me take my hat. " Immediately—do you mean to-day ? " The tone of the words was tragic—they were a cry of desolation.

" Oh no ; not so long as I can be of the least service to you."

" Well, just a day or two more—just two or three days," she panted. Then controlling herself she added in another manner : " She wanted to say something to me—the last day—something very particular. But she couldn't."

" Something very particular ? "

" Something more about the papers."

" And did you guess—have you any idea ? "

" No, I've tried to think—but I don't know. I've thought all kinds of things."

" As for instance ? "

" Well, that if you were a relation it would be different."

I wondered. " If I were a relation——? "

" If you weren't a stranger. Then it would be the same for you as for me. Anything that's mine would be yours, and you could do what you like. I shouldn't be able to prevent you—and you'd have no responsibility."

She brought out this droll explanation with a nervous rush and as if speaking words got by heart. They gave me the impression of a subtlety which at first I failed to follow. But after a moment her face helped me to see farther, and then the queerest of lights came to me. It was embarrassing, and I bent my head over Jeffrey Aspern's portrait. What an odd expression was in his face ! " Get out of it as you can, my dear fellow ! " I put the picture into the pocket of my coat and said to Miss Tina : " Yes, I'll sell it for you. I shan't get a thousand pounds by any means, but I shall get something good."

She looked at me through pitiful tears, but seemed to try to smile as she returned : " We can divide the money."

" No, no, it shall be all yours." Then I went on : " I think I know what your poor aunt wanted to say. She wanted to give directions that her papers should be buried with her."

Miss Tina appeared to weigh this suggestion ; after which she answered with striking decision, " Oh no, she wouldn't have thought that safe ! "

" It seems to me nothing could be safer."

" She had an idea that when people want to publish they're capable——! " And she paused, very red.

" Of violating a tomb ? Mercy on us, what must she have thought of me ! "

" She wasn't just, she wasn't generous ! " my companion cried with sudden passion.

The light that had come into my mind a moment before spread farther. " Ah don't say that, for we *are* a dreadful race." Then I pursued : " If she left a will, that may give you some idea."

" I've found nothing of the sort—she destroyed it. She was very fond of me," Miss Tina added with an effect of extreme inconsequence. " She wanted me to be happy. And if any person should be kind to me—she wanted to speak of that."

I was almost awestricken by the astuteness with which the good lady found herself inspired, transparent astuteness as it was and stitching, as the phrase is, with white thread. " Depend upon it she didn't want to make any provision that would be agreeable to *me*."

" No, not to you, but quite to me. She knew I should like it if you could carry out your idea. Not because she cared for you, but because she did think of me," Miss Tina went on with her unexpected persuasive volubility. " You could see the things—

you could use them." She stopped, seeing I grasped the sense of her conditional—stopped long enough for me to give some sign that I didn't give. She must have been conscious, however, that though my face showed the greatest embarrassment ever painted on a human countenance it was not set as a stone, it was also full of compassion. It was a comfort to me a long time afterwards to consider that she couldn't have seen in me the smallest symptom of disrespect. " I don't know what to do ; I'm too tormented, I'm too ashamed ! " she continued with vehemence. Then turning away from me and burying her face in her hands she burst into a flood of tears. If she didn't know what to do it may be imagined whether I knew better. I stood there dumb, watching her while her sobs resounded in the great empty hall. In a moment she was up at me again with her streaming eyes. " I'd give you everything, and she'd understand, where she is—she'd forgive me ! "

" Ah Miss Tina—ah Miss Tina," I stammered for all reply. I didn't know what to do, as I say, but at a venture I made a wild vague movement in consequence of which I found myself at the door. I remember standing there and saying, " It wouldn't do, it wouldn't do ! "—saying it pensively, awkwardly, grotesquely, while I looked away to the opposite end of the sala as at something very interesting. The next thing I remember is that I was downstairs and out of the house. My gondola was there and my gondolier, reclining on the cushions, sprang up as soon as he saw me. I jumped in and to his usual " *Dove comanda ?* " replied, in a tone that made him stare : " Anywhere, anywhere ; out into the lagoon ! "

He rowed me away and I sat there prostrate, groaning softly to myself, my hat pulled over my brow. What in the name of the preposterous did she mean if she didn't mean to offer me her hand? That was the price—that was the price! And did she think I wanted it, poor deluded infatuated extravagant lady? My gondolier, behind me, must have seen my ears red as I wondered, motionless there under the fluttering *tenda* with my hidden face, noticing nothing as we passed—wondered whether her delusion, her infatuation had been my own reckless work. Did she think I had made love to her even to get the papers? I hadn't, I hadn't; I repeated that over to myself for an hour, for two hours, till I was wearied if not convinced. I don't know where, on the lagoon, my gondolier took me; we floated aimlessly and with slow rare strokes. At last I became conscious that we were near the Lido, far up, on the right hand, as you turn your back to Venice, and I made him put me ashore. I wanted to walk, to move, to shed some of my bewilderment. I crossed the narrow strip and got to the sea-beach— I took my way toward Malamocco. But presently I flung myself down again on the warm sand, in the breeze, on the coarse dry grass. It took it out of me to think I had been so much at fault, that I had unwittingly but none the less deplorably trifled. But I hadn't given her cause—distinctly I hadn't. I had said to Mrs. Prest that I would make love to her; but it had been a joke without consequences and I had never said it to my victim. I had been as kind as possible because I really liked her; but since when had that become a crime where a woman of such an age and such an appearance was concerned? I am far from remembering clearly the succession of events and feelings during this long day of confusion, which I spent entirely in wandering about, without going home, until late at night: it only comes back to me that there were moments when I pacified my conscience and others when I lashed it into pain. I didn't laugh all day—that I do recollect ; the case, however it might have struck others, seemed to me so little amusing. I should have been better employed perhaps in taking in the comic side of it. At any rate, whether I had given cause or not, there was no doubt whatever that I couldn't pay the price. I couldn't accept the proposal. I couldn't, for a bundle of tattered papers, marry a ridiculous pathetic provincial old woman. It was a proof of how little she supposed the idea would come to me that she should have decided to suggest it herself in that practical argumentative heroic way—with the timidity, however, so much more striking than the boldness, that her reasons appeared to come first and her feelings afterward.

As the day went on I grew to wish I had never heard of Aspern's relics, and I cursed the extravagant curiosity that had put John Cumnor on the scent of them. We had more than enough material without them, and my predicament was the just punishment of that most fatal of human follies, our not having known when to stop. It was very well to say it was no predicament, that the way out was simple, that I had only to leave Venice by the first train in the morning, after addressing Miss Tina a note which should be placed in her hand as soon as I got clear of the house ; for it was strong proof of my quandary that when I tried to make up the note to my taste in advance—I would put it on paper as soon as I got home, before going to bed—I couldn't think of anything but " How can I thank you for the rare confidence you've placed in me ? " That would never do ; it sounded exactly as if an acceptance were to follow. Of course I might get off without writing at all, but that would be brutal, and my idea was still to exclude brutal solutions. As my confusion cooled I lost myself in wonder at the importance I had attached to Juliana's crumpled scraps ; the thought of them became odious to me and I was as vexed with the old witch for the superstition that had prevented her from destroying them as I was with myself for having already spent more money than I could afford in attempting to control their fate. I forget what I did, where I went after leaving the Lido and at what hour or with what recovery of composure I made my way back to my boat. I only know that in the afternoon, when the air was aglow with the sunset, I was standing before the church of Saints John and Paul and looking up at the small square-jawed face of Bartolomeo Colleoni, the terrible *condottiere* who sits so sturdily astride of his huge bronze horse on the high pedestal on which Venetian gratitude maintains him. The statue is incomparable, the finest of all mounted figures, unless that of Marcus Aurelius, who rides benignant before the Roman Capitol, be finer : but I was not thinking of that ; I only found myself staring at the triumphant captain as if he had had an oracle on his lips. The western light shines into all his grimness at that hour and makes it wonderfully personal. But he continued to look far over my head, at the red immersion of another day—he had seen so many go down into the lagoon through the centuries— and if he were thinking of battles and stratagems they were of a different quality from any I had to tell him of. He couldn't direct me what to do, gaze up at him as I might. Was it before this or after that I wandered about for an hour in the small canals, to the continued stupefaction of my gondolier, who had never seen me so restless and yet so void of a purpose and could extract from me no order but " Go any-where — everywhere — all over the place " ? He reminded me that I had not lunched, and expressed therefore respectfully the hope that I would dine earlier. He had had long periods of leisure during the day, when I had left the boat and rambled, so that I was not obliged to consider him, and I told him that till the morrow, for reasons, I should touch no meat. It was an effect of poor Miss Tina's proposal, not altogether auspicious, that I had quite lost my appetite. I don't know why it happened that on this occasion I was more than ever struck with that queer air of sociability, of cousinship and family life, which makes up half the expression of Venice. Without streets and vehicles, the uproar of wheels, the brutality of horses, and with its little winding ways where people crowd together, where voices sound as in the corridors of a house, where the human step circulates as if it skirted the angles of furniture and shoes never wear out, the place has the character of an immense collective apartment, in which Piazza San Marco is the most ornamented corner, and palaces and churches, for the rest, play the part of great divans of repose, tables of entertainment, expanses of decoration. And somehow the splendid common domicile, familiar, domestic and resonant, also resembles a theatre with its actors clicking over bridges and, in straggling processions, tripping along fondamentas. As you sit in your gondola the footways that in certain parts edge the canals assume to the eye the importance of a stage, meeting it at the same angle, and the Venetian figures, moving to and fro against the battered scenery of their little houses of comedy, strike you as members of an endless dramatic troupe.

I went to bed that night very tired and without being able to compose an address to Miss Tina. Was this failure the reason why I became conscious the next morning as soon as I awoke of a determination to see the poor lady again the first moment she would receive me ? That had something to do with it, but what had still more was the fact that during my sleep the oddest revulsion had taken place in my spirit. I found myself aware of this almost as soon as I opened my eyes : it made me jump out of my bed with the movement of a man who remembers that he has left the house-door ajar or a candle burning under a shelf. Was I still in time to save my goods ? That question was in my heart ; for what had now come to pass was that in the unconscious cerebration of sleep I had swung back to a passionate appreciation of Juliana's treasure. The pieces composing it were now more precious than ever and a positive ferocity had come into my need to acquire them. The condition Miss Tina had attached to that act no longer appeared an obstacle worth thinking of, and for an hour this morning my repentant imagination brushed it aside. It was absurd I should be able to invent nothing ; absurd to renounce so easily and turn away helpless from the idea that the only way to become possessed was to unite myself to her for life. I mightn't unite myself, yet I might still have what she had. I must add that by the time I sent down to ask if she would see me I had invented no alternative, though in fact I drew out my dressing in the interest of my wit. This failure was humiliating, yet what could the alternative be ? Miss Tina sent back word I might come ; and as I descended the stairs and crossed the sala to her door—this time she received me in her aunt's forlorn parlour — I hoped she wouldn't think my announcement was to be " favourable." She certainly would have understood my recoil of the day before.

As soon as I came into the room I saw that she had done so, but I also saw something which had not been in my forecast. Poor Miss Tina's sense of her failure had produced a rare alteration in her, but I had been too full of stratagems and spoils to think of that. Now I took it in ; I can scarcely tell how it startled me.

She stood in the middle of the room with a face of mildness bent upon me, and her look of forgiveness, of absolution, made her angelic. It beautified her; she was younger; she was not a ridiculous old woman. This trick of her expression, this magic of her spirit, transfigured her, and while I still noted it I heard a whisper somewhere in the depths of my conscience: " Why not, after all—why not ? " It seemed to me I *could* pay the price. Still more distinctly, however, than the whisper I heard Miss Tina's own voice. I was so struck with the different effect she made on me that at first I wasn't clearly aware of what she was saying; then I recognised she had bade me good-bye—she said something about hoping I should be very happy.

" Good-bye — good-bye ? " I repeated with an inflexion interrogative and probably foolish.

I saw she didn't feel the interrogation, she only heard the words : she had strung herself up to accepting our separation and they fell upon her ear as a proof. " Are you going to-day ? " she asked. " But it doesn't matter, for whenever you go I shall not see you again. I don't want to." And she smiled strangely, with an infinite gentleness. She had never doubted my having left her the day before in horror. How *could* she, since I hadn't come back before night to contradict, even as a simple form, even as an act of common humanity, such an idea ? And now she had the force of soul—Miss Tina with force of soul was a new conception—to smile at me in her abjection.

" What shall you do—where shall you go ? " I asked.

" Oh I don't know. I've done the great thing. I've destroyed the papers."

" Destroyed them ? " I wailed.

" Yes; what was I to keep them for ? I burnt them last night, one by one, in the kitchen."

" One by one ? " I coldly echoed it.

" It took a long time—there were so many." The room seemed to go round me as she said this and a real darkness for a moment descended on my eyes. When it passed Miss Tina was there still, but the transfiguration was over and she had changed back to a plain dingy elderly person. It was in this character she spoke as she said, " I can't stay with you longer, I can't " ; and it was in this character she turned her back upon me, as I had turned mine upon her twenty-four hours before, and moved to the door of her room. Here she did what I hadn't done when I quitted her—she paused long enough to give me one look. I have never forgotten it, and I sometimes still suffer from it, though it was not resentful. No, there was no resentment, nothing hard or vindictive in poor Miss Tina ; for when, later, I sent her, as the price of the portrait of Jeffrey Aspern, a larger sum of money than I had hoped to be able to gather for her, writing to her that I had sold the picture, she kept it with thanks ; she never sent it back. I wrote her that I had sold the picture, but I admitted to Mrs. Prest at the time—I met this other friend in London that autumn—that it hangs above my writing-table. When I look at it I can scarcely bear my loss—I mean of the precious papers.

THE TURN OF THE SCREW

THE story had held us, round the fire, sufficiently breathless, but except the obvious remark that it was gruesome, as on Christmas Eve in an old house a strange tale should essentially be, I remember no comment uttered till somebody happened to note it as the only case he had met in which such a visitation had fallen on a child. The case, I may mention, was that of an apparition in just such an old house as had gathered us for the occasion—an appearance, of a dreadful kind, to a little boy sleeping in the room with his mother and waking her up in the terror of it ; waking her not to dissipate his dread and soothe him to sleep again, but to encounter also herself, before she had succeeded in doing so, the same sight that had shocked him. It was this observation that drew from Douglas—not immediately, but later in the evening—a reply that had the interesting consequence to which I call attention. Some one else told a story not particularly effective, which I saw he was not following. This I took for a sign that he had himself something to produce and that we should only have to wait. We waited in fact till two nights later ; but that same evening, before we scattered, he brought out what was in his mind.

"I quite agree—in regard to Griffin's ghost, or whatever it was—that its appearing first to the little boy, at so tender an age, adds a particular touch. But it's not the first occurrence of its charming kind that I know to have been concerned with a child. If the child gives the effect another turn of the screw, what do you say to *two* children———? "

" We say of course," somebody exclaimed, " that two children give two turns ! Also that we want to hear about them."

I can see Douglas there before the fire, to which he had got up to present his back, looking down at this converser with his hands in his pockets. " Nobody but me, till now, has ever heard. It's quite too horrible." This was naturally declared by several voices to give the thing the utmost price, and our friend, with quiet art, prepared his triumph by turning his eyes over the rest of us and going on : " It's beyond everything. Nothing at all that I know touches it."

" For sheer terror ? " I remember asking.

He seemed to say it wasn't so simple as that ; to be really at a loss how to qualify it. He passed his hand over his eyes, made a little wincing grimace. " For dreadful—dreadfulness ! "

" Oh how delicious ! " cried one of the women.

He took no notice of her ; he looked at me, but as if, instead of me, he saw what he spoke of. " For general uncanny ugliness and horror and pain."

" Well then," I said, " just sit right down and begin."

He turned round to the fire, gave a kick to a log, watched it an instant. Then as he faced us again : " I can't begin. I shall have to send to town." There was a unanimous groan at this, and much reproach ; after which, in his preoccupied way, he explained. " The story's written. It's in a locked drawer—it has not been out for years. I could write to my man and enclose the key ; he could send down the packet as he finds it." It was to me in particular that he appeared to propound this—appeared almost to appeal for aid not to hesitate. He had broken a

thickness of ice, the formation of many a winter;
had had his reasons for a long silence. The others
resented postponement, but it was just his scruples
that charmed me. I adjured him to write by the
first post and to agree with us for an early hearing;
then I asked him if the experience in question had
been his own. To this his answer was prompt.
" Oh thank God, no ! "

" And is the record yours ? You took the thing
down ? "

" Nothing but the impression. I took that *here* "
—he tapped his heart. " I've never lost it."

" Then your manuscript——? "

" Is in old faded ink and in the most beautiful
hand." He hung fire again. " A woman's. She has
been dead these twenty years. She sent me the
pages in question before she died." They were all
listening now, and of course there was somebody to be
arch, or at any rate to draw the inference. But if he
put the inference by without a smile it was also
without irritation. " She was a most charming
person, but she was ten years older than I. She was
my sister's governess," he quietly said. " She was
the most agreeable woman I've ever known in her
position ; she'd have been worthy of any whatever.
It was long ago, and this episode was long before.
I was at Trinity, and I found her at home on my
coming down the second summer. I was much there
that year—it was a beautiful one ; and we had, in
her off-hours, some strolls and talks in the garden—
talks in which she struck me as awfully clever and
nice. Oh yes ; don't grin : I liked her extremely
and am glad to this day to think she liked me too.
If she hadn't she wouldn't have told me. She
had never told any one. It wasn't simply that she
said so, but that I knew she hadn't. I was sure ;
I could see. You'll easily judge why when you hear."

"Because the thing had been such a scare?"

He continued to fix me. "You'll easily judge," he repeated: "*you* will."

I fixed him too. "I see. She was in love."

He laughed for the first time. "You *are* acute. Yes, she was in love. That is she *had* been. That came out—she couldn't tell her story without its coming out. I saw it, and she saw I saw it; but neither of us spoke of it. I remember the time and the place—the corner of the lawn, the shade of the great beeches and the long hot summer afternoon. It wasn't a scene for a shudder; but oh——!" He quitted the fire and dropped back into his chair.

"You'll receive the packet Thursday morning?" I said.

"Probably not till the second post."

"Well then; after dinner——"

"You'll all meet me here?" He looked us round again. "Isn't anybody going?" It was almost the tone of hope.

"Everybody will stay!"

"*I* will—and *I* will!" cried the ladies whose departure had been fixed. Mrs. Griffin, however, expressed the need for a little more light. "Who was it she was in love with?"

"The story will tell," I took upon myself to reply.

"Oh I can't wait for the story!"

"The story *won't* tell," said Douglas; "not in any literal vulgar way."

"More's the pity then. That's the only way I ever understand."

"Won't *you* tell, Douglas?" somebody else inquired.

He sprang to his feet again. "Yes—to-morrow. Now I must go to bed. Good-night." And, quickly catching up a candlestick, he left us slightly bewildered. From our end of the great brown hall we heard his step on the stair; whereupon Mrs. Griffin spoke. "Well, if I don't know who she was in love with I know who *he* was."

"She was ten years older," said her husband.

"*Raison de plus*—at that age! But it's rather nice, his long reticence."

"Forty years!" Griffin put in.

"With this outbreak at last."

"The outbreak," I returned, "will make a tremendous occasion of Thursday night"; and every one so agreed with me that in the light of it we lost all attention for everything else. The last story, however incomplete and like the mere opening of a serial, had been told; we handshook and "candlestuck," as somebody said, and went to bed.

I knew the next day that a letter containing the key had, by the first post, gone off to his London apartments; but in spite of—or perhaps just on account of—the eventual diffusion of this knowledge we quite let him alone till after dinner, till such an hour of the evening in fact as might best accord with the kind of emotion on which our hopes were fixed. Then he became as communicative as we could desire, and indeed gave us his best reason for being so. We had it from him again before the fire in the hall, as we had had our mild wonders of the previous night. It appeared that the narrative he had promised to read us really required for a proper intelligence a few words of prologue. Let me say here distinctly, to have done with it, that this narrative, from an exact transcript of my own made much later, is what I shall presently give. Poor Douglas, before his death—when it was in sight—committed to me the manuscript that reached him on the third of these days and that, on the same spot, with immense effect, he began to read to our hushed little circle on the night of the fourth. The departing ladies who had said they would stay didn't, of course, thank heaven, stay: they departed, in consequence of arrangements made, in a rage of curiosity, as they professed, produced by the touches with which he had already worked us up. But that only made his little final auditory more compact and select, kept it, round the hearth, subject to a common thrill.

The first of these touches conveyed that the written statement took up the tale at a point after it had, in a manner, begun. The fact to be in possession of was therefore that his old friend, the youngest of several daughters of a poor country parson, had at the age of twenty, on taking service for the first time in the schoolroom, come up to London, in trepidation, to answer in person an advertisement that had already placed her in brief correspondence with the advertiser. This person proved, on her presenting herself for judgement at a house in Harley Street that impressed her as vast and imposing—this prospective patron proved a gentleman, a bachelor in the prime of life, such a figure as had never risen, save in a dream or an old novel, before a fluttered anxious girl out of a Hampshire vicarage. One could easily fix his type ; it never, happily, dies out. He was handsome and bold and pleasant, off-hand and gay and kind. He struck her, inevitably, as gallant and splendid, but what took her most of all and gave her the courage she afterwards showed was that he put the whole thing to her as a favour, an obligation he should gratefully incur. She figured him as rich, but as fearfully extravagant—saw him all in a glow of high fashion, of good looks, of expensive habits, of charming ways with women. He had for his town residence a big house filled with the spoils of travel and the trophies of the chase ; but it was to his country home, an old family place in Essex, that he wished her immediately to proceed.

134

He had been left, by the death of his parents in India, guardian to a small nephew and a small niece, children of a younger, a military brother whom he had lost two years before. These children were, by the strangest of chances for a man in his position—a lone man without the right sort of experience or a grain of patience—very heavy on his hands. It had all been a great worry and, on his own part doubtless, a series of blunders, but he immensely pitied the poor chicks and had done all he could ; had in particular sent them down to his other house, the proper place for them being of course the country, and kept them there from the first with the best people he could find to look after them, parting even with his own servants to wait on them and going down himself, whenever he might, to see how they were doing. The awkward thing was that they had practically no other relations and that his own affairs took up all his time. He had put them in possession of Bly, which was healthy and secure, and had placed at the head of their little establishment— but belowstairs only—an excellent woman, Mrs. Grose, whom he was sure his visitor would like and who had formerly been maid to his mother. She was now housekeeper and was also acting for the time as superintendent to the little girl, of whom, without children of her own, she was by good luck extremely fond. There were plenty of people to help, but of course the young lady who should go down as governess would be in supreme authority. She would also have, in holidays, to look after the small boy, who had been for a term at school—young as he was to be sent, but what else could be done ?—and who, as the holidays were about to begin, would be back from one day to the other. There had been for the two children at first a young lady whom they had had the misfortune to lose. She had done for them quite beautifully

—she was a most respectable person—till her death, the great awkwardness of which had, precisely, left no alternative but the school for little Miles. Mrs. Grose, since then, in the way of manners and things, had done as she could for Flora; and there were, further, a cook, a housemaid, a dairywoman, an old pony, an old groom, and an old gardener, all likewise thoroughly respectable.

So far had Douglas presented his picture when some one put a question. "And what did the former governess die of ? Of so much respectability?"

Our friend's answer was prompt. "That will come out. I don't anticipate."

"Pardon me—I thought that was just what you *are* doing."

"In her successor's place," I suggested, "I should have wished to learn if the office brought with it——"

"Necessary danger to life ?" Douglas completed my thought. "She did wish to learn, and she did learn. You shall hear to-morrow what she learnt. Meanwhile of course the prospect struck her as slightly grim. She was young, untried, nervous : it was a vision of serious duties and little company, of really great loneliness. She hesitated—took a couple of days to consult and consider. But the salary offered much exceeded her modest measure, and on a second interview she faced the music, she engaged." And Douglas, with this, made a pause that, for the benefit of the company, moved me to throw in—

"The moral of which was of course the seduction exercised by the splendid young man. She succumbed to it."

He got up and, as he had done the night before, went to the fire, gave a stir to a log with his foot, then stood a moment with his back to us. "She saw him only twice."

"Yes, but that's just the beauty of her passion."

A little to my surprise, on this, Douglas turned round to me. " It *was* the beauty of it. There were others," he went on, " who hadn't succumbed. He told her frankly all his difficulty—that for several applicants the conditions had been prohibitive. They were somehow simply afraid. It sounded dull—it sounded strange ; and all the more so because of his main condition."

" Which was——? "

" That she should never trouble him—but never, never : neither appeal nor complain nor write about anything ; only meet all questions herself, receive all moneys from his solicitor, take the whole thing over and let him alone. She promised to do this, and she mentioned to me that when, for a moment, disburdened, delighted, he held her hand, thanking her for the sacrifice, she already felt rewarded."

" But was that all her reward ? " one of the ladies asked.

" She never saw him again."

" Oh ! " said the lady ; which, as our friend immediately again left us, was the only other word of importance contributed to the subject till, the next night, by the corner of the hearth, in the best chair, he opened the faded red cover of a thin old-fashioned gilt-edged album. The whole thing took indeed more nights than one, but on the first occasion the same lady put another question. " What's your title ? "

" I haven't one."

" Oh *I* have ! " I said. But Douglas, without heeding me, had begun to read with a fine clearness that was like a rendering to the ear of the beauty of his author's hand.

I

I REMEMBER the whole beginning as a succession of flights and drops, a little see-saw of the right throbs and the wrong. After rising, in town, to meet his appeal I had at all events a couple of very bad days —found all my doubts bristle again, felt indeed sure I had made a mistake. In this state of mind I spent the long hours of bumping swinging coach that carried me to the stopping-place at which I was to be met by a vehicle from the house. This convenience, I was told, had been ordered, and I found, toward the close of the June afternoon, a commodious fly in waiting for me. Driving at that hour, on a lovely day, through a country the summer sweetness of which served as a friendly welcome, my fortitude revived and, as we turned into the avenue, took a flight that was probably but a proof of the point to which it had sunk. I suppose I had expected, or had dreaded, something so dreary that what greeted me was a good surprise. I remember as a thoroughly pleasant impression the broad clear front, its open windows and fresh curtains and the pair of maids looking out ; I remember the lawn and the bright flowers and the crunch of my wheels on the gravel and the clustered tree-tops over which the rooks circled and cawed in the golden sky. The scene had a greatness that made it a different affair from my own scant home, and there immediately appeared at the door, with a little girl in her hand, a civil person who dropped me as decent a curtsey as if I had been the mistress or a distinguished visitor. I had received in Harley Street a narrower notion of the place, and that, as I recalled it, made me think the proprietor still more of a gentleman, suggested that what I was to enjoy might be a matter beyond his promise.

I had no drop again till the next day, for I was carried triumphantly through the following hours by my introduction to the younger of my pupils. The little girl who accompanied Mrs. Grose affected me on the spot as a creature too charming not to make it a great fortune to have to do with her. She was the most beautiful child I had ever seen, and I afterwards wondered why my employer hadn't made more of a point to me of this. I slept little that night —I was too much excited ; and this astonished me too, I recollect, remained with me, adding to my sense of the liberality with which I was treated. The large impressive room, one of the best in the house, the great state bed, as I almost felt it, the figured full draperies, the long glasses in which, for the first time, I could see myself from head to foot, all struck me— like the wonderful appeal of my small charge—as so many things thrown in. It was thrown in as well, from the first moment, that I should get on with Mrs. Grose in a relation over which, on my way, in the coach, I fear I had rather brooded. The one appearance indeed that in this early outlook might have made me shrink again was that of her being so inordinately glad to see me. I felt within half an hour that she was so glad—stout simple plain clean wholesome woman—as to be positively on her guard against showing it too much. I wondered even then a little why she should wish *not* to show it, and that, with reflexion, with suspicion, might of course have made me uneasy.

But it was a comfort that there could be no uneasiness in a connexion with anything so beatific as the radiant image of my little girl, the vision of whose angelic beauty had probably more than anything else to do with the restlessness that, before morning, made me several times rise and wander about my room to take in the whole picture and prospect; to watch from my open window the faint summer dawn, to look at such stretches of the rest of the house as I could catch, and to listen, while in the fading dusk the first birds began to twitter, for the possible recurrence of a sound or two, less natural and not without but within, that I had fancied I heard. There had been a moment when I believed I recognised, faint and far, the cry of a child; there had been another when I found myself just consciously starting as at the passage, before my door, of a light footstep. But these fancies were not marked enough not to be thrown off, and it is only in the light, or the gloom, I should rather say, of other and subsequent matters that they now come back to me. To watch, teach, " form " little Flora would too evidently be the making of a happy and useful life. It had been agreed between us downstairs that after this first occasion I should have her as a matter of course at night, her small white bed being already arranged, to that end, in my room. What I had undertaken was the whole care of her, and she had remained just this last time with Mrs. Grose only as an effect of our consideration for my inevitable strangeness and her natural timidity. In spite of this timidity—which the child herself, in the oddest way in the world, had been perfectly frank and brave about, allowing it, without a sign of uncomfortable consciousness, with the deep sweet serenity indeed of one of Raphael's holy infants, to be discussed, to be imputed to her and to determine us—I felt quite sure she would presently like me. It was part of what I already liked Mrs. Grose herself for, the pleasure I could see her feel in my admiration and wonder as I sat at supper with four tall candles and with my pupil, in a high chair and a bib, brightly facing me between them over bread and milk. There were naturally things that in Flora's presence could pass between us only as prodigious and gratified looks, obscure and round-about allusions.

" And the little boy—does he look like her ? Is he too so very remarkable ? "

One wouldn't, it was already conveyed between us, too grossly flatter a child. " Oh Miss, *most* remarkable. If you think well of this one ! "—and she stood there with a plate in her hand, beaming at our companion, who looked from one of us to the other with placid heavenly eyes that contained nothing to check us.

" Yes ; if I do——? "

" You *will* be carried away by the little gentleman ! "

" Well, that, I think, is what I came for—to be carried away. I'm afraid, however," I remember feeling the impulse to add, " I'm rather easily carried away. I was carried away in London ! "

I can still see Mrs. Grose's broad face as she took this in. " In Harley Street ? "

" In Harley Street."

" Well, Miss, you're not the first—and you won't be the last."

" Oh I've no pretensions," I could laugh, " to being the only one. My other pupil, at any rate, as I understand, comes back to-morrow ? "

" Not to-morrow—Friday, Miss. He arrives, as you did, by the coach, under care of the guard, and is to be met by the same carriage."

I forthwith wanted to know if the proper as well as the pleasant and friendly thing wouldn't therefore be that on the arrival of the public conveyance I should await him with his little sister ; a proposition to which Mrs. Grose assented so heartily that I somehow took her manner as a kind of comforting pledge —never falsified, thank heaven !—that we should on every question be quite at one. Oh she was glad I was there !

What I felt the next day was, I suppose, nothing that could be fairly called a reaction from the cheer of my arrival ; it was probably at the most only a slight oppression produced by a fuller measure of the scale, as I walked round them, gazed up at them, took them in, of my new circumstances. They had, as it were, an extent and mass for which I had not been prepared and in the presence of which I found myself, freshly, a little scared not less than a little proud. Regular lessons, in this agitation, certainly suffered some wrong ; I reflected that my first duty was, by the gentlest arts I could contrive, to win the child into the sense of knowing me. I spent the day with her out of doors ; I arranged with her, to her great satisfaction, that it should be she, she only, who might show me the place. She showed it step by step and room by room and secret by secret, with droll delightful childish talk about it and with the result, in half an hour, of our becoming tremendous friends. Young as she was I was struck, throughout our little tour, with her confidence and courage, with the way, in empty chambers and dull corridors, on crooked staircases that made me pause and even on the summit of an old machicolated square tower that made me dizzy, her morning music, her disposition to tell me so many more things than she asked, rang out and led me on. I have not seen Bly since the day I left it, and I dare say that to my present older and more informed eyes it would show a very reduced importance. But as my little conductress, with her hair of gold and her frock of blue, danced before me round corners and pattered down passages, I had the view of a castle of romance inhabited by a rosy sprite, such a place as would somehow, for diversion of the young idea, take all colour out of story-books and fairy-tales. Wasn't it just a story-book over which I had fallen a-doze and a-dream ? No ; it was a big ugly antique but convenient house, embodying a few features of a building still older, half-displaced and half-utilised, in which I had the fancy of our being almost as lost as a handful of passengers in a great drifting ship. Well, I was strangely at the helm !

II

THIS came home to me when, two days later, I drove over with Flora to meet, as Mrs. Grose said, the little gentleman ; and all the more for an incident that, presenting itself the second evening, had deeply disconcerted me. The first day had been, on the whole, as I have expressed, reassuring ; but I was to see it wind up to a change of note. The postbag that evening—it came late—contained a letter for me which, however, in the hand of my employer, I found to be composed but of a few words enclosing another, addressed to himself, with a seal still unbroken. "This, I recognise, is from the head-master, and the head-master's an awful bore. Read him, please ; deal with him ; but mind you don't report. Not a word. I'm off ! " I broke the seal with a great effort—so great a one that I was a long time coming to it ; took the unopened missive at last up to my room and only attacked it just before going to bed. I had better have let it wait till morning, for it gave me a second sleepless night. With no counsel to take, the next day, I was full of distress ; and it finally got so the better of me that I determined to open myself at least to Mrs. Grose.

" What does it mean ? The child's dismissed his school."

She gave me a look that I remarked at the moment ;

then, visibly, with a quick blankness, seemed to try to take it back. " But aren't they all——? "

" Sent home—yes. But only for the holidays. Miles may never go back at all."

Consciously, under my attention, she reddened. " They won't take him ? "

" They absolutely decline."

At this she raised her eyes, which she had turned from me ; I saw them fill with good tears. " What has he done ? "

I cast about ; then I judged best simply to hand her my document—which, however, had the effect of making her, without taking it, simply put her hands behind her. She shook her head sadly. " Such things are not for me, Miss."

My counsellor couldn't read ! I winced at my mistake, which I attenuated as I could, and opened the letter again to repeat it to her ; then, faltering in the act and folding it up once more, I put it back in my pocket. " Is he really *bad* ? "

The tears were still in her eyes. " Do the gentlemen say so ? "

" They go into no particulars. They simply express their regret that it should be impossible to keep him. That can have but one meaning." Mrs. Grose listened with dumb emotion ; she forbore to ask me what this meaning might be ; so that, presently, to put the thing with some coherence and with the mere aid of her presence to my own mind, I went on : " That he's an injury to the others."

At this, with one of the quick turns of simple folk, she suddenly flamed up. " Master Miles !—*him* an injury ? "

There was such a flood of good faith in it that, though I had not yet seen the child, my very fears made me jump to the absurdity of the idea. I found myself, to meet my friend the better, offering it, on the spot, sarcastically. " To his poor little innocent mates ! "

" It's too dreadful," cried Mrs. Grose, " to say such cruel things ! Why, he's scarce ten years old."

" Yes, yes ; it would be incredible."

She was evidently grateful for such a profession. " See him, Miss, first. *Then* believe it ! " I felt forthwith a new impatience to see him ; it was the beginning of a curiosity that, all the next hours, was to deepen almost to pain. Mrs. Grose was aware, I could judge, of what she had produced in me, and she followed it up with assurance. " You might as well believe it of the little lady. Bless her," she added the next moment—" *look* at her ! "

I turned and saw that Flora, whom, ten minutes before, I had established in the schoolroom with a sheet of white paper, a pencil, and a copy of nice " round O's," now presented herself to view at the open door. She expressed in her little way an extraordinary detachment from disagreeable duties, looking at me, however, with a great childish light that seemed to offer it as a mere result of the affection she had conceived for my person, which had rendered necessary that she should follow me. I needed nothing more than this to feel the full force of Mrs. Grose's comparison, and, catching my pupil in my arms, covered her with kisses in which there was a sob of atonement.

None the less, the rest of the day, I watched for further occasion to approach my colleague, especially as, toward evening, I began to fancy she rather sought to avoid me. I overtook her, I remember, on the staircase ; we went down together and at the bottom I detained her, holding her there with a hand on her arm. " L take what you said to me at noon as a declaration that *you've* never known him to be bad."

She threw back her head ; she had clearly by this time, and very honestly, adopted an attitude. " Oh never known him—I don't pretend *that* ! "

I was upset again. " Then you *have* known him——? "

" Yes indeed, Miss, thank God ! "

On reflexion I accepted this. " You mean that a boy who never is——? "

" Is no boy for *me* ! "

I held her tighter. " You like them with the spirit to be naughty ? " Then, keeping pace with her answer, " So do I ! " I eagerly brought out. " But not to the degree to contaminate——"

" To contaminate ? "—my big word left her at a loss.

I explained it. " To corrupt."

She stared, taking my meaning in ; but it produced in her an odd laugh. " Are you afraid he'll corrupt *you* ? " She put the question with such a fine bold humour that with a laugh, a little silly doubtless, to match her own, I gave way for the time to the apprehension of ridicule.

But the next day, as the hour for my drive approached, I cropped up in another place. " What was the lady who was here before ? "

" The last governess ? She was also young and pretty—almost as young and almost as pretty, Miss, even as you."

" Ah then I hope her youth and her beauty helped her ! " I recollect throwing off. " " He seems to like us young and pretty ! "

" Oh he *did*," Mrs. Grose assented : " it was the way he liked every one ! " She had no sooner spoken indeed than she caught herself up. " I mean that's *his* way—the master's."

I was struck. " But of whom did you speak first ? "

She looked blank, but she coloured. " Why of *him*."

" Of the master ? "

" Of who else ? "

There was so obviously no one else that the next moment I had lost my impression of her having accidentally said more than she meant ; and I merely asked what I wanted to know. " Did *she* see anything in the boy——? "

" That wasn't right ? She never told me."

I had a scruple, but I overcame it. " Was she careful—particular ? "

Mrs. Grose appeared to try to be conscientious. " About some things—yes."

" But not about all ? "

Again she considered. " Well, Miss—she's gone. I won't tell tales."

" I quite understand your feeling," I hastened to reply ; but I thought it after an instant not opposed to this concession to pursue : " Did she die here ? "

" No—she went off."

I don't know what there was in this brevity of Mrs. Grose's that struck me as ambiguous. " Went off to die ? " Mrs. Grose looked straight out of the window, but I felt that, hypothetically, I had a right to know what young persons engaged for Bly were expected to do. " She was taken ill, you mean, and went home ? "

" She was not taken ill, so far as appeared, in this house. She left it, at the end of the year, to go home, as she said, for a short holiday, to which the time she had put in had certainly given her a right. We had then a young woman—a nursemaid who had stayed on and who was a good girl and clever ; and *she* took the children altogether for the interval. But our young lady never came back, and at the very moment

I was expecting her I heard from the master that she was dead."

I turned this over. " But of what ? "

" He never told me ! But please, Miss," said Mrs. Grose, " I must get to my work."

III

HER thus turning her back on me was fortunately not, for my just preoccupations, a snub that could check the growth of our mutual esteem. We met, after I had brought home little Miles, more intimately than ever on the ground of my stupefaction, my general emotion : so monstrous was I then ready to pronounce it that such a child as had now been revealed to me should be under an interdict. I was a little late on the scene of his arrival, and I felt, as he stood wistfully looking out for me before the door of the inn at which the coach had put him down, that I had seen him on the instant, without and within, in the great glow of freshness, the same positive fragrance of purity, in which I had from the first moment seen his little sister. He was incredibly beautiful, and Mrs. Grose had put her finger on it : everything but a sort of passion of tenderness for him was swept away by his presence. What I then and there took him to my heart for was something divine that I have never found to the same degree in any child—his indescribable little air of knowing nothing in the world but love. It would have been impossible to carry a bad name with a greater sweetness of innocence, and by the time I had got back to Bly with him I remained merely bewildered—so far, that is, as I was not outraged—by the sense of the horrible letter locked up in one of the drawers of my room. As soon as

I could compass a private word with Mrs. Grose I declared to her that it was grotesque.

She promptly understood me. " You mean the cruel charge——? "

" It doesn't live an instant. My dear woman, *look* at him ! "

She smiled at my pretension to have discovered his charm. " I assure you, Miss, I do nothing else ! What will you say then ? " she immediately added.

" In answer to the letter ? " I had made up my mind. " Nothing at all."

" And to his uncle ? "

I was incisive. " Nothing at all."

" And to the boy himself ? "

I was wonderful. " Nothing at all."

She gave with her apron a great wipe to her mouth. " Then I'll stand by you. We'll see it out."

" We'll see it out ! " I ardently echoed, giving her my hand to make it a vow.

She held me there a moment, then whisked up her apron again with her detached hand. " Would you mind, Miss, if I used the freedom——"

" To kiss me ? No ! " I took the good creature in my arms and after we had embraced like sisters felt still more fortified and indignant.

This at all events was for the time : a time so full that as I recall the way it went it reminds me of all the art I now need to make it a little distinct. What I look back at with amazement is the situation I accepted. I had undertaken, with my companion, to see it out, and I was under a charm apparently that could smooth away the extent and the far and difficult connexions of such an effort. I was lifted aloft on a great wave of infatuation and pity. I found it simple, in my ignorance, my confusion, and perhaps my conceit, to assume that I could deal with a boy whose education for the world was all on the point of beginning. I am unable even to remember at this day what proposal I framed for the end of his holidays and the resumption of his studies. Lessons with me indeed, that charming summer, we all had a theory that he was to have; but I now feel that for weeks the lessons must have been rather my own. I learnt something—at first certainly—that had not been one of the teachings of my small smothered life; learnt to be amused, and even amusing, and not to think for the morrow. It was the first time, in a manner, that I had known space and air and freedom, all the music of summer and all the mystery of nature. And then there was consideration—and consideration was sweet. Oh it was a trap—not designed but deep—to my imagination, to my delicacy, perhaps to my vanity; to whatever in me was most excitable. The best way to picture it all is to say that I was off my guard. They gave me so little trouble—they were of a gentleness so extraordinary. I used to speculate—but even this with a dim disconnectedness —as to how the rough future (for all futures are rough!) would handle them and might bruise them. They had the bloom of health and happiness; and yet, as if I had been in charge of a pair of little grandees, of princes of the blood, for whom everything, to be right, would have to be fenced about and ordered and arranged, the only form that in my fancy the after-years could take for them was that of a romantic, a really royal extension of the garden and the park. It may be of course above all that what suddenly broke into this gives the previous time a charm of stillness—that hush in which something gathers or crouches. The change was actually like the spring of a beast.

In the first weeks the days were long; they often, at their finest, gave me what I used to call my own hour, the hour when, for my pupils, tea-time and bed-time having come and gone, I had before my final retirement a small interval alone. Much as I liked my companions this hour was the thing in the day I liked most ; and I liked it best of all when, as the light faded—or rather, I should say, the day lingered and the last calls of the last birds sounded, in a flushed sky, from the old trees—I could take a turn into the grounds and enjoy, almost with a sense of property that amused and flattered me, the beauty and dignity of the place. It was a pleasure at these moments to feel myself tranquil and justified ; doubtless perhaps also to reflect that by my discretion, my quiet good sense and general high propriety, I was giving pleasure—if he ever thought of it !—to the person to whose pressure I had yielded. What I was doing was what he had earnestly hoped and directly asked of me, and that I *could*, after all, do it proved even a greater joy than I had expected. I daresay I fancied myself in short a remarkable young woman and took comfort in the faith that this would more publicly appear. Well, I needed to be remarkable to offer a front to the remarkable things that presently gave their first sign.

It was plump, one afternoon, in the middle of my very hour : the children were tucked away and I had come out for my stroll. One of the thoughts that, as I don't in the least shrink now from noting, used to be with me in these wanderings was that it would be as charming as a charming story suddenly to meet some one. Some one would appear there at the turn of a path and would stand before me and smile and approve. I didn't ask more than that—I only asked that he should *know* ; and the only way to be sure he knew would be to see it, and the kind light of it, in his handsome face. That was exactly present to me—by which I mean the face was—when, on the first of these occasions, at the end of a long June day, I

stopped short on emerging from one of the plantations and coming into view of the house. What
arrested me on the spot—and with a shock much
greater than any vision had allowed for—was the
sense that my imagination had, in a flash, turned real.
He did stand there !—but high up, beyond the lawn
and at the very top of the tower to which, on that first
morning, little Flora had conducted me. This tower
was one of a pair—square incongruous crenellated
structures—that were distinguished, for some reason,
though I could see little difference, as the new and
the old. They flanked opposite ends of the house
and were probably architectural absurdities, re-
deemed in a measure indeed by not being wholly
disengaged nor of a height too pretentious, dating, in
their gingerbread antiquity, from a romantic revival
that was already a respectable past. I admired them,
had fancies about them, for we could all profit in a
degree, especially when they loomed through the dusk,
by the grandeur of their actual battlements ; yet it
was not at such an elevation that the figure I had so
often invoked seemed most in place.

It produced in me, this figure, in the clear twilight,
I remember, two distinct gasps of emotion, which
were, sharply, the shock of my first and that of my
second surprise. My second was a violent perception
of the mistake of my first : the man who met my eyes
was not the person I had precipitately supposed.
There came to me thus a bewilderment of vision of
which, after these years, there is no living view that I
can hope to give. An unknown man in a lonely
place is a permitted object of fear to a young woman
privately bred ; and the figure that faced me was—
a few more seconds assured me—as little any one
else I knew as it was the image that had been in my
mind. I had not seen it in Harley Street—I had
not seen it anywhere. The place, moreover, in the

strangest way in the world, had on the instant and by the very fact of its appearance become a solitude. To me at least, making my statement here with a deliberation with which I have never made it, the whole feeling of the moment returns. It was as if, while I took in what I did take in, all the rest of the scene had been stricken with death. I can hear again, as I write, the intense hush in which the sounds of evening dropped. The rooks stopped cawing in the golden sky and the friendly hour lost for the unspeakable minute all its voice. But there was no other change in nature, unless indeed it were a change that I saw with a stranger sharpness. The gold was still in the sky, the clearness in the air, and the man who looked at me over the battlements was as definite as a picture in a frame. That's how I thought, with extraordinary quickness, of each person he might have been and that he wasn't. We were confronted across our distance quite long enough for me to ask myself with intensity who then he was and to feel, as an effect of my inability to say, a wonder that in a few seconds more became intense.

The great question, or one of these, is afterwards, I know, with regard to certain matters, the question of how long they have lasted. Well, this matter of mine, think what you will of it, lasted while I caught at a dozen possibilities, none of which made a difference for the better, that I could see, in there having been in the house—and for how long, above all?—a person of whom I was in ignorance. It lasted while I just bridled a little with the sense of how my office seemed to require that there should be no such ignorance and no such person. It lasted while this visitant, at all events—and there was a touch of the strange freedom, as I remember, in the sign of familiarity of his wearing no hat—seemed to fix me, from his position, with just the question, just the scrutiny through the fading light, that his own presence provoked. We were too far apart to call to each other, but there was a moment at which, at shorter range, some challenge between us, breaking the hush, would have been the right result of our straight mutual stare. He was in one of the angles, the one away from the house, very erect, as it struck me, and with both hands on the ledge. So I saw him as I see the letters I form on this page ; then, exactly, after a minute, as if to add to the spectacle, he slowly changed his place—passed, looking at me hard all the while, to the opposite corner of the platform. Yes, it was intense to me that during this transit he never took his eyes from me, and I can see at this moment the way his hand, as he went, moved from one of the crenellations to the next. He stopped at the other corner, but less long, and even as he turned away still markedly fixed me. He turned away ; that was all I knew.

IV

It was not that I didn't wait, on this occasion, for more, since I was as deeply rooted as shaken. Was there a " secret " at Bly—a mystery of Udolpho or an insane, an unmentionable relative kept in unsuspected confinement ? I can't say how long I turned it over, or how long, in a confusion of curiosity and dread, I remained where I had had my collision ; I only recall that when I re-entered the house darkness had quite closed in. Agitation, in the interval, certainly had held me and driven me, for I must, in circling about the place, have walked three miles ; but I was to be later on so much more overwhelmed that this mere dawn of alarm was a comparatively human chill. The most singular part of it in fact—singular as the rest had been—was the part I became, in the hall, aware of in meeting Mrs. Grose. This picture comes back to me in the general train—the impression, as I received it on my return, of the wide white panelled space, bright in the lamplight and with its portraits and red carpet, and of the good surprised look of my friend, which immediately told me she had missed me. It came to me straightway, under her contact, that, with plain heartiness, mere relieved anxiety at my appearance, she knew nothing whatever that could bear upon the incident I had there ready for her. I had not suspected in advance that her comfortable face would pull me up, and I somehow measured the importance of what I had seen by my thus finding myself hesitate to mention it. Scarce anything in the whole history seems to me so odd as this fact that my real beginning of fear was one, as I may say, with the instinct of sparing my companion. On the spot, accordingly, in the pleasant hall and with her eyes on me, I, for a reason that I couldn't then have phrased, achieved an inward revolution—offered a vague pretext for my lateness and, with the plea of the beauty of the night and of the heavy dew and wet feet, went as soon as possible to my room.

Here it was another affair; here, for many days after, it was a queer affair enough. There were hours, from day to day—or at least there were moments, snatched even from clear duties—when I had to shut myself up to think. It wasn't so much yet that I was more nervous than I could bear to be as that I was remarkably afraid of becoming so; for the truth I had now to turn over was simply and clearly the truth that I could arrive at no account whatever of the visitor with whom I had been so inexplicably and yet, as it seemed to me, so intimately concerned. It took me little time to see that I might easily sound, without forms of inquiry and without exciting remark, any domestic complication. The shock I had suffered must have sharpened all my senses; I felt sure, at the end of three days and as the result of mere closer attention, that I had not been practised upon by the servants nor made the object of any "game." Of whatever it was that I knew nothing was known around me. There was but one sane inference: some one had taken a liberty rather monstrous. That was what, repeatedly, I dipped into my room and locked the door to say to myself. We had been, collectively, subject to an intrusion; some unscrupulous traveller, curious in old houses, had made his way in unobserved, enjoyed the prospect from the

best point of view and then stolen out as he came.
If he had given me such a bold hard stare, that was
but a part of his indiscretion. The good thing, after
all, was that we should surely see no more of him.

This was not so good a thing, I admit, as not to
leave me to judge that what, essentially, made
nothing else much signify was simply my charming
work. My charming work was just my life with
Miles and Flora, and through nothing could I so like
it as through feeling that to throw myself into it was
to throw myself out of my trouble. The attraction
of my small charges was a constant joy, leading me
to wonder afresh at the vanity of my original fears,
the distaste I had begun by entertaining for the
probable grey prose of my office. There was to be
no grey prose, it appeared, and no long grind ; so
how could work not be charming that presented
itself as daily beauty ? It was all the romance
of the nursery and the poetry of the schoolroom.
I don't mean by this of course that we studied only
fiction and verse ; I mean that I can express no
otherwise the sort of interest my companions inspired.
How can I describe that except by saying that instead
of growing deadly used to them—and it's a marvel
for a governess : I call the sisterhood to witness !—I
made constant fresh discoveries. There was one
direction, assuredly, in which these discoveries
stopped : deep obscurity continued to cover the
region of the boy's conduct at school. It had been
promptly given me, I have noted, to face that mystery
without a pang. Perhaps even it would be nearer
the truth to say that—without a word—he himself
had cleared it up. He had made the whole charge
absurd. My conclusion bloomed there with the real
rose-flush of his innocence : he was only too fine
and fair for the little horrid unclean school-world,
and he had paid a price for it. I reflected acutely

that the sense of such individual differences, such superiorities of quality, always, on the part of the majority—which could include even stupid sordid head-masters—turns infallibly to the vindictive.

Both the children had a gentleness—it was their only fault, and it never made Miles a muff—that kept them (how shall I express it ?) almost impersonal and certainly quite unpunishable. They were like those cherubs of the anecdote who had—morally at any rate—nothing to whack ! I remember feeling with Miles in especial as if he had had, as it were, nothing to call even an infinitesimal history. We expect of a small child scant enough " antecedents," but there was in this beautiful little boy something extraordinarily sensitive, yet extraordinarily happy, that, more than in any creature of his age I have seen, struck me as beginning anew each day. He had never for a second suffered. I took this as a direct disproof of his having really been chastised. If he had been wicked he would have " caught " it, and I should have caught it by the rebound—I should have found the trace, should have felt the wound and the dishonour. I could reconstitute nothing at all, and he was therefore an angel. He never spoke of his school, never mentioned a comrade or a master ; and I, for my part, was quite too much disgusted to allude to them. Of course I was under the spell, and the wonderful part is that, even at the time, I perfectly knew I was. But I gave myself up to it ; it was an antidote to any pain, and I had more pains than one. I was in receipt in these days of disturbing letters from home, where things were not going well. But with this joy of my children what things in the world mattered ? That was the question I used to put to my scrappy retirements. I was dazzled by their loveliness.

There was a Sunday—to get on—when it rained

with such force and for so many hours that there could be no procession to church ; in consequence of which, as the day declined, I had arranged with Mrs. Grose that, should the evening show improvement, we would attend together the late service. The rain happily stopped, and I prepared for our walk, which, through the park and by the good road to the village, would be a matter of twenty minutes. Coming downstairs to meet my colleague in the hall, I remembered a pair of gloves that had required three stitches and that had received them—with a publicity perhaps not edifying—while I sat with the children at their tea, served on Sundays, by exception, in that cold clean temple of mahogany and brass, the "grown-up" dining-room. The gloves had been dropped there, and I turned in to recover them. The day was grey enough, but the afternoon light still lingered, and it enabled me, on crossing the threshold, not only to recognise, on a chair near the wide window, then closed, the articles I wanted, but to become aware of a person on the other side of the window and looking straight in. One step into the room had sufficed ; my vision was instantaneous ; it was all there. The person looking straight in was the person who had already appeared to me. He appeared thus again with I won't say greater distinctness, for that was impossible, but with a nearness that represented a forward stride in our intercourse and made me, as I met him, catch my breath and turn cold. He was the same—he was the same, and seen, this time, as he had been seen before, from the waist up, the window, though the dining-room was on the ground floor, not going down to the terrace on which he stood. His face was close to the glass, yet the effect of this better view was, strangely, just to show me how intense the former had been. He remained but a few seconds—long enough to convince me he also saw and recognised ; but it was as if I had been looking at him for years and had known him always. Something, however, happened this time that had not happened before ; his stare into my face, through the glass and across the room, was as deep and hard as then, but it quitted me for a moment during which I could still watch it, see it fix successively several other things. On the spot there came to me the added shock of a certitude that it was not for me he had come. He had come for some one else.

The flash of this knowledge—for it was knowledge in the midst of dread — produced in me the most extraordinary effect, starting, as I stood there, a sudden vibration of duty and courage. I say courage because I was beyond all doubt already far gone. I bounded straight out of the door again, reached that of the house, got in an instant upon the drive and, passing along the terrace as fast as I could rush, turned a corner and came full in sight. But it was in sight of nothing now—my visitor had vanished. I stopped, almost dropped, with the real relief of this ; but I took in the whole scene—I gave him time to reappear. I call it time, but how long was it ? I can't speak to the purpose to-day of the duration of these things. That kind of measure must have left me : they couldn't have lasted as they actually appeared to me to last. The terrace and the whole place, the lawn and the garden beyond it, all I could see of the park, were empty with a great emptiness. There were shrubberies and big trees, but I remember the clear assurance I felt that none of them concealed him. He was there or was not there : not there if I didn't see him. I got hold of this ; then, instinctively, instead of returning as I had come, went to the window. It was confusedly present to me that I ought to place myself where he had stood. I did so ; I applied my face to the pane and looked, as he had looked, into the room. As if, at this moment, to show me exactly what his range had been, Mrs. Grose, as I had done for himself just before, came in from the hall. With this I had the full image of a repetition of what had already occurred. She saw me as I had seen my own visitant ; she pulled up short as I had done ; I gave her something of the shock that I had received. She turned white, and this made me ask myself if I had blanched as much. She stared, in short, and retreated just on *my* lines, and I knew she had then passed out and come round to me and that I should presently meet her. I remained where I was, and while I waited I thought of more things than one. But there's only one I take space to mention. I wondered why *she* should be scared.

V

OH she let me know as soon as, round the corner of the house, she loomed again into view. "What in the name of goodness is the matter——?" She was now flushed and out of breath.

I said nothing till she came quite near. "With me?" I must have made a wonderful face. "Do I show it?"

"You're as white as a sheet. You look awful."

I considered; I could meet on this, without scruple, any degree of innocence. My need to respect the bloom of Mrs. Grose's had dropped, without a rustle, from my shoulders, and if I wavered for the instant it was not with what I kept back. I put out my hand to her and she took it; I held her hard a little, liking to feel her close to me. There was a kind of support in the shy heave of her surprise. "You came for me for church, of course, but I can't go."

"Has anything happened?"

"Yes. You must know now. Did I look very queer?"

"Through this window? Dreadful!"

"Well," I said, "I've been frightened." Mrs. Grose's eyes expressed plainly that *she* had no wish to be, yet also that she knew too well her place not to be ready to share with me any marked inconvenience. Oh it was quite settled that she *must* share! "Just what you saw from the dining-room a minute ago was the effect of that. What *I* saw— just before—was much worse."

Her hand tightened. " What was it ? "

" An extraordinary man. Looking in."

" What extraordinary man ? "

" I haven't the least idea."

Mrs. Grose gazed round us in vain. " Then where is he gone ? "

" I know still less."

" Have you seen him before ? "

" Yes—once. On the old tower."

She could only look at me harder. " Do you mean he's a stranger ? "

" Oh very much ! "

" Yet you didn't tell me ? "

" No — for reasons. But now that you've guessed——"

Mrs. Grose's round eyes encountered this charge. " Ah I haven't guessed ! " she said very simply. " How can I if *you* don't imagine ? "

" I don't in the very least."

" You've seen him nowhere but on the tower ? "

" And on this spot just now."

Mrs. Grose looked round again. " What was he doing on the tower ? "

" Only standing there and looking down at me."

She thought a minute. " Was he a gentleman ? "

I found I had no need to think. " No." She gazed in deeper wonder. " No."

" Then nobody about the place ? Nobody from the village ? "

" Nobody—nobody. I didn't tell you, but I made sure."

She breathed a vague relief : this was, oddly, so much to the good. It only went indeed a little way. " But if he isn't a gentleman——"

" What *is* he ? He's a horror."

" A horror ? "

" He's—God help me if I know *what* he is ! "

Mrs. Grose looked round once more ; she fixed her eyes on the duskier distance and then, pulling herself together, turned to me with full inconsequence. " It's time we should be at church."

" Oh I'm not fit for church ! "

" Won't it do you good ? "

" It won't do *them*—— ! " I nodded at the house.

" The children ? "

" I can't leave them now."

" You're afraid—— ? "

I spoke boldly. " I'm afraid of *him*."

Mrs. Grose's large face showed me, at this, for the first time, the far-away faint glimmer of a consciousness more acute : I somehow made out in it the delayed dawn of an idea I myself had not given her and that was as yet quite obscure to me. It comes back to me that I thought instantly of this as something I could get from her ; and I felt it to be connected with the desire she presently showed to know more. " When was it—on the tower ? "

" About the middle of the month. At this same hour."

" Almost at dark," said Mrs. Grose.

" Oh no, not nearly. I saw him as I see you."

" Then how did he get in ? "

" And how did he get out ? " I laughed. " I had no opportunity to ask him ! This evening, you see," I pursued, " he has not been able to get in."

" He only peeps ? "

" I hope it will be confined to that ! " She had now let go my hand ; she turned away a little. I waited an instant ; then I brought out : " Go to church. Good-bye. I must watch."

Slowly she faced me again. " Do you fear for them ? "

We met in another long look. " Don't *you* ? "
Instead of answering she came nearer to the window
and, for a minute, applied her face to the glass.
" You see how he could see," I meanwhile went on.

She didn't move. " How long was he here ? "

" Till I came out. I came to meet him."

Mrs. Grose at last turned round, and there was
still more in her face. " *I* couldn't have come out."

" Neither could I ! " I laughed again. " But I did
come. I've my duty."

" So have I mine," she replied ; after which she
added : " What's he like ? "

" I've been dying to tell you. But he's like
nobody."

" Nobody ? " she echoed.

" He has no hat." Then seeing in her face that
she already, in this, with a deeper dismay, found a
touch of picture, I quickly added stroke to stroke.
" He has red hair, very red, close-curling, and a pale
face, long in shape, with straight good features and
little rather queer whiskers that are as red as his hair.
His eyebrows are somehow darker ; they look particularly arched and as if they might move a good
deal. His eyes are sharp, strange—awfully ; but
I only know clearly that they're rather small and very
fixed. His mouth's wide, and his lips are thin, and
except for his little whiskers he's quite clean-shaven.
He gives me a sort of sense of looking like an actor."

" An actor ! " It was impossible to resemble one
less, at least, than Mrs. Grose at that moment.

" I've never seen one, but so I suppose them. He's
tall, active, erect," I continued, " but never—no,
never !—a gentleman."

My companion's face had blanched as I went on ;
her round eyes started and her mild mouth gaped.
" A gentleman ? " she gasped, confounded, stupefied :
" a gentleman *he* ? "

" You know him, then ? "

She visibly tried to hold herself. " But he *is* handsome ? "

I saw the way to help her. " Remarkably ! "

" And dressed—— ? "

" In somebody's clothes. They're smart, but they're not his own."

She broke into a breathless affirmative groan. " They're the master's ! "

I caught it up. " You *do* know him ? "

She faltered but a second. " Quint ! " she cried.

" Quint ? "

" Peter Quint—his own man, his valet, when he was here ! "

" When the master was ? "

Gaping still, but meeting me, she pieced it all together. " He never wore his hat, but he did wear —well, there were waistcoats missed ! They were both here—last year. Then the master went, and Quint was alone."

I followed, but halting a little. " Alone ? "

" Alone with *us*." Then as from a deeper depth, " In charge," she added.

" And what became of him ? "

She hung fire so long that I was still more mystified. " He went too," she brought out at last.

" Went where ? "

Her expression, at this, became extraordinary. " God knows where ! He died."

" Died ? " I almost shrieked.

She seemed fairly to square herself, plant herself more firmly to express the wonder of it. " Yes. Mr. Quint's dead."

VI

It took, of course, more than that particular passage to place us together in presence of what we had now to live with as we could, my dreadful liability to impressions of the order so vividly exemplified, and my companion's knowledge henceforth—a knowledge half consternation and half compassion — of that liability. There had been this evening, after the revelation that left me for an hour so prostrate— there had been for either of us no attendance on any service but a little service of tears and vows, of prayers and promises, a climax to the series of mutual challenges and pledges that had straightway ensued on our retreating together to the schoolroom and shutting ourselves up there to have everything out. The result of our having everything out was simply to reduce our situation to the last rigour of its elements. She herself had seen nothing, not the shadow of a shadow, and nobody in the house but the governess was in the governess's plight; yet she accepted without directly impugning my sanity the truth as I gave it to her, and ended by showing me on this ground an awestricken tenderness, a deference to my more than questionable privilege, of which the very breath has remained with me as that of the sweetest of human charities.

What was settled between us accordingly that night was that we thought we might bear things to-

169

gether; and I was not even sure that in spite of her exemption it was she who had the best of the burden. I knew at this hour, I think, as well as I knew later, what I was capable of meeting to shelter my pupils; but it took me some time to be wholly sure of what my honest comrade was prepared for to keep terms with so stiff an agreement. I was queer company enough—quite as queer as the company I received; but as I trace over what we went through I see how much common ground we must have found in the one idea that, by good fortune, *could* steady us. It was the idea, the second movement, that led me straight out, as I may say, of the inner chamber of my dread. I could take the air in the court, at least, and there Mrs. Grose could join me. Perfectly can I recall now the particular way strength came to me before we separated for the night. We had gone over and over every feature of what I had seen.

" He was looking for some one else, you say— some one who was not you ? "

" He was looking for little Miles." A portentous clearness now possessed me. " *That's* whom he was looking for."

" But how do you know ? "

" I know, I know, I know ! " My exaltation grew. " And *you* know, my dear ! "

She didn't deny this, but I required, I felt, not even so much telling as that. She took it up again in a moment. " What if *he* should see him ? "

" Little Miles ? That's what he wants ! "

She looked immensely scared again. " The child ? "

" Heaven forbid ! The man. He wants to appear to *them*." That he might was an awful conception, and yet somehow I could keep it at bay; which, more-over, as we lingered there, was what I succeeded in practically proving. I had an absolute certainty that

I should see again what I had already seen, but something within me said that by offering myself bravely as the sole subject of such experience, by accepting, by inviting, by surmounting it all, I should serve as an expiatory victim and guard the tranquillity of the rest of the household. The children in especial I should thus fence about and absolutely save. I recall one of the last things I said that night to Mrs. Grose.

" It does strike me that my pupils have never mentioned—— ! "

She looked at me hard as I musingly pulled up. " His having been here and the time they were with him ? "

" The time they were with him, and his name, his presence, his history, in any way. They've never alluded to it."

" Oh the little lady doesn't remember. She never heard or knew."

" The circumstances of his death ? " I thought with some intensity. " Perhaps not. But Miles would remember—Miles would know."

" Ah don't try him ! " broke from Mrs. Grose.

I returned her the look she had given me. " Don't be afraid." I continued to think. " It *is* rather odd."

" That he has never spoken of him ? "

" Never by the least reference. And you tell me they were ' great friends.' "

" Oh it wasn't *him* ! " Mrs. Grose with emphasis declared. " It was Quint's own fancy. To play with him, I mean—to spoil him." She paused a moment ; then she added : " Quint was much too free."

This gave me, straight from my vision of his face —*such* a face !—a sudden sickness of disgust. " Too free with *my* boy ? "

" Too free with every one ! "

I forbore for the moment to analyse this description further than by the reflexion that a part of it applied to several of the members of the household, of the half-dozen maids and men who were still of our small colony. But there was everything, for our apprehension, in the lucky fact that no discomfortable legend, no perturbation of scullions, had ever, within any one's memory, attached to the kind old place. It had neither bad name nor ill fame, and Mrs. Grose, most apparently, only desired to cling to me and to quake in silence. I even put her, the very last thing of all, to the test. It was when, at midnight, she had her hand on the schoolroom door to take leave. " I *have* it from you then—for it's of great importance— that he was definitely and admittedly bad ? "

" Oh not admittedly. *I* knew it—but the master didn't."

" And you never told him ? "

" Well, he didn't like tale-bearing—he hated complaints. He was terribly short with anything of that kind, and if people were all right to *him*——"

" He wouldn't be bothered with more ? " This squared well enough with my impression of him : he was not a trouble-loving gentleman, nor so very particular perhaps about some of the company he himself kept. All the same, I pressed my informant. " I promise you *I* would have told ! "

She felt my discrimination. " I daresay I was wrong. But really I was afraid."

" Afraid of what ? "

" Of things that man could do. Quint was so clever—he was so deep."

I took this in still more than I probably showed. " You weren't afraid of anything else ? Not of his effect—— ? "

" His effect ? " she repeated with a face of anguish and waiting while I faltered.

" On innocent little precious lives. They were in your charge."

" No, they weren't in mine ! " she roundly and distressfully returned. " The master believed in him and placed him here because he was supposed not to be quite in health and the country air so good for him. So he had everything to say. Yes "—she let me have it—" even about *them*."

" Them—that creature ? " I had to smother a kind of howl. " And you could bear it ? "

" No. I couldn't—and I can't now ! " And the poor woman burst into tears.

A rigid control, from the next day, was, as I have said, to follow them ; yet how often and how passionately, for a week, we came back together to the subject ! Much as we had discussed it that Sunday night, I was, in the immediate later hours in especial— for it may be imagined whether I slept—still haunted with the shadow of something she had not told me. I myself had kept back nothing, but there was a word Mrs. Grose had kept back. I was sure, moreover, by morning that this was not from a failure of frankness, but because on every side there were fears. It seems to me indeed, in raking it all over, that by the time the morrow's sun was high I had restlessly read into the facts before us almost all the meaning they were to receive from subsequent and more cruel occur- rences. What they gave me above all was just the sinister figure of the living man—the dead one would keep a while !—and of the months he had continuously passed at Bly, which, added up, made a formidable stretch. The limit of this evil time had arrived only when, on the dawn of a winter's morning, Peter Quint was found, by a labourer going to early work, stone dead on the road from the village : a catastrophe explained—superficially at least—by a visible wound to his head ; such a wound as might have been produced (and as, on the final evidence, *had* been) by a fatal slip, in the dark and after leaving the public-house, on the steepish icy slope, a wrong path altogether, at the bottom of which he lay. The icy slope, the turn mistaken at night and in liquor, accounted for much—practically, in the end and after the inquest and boundless chatter, for everything ; but there had been matters in his life, strange passages and perils, secret disorders, vices more than suspected, that would have accounted for a good deal more.

I scarce know how to put my story into words that shall be a credible picture of my state of mind ; but I was in these days literally able to find a joy in the extraordinary flight of heroism the occasion demanded of me. I now saw that I had been asked for a service admirable and difficult ; and there would be a greatness in letting it be seen—oh in the right quarter !—that I could succeed where many another girl might have failed. It was an immense help to me—I confess I rather applaud myself as I look back !—that I saw my response so strongly and so simply. I was there to protect and defend the little creatures in the world the most bereaved and the most lovable, the appeal of whose helplessness had suddenly become only too explicit, a deep constant ache of one's own engaged affection. We were cut off, really, together ; we were united in our danger. They had nothing but me, and I—well, I had *them*. It was in short a magnificent chance. This chance presented itself to me in an image richly material. I was a screen—I was to stand before them. The more I saw the less they would. I began to watch them in a stifled suspense, a disguised tension, that might well, had it continued too long, have turned to something like madness. What saved me, as I now see, was that it turned to another matter altogether. It didn't last as suspense—it was superseded by horrible proofs. Proofs, I say, yes—from the moment I really took hold.

This moment dated from an afternoon hour that I happened to spend in the grounds with the younger of my pupils alone. We had left Miles indoors, on the red cushion of a deep window-seat ; he had wished to finish a book, and I had been glad to encourage a purpose so laudable in a young man whose only defect was a certain ingenuity of restlessness. His sister, on the contrary, had been alert to come out, and I strolled with her half an hour, seeking the shade, for the sun was still high and the day exceptionally warm. I was aware afresh with her, as we went, of how, like her brother, she contrived—it was the charming thing in both children—to let me alone without appearing to drop me and to accompany me without appearing to oppress. They were never importunate and yet never listless. My attention to them all really went to seeing them amuse themselves immensely without me : this was a spectacle they seemed actively to prepare and that employed me as an active admirer. I walked in a world of their invention—they had no occasion whatever to draw upon mine ; so that my time was taken only with being for them some remarkable person or thing that the game of the moment required and that was merely, thanks to my superior, my exalted stamp, a happy and highly distinguished sinecure. I forget what I was on the present occasion ; I only remember that I was something very important and very quiet and that Flora was playing very hard. We were on the edge of the lake, and, as we had lately begun geography, the lake was the Sea of Azof.

Suddenly, amid these elements, I became aware that on the other side of the Sea of Azof we had an interested spectator. The way this knowledge

gathered in me was the strangest thing in the world—
the strangest, that is, except the very much stranger
in which it quickly merged itself. I had sat down
with a piece of work—for I was something or other
that could sit—on the old stone bench which overlooked the pond ; and in this position I began to take
in with certitude and yet without direct vision the
presence, a good way off, of a third person. The old
trees, the thick shrubbery, made a great and pleasant
shade, but it was all suffused with the brightness of
the hot still hour. There was no ambiguity in anything ; none whatever at least in the conviction I
from one moment to another found myself forming
as to what I should see straight before me and across
the lake as a consequence of raising my eyes. They
were attached at this juncture to the stitching in
which I was engaged, and I can feel once more the
spasm of my effort not to move them till I should so
have steadied myself as to be able to make up my
mind what to do. There was an alien object in view
—a figure whose right of presence I instantly and
passionately questioned. I recollect counting over
perfectly the possibilities, reminding myself that
nothing was more natural, for instance, than the
appearance of one of the men about the place, or
even of a messenger, a postman or a tradesman's
boy, from the village. That reminder had as little
effect on my practical certitude as I was conscious—
still even without looking—of its having upon the
character and attitude of our visitor. Nothing was
more natural than that these things should be the
other things they absolutely were not.

Of the positive identity of the apparition I would
assure myself as soon as the small clock of my courage
should have ticked out the right second ; meanwhile,
with an effort that was already sharp enough, I
transferred my eyes straight to little Flora, who, at

the moment, was about ten yards away. My heart had stood still for an instant with the wonder and terror of the question whether she too would see ; and I held my breath while I waited for what a cry from her, what some sudden innocent sign either of interest or of alarm, would tell me. I waited, but nothing came ; then in the first place—and there is something more dire in this, I feel, than in anything I have to relate—I was determined by a sense that within a minute all spontaneous sounds from her had dropped ; and in the second by the circumstance that also within the minute she had, in her play, turned her back to the water. This was her attitude when I at last looked at her—looked with the confirmed conviction that we were still, together, under direct personal notice. She had picked up a small flat piece of wood which happened to have in it a little hole that had evidently suggested to her the idea of sticking in another fragment that might figure as a mast and make the thing a boat. This second morsel, as I watched her, she was very markedly and intently attempting to tighten in its place. My apprehension of what she was doing sustained me so that after some seconds I felt I was ready for more. Then I again shifted my eyes—I faced what I had to face.

VII

I GOT hold of Mrs. Grose as soon after this as I could ; and I can give no intelligible account of how I fought out the interval. Yet I still hear myself cry as I fairly threw myself into her arms : " They *know*—it's too monstrous : they know, they know ! "

" And what on earth——? " I felt her incredulity as she held me.

" Why all that *we* know—and heaven knows what more besides ! " Then as she released me I made it out to her, made it out perhaps only now with full coherency even to myself. " Two hours ago, in the garden "—I could scarce articulate—" Flora *saw* ! "

Mrs. Grose took it as she might have taken a blow in the stomach. " She has told you ? " she panted.

" Not a word—that's the horror. She kept it to herself ! The child of eight, *that* child ! " Unutterable still for me was the stupefaction of it.

Mrs. Grose of course could only gape the wider. " Then how do you know ? "

" I was there—I saw with my eyes : saw she was perfectly aware."

" Do you mean aware of *him* ? "

" No—of *her*." I was conscious as I spoke that I looked prodigious things, for I got the slow reflexion of them in my companion's face. " Another person—this time ; but a figure of quite as unmistakable horror and evil : a woman in black, pale and dread-

178

ful—with such an air also, and such a face !—on the other side of the lake. I was there with the child —quiet for the hour ; and in the midst of it she came."

"Came how—from where ? "

"From where they come from ! She just appeared and stood there—but not so near."

"And without coming nearer ? "

"Oh for the effect and the feeling she might have been as close as you ! "

My friend, with an odd impulse, fell back a step. "Was she some one you've never seen ? "

"Never. But some one the child has. Some one *you* have." Then to show how I had thought it all out : "My predecessor—the one who died."

"Miss Jessel ? "

"Miss Jessel. You don't believe me ? " I pressed. She turned right and left in her distress. "How can you be sure ? "

This drew from me, in the state of my nerves, a flash of impatience. "Then ask Flora—*she's* sure ! " But I had no sooner spoken than I caught myself up. "No, for God's sake, *don't* ! She'll say she isn't— she'll lie ! "

Mrs. Grose was not too bewildered instinctively to protest. "Ah how *can* you ? "

"Because I'm clear. Flora doesn't want me to know."

"It's only, then, to spare you."

"No, no—there are depths, depths ! The more I go over it the more I see in it, and the more I see in it the more I fear. I don't know what I *don't* see, what I *don't* fear ! "

Mrs. Grose tried to keep up with me. "You mean you're afraid of seeing her again ? "

"Oh no ; that's nothing—now ! " Then I explained. "It's of *not* seeing her."

But my companion only looked wan. " I don't understand."

" Why, it's that the child may keep it up—and that the child assuredly *will*—without my knowing it."

At the image of this possibility Mrs. Grose for a moment collapsed, yet presently to pull herself together again as from the positive force of the sense of what, should we yield an inch, there would really be to give way to. " Dear, dear—we must keep our heads ! And after all, if she doesn't mind it——! " She even tried a grim joke. " Perhaps she likes it ! "

" Like *such* things—a scrap of an infant ! "

" Isn't it just a proof of her blest innocence ? " my friend bravely inquired.

She brought me, for the instant, almost round. " Oh, we must clutch at *that*—we must cling to it ! If it isn't a proof of what you say, it's a proof of— God knows what ! For the woman's a horror of horrors."

Mrs. Grose, at this, fixed her eyes a minute on the ground ; then at last raising them, " Tell me how you know," she said.

" Then you admit it's what she was ? " I cried.

" Tell me how you know," my friend simply repeated.

" Know ? By seeing her ! By the way she looked."

" At you, do you mean—so wickedly ? "

" Dear me, no—I could have borne that. She gave me never a glance. She only fixed the child."

Mrs. Grose tried to see it. " Fixed her ? "

" Ah, with such awful eyes ! "

She stared at mine as if they might really have resembled them. " Do you mean of dislike ? "

" God help us, no. Of something much worse."

" Worse than dislike ? "—this left her indeed at a loss.

" With a determination—indescribable. With a kind of fury of intention."

I made her turn pale. " Intention ? "

" To get hold of her." Mrs. Grose—her eyes just lingering on mine—gave a shudder and walked to the window; and while she stood there looking out I completed my statement. " *That's* what Flora knows."

After a little she turned round. " The person was in black, you say ? "

" In mourning—rather poor, almost shabby. But —yes—with extraordinary beauty." I now recognised to what I had at last, stroke by stroke, brought the victim of my confidence, for she quite visibly weighed this. " Oh handsome—very, very," I insisted ; " wonderfully handsome. But infamous."

She slowly came back to me. " Miss Jessel—*was* infamous." She once more took my hand in both her own, holding it as tight as if to fortify me against the increase of alarm I might draw from this disclosure. " They were both infamous," she finally said.

So for a little we faced it once more together ; and I found absolutely a degree of help in seeing it now so straight. " I appreciate," I said, " the great decency of your not having hitherto spoken ; but the time has certainly come to give me the whole thing." She appeared to assent to this, but still only in silence ; seeing which I went on : " I must have it now. Of what did she die ? Come, there was something between them."

" There was everything."

" In spite of the difference —— ? "

" Oh of their rank, their condition "—she brought it woefully out. " *She* was a lady."

I turned it over ; I again saw. " Yes—she was a lady."

" And he so dreadfully below," said Mrs. Grose.

I felt that I doubtless needn't press too hard, in such company, on the place of a servant in the scale ; but there was nothing to prevent an acceptance of my companion's own measure of my predecessor's abasement. There was a way to deal with that, and I dealt ; the more readily for my full vision—on the evidence—of our employer's late clever good-looking " own " man ; impudent, assured, spoiled, depraved. " The fellow was a hound."

Mrs. Grose considered as if it were perhaps a little a case for a sense of shades. " I've never seen one like him. He did what he wished."

" With *her* ? "

" With them all."

It was as if now in my friend's own eyes Miss Jessel had again appeared. I seemed at any rate for an instant to trace their evocation of her as distinctly as I had seen her by the pond ; and I brought out with decision : " It must have been also what *she* wished ! "

Mrs. Grose's face signified that it had been indeed, but she said at the same time : " Poor woman—she paid for it ! "

" Then you do know what she died of ? " I asked.

" No—I know nothing. I wanted not to know ; I was glad enough I didn't ; and I thanked heaven she was well out of this ! "

" Yet you had, then, your idea——"

" Of her real reason for leaving ? Oh yes—as to that. She couldn't have stayed. Fancy it here—for a governess ! And afterwards I imagined—and I still imagine. And what I imagine is dreadful."

" Not so dreadful as what *I* do," I replied ; on which I must have shown her—as I was indeed but too conscious—a front of miserable defeat. It brought out again all her compassion for me, and at the renewed touch of her kindness my power to resist broke down. I burst, as I had the other time made her burst, into tears ; she took me to her motherly breast, where my lamentation overflowed. " I don't do it ! " I sobbed in despair ; " I don't save or shield them ! It's far worse than I dreamed. They're lost ! "

VIII

WHAT I had said to Mrs. Grose was true enough : there were in the matter I had put before her depths and possibilities that I lacked resolution to sound ; so that when we met once more in the wonder of it we were of a common mind about the duty of resistance to extravagant fancies. We were to keep our heads if we should keep nothing else—difficult indeed as that might be in the face of all that, in our prodigious experience, seemed least to be questioned. Late that night, while the house slept, we had another talk in my room ; when she went all the way with me as to its being beyond doubt that I had seen exactly what I had seen. I found that to keep her thoroughly in the grip of this I had only to ask her how, if I had " made it up," I came to be able to give, of each of the persons appearing to me, a picture disclosing, to the last detail, their special marks—a portrait on the exhibition of which she had instantly recognised and named them. She wished, of course—small blame to her !—to sink the whole subject ; and I was quick to assure her that my own interest in it had now violently taken the form of a search for the way to escape from it. I closed with her cordially on the article of the likelihood that with recurrence—for recurrence we took for granted—I should get used to my danger ; distinctly professing that my personal exposure had suddenly become the least of my discomforts. It was my new suspicion that was intolerable ; and yet even to this complication the later hours of the day had brought a little ease.

On leaving her, after my first outbreak, I had of course returned to my pupils, associating the right remedy for my dismay with that sense of their charm which I had already recognised as a resource I could positively cultivate and which had never failed me yet. I had simply, in other words, plunged afresh into Flora's special society and there become aware— it was almost a luxury !—that she could put her little conscious hand straight upon the spot that ached. She had looked at me in sweet speculation and then had accused me to my face of having " cried." I had supposed the ugly signs of it brushed away ; but I could literally—for the time at all events—rejoice, under this fathomless charity, that they had not entirely disappeared. To gaze into the depths of blue of the child's eyes and pronounce their loveliness a trick of premature cunning was to be guilty of a cynicism in preference to which I naturally preferred to abjure my judgment and, so far as might be, my agitation. I couldn't abjure for merely wanting to, but I could repeat to Mrs. Grose—as I did there, over and over, in the small hours—that with our small friends' voices in the air, their pressure on one's heart and their fragrant faces against one's cheek, everything fell to the ground but their incapacity and their beauty. It was a pity that, somehow, to settle this once for all, I had equally to re-enumerate the signs of subtlety that, in the afternoon, by the lake, had made a miracle of my show of self-possession. It was a pity to be obliged to reinvestigate the certitude of the moment itself and repeat how it had come to me as a revelation that the inconceivable communion I then surprised must have been for both parties a matter of habit. It was a pity I should have had to quaver

out again the reasons for my not having, in my delusion, so much as questioned that the little girl saw
our visitant even as I actually saw Mrs. Grose herself,
and that she wanted, by just so much as she did thus
see, to make me suppose she didn't, and at the same
time, without showing anything, arrive at a guess as to
whether I myself did! It was a pity I needed to
recapitulate the portentous little activities by which
she sought to divert my attention—the perceptible
increase of movement, the greater intensity of play,
the singing, the gabbling of nonsense and the invitation to romp.

Yet if I had not indulged, to prove there was
nothing in it, in this review, I should have missed
the two or three dim elements of comfort that still
remained to me. I shouldn't, for instance, have been
able to asseverate to my friend that I was certain—
which was so much to the good—that *I* at least had
not betrayed myself. I shouldn't have been prompted,
by stress of need, by desperation of mind—I scarce
know what to call it—to invoke such further aid to
intelligence as might spring from pushing my colleague fairly to the wall. She had told me, bit by bit,
under pressure, a great deal; but a small shifty spot
on the wrong side of it all still sometimes brushed my
brow like the wing of a bat; and I remember how on
this occasion—for the sleeping house and the concentration alike of our danger and our watch seemed
to help—I felt the importance of giving the last jerk
to the curtain. "I don't believe anything so horrible,"
I recollect saying; "no, let us put it definitely, my
dear, that I don't. But if I did, you know, there's a
thing I should require now, just without sparing you
the least bit more—oh not a scrap, come!—to get
out of you. What was it you had in mind when, in
our distress, before Miles came back, over the letter
from his school, you said, under my insistence, that

you didn't pretend for him he hadn't literally *ever* been ' bad ' ? He has *not*, truly, ' ever,' in these weeks that I myself have lived with him and so closely watched him ; he has been an imperturbable little prodigy of delightful lovable goodness. Therefore you might perfectly have made the claim for him if you had not, as it happened, seen an exception to take. What was your exception, and to what passage in your personal observation of him did you refer ? "

It was a straight question enough, but levity was not our note, and in any case I had before the grey dawn admonished us to separate got my answer. What my friend had had in mind proved immensely to the purpose. It was neither more nor less than the particular fact that for a period of several months Quint and the boy had been perpetually together. It was indeed the very appropriate item of evidence of her having ventured to criticise the propriety, to hint at the incongruity, of so close an alliance, and even to go so far on the subject as a frank overture to Miss Jessel would take her. Miss Jessel had, with a very high manner about it, requested her to mind her business, and the good woman had on this directly approached little Miles. What she had said to him, since I pressed, was that *she* liked to see young gentlemen not forget their station.

I pressed again, of course, the closer for that. " You reminded him that Quint was only a base menial ? "

" As you might say ! And it was his answer, for one thing, that was bad."

" And for another thing ? " I waited. " He repeated your words to Quint ? "

" No, not that. It's just what he *wouldn't* ! " she could still impress on me. " I was sure, at any rate," she added, " that he didn't. But he denied certain occasions."

" What occasions ? "

" When they had been about together quite as if Quint were his tutor—and a very grand one—and Miss Jessel only for the little lady. When he had gone off with the fellow, I mean, and spent hours with him."

" He then prevaricated about it—he said he hadn't ? " Her assent was clear enough to cause me to add in a moment : " I see. He lied."

" Oh ! " Mrs. Grose mumbled. This was a suggestion that it didn't matter ; which indeed she backed up by a further remark. " You see, after all, Miss Jessel didn't mind. She didn't forbid him."

I considered. " Did he put that to you as a justification ? "

At this she dropped again. " No, he never spoke of it."

" Never mentioned her in connexion with Quint ? "

She saw, visibly flushing, where I was coming out. " Well, he didn't show anything. He denied," she repeated ; " he denied."

Lord, how I pressed her now ! " So that you could see he knew what was between the two wretches ? "

" I don't know—I don't know ! " the poor woman wailed.

" You do know, you dear thing," I replied ; " only you haven't my dreadful boldness of mind, and you keep back, out of timidity and modesty and delicacy, even the impression that in the past, when you had, without my aid, to flounder about in silence, most of all made you miserable. But I shall get it out of you yet ! There was something in the boy that suggested to you," I continued, " his covering and concealing their relation."

" Oh he couldn't prevent——"

" Your learning the truth ? I daresay ! But, heavens," I fell, with vehemence, a-thinking, " what

THE TURN OF THE SCREW

it shows that they must, to that extent, have succeeded in making of him ! "

" Ah nothing that's not nice *now* ! " Mrs. Grose lugubriously pleaded.

" I don't wonder you looked queer," I persisted, "when I mentioned to you the letter from his school!"

" I doubt if I looked as queer as you ! " she retorted with homely force. " And if he was so bad then as that comes to, how is he such an angel now ? "

" Yes indeed—and if he was a fiend at school ! How, how, how ? Well," I said in my torment, " you must put it to me again, though I shall not be able to tell you for some days. Only put it to me again ! " I cried in a way that made my friend stare. " There are directions in which I mustn't for the present let myself go." Meanwhile I returned to her first example—the one to which she had just previously referred—of the boy's happy capacity for an occasional slip. " If Quint—on your remonstrance at the time you speak of—was a base menial, one of the things Miles said to you, I find myself guessing, was that you were another." Again her admission was so adequate that I continued : " And you forgave him that ? "

" Wouldn't *you* ? "

" Oh yes ! " And we exchanged there, in the stillness, a sound of the oddest amusement. Then I went on : " At all events, while he was with the man——"

" Miss Flora was with the woman. It suited them all ! "

It suited me too, I felt, only too well ; by which I mean that it suited exactly the particular deadly view I was in the very act of forbidding myself to entertain. But I so far succeeded in checking the expression of this view that I will throw, just here, no further light on it than may be offered by the mention of my final observation to Mrs. Grose. " His having lied and been impudent are, I confess, less engaging specimens than I had hoped to have from you of the outbreak in him of the little natural man. Still," I mused, " they must do, for they make me feel more than ever that I must watch."

It made me blush, the next minute, to see in my friend's face how much more unreservedly she had forgiven him than her anecdote struck me as pointing out to my own tenderness any way to do. This was marked when, at the schoolroom door, she quitted me. " Surely you don't accuse *him*——"

" Of carrying on an intercourse that he conceals from me ? Ah remember that, until further evidence, I now accuse nobody." Then before shutting her out to go by another passage to her own place, " I must just wait," I wound up.

IX

I WAITED and waited, and the days took as they
elapsed something from my consternation. A very
few of them, in fact, passing, in constant sight of my
pupils, without a fresh incident, sufficed to give to
grievous fancies and even to odious memories a kind
of brush of the sponge. I have spoken of the surrender to their extraordinary childish grace as a thing
I could actively promote in myself, and it may be
imagined if I neglected now to apply at this source for
whatever balm it would yield. Stranger than I can
express, certainly, was the effort to struggle against
my new lights. It would doubtless have been a
greater tension still, however, had it not been so
frequently successful. I used to wonder how my
little charges could help guessing that I thought
strange things about them ; and the circumstance
that these things only made them more interesting
was not by itself a direct aid to keeping them in the
dark. I trembled lest they should see that they
were so immensely more interesting. Putting things
at the worst, at all events, as in meditation I so often
did, any clouding of their innocence could only be—
blameless and foredoomed as they were—a reason
the more for taking risks. There were moments
when I knew myself to catch them up by an irresistible impulse and press them to my heart. As soon
as I had done so I used to wonder—" What will they

think of that ? Doesn't it betray too much ? " It would have been easy to get into a sad wild tangle about how much I might betray ; but the real account, I feel, of the hours of peace I could still enjoy was that the immediate charm of my companions was a beguilement still effective even under the shadow of the possibility that it was studied. For if it occurred to me that I might occasionally excite suspicion by the little outbreaks of my sharper passion for them, so too I remember asking if I mightn't see a queerness in the traceable increase of their own demonstrations.

They were at this period extravagantly and preternaturally fond of me ; which, after all, I could reflect, was no more than a graceful response in children perpetually bowed down over and hugged. The homage of which they were so lavish succeeded in truth for my nerves quite as well as if I never appeared to myself, as I may say, literally to catch them at a purpose in it. They had never, I think, wanted to do so many things for their poor protectress ; I mean—though they got their lessons better and better, which was naturally what would please her most—in the way of diverting, entertaining, surprising her ; reading her passages, telling her stories, acting her charades, pouncing out at her, in disguises, as animals and historical characters, and above all astonishing her by the " pieces " they had secretly got by heart and could interminably recite. I should never get to the bottom—were I to let myself go even now—of the prodigious private commentary, all under still more private correction, with which I in these days overscored their full hours. They had shown me from the first a facility for everything, a general faculty which, taking a fresh start, achieved remarkable flights. They got their little tasks as if they loved them ; they indulged, from the

mere exuberance of the gift, in the most unimposed
little miracles of memory. They not only popped out
at me as tigers and as Romans, but as Shakespeareans,
astronomers and navigators. This was so singularly
the case that it had presumably much to do with the
fact as to which, at the present day, I am at a loss for
a different explanation : I allude to my unnatural
composure on the subject of another school for Miles.
What I remember is that I was content for the time
not to open the question, and that contentment must
have sprung from the sense of his perpetually striking
show of cleverness. He was too clever for a bad
governess, for a parson's daughter, to spoil ; and the
strangest if not the brightest thread in the pensive
embroidery I just spoke of was the impression I might
have got, if I had dared to work it out, that he was
under some influence operating in his small intellectual
life as a tremendous incitement.

If it was easy to reflect, however, that such a boy
could postpone school, it was at least as marked that
for such a boy to have been " kicked out " by a school-
master was a mystification without end. Let me add
that in their company now—and I was careful almost
never to be out of it—I could follow no scent very
far. We lived in a cloud of music and affection and
success and private theatricals. The musical sense
in each of the children was of the quickest, but the
elder in especial had a marvellous knack of catching
and repeating. The schoolroom piano broke into all
gruesome fancies ; and when that failed there were
confabulations in corners, with a sequel of one of
them going out in the highest spirits in order to " come
in " as something new. I had had brothers myself,
and it was no revelation to me that little girls could
be slavish idolaters of little boys. What surpassed
everything was that there was a little boy in the
world who could have for the inferior age, sex and

intelligence so fine a consideration. They were extraordinarily at one, and to say that they never either quarrelled or complained is to make the note of praise coarse for their quality of sweetness. Sometimes perhaps indeed (when I dropped into coarseness) I came across traces of little understandings between them by which one of them should keep me occupied while the other slipped away. There is a naïf side, I suppose, in all diplomacy ; but if my pupils practised upon me it was surely with the minimum of grossness. It was all in the other quarter that, after a lull, the grossness broke out.

I find that I really hang back ; but I must take my horrid plunge. In going on with the record of what was hideous at Bly I not only challenge the most liberal faith—for which I little care ; but (and this is another matter) I renew what I myself suffered, I again push my dreadful way through it to the end. There came suddenly an hour after which, as I look back, the business seems to me to have been all pure suffering ; but I have at least reached the heart of it, and the straightest road out is doubtless to advance. One evening—with nothing to lead up or prepare it —I felt the cold touch of the impression that had breathed on me the night of my arrival and which, much lighter then as I have mentioned, I should probably have made little of in memory had my subsequent sojourn been less agitated. I had not gone to bed ; I sat reading by a couple of candles. There was a roomful of old books at Bly—last-century fiction some of it, which, to the extent of a distinctly deprecated renown, but never to so much as that of a stray specimen, had reached the sequestered home and appealed to the unavowed curiosity of my youth. I remember that the book I had in my hand was Fielding's *Amelia* ; also that I was wholly awake. I recall further both a general conviction that it was horribly late and a particular objection to looking at my watch. I figure finally that the white curtain draping, in the fashion of those days, the head of Flora's little bed, shrouded, as I had assured myself long before, the perfection of childish rest. I recollect in short that though I was deeply interested in my author I found myself, at the turn of a page and with his spell all scattered, looking straight up from him and hard at the door of my room. There was a moment during which I listened, reminded of the faint sense I had had, the first night, of there being something undefinably astir in the house, and noted the soft breath of the open casement just move the half-drawn blind. Then, with all the marks of a deliberation that must have seemed magnificent had there been any one to admire it, I laid down my book, rose to my feet and, taking a candle, went straight out of the room and, from the passage, on which my light made little impression, noiselessly closed and locked the door.

I can say now neither what determined nor what guided me, but I went straight along the lobby, holding my candle high, till I came within sight of the tall window that presided over the great turn of the staircase. At this point I precipitately found myself aware of three things. They were practically simultaneous, yet they had flashes of succession. My candle, under a bold flourish, went out, and I perceived, by the uncovered window, that the yielding dusk of earliest morning rendered it unnecessary. Without it, the next instant, I knew that there was a figure on the stair. I speak of sequences, but I required no lapse of seconds to stiffen myself for a third encounter with Quint. The apparition had reached the landing halfway up and was therefore on the spot nearest the window, where, at sight of me, it stopped short and fixed me exactly as it had fixed me from the tower and from the garden. He knew me as well as I knew him; and so, in the cold faint twilight, with a glimmer in the high glass and another on the polish of the oak stair below, we faced each other in our common intensity. He was absolutely, on this occasion, a living detestable dangerous presence. But that was not the wonder of wonders ; I reserve this distinction for quite another circumstance : the circumstance that dread had unmistakably quitted me and that there was nothing in me unable to meet and measure him.

I had plenty of anguish after that extraordinary moment, but I had, thank God, no terror. And he knew I hadn't—I found myself at the end of an instant magnificently aware of this. I felt, in a fierce rigour of confidence, that if I stood my ground a minute I should cease—for the time at least—to have him to reckon with ; and during the minute, accordingly, the thing was as human and hideous as a real interview : hideous just because it *was* human, as human as to have met alone, in the small hours, in a sleeping house, some enemy, some adventurer, some criminal. It was the dead silence of our long gaze at such close quarters that gave the whole horror, huge as it was, its only note of the unnatural. If I had met a murderer in such a place and at such an hour we still at least would have spoken. Something would have passed, in life, between us ; if nothing had passed one of us would have moved. The moment was so prolonged that it would have taken but little more to make me doubt if even *I* were in life. I can't express what followed it save by saying that the silence itself—which was indeed in a manner an attestation of my strength—became the element into which I saw the figure disappear ; in which I definitely saw it turn, as I might have seen the low wretch to which it had once belonged turn on receipt of an order, and pass, with my eyes on the villainous back that no hunch could have more disfigured, straight down the staircase and into the darkness in which the next bend was lost.

X

I REMAINED a while at the top of the stair, but with the effect presently of understanding that when my visitor had gone, he had gone ; then I returned to my room. The foremost thing I saw there by the light of the candle I had left burning was that Flora's little bed was empty ; and on this I caught my breath with all the terror that, five minutes before, I had been able to resist. I dashed at the place in which I had left her lying and over which—for the small silk counterpane and the sheets were disarranged—the white curtains had been deceivingly pulled forward ; then my step, to my unutterable relief, produced an answering sound : I noticed an agitation of the window-blind, and the child, ducking down, emerged rosily from the other side of it. She stood there in so much of her candour and so little of her night-gown, with her pink bare feet and the golden glow of her curls. She looked intensely grave, and I had never had such a sense of losing an advantage acquired (the thrill of which had just been so prodigious) as on my consciousness that she addressed me with a reproach—" You naughty : where *have* you been ? " Instead of challenging her own irregularity I found myself arraigned and explaining. She herself explained, for that matter, with the loveliest eagerest simplicity. She had known suddenly, as she lay there, that I was out of the room, and had jumped up to see what had become of me. I had dropped, with the joy of her reappearance, back into my chair—feeling then, and then only, a little faint ; and she had pattered straight over to me, thrown herself upon my knee, given herself to be held with the flame of the candle full in the wonderful little°face that was still flushed with sleep. I remember closing my eyes an instant, yieldingly, consciously, as before the excess of something beautiful that shone out of the blue of her own. " You were looking for me out of the window ? " I said. " You thought I might be walking in the grounds ? "

" Well, you know, I thought some one was "—she never blanched as she smiled out that at me.

Oh how I looked at her now ! " And did you see any one ? "

" Ah *no* ! " she returned almost (with the full privilege of childish inconsequence) resentfully, though with a long sweetness in her little drawl of the negative.

At that moment, in the state of my nerves, I absolutely believed she lied ; and if I once more closed my eyes it was before the dazzle of the three or four possible ways in which I might take this up. One of these for a moment tempted me with such singular force that, to resist it, I must have gripped my little girl with a spasm that, wonderfully, she submitted to without a cry or a sign of fright. Why not break out at her on the spot and have it all over ? —give it to her straight in her lovely little lighted face ? " You see, you see, you *know* that you do and that you already quite suspect I believe it ; therefore why not frankly confess it to me, so that we may at least live with it together and learn perhaps, in the strangeness of our fate, where we are and what it means ? " This solicitation dropped, alas, as it came : if I could immediately have succumbed to it

I might have spared myself—well, you'll see what. Instead of succumbing I sprang again to my feet, looked at her bed and took a helpless middle way. " Why did you pull the curtain over the place to make me think you were still there ? "

Flora luminously considered ; after which, with her little divine smile : " Because I don't like to frighten you ! "

" But if I had, by your idea, gone out——? "

She absolutely declined to be puzzled ; she turned her eyes to the flame of the candle as if the question were as irrelevant, or at any rate as impersonal, as Mrs. Marcet or nine-times-nine. " Oh but you know," she quite adequately answered, " that you might come back, you dear, and that you *have* ! " And after a little, when she had got into bed, I had, a long time, by almost sitting on her for the retention of her hand, to show how I recognised the pertinence of my return.

You may imagine the general complexion, from that moment, of my nights. I repeatedly sat up till I didn't know when ; I selected moments when my room-mate unmistakably slept, and, stealing out, took noiseless turns in the passage. I even pushed as far as to where I had last met Quint. But I never met him there again, and I may as well say at once that I on no other occasion saw him in the house. I just missed, on the staircase, nevertheless, a different adventure. Looking down it from the top I once recognised the presence of a woman seated on one of the lower steps with her back presented to me, her body half-bowed and her head, in an attitude of woe, in her hands. I had been there but an instant, however, when she vanished without looking round at me. I knew, for all that, exactly what dreadful face she had to show ; and I wondered whether, if instead of being above I had been below, I should have had the same nerve for going up that I had lately shown

Quint. Well, there continued to be plenty of call for nerve. On the eleventh night after my latest encounter with that gentleman—they were all numbered now—I had an alarm that perilously skirted it and that indeed, from the particular quality of its unexpectedness, proved quite my sharpest shock. It was precisely the first night during this series that, weary with vigils, I had conceived I might again without laxity lay myself down at my old hour. I slept immediately and, as I afterwards knew, till about one o'clock; but when I woke it was to sit straight up, as completely roused as if a hand had shaken me. I had left a light burning, but it was now out, and I felt an instant certainty that Flora had extinguished it. This brought me to my feet and straight, in the darkness, to her bed, which I found she had left. A glance at the window enlightened me further, and the striking of a match completed the picture.

The child had again got up—this time blowing out the taper, and had again, for some purpose of observation or response, squeezed in behind the blind and was peering out into the night. That she now saw—as she had not, I had satisfied myself, the previous time—was proved to me by the fact that she was disturbed neither by my re-illumination nor by the haste I made to get into slippers and into a wrap. Hidden, protected, absorbed, she evidently rested on the sill—the casement opened forward— and gave herself up. There was a great still moon to help her, and this fact had counted in my quick decision. She was face to face with the apparition we had met at the lake, and could now communicate with it as she had not then been able to do. What I, on my side, had to care for was, without disturbing her, to reach, from the corridor, some other window turned to the same quarter. I got to the door without her hearing me ; I got out of it, closed it and listened, from the other side, for some sound from her. While I stood in the passage I had my eyes on her brother's door, which was but ten steps off and which, indescribably, produced in me a renewal of the strange impulse that I lately spoke of as my temptation. What if I should go straight in and march to *his* window ?—what if, by risking to his boyish bewilderment a revelation of my motive, I should throw across the rest of the mystery the long halter of my boldness ?

This thought held me sufficiently to make me cross to his threshold and pause again. I preternaturally listened ; I figured to myself what might portentously be ; I wondered if his bed were also empty and he also secretly at watch. It was a deep soundless minute, at the end of which my impulse failed. He was quiet ; he might be innocent ; the risk was hideous ; I turned away. There was a figure in the grounds—a figure prowling for a sight, the visitor with whom Flora was engaged ; but it wasn't the visitor most concerned with my boy. I hesitated afresh, but on other grounds and only a few seconds ; then I had made my choice. There were empty rooms enough at Bly, and it was only a question of choosing the right one. The right one suddenly presented itself to me as the lower one— though high above the gardens—in the solid corner of the house that I have spoken of as the old tower. This was a large square chamber, arranged with some state as a bedroom, the extravagant size of which made it so inconvenient that it had not for years, though kept by Mrs. Grose in exemplary order, been occupied. I had often admired it and I knew my way about in it ; I had only, after just faltering at the first chill gloom of its disuse, to pass across it and unbolt in all quietness one of the shutters. Achieving this transit I uncovered the glass without a sound and, applying my face to the pane, was able, the darkness without being much less than within, to see that I commanded the right direction. Then I saw something more. The moon made the night extraordinarily penetrable and showed me on the lawn a person, diminished by distance, who stood there motionless and as if fascinated, looking up to where I had appeared—looking, that is, not so much straight at me as at something that was apparently above me. There was clearly another person above me—there was a person on the tower; but the presence on the lawn was not in the least what I had conceived and had confidently hurried to meet. The presence on the lawn—I felt sick as I made it out—was poor little Miles himself.

XI

It was not till late next day that I spoke to Mrs. Grose; the rigour with which I kept my pupils in sight making it often difficult to meet her privately: the more as we each felt the importance of not provoking—on the part of the servants quite as much as on that of the children—any suspicion of a secret flurry or of a discussion of mysteries. I drew a great security in this particular from her mere smooth aspect. There was nothing in her fresh face to pass on to others the least of my horrible confidences. She believed me, I was sure, absolutely: if she hadn't I don't know what would have become of me, for I couldn't have borne the strain alone. But she was a magnificent monument to the blessing of a want of imagination, and if she could see in our little charges nothing but their beauty and amiability, their happiness and cleverness, she had no direct communication with the sources of my trouble. If they had been at all visibly blighted or battered she would doubtless have grown, on tracing it back, haggard enough to match them; as matters stood, however, I could feel her, when she surveyed them with her large white arms folded and the habit of serenity in all her look, thank the Lord's mercy that if they were ruined the pieces would still serve. Flights of fancy gave place, in her mind, to a steady fireside glow, and I had already begun to perceive how, with the development of the conviction that—as time went on without a public accident—our young things could, after all, look out for themselves, she addressed her greatest solicitude to the sad case presented by their deputy-guardian. That, for myself, was a sound simplification : I could engage that, to the world, my face should tell no tales, but it would have been, in the conditions, an immense added worry to find myself anxious about hers.

At the hour I now speak of she had joined me, under pressure, on the terrace, where, with the lapse of the season, the afternoon sun was now agreeable ; and we sat there together while before us and at a distance, yet within call if we wished, the children strolled to and fro in one of their most manageable moods. They moved slowly, in unison, below us, over the lawn, the boy, as they went, reading aloud from a story-book and passing his arm round his sister to keep her quite in touch. Mrs. Grose watched them with positive placidity ; then I caught the suppressed intellectual creak with which she conscientiously turned to take from me a view of the back of the tapestry. I had made her a receptacle of lurid things, but there was an odd recognition of my superiority — my accomplishments and my function — in her patience under my pain. She offered her mind to my disclosures as, had I wished to mix a witch's broth and proposed it with assurance, she would have held out a large clean saucepan. This had become thoroughly her attitude by the time that, in my recital of the events of the night, I reached the point of what Miles had said to me when, after seeing him, at such a monstrous hour, almost on the very spot where he happened now to be, I had gone down to bring him in ; choosing then, at the window, with a concentrated need of not alarming the house, rather that method than any noisier process. I had left her meanwhile in little doubt of my small hope of representing with success even to her actual sympathy my sense of the real splendour of the little inspiration with which, after I had got him into the house, the boy met my final articulate challenge. As soon as I appeared in the moonlight on the terrace he had come to me as straight as possible ; on which I had taken his hand without a word and led him, through the dark spaces, up the staircase where Quint had so hungrily hovered for him, along the lobby where I had listened and trembled, and so to his forsaken room.

Not a sound, on the way, had passed between us, and I had wondered—oh *how* I had wondered !—if he were groping about in his dreadful little mind for something plausible and not too grotesque. It would tax his invention certainly, and I felt, this time, over his real embarrassment, a curious thrill of triumph. It was a sharp trap for any game hitherto successful. He could play no longer at perfect propriety, nor could he pretend to it ; so how the deuce would he get out of the scrape ? There beat in me indeed, with the passionate throb of this question, an equal dumb appeal as to how the deuce *I* should. I was confronted at last, as never yet, with all the risk attached even now to sounding my own horrid note. I remember in fact that as we pushed into his little chamber, where the bed had not been slept in at all and the window, uncovered to the moonlight, made the place so clear that there was no need of striking a match—I remember how I suddenly dropped, sank upon the edge of the bed from the force of the idea that he must know how he really, as they say, " had " me. He could do what he liked, with all his cleverness to help him, so long as I should continue to defer to the old tradition of the criminality of those caretakers of the young who minister to superstitions and fears. He " had " me indeed, and in a cleft stick ; for who would ever absolve me, who would consent that I should go unhung, if, by the faintest tremor of an overture, I were the first to introduce into our perfect intercourse an element so dire ? No, no : it was useless to attempt to convey to Mrs. Grose, just as it is scarcely less so to attempt to suggest here, how, during our short stiff brush there in the dark, he fairly shook me with admiration. I was of course thoroughly kind and merciful ; never, never yet had I placed on his small shoulders hands of such tenderness as those with which, while I rested against the bed, I held him there well under fire. I had no alternative but, in form at least, to put it to him.

" You must tell me now—and all the truth. What did you go out for ? What were you doing there ? "

I can still see his wonderful smile, the whites of his beautiful eyes and the uncovering of his clear teeth, shine to me in the dusk. " If I tell you why, will you understand ? " My heart, at this, leaped into my mouth. *Would* he tell me why ? I found no sound on my lips to press it, and I was aware of answering only with a vague repeated grimacing nod. He was gentleness itself, and while I wagged my head at him he stood there more than ever a little fairy prince. It was his brightness indeed that gave me a respite. Would it be so great if he were really going to tell me ? " Well," he said at last, " just exactly in order that you should do this."

" Do what ? "

" Think me—for a change—*bad* ! " I shall never forget the sweetness and gaiety with which he brought out the word, nor how, on top of it, he bent forward and kissed me. It was practically the end of every-thing. I met his kiss and I had to make, while I folded him for a minute in my arms, the most stupendous effort not to cry. He had given exactly the account of himself that permitted least my going behind it, and it was only with the effect of confirming my acceptance of it that, as I presently glanced about the room, I could say:

" Then you didn't undress at all ? "

He fairly glittered in the gloom. " Not at all. I sat up and read."

" And when did you go down ? "

" At midnight. When I'm bad I *am* bad ! "

" I see, I see—it's charming. But how could you be sure I should know it ? "

" Oh I arranged that with Flora." His answers rang out with a readiness ! " She was to get up and look out."

" Which is what she did do." It was I who fell into the trap !

" So she disturbed you, and, to see what she was looking at, you also looked—you saw."

" While you," I concurred, " caught your death in the night air ! "

He literally bloomed so from this exploit that he could afford radiantly to assent. " How otherwise should I have been bad enough ? " he asked. Then, after another embrace, the incident and our interview closed on my recognition of all the reserves of goodness that, for his joke, he had been able to draw upon.

XII

The particular impression I had received proved in the morning light, I repeat, not quite successfully presentable to Mrs. Grose, though I re-enforced it with the mention of still another remark that he had made before we separated. " It all lies in half-a-dozen words," I said to her, " words that really settle the matter. ' Think, you know, what I *might* do ! ' He threw that off to show me how good he is. He knows down to the ground what he ' might do.' That's what he gave them a taste of at school."

" Lord, you do change ! " cried my friend.

" I don't change—I simply make it out. The four, depend upon it, perpetually meet. If on either of these last nights you had been with either child you'd clearly have understood. The more I've watched and waited the more I've felt that if there were nothing else to make it sure it would be made so by the systematic silence of each. *Never*, by a slip of the tongue, have they so much as alluded to either of their old friends, any more than Miles has alluded to his expulsion. Oh yes, we may sit here and look at them, and they may show off to us there to their fill ; but even while they pretend to be lost in their fairy-tale they're steeped in their vision of the dead restored to them. He's not reading to her," I declared ; " they're talking of *them*—they're talking horrors ! I go on, I know, as if I were crazy ; and it's a wonder I'm not. What I've seen would have made *you* so ; but it has only made me more lucid, made me get hold of still other things."

My lucidity must have seemed awful, but the charming creatures who were victims of it, passing and repassing in their interlocked sweetness, gave my colleague something to hold on by ; and I felt how tight she held as, without stirring in the breath of my passion, she covered them still with her eyes. " Of what other things have you got hold ? "

" Why, of the very things that have delighted, fascinated and yet, at bottom, as I now so strangely see, mystified and troubled me. Their more than earthly beauty, their absolutely unnatural goodness. It's a game," I went on ; " it's a policy and a fraud ! "

" On the part of little darlings——— ? "

" As yet mere lovely babies ? Yes, mad as that seems ! " The very act of bringing it out really helped me to trace it—follow it all up and piece it all together. " They haven't been good—they've only been absent. It has been easy to live with them because they're simply leading a life of their own. They're not mine—they're not ours. They're his and they're hers ! "

" Quint's and that woman's ? "

" Quint's and that woman's. They want to get to them."

Oh how, at this, poor Mrs. Grose appeared to study them ! " But for what ? "

" For the love of all the evil that, in those dreadful days, the pair put into them. And to ply them with that evil still, to keep up the work of demons, is what brings the others back."

" Laws ! " said my friend under her breath. The exclamation was homely, but it revealed a real accept-ance of my further proof of what, in the bad time—

for there had been a worse even than this!—must have occurred. There could have been no such justification for me as the plain assent of her experience to whatever depth of depravity I found credible in our brace of scoundrels. It was in obvious submission of memory that she brought out after a moment: "They *were* rascals! But what can they now do?" she pursued.

"Do?" I echoed so loud that Miles and Flora, as they passed at their distance, paused an instant in their walk and looked at us. "Don't they do enough?" I demanded in a lower tone, while the children, having smiled and nodded and kissed hands to us, resumed their exhibition. We were held by it a minute; then I answered: "They can destroy them!" At this my companion did turn, but the appeal she launched was a silent one, the effect of which was to make me more explicit. "They don't know as yet quite how—but they're trying hard. They're seen only across, as it were, and beyond—in strange places and on high places, the top of towers, the roof of houses, the outside of windows, the further edge of pools; but there's a deep design, on either side, to shorten the distance and overcome the obstacle: so the success of the tempters is only a question of time. They've only to keep to their suggestions of danger."

"For the children to come?"

"And perish in the attempt!" Mrs. Grose slowly got up, and I scrupulously added: "Unless, of course, we can prevent!"

Standing there before me while I kept my seat she visibly turned things over. "Their uncle must do the preventing. He must take them away."

"And who's to make him?"

She had been scanning the distance, but she now dropped on me a foolish face. "You, Miss."

" By writing to him that his house is poisoned and his little nephew and niece mad ? "

" But if they *are*, Miss ? "

" And if I am myself, you mean ?   That's charming news to be sent him by a person enjoying his confidence and whose prime undertaking was to give him no worry."

Mrs. Grose considered, following the children again.   " Yes, he do hate worry.   That was the great reason——— "

" Why those fiends took him in so long?   No doubt, though his indifference must have been awful.   As I'm not a fiend, at any rate, I shouldn't take him in."

My companion, after an instant and for all answer, sat down again and grasped my arm.   " Make him at any rate come to you."

I stared.   " To *me* ? "   I had a sudden fear of what she might do.   " ' Him ' ? "

" He ought to *be* here—he ought to help."

I quickly rose and I think I must have shown her a queerer face than ever yet.   " You see me asking him for a visit ? "   No, with her eyes on my face she evidently couldn't.   Instead of it even—as a woman reads another—she could see what I myself saw : his derision, his amusement, his contempt for the breakdown of my resignation at being left alone and for the fine machinery I had set in motion to attract his attention to my slighted charms.   She didn't know —no one knew—how proud I had been to serve him and to stick to our terms ; yet she none the less took the measure, I think, of the warning I now gave her. " If you should so lose your head as to appeal to him for me——— "

She was really frightened.   " Yes, Miss ? "

" I would leave, on the spot, both him and you."

XIII

It was all very well to join them, but speaking to them proved quite as much as ever an effort beyond my strength—offered, in close quarters, difficulties as insurmountable as before. This situation continued a month, and with new aggravations and particular notes, the note above all, sharper and sharper, of the small ironic consciousness on the part of my pupils. It was not, I am as sure to-day as I was sure then, my mere infernal imagination : it was absolutely traceable that they were aware of my predicament and that this strange relation made, in a manner, for a long time, the air in which we moved. I don't mean that they had their tongues in their cheeks or did anything vulgar, for that was not one of their dangers : I do mean, on the other hand, that the element of the unnamed and untouched became, between us, greater than any other, and that so much avoidance couldn't have been made successful without a great deal of tacit arrangement. It was as if, at moments, we were perpetually coming into sight of subjects before which we must stop short, turning suddenly out of alleys that we perceived to be blind, closing with a little bang that made us look at each other—for, like all bangs, it was something louder than we had intended — the doors we had indiscreetly opened. All roads lead to Rome, and there were times when it might have struck us that almost every branch of study or subject of conversation skirted forbidden ground. Forbidden ground was the question of the return of the dead in general and of whatever, in especial, might survive, for memory, of the friends little children had lost. There were days when I could have sworn that one of them had, with a small invisible nudge, said to the other : " She thinks she'll do it this time—but she *won't!* " To " do it " would have been to indulge, for instance—and for once in a way—in some direct reference to the lady who had prepared them for my discipline. They had a delightful endless appetite for passages in my own history to which I had again and again treated them ; they were in possession of everything that had ever happened to me, had had, with every circumstance, the story of my smallest adventures and of those of my brothers and sisters and of the cat and the dog at home, as well as many particulars of the whimsical bent of my father, of the furniture and arrangement of our house and of the conversation of the old women of our village. There were things enough, taking one with another, to chatter about, if one went very fast and knew by instinct when to go round. They pulled with an art of their own the strings of my invention and my memory ; and nothing else perhaps, when I thought of such occasions afterwards, gave me so the suspicion of being watched from under cover. It was in any case over *my* life, *my* past and *my* friends alone that we could take anything like our ease ; a state of affairs that led them sometimes without the least pertinence to break out into sociable reminders. I was invited—with no visible connexion—to repeat afresh Goody Gosling's celebrated *mot* or to confirm the details already supplied as to the cleverness of the vicarage pony.

It was partly at such junctures as these and partly at quite different ones that, with the turn my matters had now taken, my predicament, as I have called it, grew most sensible. The fact that the days passed for me without another encounter ought, it would have appeared, to have done something toward soothing my nerves. Since the light brush, that second night on the upper landing, of the presence of a woman at the foot of the stair, I had seen nothing, whether in or out of the house, that one had better not have seen. There was many a corner round which I expected to come upon Quint, and many a situation that, in a merely sinister way, would have favoured the appearance of Miss Jessel. The summer had turned, the summer had gone ; the autumn had dropped upon Bly and had blown out half our lights. The place, with its grey sky and withered garlands, its bared spaces and scattered dead leaves, was like a theatre after the performance—all strewn with crumpled playbills. There were exactly states of the air, conditions of sound and of stillness, unspeakable impressions of the *kind* of ministering moment, that brought back to me, long enough to catch it, the feeling of the medium in which, that June evening out of doors, I had had my first sight of Quint, and in which too, at those other instants, I had, after seeing him through the window, looked for him in vain in the circle of shrubbery. I recognised the signs, the portents—I recognised the moment, the spot. But they remained unaccompanied and empty, and I continued unmolested ; if unmolested one could call a young woman whose sensibility had, in the most extraordinary fashion, not declined but deepened. I had said in my talk with Mrs. Grose on that horrid scene of Flora's by the lake—and had perplexed her by so saying—that it would from that moment distress me much more to lose my power than to keep it. I had then expressed what was vividly in my mind : the truth that, whether the children really saw or not—

since, that is, it was not yet definitely proved—I greatly preferred, as a safeguard, the fulness of my own exposure. I was ready to know the very worst that was to be known. What I had then had an ugly glimpse of was that my eyes might be sealed just while theirs were most opened. Well, my eyes *were* sealed, it appeared, at present—a consummation for which it seemed blasphemous not to thank God. There was, alas, a difficulty about that : I would have thanked him with all my soul had I not had in a proportionate measure this conviction of the secret of my pupils.

How can I retrace to-day the strange steps of my obsession ? There were times of our being together when I would have been ready to swear that, literally, in my presence, but with my direct sense of it closed, they had visitors who were known and were welcome. Then it was that, had I not been deterred by the very chance that such an injury might prove greater than the injury to be averted, my exaltation would have broken out. " They're here, they're here, you little wretches," I would have cried, " and you can't deny it now ! " The little wretches denied it with all the added volume of their sociability and their tenderness, just in the crystal depths of which—like the flash of a fish in a stream—the mockery of their advantage peeped up. The shock had in truth sunk into me still deeper than I knew on the night when, looking out either for Quint or for Miss Jessel under the stars, I had seen there the boy over whose rest I watched and who had immediately brought in with him— had straightway there turned on me—the lovely upward look with which, from the battlements above us, the hideous apparition of Quint had played. If it was a question of a scare my discovery on this occasion had scared me more than any other, and it was essentially in the scared state that I drew my actual conclusions. They harassed me so that sometimes, at odd moments, I shut myself up audibly to rehearse—it was at once a fantastic relief and a renewed despair—the manner in which I might come to the point. I approached it from one side and the other while, in my room, I flung myself about, but I always broke down in the monstrous utterance of names. As they died away on my lips I said to myself that I should indeed help them to represent something infamous if by pronouncing them I should violate as rare a little case of instinctive delicacy as any schoolroom probably had ever known. When I said to myself: "*They* have the manners to be silent, and you, trusted as you are, the baseness to speak!" I felt myself crimson and covered my face with my hands. After these secret scenes I chattered more than ever, going on volubly enough till one of our prodigious palpable hushes occurred— I can call them nothing else—the strange dizzy lift or swim (I try for terms !) into a stillness, a pause of all life, that had nothing to do with the more or less noise we at the moment might be engaged in making and that I could hear through any intensified mirth or quickened recitation or louder strum of the piano. Then it was that the others, the outsiders, were there. Though they were not angels they " passed," as the French say, causing me, while they stayed, to tremble with the fear of their addressing to their younger victims some yet more infernal message or more vivid image than they had thought good enough for myself.

What it was least possible to get rid of was the cruel idea that, whatever I had seen, Miles and Flora saw *more*—things terrible and unguessable and that sprang from dreadful passages of intercourse in the past. Such things naturally left on the surface, for the time, a chill that we vociferously denied we felt ;

and we had all three, with repetition, got into such splendid training that we went, each time, to mark the close of the incident, almost automatically through the very same movements. It was striking of the children at all events to kiss me inveterately with a wild irrelevance and never to fail—one or the other—of the precious question that had helped us through many a peril. " When do you think he *will* come ? Don't you think we *ought* to write ? "—there was nothing like that inquiry, we found by experience, for carrying off an awkwardness. " He " of course was their uncle in Harley Street ; and we lived in much profusion of theory that he might at any moment arrive to mingle in our circle. It was impossible to have given less encouragement than he had administered to such a doctrine, but if we had not had the doctrine to fall back upon we should have deprived each other of some of our finest exhibitions. He never wrote to them—that may have been selfish, but it was a part of the flattery of his trust of myself ; for the way in which a man pays his highest tribute to a woman is apt to be but by the more festal celebration of one of the sacred laws of his comfort. So I held that I carried out the spirit of the pledge given not to appeal to him when I let our young friends understand that their own letters were but charming literary exercises. They were too beautiful to be posted ; I kept them myself ; I have them all to this hour. This was a rule indeed which only added to the satiric effect of my being plied with the supposition that he might at any moment be among us. It was exactly as if our young friends knew how almost more awkward than anything else that might be for me. There appears to me, moreover, as I look back no note in all this more extraordinary than the mere fact that, in spite of my tension and of their triumph, I never lost patience with them. Adorable they must in truth have been, I now feel, since I didn't in these days hate them ! Would exasperation, however, if relief had longer been postponed, finally have betrayed me ? It little matters, for relief arrived. I call it relief though it was only the relief that a snap brings to a strain or the burst of a thunderstorm to a day of suffocation. It was at least change, and it came with a rush.

XIV

WALKING to church a certain Sunday morning, I had
little Miles at my side and his sister, in advance of us
and at Mrs. Grose's, well in sight. It was a crisp clear
day, the first of its order for some time ; the night had
brought a touch of frost and the autumn air, bright
and sharp, made the church-bells almost gay. It was
an odd accident of thought that I should have happened at such a moment to be particularly and very
gratefully struck with the obedience of my little
charges. Why did they never resent my inexorable,
my perpetual society? Something or other had
brought nearer home to me that I had all but pinned
the boy to my shawl, and that in the way our companions were marshalled before me I might have
appeared to provide against some danger of rebellion.
I was like a gaoler with an eye to possible surprises
and escapes. But all this belonged—I mean their
magnificent little surrender — just to the special
array of the facts that were most abysmal. Turned
out for Sunday by his uncle's tailor, who had had a
free hand and a notion of pretty waistcoats and of his
grand little air, Miles's whole title to independence,
the rights of his sex and situation, were so stamped
upon him that if he had suddenly struck for freedom
I should have had nothing to say. I was by the
strangest of chances wondering how I should meet
him when the revolution unmistakably occurred. I

call it a revolution because I now see how, with the word he spoke, the curtain rose on the last act of my dreadful drama and the catastrophe was precipitated. " Look here, my dear, you know," he charmingly said, " when in the world, please, am I going back to school ? "

Transcribed here the speech sounds harmless enough, particularly as uttered in the sweet, high, casual pipe with which, at all interlocutors, but above all at his eternal governess, he threw off intonations as if he were tossing roses. There was something in them that always made one " catch," and I caught at any rate now so effectually that I stopped as short as if one of the trees of the park had fallen across the road. There was something new, on the spot, between us, and he was perfectly aware I recognised it, though to enable me to do so he had no need to look a whit less candid and charming than usual. I could feel in him how he already, from my at first finding nothing to reply, perceived the advantage he had gained. I was so slow to find anything that he had plenty of time, after a minute, to continue with his suggestive but inconclusive smile : " You know, my dear, that for a fellow to be with a lady *always*——! " His " my dear " was constantly on his lips for me, and nothing could have expressed more the exact shade of the sentiment with which I desired to inspire my pupils than its fond familiarity. It was so respectfully easy.

But oh how I felt that at present I must pick my own phrases ! I remember that, to gain time, I tried to laugh, and I seemed to see in the beautiful face with which he watched me how ugly and queer I looked. " And always with the same lady ? " I returned.

He neither blenched nor winked. The whole thing was virtually out between us. " Ah of course she's a jolly ' perfect ' lady ; but after all I'm a fellow, don't you see ? who's—well, getting on."

I lingered there with him an instant ever so kindly. " Yes, you're getting on." Oh but I felt helpless !

I have kept to this day the heartbreaking little idea of how he seemed to know that and to play with it. " And you can't say I've not been awfully good, can you ? "

I laid my hand on his shoulder, for though I felt how much better it would have been to walk on I was not yet quite able. " No, I can't say that, Miles."

" Except just that one night, you know——! "

" That one night ? " I couldn't look as straight as he.

" Why, when I went down—went out of the house."

" Oh yes. But I forget what you did it for."

" You forget ? "—he spoke with the sweet extravagance of childish reproach. " Why, it was just to show you I could ! "

" Oh yes—you could."

" And I can again."

I felt I might perhaps after all succeed in keeping my wits about me. " Certainly. But you won't."

" No, not *that* again. It was nothing."

" It was nothing," I said. " But we must go on."

He resumed our walk with me, passing his hand into my arm. " Then when *am* I going back ? "

I wore, in turning it over, my most responsible air. " Were you very happy at school ? "

He just considered. " Oh I'm happy enough anywhere ! "

" Well then," I quavered, " if you're just as happy here——! "

" Ah but that isn't everything ! Of course *you* know a lot——"

" But you hint that you know almost as much ? "
I risked as he paused.

" Not half I want to ! " Miles honestly professed.
" But it isn't so much that."

" What is it, then ? "

" Well—I want to see more life."

" I see ; I see." We had arrived within sight of the
church and of various persons, including several of
the household of Bly, on their way to it and clustered
about the door to see us go in. I quickened our step ;
I wanted to get there before the question between us
opened up much further ; I reflected hungrily that he
would have for more than an hour to be silent ; and I
thought with envy of the comparative dusk of the
pew and of the almost spiritual help of the hassock on
which I might bend my knees. I seemed literally to
be running a race with some confusion to which he
was about to reduce me, but I felt he had got in first
when, before we had even entered the churchyard,
he threw out :

" I want my own sort ! "

It literally made me bound forward. " There
aren't many of your own sort, Miles ! " I laughed.
" Unless perhaps dear little Flora ! "

" You really compare me to a baby girl ? "

This found me singularly weak. " Don't you,
then, *love* our sweet Flora ? "

" If I didn't—and you too ; if I didn't——! " he
repeated as if retreating for a jump, yet leaving his
thought so unfinished that, after we had come into the
gate, another stop, which he imposed on me by the
pressure of his arm, had become inevitable. Mrs.
Grose and Flora had passed into the church, the other
worshippers had followed and we were, for the minute,
alone among the old thick graves. We had paused,
on the path from the gate, by a low oblong table-like
tomb.

" Yes, if you didn't——? "

He looked, while I waited, about at the graves. " Well, you know what ! " But he didn't move, and he presently produced something that made me drop straight down on the stone slab as if suddenly to rest. " Does my uncle think what *you* think ? "

I markedly rested. " How do you know what I think ? "

" Ah well, of course I don't ; for it strikes me you never tell me. But I mean does *he* know ? "

" Know what, Miles ? "

" Why, the way I'm going on."

I recognised quickly enough that I could make, to this inquiry, no answer that wouldn't involve something of a sacrifice of my employer. Yet it struck me that we were all, at Bly, sufficiently sacrificed to make that venial. " I don't think your uncle much cares."

Miles, on this, stood looking at me. " Then don't you think he can be made to ? "

" In what way ? "

" Why, by his coming down."

" But who'll get him to come down ? "

" *I* will ! " the boy said with extraordinary brightness and emphasis. He gave me another look charged with that expression and then marched off alone into church.

XV

THE business was practically settled from the moment
I never followed him. It was a pitiful surrender to
agitation, but my being aware of this had somehow
no power to restore me. I only sat there on my tomb
and read into what our young friend had said to me
the fulness of its meaning ; by the time I had grasped
the whole of which I had also embraced, for absence,
the pretext that I was ashamed to offer my pupils and
the rest of the congregation such an example of delay.
What I said to myself above all was that Miles had got
something out of me and that the gage of it for him
would be just this awkward collapse. He had got out
of me that there was something I was much afraid of,
and that he should probably be able to make use of
my fear to gain, for his own purpose, more freedom.
My fear was of having to deal with the intolerable
question of the grounds of his dismissal from school,
since that was really but the question of the horrors
gathered behind. That his uncle should arrive to
treat with me of these things was a solution that,
strictly speaking, I ought now to have desired to
bring on ; but I could so little face the ugliness and
the pain of it that I simply procrastinated and lived
from hand to mouth. The boy, to my deep dis-
composure, was immensely in the right, was in a
position to say to me : " Either you clear up with
my guardian the mystery of this interruption of my

studies, or you cease to expect me to lead with you a life that's so unnatural for a boy." What was so unnatural for the particular boy I was concerned with was this sudden revelation of a consciousness and a plan.

That was what really overcame me, what prevented my going in. I walked round the church, hesitating, hovering ; I reflected that I had already, with him, hurt myself beyond repair. Therefore I could patch up nothing and it was too extreme an effort to squeeze beside him into the pew : he would be so much more sure than ever to pass his arm into mine and make me sit there for an hour in close mute contact with his commentary on our talk. For the first minute since his arrival I wanted to get away from him. As I paused beneath the high east window and listened to the sounds of worship I was taken with an impulse that might master me, I felt, and completely, should I give it the least encouragement. I might easily put an end to my ordeal by getting away altogether. Here was my chance ; there was no one to stop me ; I could give the whole thing up—turn my back and bolt. It was only a question of hurrying again, for a few preparations, to the house which the attendance at church of so many of the servants would practically have left unoccupied. No one, in short, could blame me if I should just drive desperately off. What was it to get away if I should get away only till dinner ? That would be in a couple of hours, at the end of which—I had the acute prevision—my little pupils would play at innocent wonder about my non-appearance in their train.

" What *did* you do, you naughty bad thing ? Why in the world, to worry us so—and take our thoughts off too, don't you know ?—did you desert us at the very door ? " I couldn't meet such questions nor, as they asked them, their false little lovely eyes ;

yet it was all so exactly what I should have to meet that, as the prospect grew sharp to me, I at last let myself go.

I got, so far as the immediate moment was concerned, away ; I came straight out of the churchyard and, thinking hard, retraced my steps through the park. It seemed to me that by the time I reached the house I had made up my mind to cynical flight. The Sunday stillness both of the approaches and of the interior, in which I met no one, fairly stirred me with a sense of opportunity. Were I to get off quickly this way I should get off without a scene, without a word. My quickness would have to be remarkable, however, and the question of a conveyance was the great one to settle. Tormented, in the hall, with difficulties and obstacles, I remember sinking down at the foot of the staircase—suddenly collapsing there on the lowest step and then, with a revulsion, recalling that it was exactly where, more than a month before, in the darkness of night and just so bowed with evil things, I had seen the spectre of the most horrible of women. At this I was able to straighten myself ; I went the rest of the way up ; I made, in my turmoil, for the schoolroom, where there were objects belonging to me that I should have to take. But I opened the door to find again, in a flash, my eyes unsealed. In the presence of what I saw I reeled straight back upon resistance.

Seated at my own table in the clear noonday light I saw a person whom, without my previous experience, I should have taken at the first blush for some housemaid who might have stayed at home to look after the place and who, availing herself of rare relief from observation and of the schoolroom table and my pens, ink and paper, had applied herself to the considerable effort of a letter to her sweetheart. There was an effort in the way that, while her arms rested on the table, her hands, with evident weariness, supported her head; but at the moment I took this in I had already become aware that, in spite of my entrance, her attitude strangely persisted. Then it was—with the very act of its announcing itself— that her identity flared up in a change of posture. She rose, not as if she had heard me, but with an indescribable grand melancholy of indifference and detachment, and, within a dozen feet of me, stood there as my vile predecessor. Dishonoured and tragic, she was all before me; but even as I fixed and, for memory, secured it, the awful image passed away. Dark as midnight in her black dress, her haggard beauty and her unutterable woe, she had looked at me long enough to appear to say that her right to sit at my table was as good as mine to sit at hers. While these instants lasted indeed I had the extraordinary chill of a feeling that it was I who was the intruder. It was as a wild protest against it that, actually addressing her—" You terrible miserable woman!" —I heard myself break into a sound that, by the open door, rang through the long passage and the empty house. She looked at me as if she heard me, but I had recovered myself and cleared the air. There was nothing in the room the next minute but the sunshine and the sense that I must stay.

XVI

I HAD so perfectly expected the return of the others to be marked by a demonstration that I was freshly upset at having to find them merely dumb and discreet about my desertion. Instead of gaily denouncing and caressing me they made no allusion to my having failed them, and I was left, for the time, on perceiving that she too said nothing, to study Mrs. Grose's odd face. I did this to such purpose that I made sure they had in some way bribed her to silence; a silence that, however, I would engage to break down on the first private opportunity. This opportunity came before tea: I secured five minutes with her in the housekeeper's room, where, in the twilight, amid a smell of lately-baked bread, but with the place all swept and garnished, I found her sitting in pained placidity before the fire. So I see her still, so I see her best: facing the flame from her straight chair in the dusky shining room, a large clean picture of the " put away "—of drawers closed and locked and rest without a remedy.

" Oh yes, they asked me to say nothing; and to please them—so long as they were there—of course I promised. But what had happened to you ? "

" I only went with you for the walk," I said. " I had then to come back to meet a friend."

She showed her surprise. " A friend—*you* ? "

" Oh yes, I've a couple ! " I laughed. " But did the children give you a reason ? "

" For not alluding to your leaving us ? Yes ; they said you'd like it better. *Do* you like it better ? "

My face had made her rueful. " No, I like it worse ! " But after an instant I added : " Did they say why I should like it better ? "

" No ; Master Miles only said ' We must do nothing but what she likes ! ' "

" I wish indeed he would ! And what did Flora say ? "

" Miss Flora was too sweet. She said ' Oh of course, of course ! '—and I said the same."

I thought a moment. " You were too sweet too —I can hear you all. But none the less, between Miles and me, it's now all out."

" All out ? " My companion stared. " But what, Miss ? "

" Everything. It doesn't matter. I've made up my mind. I came home, my dear," I went on, " for a talk with Miss Jessel."

I had by this time formed the habit of having Mrs. Grose literally well in hand in advance of my sounding that note ; so that even now, as she bravely blinked under the signal of my word, I could keep her comparatively firm. " A talk ! Do you mean she spoke ? "

" It came to that. I found her, on my return, in the schoolroom."

" And what did she say ? " I can hear the good woman still, and the candour of her stupefaction.

" That she suffers the torments——! "

It was this, of a truth, that made her, as she filled out my picture, gape. " Do you mean," she faltered " —of the lost ? "

" Of the lost. Of the damned. And that's why,

to share them——" I faltered myself with the horror of it.

But my companion, with less imagination, kept me up. " To share them——? "

" She wants Flora." Mrs. Grose might, as I gave it to her, fairly have fallen away from me had I not been prepared. I still held her there, to show I was. " As I've told you, however, it doesn't matter."

" Because you've made up your mind ? But to what ? "

" To everything."

" And what do you call ' everything ' ? "

" Why, to sending for their uncle."

" Oh Miss, in pity do," my friend broke out.

" Ah but I will, I *will* ! I see it's the only way. What's ' out,' as I told you, with Miles is that if he thinks I'm afraid to—and has ideas of what he gains by that—he shall see he's mistaken. Yes, yes ; his uncle shall have it here from me on the spot (and before the boy himself if necessary) that if I'm to be reproached with having done nothing again about more school——"

" Yes, Miss——" my companion pressed me.

" Well, there's that awful reason."

There were now clearly so many of these for my poor colleague that she was excusable for being vague. " But—a—which ? "

" Why, the letter from his old place."

" You'll show it to the master ? "

" I ought to have done so on the instant."

" Oh no ! " said Mrs. Grose with decision.

" I'll put it before him," I went on inexorably, " that I can't undertake to work the question on behalf of a child who has been expelled——"

" For we've never in the least known what ! " Mrs. Grose declared.

" For wickedness. For what else—when he's so

clever and beautiful and perfect ? Is he stupid ? Is he untidy ? Is he infirm ? Is he ill-natured ? He's exquisite—so it can be only *that*; and that would open up the whole thing. After all," I said, " it's their uncle's fault. If he left here such people——! "

" He didn't really in the least know them. The fault's mine." She had turned quite pale.

" Well, you shan't suffer," I answered.

" The children shan't ! " she emphatically returned.

I was silent a while ; we looked at each other. " Then what am I to tell him ? "

" You needn't tell him anything. *I'll* tell him."

I measured this. " Do you mean you'll write——? " Remembering she couldn't, I caught myself up. " How do you communicate ? "

" I tell the bailiff. *He* writes."

" And should you like him to write our story ? "

My question had a sarcastic force that I had not fully intended, and it made her after a moment inconsequently break down. The tears were again in her eyes. " Ah Miss, *you* write ! "

" Well—to-night," I at last returned ; and on this we separated.

XVII

I WENT so far, in the evening, as to make a beginning. The weather had changed back, a great wind was abroad, and beneath the lamp, in my room, with Flora at peace beside me, I sat for a long time before a blank sheet of paper and listened to the lash of the rain and the batter of the gusts. Finally I went out, taking a candle ; I crossed the passage and listened a minute at Miles's door. What, under my endless obsession, I had been impelled to listen for was some betrayal of his not being at rest, and I presently caught one, but not in the form I had expected. His voice tinkled out. " I say, you there—come in." It was gaiety in the gloom !

I went in with my light and found him in bed, very wide awake but very much at his ease. " Well, what are *you* up to ? " he asked with a grace of sociability in which it occurred to me that Mrs. Grose, had she been present, might have looked in vain for proof that anything was " out."

I stood over him with my candle. " How did you know I was there ? "

" Why of course I heard you. Did you fancy you made no noise ? You're like a troop of cavalry ! " he beautifully laughed.

" Then you weren't asleep ? "

" Not much ! I lie awake and think."

I had put my candle, designedly, a short way off, and then, as he held out his friendly old hand to me, had sat down on the edge of his bed. "What is it," I asked, "that you think of?"

"What in the world, my dear, but *you*?"

"Ah, the pride I take in your appreciation doesn't insist on that! I had so far rather you slept."

"Well, I think also, you know, of this queer business of ours."

I marked the coolness of his firm little hand. "Of what queer business, Miles?"

"Why, the way you bring me up. And all the rest!"

I fairly held my breath a minute, and even from my glimmering taper there was light enough to show how he smiled up at me from his pillow. "What do you mean by all the rest?"

"Oh you know, you know!"

I could say nothing for a minute, though I felt as I held his hand and our eyes continued to meet that my silence had all the air of admitting his charge and that nothing in the whole world of reality was perhaps at that moment so fabulous as our actual relation. "Certainly you shall go back to school," I said, "if it be that that troubles you. But not to the old place—we must find another, a better. How could I know it did trouble you, this question, when you never told me so, never spoke of it at all?" His clear listening face, framed in its smooth whiteness, made him for the minute as appealing as some wistful patient in a children's hospital; and I would have given, as the resemblance came to me, all I possessed on earth really to be the nurse or the sister of charity who might have helped to cure him. Well, even as it was I perhaps might help! "Do you know you've never said a word to me about your school—I mean the old one; never mentioned it in any way?"

He seemed to wonder; he smiled with the same loveliness. But he clearly gained time; he waited, he called for guidance. " Haven't I ? " It wasn't for *me* to help him—it was for the thing I had met !

Something in his tone and the expression of his face, as I got this from him, set my heart aching with such a pang as it had never yet known; so unutterably touching was it to see his little brain puzzled and his little resources taxed to play, under the spell laid on him, a part of innocence and consistency. " No, never—from the hour you came back. You've never mentioned to me one of your masters, one of your comrades, nor the least little thing that ever happened to you at school. Never, little Miles — no, never—have you given me an inkling of anything that *may* have happened there. Therefore you can fancy how much I'm in the dark. Until you came out, that way, this morning, you had since the first hour I saw you scarce even made a reference to anything in your previous life. You seemed so perfectly to accept the present." It was extraordinary how my absolute conviction of his secret precocity—or whatever I might call the poison of an influence that I dared but half-phrase — made him, in spite of the faint breath of his inward trouble, appear as accessible as an older person, forced me to treat him as an intelligent equal. " I thought you wanted to go on as you are."

It struck me that at this he just faintly coloured. He gave, at any rate, like a convalescent slightly fatigued, a languid shake of his head. " I don't—I don't. I want to get away."

" You're tired of Bly ? "

" Oh no, I like Bly."

" Well then——? "

" Oh *you* know what a boy wants ! "

I felt I didn't know so well as Miles, and I took

temporary refuge. "You want to go to your uncle ? "

Again, at this, with his sweet ironic face, he made a movement on the pillow. "Ah you can't get off with that ! "

I was silent a little, and it was I now, I think, who changed colour. "My dear, I don't want to get off ! "

"You can't even if you do. You can't, you can't ! "—he lay beautifully staring. "My uncle must come down and you must completely settle things."

"If we do," I returned with some spirit, " you may be sure it will be to take you quite away."

"Well, don't you understand that that's exactly what I'm working for ? You'll have to *tell* him— about the way you've let it all drop : you'll have to tell him a tremendous lot ! "

The exultation with which he uttered this helped me somehow for the instant to meet him rather more. "And how much will *you*, Miles, have to tell him ? There are things he'll ask you ! "

He turned it over. "Very likely. But what things ? "

"The things you've never told me. To make up his mind what to do with you. He can't send you back——"

"I don't want to go back ! " he broke in. "I want a new field."

He said it with admirable serenity, with positive unimpeachable gaiety ; and doubtless it was that very note that most evoked for me the poignancy, the unnatural childish tragedy, of his probable reappearance at the end of three months with all this bravado and still more dishonour. It overwhelmed me now that I should never be able to bear that, and it made me let myself go. I threw myself upon him and in the tenderness of my pity I embraced him. " Dear little Miles, dear little Miles——! "

My face was close to his, and he let me kiss him, simply taking it with indulgent good humour. " Well, old lady ? "

" Is there nothing—nothing at all that you want to tell me ? "

He turned off a little, facing round toward the wall and holding up his hand to look at as one had seen sick children look. " I've told you—I told you this morning."

Oh I was sorry for him ! " That you just want me not to worry you ? "

He looked round at me now as if in recognition of my understanding him ; then ever so gently, " To let me alone," he replied.

There was even a strange little dignity in it, something that made me release him, yet, when I had slowly risen, linger beside him. God knows *I* never wished to harass him, but I felt that merely, at this, to turn my back on him was to abandon or, to put it more truly, lose him. " I've just begun a letter to your uncle," I said.

" Well then, finish it ! "

I waited a minute. " What happened before ? "

He gazed up at me again. " Before what ? "

" Before you came back. And before you went away."

For some time he was silent, but he continued to meet my eyes. " What happened ? "

It made me, the sound of the words, in which it seemed to me I caught for the very first time a small faint quaver of consenting consciousness—it made me drop on my knees beside the bed and seize once more the chance of possessing him. " Dear little Miles, dear little Miles, if you *knew* how I want to help you ! It's only that, it's nothing but that, and I'd

rather die than give you a pain or do you a wrong—
I'd rather die than hurt a hair of you. Dear little
Miles "—oh I brought it out now even if I *should* go
too far—" I just want you to help me to save you ! "
But I knew in a moment after this that I had gone too
far. The answer to my appeal was instantaneous,
but it came in the form of an extraordinary blast and
chill, a gust of frozen air and a shake of the room as
great as if, in the wild wind, the casement had crashed
in. The boy gave a loud high shriek which, lost in
the rest of the shock of sound, might have seemed,
indistinctly, though I was so close to him, a note either
of jubilation or of terror. I jumped to my feet again
and was conscious of darkness. So for a moment we
remained, while I stared about me and saw the drawn
curtains unstirred and the window still tight. " Why,
the candle's out ! " I then cried.

" It was I who blew it, dear ! " said Miles.

XVIII

THE next day, after lessons, Mrs. Grose found a
moment to say to me quietly: "Have you written,
Miss?"

"Yes—I've written." But I didn't add—for the
hour—that my letter, sealed and directed, was still
in my pocket. There would be time enough to send
it before the messenger should go to the village.
Meanwhile there had been on the part of my pupils
no more brilliant, more exemplary morning. It was
exactly as if they had both had at heart to gloss
over any recent little friction. They performed the
dizziest feats of arithmetic, soaring quite out of *my*
feeble range, and perpetrated, in higher spirits than
ever, geographical and historical jokes. It was
conspicuous of course in Miles in particular that he
appeared to wish to show how easily he could let me
down. This child, to my memory, really lives in a
setting of beauty and misery that no words can
translate; there was a distinction all his own in
every impulse he revealed; never was a small natural
creature, to the uninformed eye all frankness and
freedom, a more ingenious, a more extraordinary
little gentleman. I had perpetually to guard against
the wonder of contemplation into which my initiated
view betrayed me; to check the irrelevant gaze and
discouraged sigh in which I constantly both attacked
and renounced the enigma of what such a little

gentleman could have done that deserved a penalty.
Say that, by the dark prodigy I knew, the imagination
of all evil *had* been opened up to him : all the justice
within me ached for the proof that it could ever have
flowered into an act.

He had never at any rate been such a little gentleman as when, after our early dinner on this dreadful
day, he came round to me and asked if I shouldn't
like him for half an hour to play to me.   David playing to Saul could never have shown a finer sense of
the occasion.   It was literally a charming exhibition
of tact, of magnanimity, and quite tantamount to his
saying outright : " The true knights we love to read
about never push an advantage too far.   I know what
you mean now : you mean that—to be let alone
yourself and not followed up—you'll cease to worry
and spy upon me, won't keep me so close to you, will
let me go and come.   Well, I ' come,' you see—but I
don't go !   There'll be plenty of time for that.   I do
really delight in your society and I only want to show
you that I contended for a principle."   It may be
imagined whether I resisted this appeal or failed to
accompany him again, hand in hand, to the schoolroom.   He sat down at the old piano and played as
he had never played ; and if there are those who
think he had better have been kicking a football I can
only say that I wholly agree with them.   For at the
end of a time that under his influence I had quite
ceased to measure I started up with a strange sense
of having literally slept at my post.   It was after
luncheon, and by the school-room fire, and yet I
hadn't really in the least slept ; I had only done
something much worse—I had forgotten.   Where all
this time was Flora ?   When I put the question to
Miles he played on a minute before answering, and
then could only say : " Why, my dear, how do *I*
know ? "—breaking, moreover, into a happy laugh

which immediately after, as if it were a vocal accompaniment, he prolonged into incoherent extravagant song.

I went straight to my room, but his sister was not there ; then, before going downstairs, I looked into several others. As she was nowhere about she would surely be with Mrs. Grose, whom in the comfort of that theory I accordingly proceeded in quest of. I found her where I had found her the evening before, but she met my quick challenge with blank scared ignorance. She had only supposed that, after the repast, I had carried off both the children ; as to which she was quite in her right, for it was the very first time I had allowed the little girl out of my sight without some special provision. Of course now indeed she might be with the maids, so that the immediate thing was to look for her without an air of alarm. This we promptly arranged between us ; but when, ten minutes later and in pursuance of our arrangement, we met in the hall, it was only to report on either side that after guarded inquiries we had altogether failed to trace her. For a minute there, apart from observation, we exchanged mute alarms, and I could feel with what high interest my friend returned me all those I had from the first given her.

" She'll be above," she presently said—" in one of the rooms you haven't searched."

" No ; she's at a distance." I had made up my mind. " She has gone out."

Mrs. Grose stared. " Without a hat ? "

I naturally also looked volumes. " Isn't that woman always without one ? "

" She's with *her* ? "

" She's with *her* ! " I declared. " We must find them."

My hand was on my friend's arm, but she failed for the moment, confronted with such an account of the matter, to respond to my pressure. She communed, on the contrary, where she stood, with her uneasiness. " And where's Master Miles ? "

"Oh *he's* with Quint. They'll be in the schoolroom."

" Lord, Miss ! " My view, I was myself aware— and therefore I suppose my tone — had never yet reached so calm an assurance.

" The trick's played," I went on ; " they've successfully worked their plan. He found the most divine little way to keep me quiet while she went off."

" ' Divine ' ? " Mrs. Grose bewilderedly echoed.

" Infernal, then ! " I almost cheerfully rejoined. " He has provided for himself as well. But come ! "

She had helplessly gloomed at the upper regions. " You leave him——? "

" So long with Quint ? Yes—I don't mind that now."

She always ended at these moments by getting possession of my hand, and in this manner she could at present still stay me. But after gasping an instant at my sudden resignation, " Because of your letter ? " she eagerly brought out.

I quickly, by way of answer, felt for my letter, drew it forth, held it up, and then, freeing myself, went and laid it on the great hall-table. " Luke will take it," I said as I came back. I reached the house-door and opened it ; I was already on the steps.

My companion still demurred : the storm of the night and the early morning had dropped, but the afternoon was damp and grey. I came down to the drive while she stood in the doorway. " You go with nothing on ? "

" What do I care when the child has nothing ? I can't wait to dress," I cried, " and if you must do so I leave you. Try meanwhile yourself upstairs."

" With *them* ? " Oh on this the poor woman promptly joined me !

XIX

WE went straight to the lake, as it was called at Bly,
and I daresay rightly called, though it may have been
a sheet of water less remarkable than my untravelled
eyes supposed it. My acquaintance with sheets of
water was small, and the pool of Bly, at all events on
the few occasions of my consenting, under the protection of my pupils, to affront its surface in the old
flat-bottomed boat moored there for our use, had
impressed me both with its extent and its agitation.
The usual place of embarkation was half a mile from
the house, but I had an intimate conviction that,
wherever Flora might be, she was not near home.
She had not given me the slip for any small adventure,
and, since the day of the very great one that I had
shared with her by the pond, I had been aware, in
our walks, of the quarter to which she most inclined.
This was why I had now given to Mrs. Grose's steps
so marked a direction—a direction making her, when
she perceived it, oppose a resistance that showed
me she was freshly mystified. " You're going to the
water, Miss ?—you think she's *in*——? "

" She may be, though the depth is, I believe,
nowhere very great. But what I judge most likely is
that she's on the spot from which, the other day, we
saw together what I told you."

" When she pretended not to see——? "

" With that astounding self-possession ! I've

always been sure she wanted to go back alone. And now her brother has managed it for her."

Mrs. Grose still stood where she had stopped. " You suppose they really *talk* of them ? "

I could meet this with an assurance ! " They say things that, if we heard them, would simply appal us."

" And if she *is* there——? "

" Yes ? "

" Then Miss Jessel is ? "

" Beyond a doubt. You shall see."

" Oh thank you ! " my friend cried, planted so firm that, taking it in, I went straight on without her. By the time I reached the pool, however, she was close behind me, and I knew that, whatever, to her apprehension, might befall me, the exposure of sticking to me struck her as her least danger. She exhaled a moan of relief as we at last came in sight of the greater part of the water without a sight of the child. There was no trace of Flora on that nearer side of the bank where my observation of her had been most startling, and none on the opposite edge, where, save for a margin of some twenty yards, a thick copse came down to the pond. This expanse, oblong in shape, was so narrow compared to its length that, with its ends out of view, it might have been taken for a scant river. We looked at the empty stretch, and then I felt the suggestion in my friend's eyes. I knew what she meant and I replied with a negative headshake.

" No, no ; wait ! She has taken the boat."

My companion stared at the vacant mooring-place and then again across the lake. " Then where is it ? "

" Our not seeing it is the strongest of proofs. She has used it to go over, and then has managed to hide it."

" All alone—that child ? "

" She's not alone, and at such times she's not a
child : she's an old, old woman." I scanned all the
visible shore while Mrs. Grose took again, into the
queer element I offered her, one of her plunges of
submission ; then I pointed out that the boat might
perfectly be in a small refuge formed by one of the
recesses of the pool, an indentation masked, for the
hither side, by a projection of the bank and by a
clump of trees growing close to the water.

" But if the boat's there, where on earth's *she* ? "
my colleague anxiously asked.

" That's exactly what we must learn." And I
started to walk further.

" By going all the way round ? "

" Certainly, far as it is. It will take us but ten
minutes, yet it's far enough to have made the child
prefer not to walk. She went straight over."

" Laws ! " cried my friend again : the chain of my
logic was ever too strong for her. It dragged her at
my heels even now, and when we had got halfway
round—a devious tiresome process, on ground much
broken and by a path choked with overgrowth—I
paused to give her breath. I sustained her with a
grateful arm, assuring her that she might hugely
help me ; and this started us afresh, so that in the
course of but few minutes more we reached a point
from which we found the boat to be where I had
supposed it. It had been intentionally left as much
as possible out of sight and was tied to one of the
stakes of a fence that came, just there, down to the
brink and that had been an assistance to disembarking.
I recognised, as I looked at the pair of short thick
oars, quite safely drawn up, the prodigious character
of the feat for a little girl ; but I had by this time
lived too long among wonders and had panted to too
many livelier measures. There was a gate in the
fence, through which we passed, and that brought us

after a trifling interval more into the open. Then " There she is ! " we both exclaimed at once.

Flora, a short way off, stood before us on the grass and smiled as if her performance had now become complete. The next thing she did, however, was to stoop straight down and pluck—quite as if it were all she was there for—a big ugly spray of withered fern. I at once felt sure she had just come out of the copse. She waited for us, not herself taking a step, and I was conscious of the rare solemnity with which we presently approached her. She smiled and smiled, and we met ; but it was all done in a silence by this time flagrantly ominous. Mrs. Grose was the first to break the spell : she threw herself on her knees and, drawing the child to her breast, clasped in a long embrace the little tender yielding body. While this dumb convulsion lasted I could only watch it—which I did the more intently when I saw Flora's face peep at me over our companion's shoulder. It was serious now—the flicker had left it ; but it strengthened the pang with which I at that moment envied Mrs. Grose the simplicity of *her* relation. Still, all this while, nothing more passed between us save that Flora had let her foolish fern again drop to the ground. What she and I had virtually said to each other was that pretexts were useless now. When Mrs. Grose finally got up she kept the child's hand, so that the two were still before me ; and the singular reticence of our communion was even more marked in the frank look she addressed me. " I'll be hanged," it said, " if *I'll* speak ! "

It was Flora who, gazing all over me in candid wonder, was the first. She was struck with our bareheaded aspect. " Why, where are your things ? "

" Where yours are, my dear ! " I promptly returned.

She had already got back her gaiety and appeared

to take this as an answer quite sufficient. " And where's Miles ? " she went on.

There was something in the small valour of it that quite finished me : these three words from her were in a flash like the glitter of a drawn blade the jostle of the cup that my hand for weeks and weeks had held high and full to the brim and that now, even before speaking, I felt overflow in a deluge. " I'll tell you if you'll tell *me*——" I heard myself say, then heard the tremor in which it broke.

" Well, what ? "

Mrs. Grose's suspense blazed at me, but it was too late now, and I brought the thing out handsomely. " Where, my pet, is Miss Jessel ? "

XX

Just as in the churchyard with Miles, the whole
thing was upon us. Much as I had made of the fact
that this name had never once, between us, been
sounded, the quick smitten glare with which the
child's face now received it fairly likened my breach
of the silence to the smash of a pane of glass. It
added to the interposing cry, as if to stay the blow,
that Mrs. Grose at the same instant uttered over my
violence—the shriek of a creature scared, or rather
wounded, which, in turn, within a few seconds, was
completed by a gasp of my own. I seized my colleague's arm. "She's there, she's there!"

Miss Jessel stood before us on the opposite bank
exactly as she had stood the other time, and I remember, strangely, as the first feeling now produced
in me, my thrill of joy at having brought on a proof.
She was there, so I was justified; she was there, so
I was neither cruel nor mad. She was there for poor
scared Mrs. Grose, but she was there most for Flora;
and no moment of my monstrous time was perhaps
so extraordinary as that in which I consciously threw
out to her—with the sense that, pale and ravenous
demon as she was, she would catch and understand
it—an inarticulate message of gratitude. She rose
erect on the spot my friend and I had lately quitted,
and there wasn't in all the long reach of her desire
an inch of her evil that fell short. This first vividness

of vision and emotion were things of a few seconds, during which Mrs. Grose's dazed blink across to where I pointed struck me as showing that she too at last saw, just as it carried my own eyes precipitately to the child. The revelation then of the manner in which Flora was affected startled me in truth far more than it would have done to find her also merely agitated, for direct dismay was of course not what I had expected. Prepared and on her guard as our pursuit had actually made her, she would repress every betrayal ; and I was therefore at once shaken by my first glimpse of the particular one for which I had not allowed. To see her, without a convulsion of her small pink face, not even feign to glance in the direction of the prodigy I announced, but only, instead of that, turn at *me* an expression of hard still gravity, an expression absolutely new and unprecedented and that appeared to read and accuse and judge me—this was a stroke that somehow converted the little girl herself into a figure portentous. I gaped at her coolness even though my certitude of her thoroughly seeing was never greater than at that instant, and then, in the immediate need to defend myself, I called her passionately to witness. " She's there, you little unhappy thing—there, there, *there*, and you know it as well as you know me ! " I had said shortly before to Mrs. Grose that she was not at these times a child, but an old, old woman, and my description of her couldn't have been more strikingly confirmed than in the way in which, for all notice of this, she simply showed me, without an expressional concession or admission, a countenance of deeper and deeper, of indeed suddenly quite fixed reprobation. I was by this time—if I can put the whole thing at all together—more appalled at what I may properly call her manner than at anything else, though it was quite simultaneously that I became aware of having Mrs. Grose also, and very formidably, to reckon with. My elder companion, the next moment, at any rate, blotted out everything but her own flushed face and her loud shocked protest, a burst of high disapproval. " What a dreadful turn, to be sure, Miss ! Where on earth do you see anything ? "

I could only grasp her more quickly yet, for even while she spoke the hideous plain presence stood undimmed and undaunted. It had already lasted a minute, and it lasted while I continued, seizing my colleague, quite thrusting her at it and presenting her to it, to insist with my pointing hand. " You don't see her exactly as *we* see ?—you mean to say you don't now—*now*? She's as big as a blazing fire ! Only look, dearest woman, *look*—— ! " She looked, just as I did, and gave me, with her deep groan of negation, repulsion, compassion—the mixture with her pity of her relief at her exemption—a sense, touching to me even then, that she would have backed me up if she had been able. I might well have needed that, for with this hard blow of the proof that her eyes were hopelessly sealed I felt my own situation horribly crumble, I felt—I *saw*—my livid predecessor press, from her position, on my defeat, and I took the measure, more than all, of what I should have from this instant to deal with in the astounding little attitude of Flora. Into this attitude Mrs. Grose immediately and violently entered, breaking, even while there pierced through my sense of ruin a prodigious private triumph, into breathless reassurance.

" She isn't there, little lady, and nobody's there— and you never see nothing, my sweet ! How can poor Miss Jessel—when poor Miss Jessel's dead and buried ? *We* know, don't we, love ? "—and she appealed, blundering in, to the child. " It's all a mere mistake and a worry and a joke—and we'll go home as fast as we can ! "

Our companion, on this, had responded with a strange quick primness of propriety, and they were again, with Mrs. Grose on her feet, united, as it were, in shocked opposition to me. Flora continued to fix me with her small mask of disaffection, and even at that minute I prayed God to forgive me for seeming to see that, as she stood there holding tight to our friend's dress, her incomparable childish beauty had suddenly failed, had quite vanished. I've said it already—she was literally, she was hideously hard ; she had turned common and almost ugly. " I don't know what you mean. I see nobody. I see nothing. I never *have*. I think you're cruel. I don't like you ! " Then, after this deliverance, which might have been that of a vulgarly pert little girl in the street, she hugged Mrs. Grose more closely and buried in her skirts the dreadful little face. In this position she launched an almost furious wail. " Take me away, take me away—oh take me away from *her* ! "

" From *me* ? " I panted.

" From you—from you ! " she cried.

Even Mrs. Grose looked across at me dismayed ; while I had nothing to do but communicate again with the figure that, on the opposite bank, without a movement, as rigidly still as if catching, beyond the interval, our voices, was as vividly there for my disaster as it was not there for my service. The wretched child had spoken exactly as if she had got from some outside source each of her stabbing little words, and I could therefore, in the full despair of all I had to accept, but sadly shake my head at her. " If I had ever doubted all my doubt would at present have gone. I've been living with the miserable truth, and now it has only too much closed round me. Of course I've lost you : I've interfered, and you've seen, under *her* dictation "—with which I faced, over the pool again, our infernal witness—" the easy and perfect way to meet it. I've done my best, but I've lost you. Good-bye." For Mrs. Grose I had an imperative, an almost frantic "Go, go!" before which, in infinite distress, but mutely possessed of the little girl and clearly convinced, in spite of her blindness, that something awful had occurred and some collapse engulfed us, she retreated, by the way we had come, as fast as she could move.

Of what first happened when I was left alone I had no subsequent memory. I only knew that at the end of, I suppose, a quarter of an hour, an odorous dampness and roughness, chilling and piercing my trouble, had made me understand that I must have thrown myself, on my face, to the ground and given way to a wildness of grief. I must have lain there long and cried and wailed, for when I raised my head the day was almost done. I got up and looked a moment, through the twilight, at the grey pool and its blank haunted edge, and then I took, back to the house, my dreary and difficult course. When I reached the gate in the fence the boat, to my surprise, was gone, so that I had a fresh reflexion to make on Flora's extraordinary command of the situation. She passed that night, by the most tacit and, I should add, were not the word so grotesque a false note, the happiest of arrangements, with Mrs. Grose. I saw neither of them on my return, but on the other hand I saw, as by an ambiguous compensation, a great deal of Miles. I saw—I can use no other phrase—so much of him that it fairly measured more than it had ever measured. No evening I had passed at Bly was to have had the portentous quality of this one; in spite of which—and in spite also of the deeper depths of consternation that had opened beneath my feet—there was literally, in the ebbing actual, an extraordinarily sweet sadness. On reaching the house I had never so much as looked for the boy; I had simply gone straight to my room to change what I was wearing and to take in, at a glance, much material testimony to Flora's rupture. Her little belongings had all been removed. When later, by the schoolroom fire, I was served with tea by the usual maid, I indulged, on the article of my other pupil, in no inquiry whatever. He had his freedom now—he might have it to the end! Well, he did have it; and it consisted—in part at least—of his coming in at about eight o'clock and sitting down with me in silence. On the removal of the tea-things I had blown out the candles and drawn my chair closer: I was conscious of a mortal coldness and felt as if I should never again be warm. So when he appeared I was sitting in the glow with my thoughts. He paused a moment by the door as if to look at me; then—as if to share them—came to the other side of the hearth and sank into a chair. We sat there in absolute stillness; yet he wanted, I felt, to be with me.

XXI

BEFORE a new day, in my room, had fully broken, my eyes opened to Mrs. Grose, who had come to my bedside with worse news. Flora was so markedly feverish that an illness was perhaps at hand ; she had passed a night of extreme unrest, a night agitated above all by fears that had for their subject not in the least her former but wholly her present governess. It was not against the possible re-entrance of Miss Jessel on the scene that she protested—it was conspicuously and passionately against mine. I was at once on my feet, and with an immense deal to ask ; the more that my friend had discernibly now girded her loins to meet me afresh. This I felt as soon as I had put to her the question of her sense of the child's sincerity as against my own. "She persists in denying to you that she saw, or has ever seen, anything ? "

My visitor's trouble truly was great. "Ah Miss, it isn't a matter on which I can push her ! Yet it isn't either, I must say, as if I much needed to. It has made her, every inch of her, quite old."

"Oh I see her perfectly from here. She resents, for all the world like some high little personage, the imputation on her truthfulness and, as it were, her respectability. 'Miss Jessel indeed—*she* ! ' Ah she's 'respectable,' the chit ! The impression she gave me there yesterday was, I assure you, the very strangest of all : it was quite beyond any of the others. I *did* put my foot in it ! She'll never speak to me again."

Hideous and obscure as it all was, it held Mrs. Grose briefly silent ; then she granted my point with a frankness which, I made sure, had more behind it. " I think indeed, Miss, she never will. She do have a grand manner about it ! "

" And that manner " — I summed it up — " is practically what's the matter with her now."

Oh that manner, I could see in my visitor's face, and not a little else besides ! " She asks me every three minutes if I think you're coming in."

" I see—I see." I too, on my side, had so much more than worked it out. " Has she said to you since yesterday—except to repudiate her familiarity with anything so dreadful—a single other word about Miss Jessel ? "

" Not one, Miss. And of course, you know," my friend added, " I took it from her by the lake that just then and there at least there *was* nobody."

" Rather ! And naturally you take it from her still."

" I don't contradict her. What else can I do ? "

" Nothing in the world ! You've the cleverest little person to deal with. They've made them— their two friends, I mean—still cleverer even than nature did ; for it was wondrous material to play on ! Flora has now her grievance, and she'll work it to the end."

" Yes, Miss ; but to *what* end ? "

" Why that of dealing with me to her uncle. She'll make me out to him the lowest creature——— ! "

I winced at the fair show of the scene in Mrs. Grose's face ; she looked for a minute as if she sharply saw them together. " And him who thinks so well of you ! "

" He has an odd way—it comes over me now," I laughed, "—of proving it ! But that doesn't matter. What Flora wants of course is to get rid of me."

My companion bravely concurred. " Never again to so much as look at you."

" So that what you've come to me now for," I asked, " is to speed me on my way ? " Before she had time to reply, however, I had her in check. " I've a better idea—the result of my reflexions. My going *would* seem the right thing, and on Sunday I was terribly near it. Yet that won't do. It's *you* who must go. You must take Flora."

My visitor, at this, did speculate. " But where in the world——? "

" Away from here. Away from *them*. Away, even most of all, now, from me. Straight to her uncle."

" Only to tell on you——? "

" No, not ' only ' ! To leave me, in addition, with my remedy."

She was still vague. " And what *is* your remedy ? "

" Your loyalty, to begin with. And then Miles's."

She looked at me hard. " Do you think he——? "

" Won't, if he has the chance, turn on me ? Yes, I venture still to think it. At all events I want to try. Get off with his sister as soon as possible and leave me with him alone." I was amazed, myself, at the spirit I had still in reserve, and therefore perhaps a trifle the more disconcerted at the way in which, in spite of this fine example of it, she hesitated. " There's one thing, of course," I went on : " they mustn't, before she goes, see each other for three seconds." Then it came over me that, in spite of Flora's presumable sequestration from the instant of her return from the pool, it might already be too late. " Do you mean," I anxiously asked, " that they *have* met ? "

At this she quite flushed. " Ah, Miss, I'm not such a fool as that ! If I've been obliged to leave her three or four times, it has been each time with one of the maids, and at present, though she's alone, she's locked in safe. And yet—and yet!" There were too many things.

"And yet what?"

"Well, are you so sure of the little gentleman?"

"I'm not sure of anything but *you*. But I have, since last evening, a new hope. I think he wants to give me an opening. I do believe that—poor little exquisite wretch!—he wants to speak. Last evening, in the firelight and the silence, he sat with me for two hours as if it were just coming."

Mrs. Grose looked hard through the window at the grey gathering day. "And did it come?"

"No, though I waited and waited I confess it didn't, and it was without a breach of the silence, or so much as a faint allusion to his sister's condition and absence, that we at last kissed for good-night. All the same," I continued, "I can't, if her uncle sees her, consent to his seeing her brother without my having given the boy—and most of all because things have got so bad—a little more time."

My friend appeared on this ground more reluctant than I could quite understand. "What do you mean by more time?"

"Well, a day or two—really to bring it out. He'll then be on *my* side—of which you see the importance. If nothing comes I shall only fail, and you at the worst have helped me by doing on your arrival in town whatever you may have found possible." So I put it before her, but she continued for a little so lost in other reasons that I came again to her aid. "Unless indeed," I wound up, "you really want *not* to go."

I could see it, in her face, at last clear itself: she put out her hand to me as a pledge. "I'll go—I'll go. I'll go this morning."

I wanted to be very just. "If you *should* wish still to wait I'd engage she shouldn't see me."

"No, no : it's the place itself. She must leave it." She held me a moment with heavy eyes, then brought out the rest. "Your idea's the right one. I myself, Miss——"

"Well ? "

"I can't stay."

The look she gave me with it made me jump at possibilities. "You mean that, since yesterday, you *have* seen—— ? "

She shook her head with dignity. "I've *heard*——!"

"Heard ? "

"From that child—horrors ! There ! " she sighed with tragic relief. "On my honour, Miss, she says things——!" But at this evocation she broke down ; she dropped with a sudden cry upon my sofa and, as I had seen her do before, gave way to all the anguish of it.

It was quite in another manner that I for my part let myself go. "Oh thank God ! "

She sprang up again at this, drying her eyes with a groan. "'Thank God'? "

"It so justifies me ! "

"It does that, Miss ! "

I couldn't have desired more emphasis, but I just waited. "She's so horrible ? "

I saw my colleague scarce knew how to put it. "Really shocking."

"And about me ? "

"About you, Miss—since you must have it. It's beyond everything, for a young lady ; and I can't think wherever she must have picked up——"

"The appalling language she applies to me ? I can, then ! " I broke in with a laugh that was doubtless significant enough.

It only in truth left my friend still more grave. "Well, perhaps I ought to also—since I've heard some of it before ! Yet I can't bear it," the poor woman went on while with the same movement she glanced, on my dressing-table, at the face of my watch. " But I must go back."

I kept her, however. "Ah if you can't bear it——!"

" How can I stop with her, you mean ? Why just *for* that : to get her away. Far from this," she pursued, " far from *them*——"

" She may be different ? she may be free ? " I seized her almost with joy. " Then in spite of yesterday you *believe*——"

" In such doings ? " Her simple description of them required, in the light of her expression, to be carried no farther, and she gave me the whole thing as she had never done. " I believe."

Yes, it was a joy, and we were still shoulder to shoulder : if I might continue sure of that I should care but little what else happened. My support in the presence of disaster would be the same as it had been in my early need of confidence, and if my friend would answer for my honesty I would answer for all the rest. On the point of taking leave of her, none the less, I was to some extent embarrassed. " There's one thing of course—it occurs to me—to remember. My letter giving the alarm will have reached town before you."

I now felt still more how she had been beating about the bush and how weary at last it had made her. " Your letter won't have got there. Your letter never went."

" What, then, became of it ? "

" Goodness knows ! Master Miles——"

" Do you mean *he* took it ? " I gasped.

She hung fire, but she overcame her reluctance. " I mean that I saw yesterday, when I came back with Miss Flora, that it wasn't where you had put it. Later in the evening I had the chance to question Luke, and he declared that he had neither noticed nor touched it." We could only exchange, on this, one of our deeper mutual soundings, and it was Mrs. Grose who first brought up the plumb with an almost elate " You see ! "

" Yes, I see that if Miles took it instead he probably will have read it and destroyed it."

" And don't you see anything else ? "

I faced her a moment with a sad smile. " It strikes me that by this time your eyes are open even wider than mine."

They proved to be so indeed, but she could still almost blush to show it. " I make out now what he must have done at school." And she gave, in her simple sharpness, an almost droll disillusioned nod. " He stole ! "

I turned it over—I tried to be more judicial. " Well—perhaps."

She looked as if she found me unexpectedly calm. " He stole *letters* ! "

She couldn't know my reasons for a calmness after all pretty shallow ; so I showed them off as I might. " I hope, then, it was to more purpose than in this case ! The note, at all events, that I put on the table yesterday," I pursued, " will have given him so scant an advantage—for it contained only the bare demand for an interview—that he's already much ashamed of having gone so far for so little, and that what he had on his mind last evening was precisely the need of confession." I seemed to myself for the instant to have mastered it, to see it all. " Leave us, leave us " —I was already, at the door, hurrying her off. " I'll get it out of him. He'll meet me. He'll confess. If he confesses he's saved. And if he's saved——"

" Then *you* are ? " The dear woman kissed me on this, and I took her farewell. " I'll save you without him ! " she cried as she went.

XXII

YET it was when she had got off—and I missed her on the spot—that the great pinch really came. If I had counted on what it would give me to find myself alone with Miles I quickly recognised that it would give me at least a measure. No hour of my stay in fact was so assailed with apprehensions as that of my coming down to learn that the carriage containing Mrs. Grose and my younger pupil had already rolled out of the gates. Now I *was*, I said to myself, face to face with the elements, and for much of the rest of the day, while I fought my weakness, I could consider that I had been supremely rash. It was a tighter place still than I had yet turned round in ; all the more that, for the first time, I could see in the aspect of others a confused reflexion of the crisis. What had happened naturally caused them all to stare ; there was too little of the explained, throw out whatever we might, in the suddenness of my colleague's act. The maids and the men looked blank ; the effect of which on my nerves was an aggravation until I saw the necessity of making it a positive aid. It was in short by just clutching the helm that I avoided total wreck ; and I daresay that, to bear up at all, I became that morning very grand and very dry. I welcomed the consciousness that I was charged with much to do, and I caused it to be known as well that, left thus to myself, I was quite remarkably firm. I wandered with that manner, for the next hour or two, all over the place and looked, I have no doubt, as if I were ready for any onset. So, for the benefit of whom it might concern, I paraded with a sick heart.

The person it appeared least to concern proved to be, till dinner, little Miles himself. My perambulations had given me meanwhile no glimpse of him, but they had tended to make more public the change taking place in our relation as a consequence of his having at the piano, the day before, kept me, in Flora's interest, so beguiled and befooled. The stamp of publicity had of course been fully given by her confinement and departure, and the change itself was now ushered in by our non-observance of the regular custom of the schoolroom. He had already disappeared when, on my way down, I pushed open his door, and I learned below that he had breakfasted —in the presence of a couple of the maids—with Mrs. Grose and his sister. He had then gone out, as he said, for a stroll ; than which nothing, I reflected, could better have expressed his frank view of the abrupt transformation of my office. What he would now permit this office to consist of was yet to be settled : there was at the least a queer relief—I mean for myself in especial—in the renouncement of one pretension. If so much had sprung to the surface I scarce put it too strongly in saying that what had perhaps sprung highest was the absurdity of our prolonging the fiction that I had anything more to teach him. It sufficiently stuck out that, by tacit little tricks in which even more than myself he carried out the care for my dignity, I had had to appeal to him to let me off straining to meet him on the ground of his true capacity. He had at any rate his freedom now ; I was never to touch it again : as I had amply shown, moreover, when, on his joining me in the schoolroom the previous night, I uttered, in reference to the interval just concluded, neither challenge nor hint. I had too much, from this moment, my other ideas. Yet when he at last arrived the difficulty of applying them, the accumulations of my problem, were brought straight home to me by the beautiful little presence on which what had occurred had as yet, for the eye, dropped neither stain nor shadow.

To mark, for the house, the high state I cultivated I decreed that my meals with the boy should be served, as we called it, downstairs; so that I had been awaiting him in the ponderous pomp of the room outside the window of which I had had from Mrs. Grose, that first scared Sunday, my flash of something it would scarce have done to call light. Here at present I felt afresh—for I had felt it again and again—how my equilibrium depended on the success of my rigid will, the will to shut my eyes as tight as possible to the truth that what I had to deal with was, revoltingly, against nature. I could only get on at all by taking " nature " into my confidence and my account, by treating my monstrous ordeal as a push in a direction unusual, of course, and unpleasant, but demanding after all, for a fair front, only another turn of the screw of ordinary human virtue. No attempt, none the less, could well require more tact than just this attempt to supply, one's self, *all* the nature. How could I put even a little of that article into a suppression of reference to what had occurred ? How, on the other hand, could I make a reference without a new plunge into the hideous obscure ? Well, a sort of answer, after a time, had come to me, and it was so far confirmed as that I was met, incontestably, by the quickened vision of what was rare in my little companion. It was indeed as if he had found even now—as he had so often found at lessons—still some other delicate way to ease me off. Wasn't there light in the fact which, as we shared our solitude, broke out with a specious glitter it had never yet quite worn ?—the fact that (opportunity aiding, precious opportunity which had now come) it would be preposterous, with a child so endowed, to forgo the help one might wrest from absolute intelligence ? What had his intelligence been given him for but to save him ? Mightn't one, to reach his mind, risk the stretch of a stiff arm across his character ? It was as if, when we were face to face in the dining-room, he had literally shown me the way. The roast mutton was on the table and I had dispensed with attendance. Miles, before he sat down, stood a moment with his hands in his pockets and looked at the joint, on which he seemed on the point of passing some humorous judgement. But what he presently produced was : " I say, my dear, is she really very awfully ill ? "

" Little Flora ? Not so bad but that she'll presently be better. London will set her up. Bly had ceased to agree with her. Come here and take your mutton."

He alertly obeyed me, carried the plate carefully to his seat and, when he was established, went on : " Did Bly disagree with her so terribly all at once ? "

" Not so suddenly as you might think. One had seen it coming on."

" Then why didn't you get her off before ? "

" Before what ? "

" Before she became too ill to travel."

I found myself prompt. " She's *not* too ill to travel ; she only might have become so if she had stayed. This was just the moment to seize. The journey will dissipate the influence "—oh I was grand !—" and carry it off."

" I see, I see "—Miles, for that matter, was grand

too. He settled to his repast with the charming little
" table manner " that, from the day of his arrival,
had relieved me of all grossness of admonition.
Whatever he had been expelled from school for, it
wasn't for ugly feeding. He was irreproachable, as
always, to-day ; but was unmistakably more conscious. He was discernibly trying to take for granted
more things than he found, without assistance, quite
easy ; and he dropped into peaceful silence while he
felt his situation. Our meal was of the briefest—
mine a vain pretence, and I had the things immediately removed. While this was done Miles
stood again with his hands in his little pockets and
his back to me—stood and looked out of the wide
window through which, that other day, I had seen
what pulled me up. We continued silent while the
maid was with us—as silent, it whimsically occurred
to me, as some young couple who, on their wedding-
journey, at the inn, feel shy in the presence of the
waiter. He turned round only when the waiter had
left us. " Well—so we're alone ! "

XXIII

"Oh more or less." I imagine my smile was pale. "Not absolutely. We shouldn't like that!" I went on.

"No—I suppose we shouldn't. Of course we've the others."

"We've the others—we've indeed the others," I concurred.

"Yet even though we have them," he returned, still with his hands in his pockets and planted there in front of me, "they don't much count, do they?"

I made the best of it, but I felt wan. "It depends on what you call 'much'!"

"Yes"—with all accommodation—"everything depends!" On this, however, he faced to the window again and presently reached it with his vague restless cogitating step. He remained there a while with his forehead against the glass, in contemplation of the stupid shrubs I knew and the dull things of November. I had always my hypocrisy of "work," behind which I now gained the sofa. Steadying myself with it there as I had repeatedly done at those moments of torment that I have described as the moments of my knowing the children to be given to something from which I was barred, I sufficiently obeyed my habit of being prepared for the worst. But an extraordinary impression dropped on me as I extracted a meaning from the boy's embarrassed back—none other than the impression that I was not barred now. This inference grew in a few minutes to sharp intensity and seemed bound up with the direct perception that it was positively *he* who was. The frames and squares of the great window were a kind of image, for him, of a kind of failure. I felt that I saw him, in any case, shut in or shut out. He was admirable but not comfortable : I took it in with a throb of hope. Wasn't he looking through the haunted pane for something he couldn't see ?—and wasn't it the first time in the whole business that he had known such a lapse ? The first, the very first : I found it a splendid portent. It made him anxious, though he watched himself ; he had been anxious all day and, even while in his usual sweet little manner he sat at table, had needed all his small strange genius to give it a gloss. When he at last turned round to meet me it was almost as if this genius had succumbed. " Well, I think I'm glad Bly agrees with *me* ! "

" You'd certainly seem to have seen, these twenty-four hours, a good deal more of it than for some time before. I hope," I went on bravely, " that you've been enjoying yourself."

" Oh yes, I've been ever so far ; all round about— miles and miles away. I've never been so free."

He had really a manner of his own, and I could only try to keep up with him. " Well, do you like it ? "

He stood there smiling ; then at last he put into two words—" Do *you* ? "—more discrimination than I had ever heard two words contain. Before I had time to deal with that, however, he continued as if with the sense that this was an impertinence to be softened. " Nothing could be more charming than the way you take it, for of course if we're alone together now it's you that are alone most. But I hope," he threw in, " you don't particularly mind ! "

" Having to do with you ? " I asked. " My dear child, how can I help minding ? Though I've renounced all claim to your company—you're so beyond me—I at least greatly enjoy it. What else should I stay on for ? "

He looked at me more directly, and the expression of his face, graver now, struck me as the most beautiful I had ever found in it. " You stay on just for *that* ? "

" Certainly. I stay on as your friend and from the tremendous interest I take in you till something can be done for you that may be more worth your while. That needn't surprise you." My voice trembled so that I felt it impossible to suppress the shake. " Don't you remember how I told you, when I came and sat on your bed the night of the storm, that there was nothing in the world I wouldn't do for you ? "

" Yes, yes ! " He, on his side, more and more visibly nervous, had a tone to master ; but he was so much more successful than I that, laughing out through his gravity, he could pretend we were pleasantly jesting. " Only that, I think, was to get me to do something for *you* ! "

" It was partly to get you to do something," I conceded. " But, you know, you didn't do it."

" Oh yes," he said with the brightest superficial eagerness, " you wanted me to tell you something."

" That's it. Out, straight out. What you have on your mind, you know."

" Ah, then, is *that* what you've stayed over for ? "

He spoke with a gaiety through which I could still catch the finest little quiver or resentful passion ; but I can't begin to express the effect upon me of an implication of surrender even so faint. It was as if what I had yearned for had come at last only to astonish me. " Well, yes—I may as well make a clean breast of it. It was precisely for that."

He waited so long that I supposed it for the purpose

of repudiating the assumption on which my action had been founded ; but what he finally said was : " Do you mean now—here ? "

" There couldn't be a better place or time." He looked round him uneasily, and I had the rare—oh the queer !—impression of the very first symptom I had seen in him of the approach of immediate fear. It was as if he were suddenly afraid of me—which struck me indeed as perhaps the best thing to make him. Yet in the very pang of the effort I felt it vain to try sternness, and I heard myself the next instant so gentle as to be almost grotesque. " You want so to go out again ? "

" Awfully ! " He smiled at me heroically, and the touching little bravery of it was enhanced by his actually flushing with pain. He had picked up his hat, which he had brought in, and stood twirling it in a way that gave me, even as I was just nearly reaching port, a perverse horror of what I was doing. To do it in *any* way was an act of violence, for what did it consist of but the obtrusion of the idea of grossness and guilt on a small helpless creature who had been for me a revelation of the possibilities of beautiful intercourse ? Wasn't it base to create for a being so exquisite a mere alien awkwardness ? I suppose I now read into our situation a clearness it couldn't have had at the time, for I seem to see our poor eyes already lighted with some spark of a prevision of the anguish that was to come. So we circled about with terrors and scruples, fighters not daring to close. But it was for each other we feared ! That kept us a little longer suspended and unbruised. " I'll tell you everything," Miles said—" I mean I'll tell you any-thing you like. You'll stay on with me, and we shall both be all right, and I *will* tell you—I *will*. But not now."

" Why not now ? "

My insistence turned him from me and kept him once more at his window in a silence during which, between us, you might have heard a pin drop. Then he was before me again with the air of a person for whom, outside, some one who had frankly to be reckoned with was waiting. " I have to see Luke."

I had not yet reduced him to quite so vulgar a lie, and I felt proportionately ashamed. But, horrible as it was, his lies made up my truth. I achieved thoughtfully a few loops of my knitting. " Well then, go to Luke, and I'll wait for what you promise. Only in return for that satisfy, before you leave me, one very much smaller request."

He looked as if he felt he had succeeded enough to be able still a little to bargain. " Very much smaller——? "

" Yes, a mere fraction of the whole. Tell me "— oh my work preoccupied me, and I was off-hand !— " if yesterday afternoon, from the table in the hall, you took, you know, my letter."

XXIV

MY grasp of how he received this suffered for a minute
from something that I can describe only as a fierce
split of my attention—a stroke that at first, as I
sprang straight up, reduced me to the mere blind
movement of getting hold of him, drawing him close
and, while I just fell for support against the nearest
piece of furniture, instinctively keeping him with his
back to the window. The appearance was full upon
us that I had already had to deal with here : Peter
Quint had come into view like a sentinel before a
prison. The next thing I saw was that, from outside,
he had reached the window, and then I knew that,
close to the glass and glaring in through it, he offered
once more to the room his white face of damnation.
It represents but grossly what took place within me
at the sight to say that on the second my decision
was made ; yet I believe that no woman so overwhelmed ever in so short a time recovered her command of the *act*. It came to me in the very horror of
the immediate presence that the act would be, seeing
and facing what I saw and faced, to keep the boy
himself unaware. The inspiration—I can call it by
no other name—was that I felt how voluntarily, how
transcendently, I *might*. It was like fighting with
a demon for a human soul, and when I had fairly so
appraised it I saw how the human soul—held out, in
the tremor of my hands, at arms' length—had a

perfect dew of sweat on a lovely childish forehead. The face that was close to mine was as white as the face against the glass, and out of it presently came a sound, not low nor weak, but as if from much farther away, that I drank like a waft of fragrance.

" Yes—I took it."

At this, with a moan of joy, I enfolded, I drew him close ; and while I held him to my breast, where I could feel in the sudden fever of his little body the tremendous pulse of his little heart, I kept my eyes on the thing at the window and saw it move and shift its posture. I have likened it to a sentinel, but its slow wheel, for a moment, was rather the prowl of a baffled beast. My present quickened courage, however, was such that, not too much to let it through, I had to shade, as it were, my flame. Meanwhile the glare of the face was again at the window, the scoundrel fixed as if to watch and wait. It was the very confidence that I might now defy him, as well as the positive certitude, by this time, of the child's unconsciousness, that made me go on. " What did you take it for ? "

" To see what you said about me."

" You opened the letter ? "

" I opened it."

My eyes were now, as I held him off a little again, on Miles's own face, in which the collapse of mockery showed me how complete was the ravage of uneasiness. What was prodigious was that at last, by my success, his sense was sealed and his communication stopped : he knew that he was in presence, but knew not of what, and knew still less that I also was and that I did know. And what did this strain of trouble matter when my eyes went back to the window only to see that the air was clear again and—by my personal triumph—the influence quenched ? There was nothing there. I felt that the cause was mine and that I should surely get *all*. " And you found nothing ! "—I let my elation out.

He gave the most mournful thoughtful little headshake. " Nothing."

" Nothing, nothing ! " I almost shouted in my joy.

" Nothing, nothing," he sadly repeated.

I kissed his forehead ; it was drenched. " So what have you done with it ? "

" I've burnt it."

" Burnt it ? " It was now or never. " Is that what you did at school ? "

Oh what this brought up ! " At school ? "

" Did you take letters ?—or other things ? "

" Other things ? " He appeared now to be thinking of something far off and that reached him only through the pressure of his anxiety. Yet it did reach him. " Did I *steal* ? "

I felt myself redden to the roots of my hair as well as wonder if it were more strange to put to a gentleman such a question or to see him take it with allowances that gave the very distance of his fall in the world. " Was it for that you mightn't go back ? "

The only thing he felt was rather a dreary little surprise. " Did you know I mightn't go back ? "

" I know everything."

He gave me at this the longest and strangest look. " Everything ? "

" Everything. Therefore *did* you——? " But I couldn't say it again.

Miles could, very simply. " No. I didn't steal."

My face must have shown him I believed him utterly ; yet my hands—but it was for pure tenderness—shook him as if to ask him why, if it was all for nothing, he had condemned me to months of torment. " What, then, did you do ? "

He looked in vague pain all round the top of the

room and drew his breath, two or three times over, as if with difficulty. He might have been standing at the bottom of the sea and raising his eyes to some faint green twilight. " Well—I said things."

" Only that ? "

" They thought it was enough ! "

" To turn you out for ? "

Never, truly, had a person " turned out " shown so little to explain it as this little person ! He appeared to weigh my question, but in a manner quite detached and almost helpless. " Well, I suppose I oughtn't."

" But to whom did you say them ? "

He evidently tried to remember, but it dropped— he had lost it. " I don't know ! "

He almost smiled at me in the desolation of his surrender, which was indeed practically, by this time, so complete that I ought to have left it there. But I was infatuated—I was blind with victory, though even then the very effect that was to have brought him so much nearer was already that of added separation. " Was it to every one ? " I asked.

" No ; it was only to——" But he gave a sick little headshake. " I don't remember their names."

" Were they, then, so many ? "

" No—only a few. Those I liked."

Those he liked ? I seemed to float, not into clearness, but into a darker obscure, and within a minute there had come to me out of my very pity the appalling alarm of his being perhaps innocent. It was for the instant confounding and bottomless, for if he *were* innocent what then on earth was I ? Paralysed, while it lasted, by the mere brush of the question, I let him go a little, so that, with a deep-drawn sigh, he turned away from me again ; which, as he faced toward the clear window, I suffered, feeling that I had nothing now there to keep him from. " And did they repeat what you said ? " I went on after a moment.

He was soon at some distance from me, still breathing hard and again with the air, though now without anger for it, of being confined against his will. Once more, as he had done before, he looked up at the dim day as if, of what had hitherto sustained him, nothing was left but an unspeakable anxiety. " Oh yes," he nevertheless replied—" they must have repeated them. To those *they* liked," he added.

There was somehow less of it than I had expected ; but I turned it over. " And these things came round——? "

" To the masters ? Oh yes ! " he answered very simply. " But I didn't know they'd tell."

" The masters ? They didn't—they've never told. That's why I ask you."

He turned to me again his little beautiful fevered face. " Yes, it was too bad."

" Too bad ? "

" What I suppose I sometimes said. To write home."

I can't name the exquisite pathos of the contradiction given to such a speech by such a speaker; I only know that the next instant I heard myself throw off with homely force : " Stuff and nonsense ! " But the next after that I must have sounded stern enough. " What *were* these things ? "

My sternness was all for his judge, his executioner ; yet it made him avert himself again, and that movement made *me*, with a single bound and an irrepressible cry, spring straight upon him. For there again, against the glass, as if to blight his confession and stay his answer, was the hideous author of our woe—the white face of damnation. I felt a sick swim at the drop of my victory and all the return of my battle, so that the wildness of my veritable leap only served as a great betrayal. I saw him, from the midst of my act, meet it with a divination, and on the perception that even now he only guessed, and that the window was still to his own eyes free, I let the impulse flame up to convert the climax of his dismay into the very proof of his liberation. "No more, no more, no more!" I shrieked to my visitant as I tried to press him against me.

"Is she *here*?" Miles panted as he caught with his sealed eyes the direction of my words. Then as his strange "she" staggered me and, with a gasp, I echoed it, "Miss Jessel, Miss Jessel!" he with sudden fury gave me back.

I seized, stupefied, his supposition—some sequel to what we had done to Flora, but this made me only want to show him that it was better still than that. "It's not Miss Jessel! But it's at the window— straight before us. It's *there*—the coward horror, there for the last time!"

At this, after a second in which his head made the movement of a baffled dog's on a scent and then gave a frantic little shake for air and light, he was at me in a white rage, bewildered, glaring vainly over the place and missing wholly, though it now, to my sense, filled the room like the taste of poison, the wide overwhelming presence. "It's *he*?"

I was so determined to have all my proof that I flashed into ice to challenge him. "Whom do you mean by 'he'?"

"Peter Quint—you devil!" His face gave again, round the room, its convulsed supplication. "*Where?*"

They are in my ears still, his supreme surrender of the name and his tribute to my devotion. "What does he matter now, my own?—what will he *ever* matter? *I* have you," I launched at the beast, "but he has lost you for ever!" Then for the demonstration of my work, " There, *there* ! " I said to Miles.

But he had already jerked straight round, stared, glared again, and seen but the quiet day. With the stroke of the loss I was so proud of he uttered the cry of a creature hurled over an abyss, and the grasp with which I recovered him might have been that of catching him in his fall. I caught him, yes, I held him— it may be imagined with what a passion ; but at the end of a minute I began to feel what it truly was that I held. We were alone with the quiet day, and his little heart, dispossessed, had stopped.

THE SPOILS OF POYNTON

MRS. GERETH had said she would go with the rest to church, but suddenly it seemed to her she shouldn't be able to wait even till church-time for relief : breakfast was at Waterbath a punctual meal and she had still nearly an hour on her hands. Knowing the church to be near she prepared in her room for the little rural walk, and on her way down again, passing through corridors and observing imbecilities of decoration, the esthetic misery of the big commodious house, she felt a return of the tide of last night's irritation, a renewal of everything she could secretly suffer from ugliness and stupidity. Why did she consent to such contacts ? why did she so rashly expose herself ? She had had, heaven knew, her reasons, but the whole experience was to be sharper than she had feared. To get away from it and out into the air, into the presence of sky and trees, flowers and birds, was a necessity of every nerve. The flowers at Waterbath would probably go wrong in colour and the nightingales sing out of tune ; but she remembered to have heard the place described as possessing those advantages that are usually spoken of as natural. There were advantages enough it clearly didn't possess. It was hard for her to believe a woman could look presentable who had been kept awake for hours by the wall-paper in her room ; yet none the less, as she rustled in her fresh widow's weeds across the hall, she was sustained by the consciousness, which always added to the unction of her social Sundays, that she was, as usual, the only person in the house incapable of wearing in her preparation the horrible stamp of the same exceptional smartness that would be conspicuous in a grocer's wife. She would rather have perished than have looked *endimanchée*.

She was fortunately not challenged, the hall being empty of the other women, who were engaged precisely in arraying themselves to that dire end. Once in the grounds she recognised that, with a site, a view, that struck the note, set an example to all inmates, Waterbath ought to have been charming. How she herself, with such elements to handle, would have taken the fine hint of nature ! Suddenly, at the turn of a walk, she came on a member of the party, a young lady seated on a bench in deep and lonely meditation. She had observed the girl at dinner and afterwards : she was always looking at girls with reference, apprehensive or speculative, to her son. Deep in her heart was a conviction that Owen would, in spite of all her spells, marry at last a frump ; and this from no evidence she could have represented as adequate, but simply from her deep uneasiness, her belief that such a special sensibility as her own could have been inflicted on a woman only as a source of anguish. It would be her fate, her discipline, her cross, to have a frump brought hideously home to her. This girl, one of the two Vetches, had no beauty, but Mrs. Gereth, scanning the dulness for a sign of life, had been straightway able to classify such a figure as for the moment the least of her afflictions. Fleda Vetch was dressed with an idea, though perhaps not with much else ; and that made a bond when there was none other, especially as in this case the idea was real, not imitation. Mrs. Gereth had long ago generalised the truth that the temperament of the frump may easily consort with a certain casual prettiness. There were five girls in the party, and the prettiness of this one, slim, pale, and black-haired, was less likely than that of the others ever to occasion an exchange of platitudes. The two less developed Brigstocks, daughters of the house, were in particular tiresomely " lovely." A second glance, a sharp one, at the young lady before her conveyed to Mrs. Gereth the soothing assurance that she also was guiltless of looking hot and fine. They had had no talk as yet, but here was a note that would effectually introduce them if the girl should show herself in the least conscious of their community. She got up from her seat with a smile that but partly dissipated the prostration Mrs. Gereth had recognised in her attitude. The elder woman drew her down again, and for a minute, as they sat together, their eyes met and sent out mutual soundings. " Are you safe ? Can I utter it ? " each of them said to the other, quickly recognising, almost proclaiming, their common need to escape. The tremendous fancy, as it came to be called, that Mrs. Gereth was destined to take to Fleda Vetch virtually began with this discovery that the poor child had been moved to flight even more promptly than herself. That the poor child no less quickly perceived how far she could now go was proved by the immense friendliness with which she instantly broke out : " Isn't it too dreadful ? "

" Horrible—horrible ! " cried Mrs. Gereth with a laugh ; " and it's really a comfort to be able to say it." She had an idea, for it was her ambition, that she successfully made a secret of that awkward oddity her proneness to be rendered unhappy by the presence of the dreadful. Her passion for the exquisite was the cause of this, but it was a passion she considered she never advertised nor gloried in, contenting herself with letting it regulate her steps and show quietly in her life, remembering at all times that there are few things more soundless than a deep devotion. She was therefore struck with the acuteness of the little girl who had already put a finger on her hidden spring. What was dreadful now, what was horrible, was the intimate ugliness of Waterbath, and it was of that phenomenon these ladies talked while they sat in the shade and drew refreshment from the great tranquil sky, whence no cheap blue plates depended. It was an ugliness fundamental and systematic, the result of the abnormal nature of the Brigstocks, from whose composition the principle of taste had been extravagantly omitted. In the arrangement of their home some other principle, remarkably active, but uncanny and obscure, had operated instead, with consequences depressing to behold, consequences that took the form of a universal futility. The house was bad in all conscience, but it might have passed if they had only let it alone. This saving mercy was beyond them ; they had smothered it with trumpery ornament and scrapbook art, with strange excrescences and bunchy draperies, with gimcracks that might have been keepsakes for maid-servants and nondescript conveniences that might have been prizes for the blind. They had gone wildly astray over carpets and curtains ; they had an infallible instinct for gross deviation and were so cruelly doom-ridden that it rendered them almost tragic. Their drawing-room, Mrs. Gereth lowered her voice to mention, caused her face to burn, and each of the new friends confided to the other that in her own apartment she had given way to tears. There was in the elder lady's a set of comic water-colours, a family joke by a family genius, and in the younger's a souvenir from some centennial or other Exhibition, that they shudderingly alluded to. The house was perversely full of souvenirs of places even more ugly than itself and of things it would have been a pious duty to forget. The worst horror was the acres of varnish, something advertised and smelly, with which everything was smeared : it was Fleda Vetch's conviction that the application of it, by their own hands and hilariously shoving each other, was the amusement of the Brigstocks on rainy days.

When, as criticism deepened, Fleda dropped the suggestion that some people would perhaps see something in Mona, Mrs. Gereth caught her up with a groan of protest, a smothered familiar cry of " Oh my dear ! " Mona was the eldest of the three, the one Mrs. Gereth most suspected. She confided to her young friend how it was her suspicion that had brought her to Waterbath ; and this was going very far, for on the spot, as a refuge, a remedy, she had clutched at the idea that something might be done with the girl before her. It was her fancied exposure at any rate that had sharpened the shock, made her ask herself with a terrible chill if fate could really be plotting to saddle her with a daughter-in-law brought up in such a place. She had seen Mona in her appropriate setting and had seen Owen, handsome and heavy, dangle beside her ; but the effect of these first hours had happily not been to darken the prospect. It was clearer to her that she could never accept Mona, but it was after all by no means certain Owen would ask her to. He had sat by somebody else at dinner and afterwards had talked to Mrs. Firmin, who was as dreadful as all the rest, but redeemingly married. His heaviness, which in her need of expansion she freely named, had two aspects : one of them his monstrous lack of taste, the other his exaggerated prudence. If it should come to a question of carrying Mona with a high hand there would be no need to worry, for that was rarely his mode of proceeding.

Invited by her companion, who had asked if it weren't wonderful, Mrs. Gereth had begun to say a word about Poynton ; but she heard a sound of voices that made her stop short. The next moment she rose to her feet, and Fleda could then see her alarm to be by no means quenched. Behind the place where they had been sitting the ground dropped with some steepness, forming a long grassy bank up which Owen Gereth and Mona Brigstock, dressed for church but making a familiar joke of it, were in the act of scrambling and helping each other. When they had reached the even ground Fleda was able to read the meaning of the exclamation in which Mrs. Gereth had expressed her reserves on the subject of Miss Brigstock's personality. Miss Brigstock had been laughing and even romping, but the circumstance hadn't contributed the ghost of an expression to her countenance. Tall, straight and fair, long-limbed and strangely festooned, she stood there without a look in her eye or any perceptible intention of any sort in any other feature. She belonged to the type in which speech is an unaided emission of sound, in which the secret of being is impenetrably and incorruptibly kept. Her expression would probably have been beautiful if she had had one, but whatever she communicated she communicated, in a manner best known to herself, without signs. This was not the case with Owen Gereth, who had plenty of them, and all very simple and immediate. Robust and artless, eminently natural yet perfectly correct, he looked pointlessly active and pleasantly dull. Like his mother and like Fleda Vetch, but not for the same reason, this young pair had come out to take a turn before church.

The meeting of the two couples was sensibly

awkward, and Fleda, who had perceptions, and these now more and more roused, took the measure of the shock inflicted on Mrs. Gereth. There had been intimacy—oh yes, intimacy as well as puerility—in the horse-play of which they had just had a glimpse. The party began to stroll together to the house, and Fleda had again a sense of Mrs. Gereth's quick management in the way the lovers, or whatever they were, found themselves separated. She strolled behind with Mona, the mother possessing herself of her son, her exchange of remarks with whom, however, remained, as they went, vividly inaudible. That member of the party in whose intenser consciousness we shall most profitably seek a reflexion of the little drama with which we are concerned drew a yet livelier impression of Mrs. Gereth's intervention from the fact that ten minutes later, on the way to church, still another pairing had been effected. Owen walked with Fleda, and it was an amusement to the girl to feel sure this was by his mother's direction. Fleda had other amusements as well : such as noting that Mrs. Gereth was now with Mona Brigstock ; such as observing that she was all affability to that young woman ; such as reflecting that, masterful and clever, with a great bright spirit, she was one of those who impose, who interfuse themselves ; such as feeling finally that Owen Gereth was absolutely beautiful and delightfully dense. This young person had even from herself wonderful secrets of delicacy and pride ; but she came as near distinctness as in the consideration of such matters she had ever come at all in now embracing the idea that it was of a pleasant effect and rather remarkable to be stupid without offence —of a pleasanter effect and more remarkable indeed than to be clever and horrid. Owen Gereth at any rate, with his inches, his features and his lapses, was neither of these latter things. She herself was prepared, if she should ever marry, to contribute all the cleverness, and she liked to figure it out that her husband would be a force grateful for direction. She was in her small way a spirit of the same family as Mrs. Gereth. On that flushed and huddled Sunday a great matter occurred ; her little life became aware of a singular quickening. Her meagre past fell away from her like a garment of the wrong fashion, and as she came up to town on the Monday what she stared at from the train in the suburban fields was a future full of the things she particularly loved.

II

THESE were neither more nor less than the things with which she had had time to learn from Mrs. Gereth that Poynton overflowed. Poynton, in the south of England, was this lady's established, or rather her disestablished, home: it had recently passed into the possession of her son. The father of the boy, an only child, had died two years before, and in London, with his mother, Owen was occupying for May and June a house good-naturedly lent them by Colonel Gereth, their uncle and brother-in-law. His mother had laid her hand so engagingly on Fleda Vetch that in a very few days the girl knew it was possible they should suffer together in Cadogan Place almost as much as they had suffered together at Waterbath. The kind soldier's house was also an ordeal, but the two women, for the ensuing month, had at least the relief of their confessions. The great drawback of Mrs. Gereth's situation was that, thanks to the rare perfection of Poynton, she was condemned to wince wherever she turned. She had lived for a quarter of a century in such warm closeness with the beautiful that, as she frankly admitted, life had become for her a true fool's paradise. She couldn't leave her own house without peril of exposure. She didn't say it in so many words, but Fleda could see she held nothing in England really comparable to Poynton. There were places much grander and richer, but no such complete work of art, nothing that would appeal so to those really informed. In putting such elements into her hand destiny had given her an inestimable chance ; she knew how rarely well things had gone with her and that she had enjoyed an extraordinary fortune.

There had been in the first place the exquisite old house itself, early Jacobean, supreme in every part ; a provocation, an inspiration, the matchless canvas for a picture. Then there had been her husband's sympathy and generosity, his knowledge and love, their perfect accord and beautiful life together, twenty-six years of planning and seeking, a long, sunny harvest of taste and curiosity. Lastly, she never denied, there had been her personal gift, the genius, the passion, the patience of the collector— a patience, an almost infernal cunning, that had enabled her to do it all with a limited command of money. There wouldn't have been money enough for any fumbler, she said with pride, but there had been money enough for her. They had saved on lots of things in life, and there were lots of things they hadn't had at all, but they had had in every corner of Europe their swing among the demons of Jews. It was fascinating to poor Fleda, who hadn't a penny in the world nor anything nice at home, and whose only treasure was her subtle mind, to hear this genuine English lady, fresh and fair, young in the fifties, admit with gaiety and conviction that she was herself the craftiest stalker who had ever tracked big game. Fleda, with her mother dead, hadn't so much even as a home, and her nearest chance of one was that there was some appearance her sister would become engaged to a curate whose eldest brother was supposed to have property and would perhaps allow him something. Her father paid some of her bills but didn't like her to live with him ; and she had lately, in Paris, with several hundred other young women, spent a year at a studio, arming herself for the battle of life by a course with an impressionist painter. She was determined to work, but her impressions, or somebody's else, were as yet her only material. Mrs. Gereth had told her she liked her because she had an extraordinary *flair* ; but under the circumstances a *flair* was a questionable boon : in the dry spaces in which she had mainly moved she could have borne a chronic catarrh   She was now much summoned to Cadogan Place and before the month elapsed was kept to stay, to pay a visit of which the end, it was agreed, should have nothing to do with the beginning. She had a sense partly exultant and partly alarmed of having quickly become necessary to her imperious friend, who indeed gave a reason quite sufficient for it in telling her there was nobody else who understood. From Mrs. Gereth there was in these days an immense deal to understand, though it might freely be summed up in the circumstance that she was wretched. Fleda was thus assured she couldn't completely know why till she should have seen the things at Poynton. She could perfectly grasp this connexion, which was exactly one of the matters that, in their inner mystery, were a blank to everybody else.

The girl had a promise that the wonderful house should be shown her early in July, when Mrs. Gereth would return to it as to her home ; but even before this initiation she put her finger on the spot that in the poor lady's troubled soul ached hardest. This was the misery haunting her, the dread of the inevitable surrender. What Fleda had to sit up to was the confirmed appearance that Owen Gereth would marry Mona Brigstock, marry her in his mother's teeth, and that such an act would have incalculable bearings. They were present to Mrs. Gereth, her companion could see, with a vividness that at moments almost ceased to be that of sanity. She would have to give up Poynton, and give it up to a product of Waterbath—that was the wrong that rankled, the humiliation at which one would be able adequately to shudder only when one should know the place. She did know Waterbath and despised it—she had that qualification for sympathy. Her sympathy was intelligent, for she read deep into the matter : she stared, aghast, as it came home to her for the first time, at the cruel English custom of the expropriation of the lonely mother. Mr. Gereth had apparently been a very amiable man, but Mr. Gereth had left things in a way that made the girl marvel. The house and its contents had been treated as a single splendid object ; everything was to go straight to his son, his widow being assured but a maintenance and a cottage in another county. No account whatever had been taken of her relation to her treasures, of the passion with which she had waited for them, worked for them, picked them over, made them worthy of each other and the house, watched them, loved them, lived with them. He appeared to have assumed she would settle questions with her son and that he could depend on Owen's affection and Owen's fairness. And in truth, as poor Mrs. Gereth inquired, how could he possibly have had a prevision—he who turned his eyes instinctively from everything repulsive—of anything so abnormal either as a Waterbath Brigstock or as a Brigstock Waterbath ? He had been in ugly houses enough, but had escaped that particular nightmare. Nothing so perverse could have been expected to happen as that the heir to the loveliest thing in England should be inspired to hand it over to a girl so exceptionally tainted. Mrs. Gereth spoke of poor Mona's taint as if to mention it were almost a violation of decency,

and a person who had listened without enlighten-
ment would have wondered of what fault the girl
had been or had indeed not been guilty. But Owen
had from a boy never cared, never taken the least
pride or pleasure in his home.

" Well then if he doesn't care—— ! " Fleda exclaimed with some impetuosity ; stopping short,
however, before she completed her sentence.

Mrs. Gereth looked at her rather hard. " If he
doesn't care ? "

Fleda cast about ; she had not quite had a definite
idea. " Well—he'll give them up."

" Give what up ? "

" Why, those beautiful things."

" Give them up to whom ? " Mrs. Gereth more
boldly stared.

" To you of course—to enjoy, to keep for yourself."

" And leave his house as bare as your hand ?
There's nothing in it that isn't precious."

Fleda considered ; her friend had taken her up
with a smothered ferocity by which she was slightly
disconcerted. " I don't mean, naturally, that he
should surrender everything ; but he might let you
pick out the things to which you're most attached."

" I think he would if he were free," said Mrs.
Gereth.

" And do you mean, as it is, that she'll prevent
him ? " Mona Brigstock, between these ladies, was
now nothing but " she."

" By every means in her power."

" But surely not because she understands and
appreciates them ? "

" No," Mrs. Gereth replied, " but because they
belong to the house and the house belongs to Owen.
If I should wish to take anything she would simply
say, with that motionless mask, ' It goes with the

house.' And day after day, in the face of every
argument, of every consideration of generosity, she
would repeat, without winking, in that voice like the
squeeze of a doll's stomach, ' It goes with the house
—it goes with the house.' In that attitude they'll
shut themselves up.''

Fleda was struck, was even a little startled by the
way Mrs. Gereth had turned this over—had faced,
if indeed only to recognise its futility, the notion of
a battle with her only son. These words led her to
take a sounding she had not thought it discreet to
take before : she brought out the idea of the possibility, after all, of her friend's continuing to live
at Poynton. Would they really wish to proceed to
extremities ? Was no good-humoured graceful compromise to be imagined or brought about ? Couldn't
the same roof cover them ? Was it so very inconceivable that a married son should for the rest of her
days share with so charming a mother the home she
had devoted more than a score of years to making
beautiful for him ? Mrs. Gereth hailed this question
with a wan compassionate smile : she replied that a
common household was in such a case just so inconceivable that Fleda had only to glance over the fair
face of the English land to see how few people had
ever conceived it. It was always thought a wonder, a
" mistake," a piece of overstrained sentiment ; and
she confessed she was as little capable of a flight of
that sort as Owen himself. Even if they both had
been capable they would still have Mona's hatred to
reckon with. Fleda's breath was sometimes taken
away by the great fierce bounds and elisions which,
on Mrs. Gereth's lips, the course of discussion could
take.

This was the first she had heard of Mona's hatred,
though she certainly had not needed Mrs. Gereth to
tell her that in close quarters that young lady would

prove secretly mulish. Later Fleda perceived indeed
that perhaps almost any girl would hate a person
who should be so markedly averse to having anything
to do with her. Before this, however, in conversation
with her young friend, Mrs. Gereth furnished a more
vivid motive for her despair by asking how she could
possibly be expected to sit there with the new pro-
prietors and accept—or call it, for a day, endure—
the horrors they would perpetrate in the house.
Fleda argued that they wouldn't after all smash things
nor burn them up ; and Mrs. Gereth admitted when
pushed that she didn't quite suppose they would.
What she meant was that they would neglect them,
ignore them, leave them to clumsy servants—there
wasn't an object of them all but should be handled
with perfect love—and in many cases probably wish
to replace them by pieces answerable to some vulgar
modern notion of the " handy." Above all she saw
in advance with dilated eyes the abominations they
would inevitably mix up with them—the maddening
relics of Waterbath, the little brackets and pink vases,
the sweepings of bazaars, the family photographs and
illuminated texts, the " household art " and household
piety of Mona's hideous home. Wasn't it enough
simply to contend that Mona would approach Poynton
in the spirit of a Brigstock and that in the spirit of a
Brigstock she would deal with her acquisition ? Did
Fleda really see *her*, Mrs. Gereth demanded, spending
the remainder of her days with such a creature's
elbow half-way down her throat ?

Fleda had to declare that she certainly didn't and
that Waterbath had been a warning it would be
frivolous to overlook. At the same time she privately
reflected that they were taking a great deal for granted
and that, inasmuch as to her knowledge Owen Gereth
had positively denied his betrothal, the ground of
their speculations was by no means firm. It struck

our young lady that in a difficult position Owen conducted himself with some natural art ; treating this domesticated confidant of his mother's wrongs with a simple civility that almost troubled her conscience, so deeply she felt she might have had for him the air of siding with that lady against him. She wondered if he would ever know how little really she did this and that she was there, since Mrs. Gereth had insisted, not to betray but essentially to plead and protect. The fact that his mother disliked Mona Brigstock might have made him dislike the object of her preference, and it was detestable to Fleda to remember that she might have appeared to him to offer herself as an exemplary contrast. It was clear enough, however, that the happy youth had no more sense for a motive than a deaf man for a tune ; a limitation by which, after all, she could gain as well as lose. He came and went very freely on the business with which London abundantly furnished him, but he found time more than once to say to her " It's awfully nice of you to look after poor Mummy." As well as his quick speech, which shyness made obscure—it was usually as desperate as a "rush" at some violent game—his child's eyes in his man's face put it to her that, you know, this really meant a good deal for him and that he hoped she would stay on. With a person in the house who, like herself, was clever, poor Mummy was conveniently occupied. Fleda found a beauty in the candour and even in the modesty which apparently kept him from suspecting that two such wiseheads could possibly be occupied with Owen Gereth.

III

THEY went at last, the wiseheads, down to Poynton, where the palpitating girl had the full revelation. " *Now* do you know how I feel ? " Mrs. Gereth asked when in the wondrous hall, three minutes after their arrival, her pretty associate dropped on a seat with a soft gasp and a roll of dilated eyes. The answer came clearly enough, and in the rapture of that first walk through the house Fleda took a prodigious span. She perfectly understood how Mrs. Gereth felt— she had understood but meagrely before ; and the two women embraced with tears over the tightening of their bond—tears which on the younger one's part were the natural and usual sign of her submission to perfect beauty. It was not the first time she had cried for the joy of admiration, but it was the first time the mistress of Poynton, often as she had shown her house, had been present at such an exhibition. She exulted in it ; it quickened her own tears ; she assured her companion that such an occasion made the poor old place fresh to her again and more precious than ever. Yes, nobody had ever, that way, *cared*, ever felt what she had achieved : people were so grossly ignorant, and everybody, even the knowing ones as they thought themselves, more or less dense. What Mrs. Gereth had achieved was indeed a supreme result ; and in such an art of the treasure-hunter, in selection and comparison refined to that point, there was an

element of creation, of personality. She had commended Fleda's *flair*, and Fleda now gave herself
up to satiety. Preoccupations and scruples fell away
from her ; she had never known a greater happiness
than the week passed in this initiation.

Wandering through clear chambers where the
general effect made preferences almost as impossible
as if they had been shocks, pausing at open doors
where vistas were long and bland, she would, even
hadn't she already known, have discovered for herself that Poynton was the record of a life. It was
written in great syllables of colour and form, the
tongues of other countries and the hands of rare
artists. It was all France and Italy with their ages
composed to rest. For England you looked out of
old windows—it was England that was the wide
embrace. While outside, on the low terraces, she
contradicted gardeners and refined on nature, Mrs.
Gereth left her guest to finger fondly the brasses that
Louis Quinze might have thumbed, to sit with Venetian velvets just held in a loving palm, to hang over
cases of enamels and pass and repass before cabinets.
There were not many pictures—the panels and the
stuffs were themselves the picture ; and in all the great
wainscoted house there was not an inch of pasted
paper. What struck Fleda most in it was the high
pride of her friend's taste, a fine arrogance, a sense
of style which, however amused and amusing, never
compromised nor stooped. She felt indeed, as this
lady had promised her she should, both a respect and
a compassion she had not known before ; thus the
vision of the coming surrender could but fill her with
an equal pain. To give it all up, to die to it—that
thought ached in her breast. She herself could imagine clinging there with a clutch indifferent to dignity.
To have created such a place was to have had dignity
enough ; when there was a question of defending it

the fiercest attitude was the right one. After so intense a taking of possession she too was to give it up ; for she reflected that if Mrs. Gereth's remaining would have offered her an apology for a future—stretching away in safe years on the other side of a gulf— the advent of the others could only be, by the same law, a great vague menace, the ruffling of a still water. Such were the emotions of a hungry girl whose sensibility was almost as great as her opportunities for comparison had been small. The museums had done something for her, but nature had done more.

If Owen had not come down with them nor joined them later it was because he still found London jolly ; yet the question remained of whether the jollity of London were not merely the only name his small vocabulary yielded for the jollity of Mona Brigstock. There was indeed in his conduct another ambiguity —something that required explaining so long as his motive didn't come to the surface. If he was in love what was the matter ? And what was the matter still more if he wasn't ? The mystery was at last cleared up : this Fleda gathered from the tone in which, one morning at breakfast, a letter just opened made Mrs. Gereth cry out. Her dismay was almost a shriek : " Why he's bringing her down—he wants her to see the house ! " They flew, the two women, into each other's arms and, with their heads together, soon made out the reason, the baffling reason why nothing had yet happened, to be that Mona didn't know, or Owen didn't, whether Poynton would really please her. She was coming down to judge ; and could anything in the world be more like poor Owen than the ponderous probity that had kept him from pressing her for a reply till she should have learned if she approved what he had to offer her ? That was a scruple it had naturally been impossible to impute. If only they might fondly hope, Mrs. Gereth wailed, that the girl's expectations would be dashed ! There was a fine consistency, a sincerity quite affecting, in her arguing that the better the place should happen to look, the better it should express the conceptions to which it owed its origin, the less it would speak to an intelligence so primitive. How could a Brigstock possibly understand what it was all about ? How, really, could a Brigstock logically do anything but hate it ? Mrs. Gereth, even as she whisked away linen shrouds, persuaded herself of the likelihood on Mona's part of some bewildered blankness, some collapse of admiration that would prove disconcerting to her swain—a hope of which Fleda at least could see the absurdity and which gave the measure of the poor lady's strange, almost maniacal disposition to thrust in everywhere the question of " things," to read all behaviour in the light of some fancied relation to them. " Things " were of course the sum of the world ; only, for Mrs. Gereth, the sum of the world was rare French furniture and oriental china. She could at a stretch imagine people's not " having," but she couldn't imagine their not wanting and not missing.

The young people were to be accompanied by Mrs. Brigstock, and with a prevision of how fiercely they would be watched Fleda became conscious, before the party arrived, of an amused diplomatic pity for them. Almost as much as Mrs. Gereth's her taste was her life, though her life was somehow the larger for it. Besides, she had another care now : there was some one she wouldn't have liked to see humiliated even in the person of a young lady formed to foster his never suspecting so much delicacy. When this young lady appeared Fleda tried, so far as the wish to efface herself allowed, to be mainly the person to take her about, show her the house and cover up her ignorance. Owen's announcement had been that, as trains made it convenient, they would present themselves for luncheon and depart before dinner; but Mrs. Gereth, true to her system of glaring civility, proposed and obtained an extension, a dining and a spending of the night. She made her young friend wonder against what rebellion of fact she was sacrificing in advance so profusely to appearance. Fleda was appalled after the first hour by the rash innocence with which Mona had accepted the responsibility of observation, and indeed by the large levity with which, sitting there like a bored tourist in fine scenery, she exercised it. She felt in her nerves the effect of such a manner on her companion's, and it was this that made her want to entice the girl away, give her some merciful warning or some jocular cue. Mona met intense looks, however, with eyes that might have been blue beads, the only ones she had—eyes into which Fleda thought it strange Owen Gereth should have to plunge for his fate and his mother for a confession of whether Poynton were a success. She made no remark that helped to supply this light; her impression at any rate had nothing in common with the feeling that, as the beauty of the place throbbed out like music, had caused Fleda Vetch to burst into tears. She was as content to say nothing as if, their hostess afterwards exclaimed, she had been keeping her mouth shut in a railway tunnel. Mrs. Gereth contrived at the end of an hour to convey to Fleda that it was plain she was brutally ignorant; but Fleda more finely discovered that her ignorance was obscurely active.

Mona was not so stupid as not to see that something, though she scarcely knew what, was expected of her that she couldn't give; and the only mode her intelligence suggested of meeting the expectation was to plant her big feet and pull another way. Mrs. Gereth wanted her to rise, somehow or somewhere, and was prepared to hate her if she didn't: very well, she couldn't, wouldn't rise; she had already moved at the altitude that suited her and was able to see that since she was exposed to the hatred she might at least enjoy the calm. The smallest trouble, for a girl with no nonsense about her, was to earn what she incurred ; so that, a dim instinct teaching her she would earn it best by no fond overflow, and combining with the conviction that she now definitely held Owen, and therefore the place, she had the pleasure of her honesty as well as of her security. Didn't her very honesty lead her to be belligerently blank about Poynton, inasmuch as it was just Poynton that was forced upon her as a subject for effusiveness ? Such subjects, to Miss Brigstock, had an air almost of indecency ; so that the house became uncanny to her by the very appeal in its name—an appeal that somewhere in the twilight of her being, as Fleda was sure, Mona thanked heaven she *was* the girl stiffly to draw back from. She was a person whom pressure at a given point infallibly caused to expand in the wrong place instead of, as it is usually administered in the hope of doing, the right one. Her mother, to make up for this, broke out universally, pronounced everything " most striking," and was visibly happy that Owen's captor should be so far on the way to strike : but she jarred upon Mrs. Gereth by her formula of admiration, which was that anything she looked at was " in the style " of something else. This was to show how much she had seen, but it only showed she had seen nothing ; everything at Poynton was in the style of Poynton, and poor Mrs. Brigstock, who at least was determined to rise and had brought with her a trophy of her journey, a " lady's magazine " purchased at the station, a horrible thing with patterns of antimacassars, which, as it was quite new, the first number, and seemed so clever, she kindly offered to leave for the house, was in the style of a vulgar old woman who wore silver jewelry and tried to pass off a gross avidity as a sense of the beautiful.

By the day's end it was clear to Fleda Vetch that, however Mona judged, the day had been determinant. Whether or no she felt the charm she felt the challenge : at an early moment Owen Gereth would be able to tell his mother the worst. Nevertheless when the elder lady, at bedtime, coming in a dressing-gown and a high fever to the younger one's room, cried out "She hates it ; but what will she do ? " Fleda pretended vagueness, played at obscurity and assented disingenuously to the proposition that they at least had a respite. The future was dark to her, but there was a silken thread she could clutch in the gloom—she would never give Owen away. He might give himself—he even certainly would ; but that was his own affair, and his blunders, his innocence, only added to the appeal he made to her. She would cover him, she would protect him, and beyond thinking her a cheerful inmate he would never guess her intention, any more than, beyond thinking her clever enough for anything, his astute mother would discover it. From this hour, with Mrs. Gereth, there was a flaw in her frankness. Her admirable friend continued to know everything she did : what was to remain unknown was her general motive.

From the window of her room, the next morning before breakfast, the girl saw Owen in the garden with Mona, who strolled beside him under a listening parasol but without a visible look for the great florid picture hung there from so far back by Mrs. Gereth's hand. Mona kept dropping her eyes, as she walked, to catch the sheen of her patent-leather shoes, which resembled a man's and which she kicked forward a little—it gave her an odd movement—to help her see what she thought of them. When Fleda came down Mrs. Gereth was in the breakfast-room ; and

at that moment Owen, through a long window, passed
in alone from the terrace and very endearingly kissed
his mother. It immediately struck their guest that
she was in their way, for hadn't he been borne on a
wave of joy exactly to announce, before the Brigstocks departed, that Mona had at last faltered out the
sweet word he had been waiting for ? He shook
hands with his friendly violence, but Fleda contrived not to look into his face : what she liked most
to see in it was not the reflexion of Mona's big boot-
toes. She could bear well enough that young lady
herself, but she couldn't bear Owen's opinion of her.
She was on the point of slipping into the garden
when the movement was checked by Mrs. Gereth's
suddenly drawing her close, as if for the morning
embrace, and then, while she kept her there with the
bravery of the night's repose, breaking out : " Well,
my dear boy, what *does* your young friend there
make of our odds and ends ? "

" Oh she thinks they're all right ! "

Fleda immediately guessed from his tone that he
had not come in to say what she supposed : there was
even something in it to confirm Mrs. Gereth's belief
that their danger had dropped. She was sure, moreover, that his tribute to Mona's taste was a repetition
of the eloquent words in which the girl had herself
recorded it ; she could indeed hear with all vividness the probable pretty passage between the pair.
" Don't you think it's rather jolly, the old shop ? "
" Oh it's all right ! " Mona had graciously remarked ;
and then they had probably, with a slap on a back,
run another race up or down a green bank. Fleda
knew Mrs. Gereth hadn't yet uttered a word to her
son that would have shown him how much she feared ;
but it was impossible to feel her friend's arm round
her and not become aware that this friend was now
throbbing with a strange intention. Owen's reply

had scarcely been of a nature to usher in a discussion of Mona's sensibilities, but Mrs. Gereth went on in a moment with an innocence of which Fleda could measure the cold hypocrisy. " Has she any sort of feeling for nice old things ? " The question was as fresh as the morning light.

" Oh of course she likes everything that's nice." And Owen, who constitutionally shirked questions—an answer was almost as hateful to him as a " trick " to a big dog—smiled kindly at Fleda and conveyed that she'd understand what he meant even if his mother didn't. Fleda, however, mainly understood that Mrs. Gereth, with an odd wild laugh, held her so hard as to hurt her.

" I could give up everything without a pang, I think, to a person I could trust, I could respect." The girl heard her voice tremble under the effort to show nothing but what she wanted to show, and felt the sincerity of her implication that the piety most real to her was to be on one's knees before one's high standard. " The best things here, as you know, are the things your father and I collected, things all that we worked for and waited for and suffered for. Yes," cried Mrs. Gereth with a fine freedom of fancy, " there are things in the house that we almost starved for ! They were our religion, they were our life, they were *us* ! And now they're only *me*—except that they're also *you*, thank God, a little, you dear ! " she continued, suddenly inflicting on Fleda a kiss intended by every sign to knock her into position. " There isn't one of them I don't know and love— yes, as one remembers and cherishes the happiest moments of one's life. Blindfold, in the dark, with the brush of a finger, I could tell one from another. They're living things to me ; they know me, they return the touch of my hand. But I could let them all go, since I have to so strangely, to another affection, another conscience. There's a care they want, there's a sympathy that draws out their beauty. Rather than make them over to a woman ignorant and vulgar I think I'd deface them with my own hands. Can't you see me, Fleda, and wouldn't you do it yourself ? ''—she appealed to her companion with glittering eyes. " I couldn't bear the thought of such a woman here—I *could*n't. I don't know what she'd do ; she'd be sure to invent some deviltry, if it should be only to bring in her own little belongings and horrors ! The world is full of cheap gimcracks in this awful age, and they're thrust in at one at every turn. They'd be thrust in here on top of my treasures, my own. Who'd save *them* for me—I ask you who *would* ? '' and she turned again to Fleda with a dry strained smile. Her handsome high-nosed excited face might have been that of Don Quixote tilting at a windmill. Drawn into the eddy of this outpouring the girl, scared and embarrassed, laughed off her exposure ; but only to feel herself more passionately caught up and, as it seemed to her, thrust down the fine open mouth (it showed such perfect teeth) with which poor Owen's slow cerebration gaped. " *You* would, of course—only you, in all the world, because you know, you feel as I do myself, what's good and true and pure.'' No severity of the moral law could have taken a higher tone in this implication of the young lady who lacked the only virtue Mrs. Gereth actively esteemed. " *You* would replace me, *you* would watch over them, *you* would keep the place right,'' she austerely pursued, " and with you here —yes, with you, I believe I might rest at last in my grave ! '' She threw herself on Fleda's neck, and before that witness, horribly shamed, could shake her off, had burst into tears which couldn't have been explained but which might perhaps have been understood.

IV

A WEEK later Owen came down to inform his mother
he had settled with Mona Brigstock ; but it was not
at all a joy to Fleda, aware of how much to himself
it would be a surprise, that he should find her still
in the house. That dreadful scene before breakfast
had made her position false and odious ; it had been
followed, after they were left alone, by a scene of
her own making with her extravagant friend. She
notified Mrs. Gereth of her instant departure : she
couldn't possibly remain after being offered to Owen
so distinctly, before her very face, as his mother's
candidate for the honour of his hand. That was all
he could have seen in such an outbreak and in the
indecency of her standing there to enjoy it. Fleda
had on the prior occasion dashed out of the room
by the shortest course and, while still upset, had
fallen on Mona in the garden. She had taken an
aimless turn with her and they had had some talk,
rendered at first difficult, thoroughly thankless, by
Mona's apparent suspicion that she had been sent out
to spy, as Mrs. Gereth had tried to spy, into her
opinions. Fleda was wise enough to treat these
opinions as a mystery almost awful ; which had an
effect so much more than reassuring that at the end
of five minutes the young lady from Waterbath
suddenly and perversely said : " Why has she never
had a winter garden thrown out ? If ever I have a

place of my own I mean to have one." Fleda, dismayed, could see the thing—something glazed and piped, on iron pillars, with untidy plants and cane sofas; a shiny excrescence on the noble face of Poynton. She remembered at Waterbath a conservatory where she had caught a bad cold in the company of a stuffed cockatoo fastened to a tropical bough and a waterless fountain composed of shells stuck into some hardened paste. She asked Mona if her idea would be to make something like this conservatory; to which Mona replied: "Oh no, much finer; we haven't got a winter garden at Waterbath." Fleda wondered if she meant to convey that it was the only grandeur they lacked, and in a moment she went on: "But we *have* got a billiard-room—that I *will* say for us!" There was no billiard-room at Poynton, but there would evidently be one, and it would have, hung on its walls, framed at the "Stores," caricature-portraits of celebrities taken from a "society paper."

When the two girls had gone in to breakfast it was for Fleda to see at a glance that there had been a further passage, of some high colour, between Owen and his mother; and she had turned pale in guessing to what extremity, at her expense, Mrs. Gereth had found occasion to proceed. Hadn't she after her clumsy flight been pressed upon Owen in still clearer terms? Mrs. Gereth would practically have said to him: "If you'll take *her* I'll move away without a sound. But if you take any one else, any one I'm not sure of as I am of her—heaven help me, I'll fight to the death!" Breakfast this morning at Poynton had been a meal singularly silent, in spite of the vague little cries with which Mrs. Brigstock turned up the underside of plates and the knowing but alarming raps administered by her big knuckles to porcelain cups. Some one had to respond to her, and the duty assigned itself to Fleda, who, while pretending to meet her on the ground of explanation, wondered what Owen thought of a girl still indelicately anxious, after she had been grossly hurled at him, to prove by exhibitions of her fine taste that she was really what his mother pretended. This time at any rate their fate was sealed : Owen, as soon as he should get out of the house, would describe to Mona the extraordinary display made to him, and if anything more had been wanted to " fetch " her, as he would call it, the deficiency was now made up. Mrs. Gereth in fact took care of that—took care of it by the way, at the last, on the threshold, she said to the younger of her departing guests, with an irony of which the sting was wholly in the sense, not at all in the sound : " We haven't had the talk we might have had, have we ? You'll feel I've neglected you and you'll treasure it up against me. *Don't*, because really, you know, it has been quite an accident, and I've all sorts of information at your disposal. If you should come down again (only you won't, ever—I feel that !) I should give you plenty of time to worry it out of me. Indeed there are some things I should quite insist on your learning ; not permit you at all, in any settled way, *not* to learn. Yes indeed, you'd put me through, and I should put you, my dear ! We should have each other to reckon with and you'd see me as I really am. I'm not a bit the vague mooning easy creature I daresay you think. However, if you won't come you won't ; *n'en parlons plus*. It *is* stupid here after what you're accustomed to. We can only, all round, do *what* we can, eh ? For heaven's sake don't let your mother forget her precious publication, the female magazine with the what - do - you - call - 'em ? — the greasecatchers. There ! "

Mrs. Gereth, delivering herself from the doorstep, had tossed the periodical higher in air than was absolutely needful — tossed it toward the carriage the retreating party was about to enter. Mona, from the force of habit, the reflex action of the custom of sport, had popped out, with a little spring, a long arm and intercepted the missile as easily as she would have caused a tennis-ball to rebound from a racket. " Good catch ! " Owen had cried, so genuinely pleased that practically no notice was taken of his mother's impressive remarks. It was to the accompaniment of romping laughter, as Mrs. Gereth afterwards said, that the carriage had rolled away ; but it was while that laughter was still in the air that Fleda Vetch, white and terrible, had turned on her hostess with her scorching " How *could* you ?   Great God, how *could* you ? "   This lady's perfect blankness was from the first a sign of her smooth conscience ; and the fact that till indoctrinated she didn't even know what Fleda meant by resenting her late offence to every susceptibility gave our young woman a sore scared perception that her own value in the house was the mere value, as one might say, of a good agent. Mrs. Gereth was generously sorry, but was still more surprised — surprised at Fleda's not having liked to be shown off to Owen as the right sort of wife for him.   Why not, in the name of wonder, if she absolutely *was* the right sort ?   She had admitted on explanation that she could see what her young friend meant by having been laid, as Fleda called it, at his feet ; but it struck the girl that the admission was only made to please her and that Mrs. Gereth was secretly surprised at her not being as happy to be sacrificed to the supremacy of a high standard as she was happy to sacrifice her.   She had taken a tremendous fancy to her, but that was on account of the fancy—to Poynton of course—taken by Fleda herself.   Wasn't this latter fancy then so great after all ?   Fleda felt she could pronounce it great indeed when really forgiving for the sake of it what she had suffered and, after reproaches and tears, asseverations and kisses, after practical proof that she was cared for only as a priestess of the altar and a view of her bruised dignity which left no alternative to flight, accepting the shame with the balm, consenting not to depart, taking refuge in the thin comfort of the truth at least brought home to her. The truth was simply that all Mrs. Gereth's scruples were on one side and that her ruling passion had in a manner despoiled her of her humanity. On the second day, when the tide of emotion had somewhat ebbed, she said soothingly to her companion : " But you *would*, after all, marry him, you know, darling, wouldn't you, if that girl were not there ? I mean of course if he were to ask you," Mrs. Gereth had thoughtfully added. Yet she made the strangest free reach over all such preliminaries.

" Marry him if he were to ask me ? Most distinctly not ! "

The question had not come up with this definiteness before, and Mrs. Gereth was clearly more surprised than ever. She marvelled a moment. " Not even to have Poynton ? "

" Not even to have Poynton."

" But why on earth ? " Mrs. Gereth's sad eyes were fixed on her.

Fleda coloured ; she hung fire. " Because he's too stupid ! " Save on one other occasion at which we shall in time arrive she never came nearer to betraying to Mrs. Gereth that she was in love with Owen. She found a vain charm in reflecting that if Mona had not been there and he had not been too stupid and he verily had asked her, she might, should she have wished to keep her secret, have found it possible to pass off the motive of her conduct as a mere passion for his property.

311

Mrs. Gereth evidently thought in these days of little but things hymeneal ; for she broke out with sudden rapture in the middle of the week : " I know what they'll do : they *will* marry, but they'll go and live at Waterbath ! " There was positive joy in that form of the idea, which she embroidered and developed : it seemed so much the safest thing that could happen. " Yes, I'll have you, but I won't go *there* ! " Mona would have said with a vicious nod at the southern horizon : " we'll leave your horrid mother alone there for life." It would be an ideal solution, this ingress the lively pair, with their spiritual need of a warmer medium, would playfully punch in the ribs of her ancestral home ; for it would not only prevent recurring panic at Poynton—it would offer them, as in one of their gimcrack baskets or other vessels of ugliness, a diurnal round of felicity that Poynton could never give. Owen might manage his estate just as he managed it now, and Mrs. Gereth would manage everything else. When in the hall, on the unforgettable day of his return, she had heard his voice ring out like a call to a terrier she had still, as Fleda afterwards learned, clutched frantically at the conceit that he had come, at the worst, to announce some compromise ; to tell her she would have to put up with the girl yes, but that some way would be arrived at of leaving her in personal possession. Fleda Vetch, whom from the earliest hour no illusion had brushed with its wing, now held her breath, went on tiptoe, wandered in outlying parts of the house and through delicate muffled rooms while the mother and son faced each other below. From time to time she stopped to listen ; but all was so quiet she was almost frightened : she had vaguely expected a sound of contention. It lasted longer than she would have supposed, whatever it was they were doing ; and when finally, from a window, she saw Owen stroll out of the house, stop and light a cigarette and then pensively lose himself in the plantations, she found other matter for trepidation in the fact that Mrs. Gereth didn't immediately come rushing up into her arms. She wondered if she oughtn't to go down to her, and measured the gravity of what had occurred by the circumstance, which she presently ascertained, that the poor lady had retired to her room and wished not to be disturbed. This admonition had been for her maid, with whom Fleda conferred as at the door of a death-chamber ; but the girl, without either fatuity or resentment, judged that, since it could render Mrs. Gereth indifferent even to the ministrations of disinterested attachment, the scene had been tremendous.

She was absent from luncheon, where indeed Fleda had enough to do to look Owen in the face : there would be so much to make that hateful in their common memory of the passage in which his last visit had terminated. This had been her apprehension at least ; but as soon as he stood there she was constrained to surprise at the practical simplicity of the ordeal—a simplicity that was altogether his own simplicity, the particular thing that, for Fleda Vetch, some other things of course aiding, made almost any direct relation with him pleasant. He had neither wit nor tact nor inspiration : all she could say was that in his presence, uncontrolled as it might be, the alienation these charms were usually depended on to allay didn't occur. On this occasion for instance he did so much better than " carry off " an awkward remembrance : he simply didn't have it. He had clean forgotten she was the girl his mother would have fobbed off on him ; he was conscious only of her being there as for decent service—conscious of the dumb instinct that from the first had made him regard her not as complicating his intercourse with that personage, but as simplifying it. Fleda found it beautiful

that this theory should have survived the incident of
the other day ; found it exquisite that whereas she
was aware, through faint reverberations, that for her
kind little circle at large, who didn't now at all matter,
her tendency had begun to define itself as parasitical,
this strong young man, who had a right to judge
and even a reason to loathe her, didn't judge and didn't
loathe, let her down gently, treated her as if she
pleased him—in fact evidently liked her to be just
where she was. She asked herself what he did when
Mona denounced her, and the only answer to the
question was that perhaps Mona didn't denounce
her. If Mona was inarticulate he wasn't such a fool
then to marry her. That he was glad Fleda was there
was at any rate sufficiently shown by the domestic
familiarity with which he said to her : " I must tell
you I've been having an awful row with my mother.
I'm engaged to be married to Miss Brigstock."

" Ah really ? " cried Fleda, achieving a radiance
of which she was secretly proud. " How very
exciting ! "

" Too exciting for poor Mummy.· She won't hear
of it. She has been slating her fearfully. She says
she's a regular barbarian."

" Why she's lovely ! " Fleda exclaimed.

" Oh she's all right. Mother must come round."

" Only give her time," said Fleda. She had
advanced to the threshold of the door thus thrown
open to her and, without exactly crossing it, she threw
in an appreciative glance. She asked Owen when his
marriage would take place, and in the light of his
reply read that Mrs. Gereth's wretched attitude
would have no influence at all on the event, absolutely
fixed when he had come down and distant by only
three months. He liked Fleda's seeming to be on
his side, though that was a secondary matter ; for
what actually most concerned him was the line his

mother took about Poynton, her declared unwillingness to give it up.

" Naturally I want my own house, you know," he
said, " and my father made every arrangement for
me to have it. But she may make it devilish
awkward. What in the world's a fellow to do ? "
This it was that Owen wanted to know, and there
could be no better proof of his friendliness than his
air of depending so utterly on Fleda Vetch to tell him.
She questioned him, they spent an hour together, and,
as he spoke of the force of the concussion from which
he had rebounded she found herself scared and depressed by the material he seemed to offer her to deal
with. It *was* devilish awkward, and it was so in part
because Owen had no imagination. It had lodged
itself in that empty chamber that his mother hated
the surrender because she hated Mona. He didn't
of course understand why she hated Mona, but this
belonged to an order of mysteries that never troubled
him : there were lots of things, especially in people's
minds, that a fellow didn't understand. Poor Owen
went through life with a frank dread of people's
minds : there were explanations he would have been
almost as shy of receiving as of giving. There was
therefore nothing that accounted for anything, though
on its own free lines it was vivid enough, his picture
to Fleda of his mother's all but express refusal to move.
That was what it came to ; for didn't she refuse to
move when she as good as declared that she would
move only with the furniture ? It was the furniture
he wouldn't give up ; and what was the good of
Poynton pray without the furniture ? Besides, the
furniture happened to be his, just as everything else
happened to be. The furniture—the word, on his
lips, had somehow to Fleda the sound of washing-
stands and copious bedding, and she could well
imagine the note it might have struck for Mrs. Gereth.

The girl herself, in this interview with him, spoke of the contents of the house only as " the works of art." It didn't, however, in the least matter to Owen what they were called ; what did matter, she easily guessed, was that it had been laid upon him by Mona, been made in effect a condition of her consent, that he should hold his mother to the strictest accountability for them. Mona had already entered upon the enjoyment of her rights. She had made him feel that Mrs. Gereth had been liberally provided for, and had asked him strikingly enough what room there would be at Ricks for the innumerable treasures of the big house. Ricks, the sweet little place offered to the mistress of Poynton as the refuge of her declining years, had been left to the late Mr. Gereth a considerable time before his death by an old maternal aunt, a good lady who had spent most of her life there. The house had in recent times been let, but it was amply furnished, it contained all the defunct aunt's possessions. Owen had lately inspected it, and he communicated to Fleda that he had quietly taken Mona to see it. It wasn't a place like Poynton—what dower-house ever was ?—but it was an awfully jolly little place, and Mona had taken a tremendous fancy to it. If there were a few things at Poynton that were Mrs. Gereth's peculiar property she must of course take them away with her ; but one of the matters that became clear to Fleda was that this transfer would be now wholly subject to Miss Brigstock's approval. The special business she herself thus became aware of being charged with was that of seeing Mrs. Gereth safely and singly off the premises.

Her heart failed her, after Owen had returned to London, with the ugliness of this duty—with the ugliness indeed of the whole close contest. She saw nothing of Mrs. Gereth that day ; she spent it in roaming with sick sighs, in feeling, as she passed from room to room, that what was expected of her companion was really dreadful. It would have been better never to have had such a place than to have had it and lose it. It was odious to *her* to have to look for solutions : what a strange relation between mother and son when there was no fundamental tenderness out of which a solution would irrepressibly spring ! Was it Owen who was mainly responsible for that poverty ? Fleda couldn't think so when she remembered that, so far as he was concerned, Mrs. Gereth would still have been welcome to keep her seat by the Poynton fire. The fact that from the moment one accepted his marrying one saw no very different course for him to take—this fact made her all the rest of that aching day find her best relief in the mercy of not having yet to face her hostess. She dodged and dreamed and fabled and trifled away the time. Instead of inventing a remedy or a compromise, instead of preparing a plan by which a scandal might be averted, she gave herself, in her sacred solitude, up to a mere fairy-tale, up to the very taste of the beautiful peace she would have scattered on the air if only something might have been that could never have been.

V

" I'll give up the house if they'll let me take what
I require ! "—that, on the morrow, was what Mrs.
Gereth's stifled night had qualified her to say with a
tragic face at breakfast. Fleda reflected that what
she " required " was simply every object that sur-
rounded them. The poor woman would have admitted this truth and accepted the conclusion to be
drawn from it, the reduction to the absurd of her
attitude, the exaltation of her claim. The girl's dread
of a scandal, of spectators and critics, grew less the
more she saw how little vulgar avidity had to do
with this rigour. It was not the crude love of possession ; it was the need to be faithful to a trust and
loyal to an idea. The idea was surely noble ; it was
that of the beauty Mrs. Gereth had so patiently and
consummately wrought. Pale but radiant, her back
to the wall, she planted herself there as a heroine
guarding a treasure. To give up the ship was to
flinch from her duty ; there was something in her
eyes that declared she would die at her post. If their
difference should become public the shame would
be all for the others. If Waterbath thought it could
afford to expose itself, then Waterbath was welcome
to the folly. Her fanaticism gave her a new distinction, and Fleda remarked almost with awe that she
had never carried herself so well. She trod the place
like a reigning queen or a proud usurper ; full as it

318

was of splendid pieces it could show in these days no ornament so effective as its menaced mistress.

Our young lady's spirit was strangely divided ; she had a tenderness for Owen which she deeply concealed, yet it left her occasion to marvel at the way a man was made who could care in any relation for a creature like Mona Brigstock when he had known in any relation a creature like Adela Gereth. With such a mother to give him the pitch how could he take it so low ? She wondered she didn't despise him for this, but there was something that kept her from it. If there had been nothing else it would have sufficed that she really found herself from this moment, between the pair, the sole messenger and mediator.

" He'll come back to assert himself," Mrs. Gereth had said ; and the following week Owen in fact reappeared. He might merely have written, Fleda could see, but he had come in person because it was at once " nicer " for his mother and stronger for his cause. He didn't like such a row, though Mona probably did ; if he hadn't a sense of beauty he had after all a sense of justice ; but it was inevitable he should clearly announce at Poynton the date at which he must look to find the house vacant. " You don't think I'm rough or hard, do you ? " he asked of Fleda, his impatience shining in his idle eyes as the dining-hour shines in club-windows. " The place at Ricks stands there with open arms. And then I give her lots of time. Tell her she can remove everything that belongs to her." Fleda recognised the elements of the sort of case the newspapers called a deadlock in the circumstance that nothing at Poynton belonged to Mrs. Gereth either more or less than anything else. She must either take everything or nothing, and the girl's suggestion was that it might perhaps be an inspiration to do the latter and begin again on a clean page. What, however, was the poor woman in that event to begin with ? What was she to do at all on her meagre income but make the best of the *objets d'art* of Ricks, the treasures collected by Mr. Gereth's maiden-aunt ? She had never been near the place : for long years it had been let to strangers, and after this the foreboding that it would be her doom had kept her from positively courting abasement. She had felt she should see it soon enough, but Fleda (who was careful not to betray to her that Mona had seen it and had been gratified) knew her reasons for believing that the maiden-aunt's principles had had much in common with the principles of Waterbath. In short the only thing she would ever have to do with the *objets d'art* of Ricks would be to turn them out into the road. What belonged to her at Poynton, as Owen said, would conveniently mitigate the void resulting from that demonstration.

The exchange of observations between the friends had grown very direct by the time Fleda asked Mrs. Gereth if she literally meant to shut herself up and stand a siege, or if it might be her idea to expose herself, more informally, to be dragged out of the house by constables. " Oh I prefer the constables and the dragging ! " the heroine of Poynton had readily answered. " I want to make Owen and Mona do everything that will be most publicly odious." She gave it out as her one thought now to force them to a line that would dishonour them and dishonour the tradition they embodied, though Fleda was privately sure she had visions of an alternative policy. The strange thing was that, proud and fastidious all her life, she now showed so little distaste for the world's hearing of the broil. What had taken place in her above all was that a long resentment had ripened. She hated the effacement to which English usage reduced the widowed mother ; she had discoursed of it passionately to Fleda ; contrasted it with the beautiful homage paid by other countries to women in that position, women no better than herself, whom she had seen acclaimed and enthroned, whom she had known and envied ; made in short as little as possible a secret of the injury, the bitterness she found in it. The great wrong Owen had done her was not his " taking up " with Mona—that was disgusting, but it was a detail, an accidental form ; it was his failure from the first to understand what it was to have a mother at all, to appreciate the beauty and sanctity of the character. She was just his mother as his nose was just his nose, and he had never had the least imagination or tenderness or gallantry about her. One's mother, gracious goodness, if one were the kind of fine young man one ought to be, the only kind Mrs. Gereth cared for, was a subject for poetry, for idolatry. Hadn't she often told Fleda of her friend Madame de Jaume, the wittiest of women, but a small black crooked person, each of whose three boys, when absent, wrote to her every day of their lives ? She had the house in Paris, she had the house in Poitou, she had more than in the lifetime of her husband—to whom, in spite of her appearance, she had afforded repeated cause for jealousy—because she was to have till the end of her days the supreme word about everything. It was easy to see how Mrs. Gereth would have given again and again her complexion, her figure, and even perhaps the spotless virtue she had still more successfully retained, to have been the consecrated Madame de Jaume. She wasn't, alas, and this was what she had at present a splendid occasion to protest against. She was of course fully aware of Owen's concession, his willingness to let her take away with her the few things she liked best ; but as yet she only declared that to meet him on this ground would be to give him a triumph, to put him impossibly in the right. " Liked best ? "

There wasn't a thing in the house she didn't like best, and what she liked better still was to be left where she was. How could Owen use such an expression without being conscious of his hypocrisy ? Mrs. Gereth, whose criticism was often gay, dilated with sardonic humour on the happy look a dozen objects from Poynton would wear, and the charming effect they would conduce to, when interspersed with the peculiar features of Ricks. What had her whole life been but an effort toward completeness and perfection ? Better Waterbath at once, in its cynical sameness, than the ignominy of such a mixture !

All this was of no great help to Fleda, in so far as Fleda tried to rise to her mission of finding a way out. When at the end of a fortnight Owen came down once more it was ostensibly to tackle a tenant on the property whose course with them had not been straight ; the girl was sure, however, that he had really come, on the instance of Mona, to see what his mother was up to. He wanted to convince himself that she was preparing her departure, and he desired to perform a duty, distinct but not less imperative, in regard to the question of the perquisites with which she would retreat. The tension between them was now such that he had thus to reconnoitre without meeting the enemy. Mrs. Gereth was as willing as himself that he should address to Fleda Vetch whatever cruel remarks he might have to make ; she only pitied her poor young friend for repeated encounters with a person as to whom she perfectly understood the girl's repulsion. Fleda found it of a fine dim inspiration on Owen's part not to have expected her to write to him : he wouldn't have wished any more than herself that she should have the air of spying on his mother in his interest. What made it of good effect to deal with him in this more familiar way was the sense that she understood so perfectly how poor Mrs. Gereth suffered and that she measured so adequately the sacrifice the other side did take rather monstrously for granted. She understood equally how Owen himself suffered, now that Mona had already begun to make him do things he didn't like. Vividly Fleda apprehended how *she* would have first made him like anything she would have made him do ; anything even as disagreeable as this appearing there to state, virtually on Mona's behalf, that of course there must be a definite limit to the number of articles appropriated. She took a longish stroll with him in order to talk the matter over ; to say if she didn't think a dozen pieces, chosen absolutely at will, would be a handsome allowance ; and above all to consider the very delicate question of whether the advantage enjoyed by Mrs. Gereth mightn't be left—well, to her honour. To leave it so was what Owen wished ; but there was plainly a young lady at Waterbath to whom, on his side, he already had to render an account. He was as touching in his off-hand annoyance as his mother was tragic in her intensity ; for if he couldn't help having a sense of propriety about the whole matter he could as little help hating it. It was for his hating it, Fleda reasoned, that she liked him so, and her insistence to his mother on the hatred perilously resembled on one or two occasions a revelation of the liking. There were moments when, in conscience, that revelation pressed her ; inasmuch as it was just on the ground of her not liking him that Mrs. Gereth trusted her so much. Mrs. Gereth herself didn't in these days like him at all, and she was of course always on Mrs. Gereth's side. He ended really, while the preparations for his marriage went on, by quite a little custom of coming and going ; but at no one of these junctures would his mother receive him. He talked only with Fleda and strolled with Fleda ;

and when he asked her, in regard to the great matter, if Mrs. Gereth were really doing nothing, the girl usually replied : " She pretends not to be, if I may say so ; but I think she's really thinking over what she'll take." When her friend at the great house asked her in turn what " those monsters " were doing she could have but one answer. " They're waiting, dear lady, to see what *you* do ! "

Mrs. Gereth, a month after she had received her great shock, did something abrupt and extraordinary : she caught up her companion and went over to have a look at Ricks. They had come to London first and taken a train from Liverpool Street, and the least of the sufferings they were armed against was that of passing the night. Fleda's admirable dressing-bag had been given her by her high benefactress. " Why it's charming ! " she exclaimed a few hours later, turning back again into the small prim parlour from a friendly advance to the single plate of the window. Mrs. Gereth hated such windows, the one flat glass sliding up and down, especially when they enjoyed a view of four iron pots on pedestals, painted white and containing ugly geraniums, ranged on the edge of a gravel path and doing their best to give it the air of a terrace. Fleda had instantly averted her eyes from these ornaments, but Mrs. Gereth grimly gazed, wondering of course how a place in the deepest depths of Essex and three miles from a small station could contrive to look so suburban. The room was practically a shallow box, with the junction of the walls and ceiling guiltless of curve or cornice and marked merely by the little band of crimson paper glued round the top of the other paper, a turbid grey sprigged with silver flowers. This decoration was rather new and quite fresh ; and there was in the centre of the ceiling a big square beam papered over in white, as to which Fleda hesitated about throwing out that it was rather picturesque. She recognised in time that this venture would be weak and that she should, all through, be able to say nothing either for the mantelpieces or for the doors, of which she saw her companion become sensible with a soundless moan. On the subject of doors especially Mrs. Gereth had the finest views : the thing in the world she most despised was the meanness of the undivided opening. From end to end of Poynton there swung high double leaves. At Ricks the entrances to the rooms were like the holes of rabbit-hutches.

It was all, none the less, not so bad as Fleda had feared ; it was faded and melancholy, whereas there had been a danger it would be contradictious and positive, cheerful and loud. The place was crowded with objects of which the aggregation somehow made a thinness and the futility a grace ; things that told her they had been gathered as slowly and as lovingly as the golden flowers of the other house. She too, for a home, could have lived with them : they made her fond of the old maiden-aunt ; they made her even wonder if it didn't work more for happiness not to have tasted, as she herself had done, of knowledge. Without resources, without a stick, as she said, of her own, Fleda was moved, after all, to some secret surprise at the pretensions of a shipwrecked woman who could hold such an asylum cheap. The more she looked about the surer she felt of the character of the maiden-aunt, the sense of whose dim presence urged her to pacification : the maiden-aunt had been a dear ; she should have adored the maiden-aunt. The poor lady had passed shyly, yet with some bruises, through life ; had been sensitive and ignorant and exquisite : that too was a sort of origin, a sort of atmosphere for relics and rarities, though different from the sorts most prized at Poynton. Mrs. Gereth had of course more than once said that one of the deepest mysteries of life was the way that—given certain natures—hideous objects could be loved. But it wasn't a question of love at present for these ; it was only a question of some practical patience. Perhaps a thought of that kind had stolen over her when, at the end of a brooding hour, she exclaimed, taking in the house with a strenuous sigh : " Well, something can be done with it ! " Fleda had repeated to her more than once the indulgent fancy about the maiden-aunt—she was so sure she had deeply suffered. " I'm sure I thoroughly hope she did ! " was, however, all the more austere of the pilgrims to Ricks had replied.

VI

It was a great relief to the girl at last to feel sure
that the dreadful move would really be made. What
might happen if it shouldn't had been from the first
indefinite. It was absurd to pretend that any violence was probable—a tussle, dishevelment, pushes,
scratches, shrieks ; yet Fleda had an imagination
of drama, of a " great scene," a thing, somehow, of
indignity and misery, of wounds inflicted and received, in which indeed, though Mrs. Gereth's presence, with movements and sounds, loomed large to
her, Owen remained indistinct and on the whole un-
aggressive. He wouldn't be there with a cigarette in
his teeth, very handsome and insolently quiet : that
was only the way he would be in a novel, across
whose interesting page some such figure, as she half-
closed her eyes, seemed to her to walk. Fleda har-
boured rather, and indeed with shame, the confused,
pitying vision of Mrs. Gereth with her great scene
left in a manner on her hands, Mrs. Gereth missing
her effect and having to appear merely hot and in-
jured and in the wrong. The symptoms that she
would be spared even that spectacle resided not so
much, through the chambers of Poynton, in an air of
concentration as in the hum of uneasy alternatives.
There was no common preparation, but one day, at
the turn of a corridor, she found her hostess standing
very still, with the hanging hands of despair and yet

with the active eyes of adventure. These eyes appeared to Fleda to meet her own with a strange dim bravado, and there was a silence almost awkward before either of the friends spoke. The girl afterwards thought of the moment as one in which her hostess mutely accused her of an accusation, meeting it at the same time, however, by a kind of defiant acceptance. Yet it was with mere melancholy candour that Mrs. Gereth at last sighingly exclaimed : " I'm thinking over what I had better take ! " Fleda could have embraced her for this virtual promise of a concession, the announcement that she had finally accepted the problem of knocking together a shelter with the small salvage of the wreck.

It was true that when after their return from Ricks they tried to lighten the ship the great embarrassment was still immutably there, the odiousness of sacrificing the exquisite things one wouldn't take to the exquisite things one would. This immediately made the things one wouldn't the very things one ought to, and, as Mrs. Gereth said, condemned one, in the whole business, to an eternal vicious circle. In such a circle, for days, she had been tormentedly moving, prowling up and down, comparing incomparables. It was for that one had to cling to them—for their faces of supplication. Fleda herself could judge of these faces, so conscious of their race and their danger, and she had little enough to say when her companion asked her if the place, all perversely fair on October afternoons, looked like a place to give up. It looked, to begin with, through some effect of season and light, larger than ever, immense, and it brimmed over as with the hush of sorrow, which was in turn all charged with memories. Everything was in the air—each history of each find, each circumstance of each capture. Mrs. Gereth had drawn back every curtain and removed every cover ; she prolonged the vistas, opened wide the whole house, gave it an appearance of awaiting a royal visit. The shimmer of wrought substances spent itself in the brightness ; the old golds and brasses, old ivories and bronzes, the fresh old tapestries and deep old damasks threw out a radiance in which the poor woman saw in solution all her old loves and patiences, all her old tricks and triumphs.

Fleda had a depressed sense of not, after all, helping her much : this was relieved indeed by the fact that Mrs. Gereth, letting her off easily, didn't now seem to expect it. Her sympathy, her interest, her feeling for everything for which her hostess felt, were a force that really worked to prolong the deadlock. " I only wish I bored you and my possessions bored you," that lady declared with some humour ; " then you'd make short work with me, bundle me off, tell me just to pile certain things into a cart and have done." Fleda's sharpest difficulty was in having to act up to the character of thinking Owen a brute, or in having at least to carry off the inconsistency of seeing him when he came down. By good fortune it was her indicated duty, her prescribed function, as well as a due protection to Mrs. Gereth. She thought of him perpetually and her eyes had come to rejoice in his manly magnificence more even than they rejoiced in the royal cabinets of the red saloon. She wondered, very faintly at first, why he came so often ; but of course she knew nothing of the business he had in hand, over which, with men red-faced and leather-legged, he was sometimes closeted for an hour in a room of his own that was the one monstrosity of Poynton : all tobacco-pots and bootjacks, his mother had said—such an array of arms of aggression and castigation that he himself had confessed to eighteen rifles and forty whips. He was arranging for settlements on his wife, he was doing things that would meet the views of the Brigstocks. Considering the house was his own Fleda thought it nice of him to keep himself in the background while his mother remained ; making his visits, at some cost of ingenuity about trains from town, only between meals, taking pains to let it press lightly on her that he was there. This was rather a check to her meeting Mrs. Gereth on the ground of his being a brute ; the most possible really at last was not to contradict her when she repeated that he was posted—just insultingly posted to watch. He *was* watching, no doubt ; but he watched somehow with his head turned away. He knew Fleda to know at present what he wanted of her, so that it would be gross of him to say it over and over. It existed as a confidence between them and made him sometimes, with his wandering stare, meet her eyes as if a silence so pleasant could only unite them the more. He had no great flow of speech, certainly, and at first the girl took for granted that this only exhausted any conceivable statement of the matter. Yet little by little she speculated as to whether, with a person who, like herself, could after all put him at some domestic ease, it was not supposable he would have more conversation if he were not keeping some of it back for Mona.

From the moment she suspected he might be thinking how Mona would judge his chattering so to an underhand " companion," an inmate all but paid in shillings, this young lady's repressed emotion began to require still more repression. She grew impatient of her posture at Poynton, privately pronouncing it false and horrid. She said to herself that she had let Owen know of her having, to the best of her power, directed his mother in the general sense he desired ; that he quite understood this and that he also understood how unworthy it was of either of them to stand over the good lady with a note-book and a lash. Wasn't this practical unanimity just practical success ? Fleda became aware of a sudden desire, as well as of pressing reasons, for the cessation of her long stay. She had not, on the one hand, like a minion of the law, undertaken to see Mrs. Gereth down to the train and locked, in sign of her abdication, into a compartment ; neither had she on the other committed herself to hold Owen indefinitely in dalliance while his mother gained time or worked with the spade at a counter-mine. Besides, people *were* saying that she fastened like a leech on other people — people who had houses where something was to be picked up : this disclosure was frankly made her by her sister, now distinctly doomed to the curate and in view of whose nuptials she had almost finished, as a present, a wonderful piece of embroidery suggested, and precisely at Poynton, by an old Spanish altar-cloth. She would have to exert herself still further for the intended recipient of this offering, turn her out for the altar and subsequent straits with more than that drapery. She would go up to town, in short, to dress Maggie ; and their father, in lodgings at West Kensington, would stretch a point and take them in. He, to do him justice, never reproached her with profitable devotions ; so far as they existed he rather studied to glean from the same supposed harvest. Mrs. Gereth gave her up as heroically as if she had been a great bargain, and Fleda knew she shouldn't herself miss any imminent visit of the young man's, since the young man was shooting at Waterbath. Owen shooting was Owen lost, and there was scant sport at Poynton.

The first news she had from Mrs. Gereth was news of that lady's having accomplished, in form at least, her dread migration. The letter was dated from Ricks, to which place she had been transported by an impulse apparently as sudden as the inspiration she had obeyed before. " Yes, I've literally come," she wrote, " with a band-box and a kitchen-maid ; I've crossed the Rubicon, I've taken possession. It has been like plumping into cold water. I saw the only thing was to do it, not to stand shivering. I shall have warmed the place a little by simply being here for a week ; when I come back the ice will have been broken. I didn't write to you to meet me on my way through town, because I know how busy you are and because, besides, I'm too savage and odious to be fit company even for you. You'd say I really go too far, and there's no doubt whatever I do. I'm here, at any rate, just to look round once more, to see certain things done before I enter in force. I shall probably be at Poynton all next week. There's more room than I quite measured the other day, and a rather good set of old Worcester. But what are space and time, what's even old Worcester, to your wretched and affectionate A. G. ? "

The day after Fleda received this letter she had occasion to enter a big shop in Oxford Street—a journey she achieved circuitously, first on foot and then by the aid of two omnibuses. The second of these vehicles put her down on the side of the street opposite her shop, and while, on the curbstone, she humbly waited, with a parcel, an umbrella and a tucked-up frock, to cross in security, she became aware that, close beside her, a hansom had pulled up short and in obedience to the brandished stick of a demonstrative occupant. This occupant was exactly Owen Gereth, who had caught sight of her as he rattled along and who, with an exhibition of white teeth that, from under the hood of the cab, had almost flashed through the fog, now alighted to ask her if he couldn't give her a lift. On learning her destination to be just over the way he dismissed his vehicle and joined her, not only piloting her to the shop but taking her in : with the assurance that his errands didn't matter and that it amused him to be concerned with hers. She told him she had come to buy a trimming for her sister's frock, and he expressed a joyous interest in the purchase. His joy, always hilarious, was apt to be out of proportion to the case, but it struck her at present as higher-pitched than ever ; especially when she had suggested he might find it a good time to buy a garnishment of some sort for Mona. After wondering an instant whether he read the full satiric meaning, such as it was, into this remark, Fleda dismissed the possibility as inconceivable. He stammered out that it was for *her* he should like to buy something, something " ripping," and that she must give him the pleasure of telling him what would best please her. He couldn't have a better opportunity for making her a present—the tribute of recognition of all she had done for Mummy that he had had in his head for weeks.

Fleda had more than one small errand in the big bazaar, and he went up and down with her, pointedly patient, pretending to be interested in questions of tape and of change. She had now not the least hesitation in wondering what Mona would think of such proceedings. But they were not her doing—they were Owen's ; and Owen, inconsequent and even extravagant, was unlike anything she had ever seen him before. He broke off, he came back, he repeated questions without heeding answers, he made vague and abrupt remarks about the resemblances of shop-girls and the uses of chiffon. He unduly prolonged their business together, giving Fleda a sense of his putting off something particular that he had to face. If she had ever dreamed of Owen Gereth as finely fluttered she would have seen him with some such manner as this. But why should he be finely fluttered ?

Even at the height of the crisis his mother hadn't made him flagrantly nervous, and at present he was satisfied about his mother. The one idea he stuck to was that Fleda should mention something she would let him give her : there was everything in the world in the wonderful place, and he made her incongruous offers—a travelling-rug, a massive clock, a table for breakfast in bed, and above all, in a resplendent binding, a set of somebody's "works." His notion was a testimonial, something of the sort usually done by subscription—and in this case indeed perhaps the Brigstocks would contribute ; so that the "works" in especial would be a graceful intimation that it was her cleverness he wished above all to commemorate. He was immensely in earnest, but the articles he pressed upon her betrayed a delicacy that went to her heart : what he would really have liked, as he saw them tumbled about, was one of the splendid stuffs for a gown—a choice proscribed by his fear of seeming to patronise her, to refer to her small means and her deficiencies. Fleda found it easy to chaff him about his exaggeration of her deserts ; she gave the just measure of them in consenting to accept a small pin-cushion, costing sixpence, in which the letter F was marked out with pins. A sense of loyalty to Mona was not needed to enforce this discretion, and she was careful not to renew her reference to their beautiful friend. She noticed on this occasion more things in Owen Gereth than she had ever noticed before, but what she noticed most was that he said no word of his intended. She asked herself what he had done, in so long a parenthesis, with his loyalty or at least with his "form" ; and then reflected that even had he done something very good the situation in which such a question could come up was already a little strange. Of course he wasn't thinking of anything so vulgar as to make love to her ; but there was a kind of punctilio for a man known to be engaged.

That punctilio didn't prevent Owen's remaining with her after they had left the shop, nor his hoping she had a lot more to do, nor yet his pressing her to look with him, for a possible glimpse of something she might really let him give her, into the windows of other establishments. There was a moment when, under this pressure, she made up her mind that his tribute would be, if analysed, a tribute to her insignificance. But all the same he wanted her to come somewhere and have luncheon with him : what was that a tribute to ? She must have counted very little if she didn't count too much for a romp in a restaurant. She had to get home with her trimming, and the most she was amenable to in his company was a retracing of her steps to the Marble Arch and then, after a discussion when they had reached it, a walk with him across the Park. She knew Mona would have considered she ought now to take the " penny bus " again ; but she had by this time to think for Owen as well as for herself—she couldn't think for Mona. Even in the Park the autumn air was thick, and as they moved westward over the grass, which was what Owen preferred, the cool greyness made their words soft, made them at last rare and everything else dim. He wanted to stay with her—he wanted not to leave her : he had dropped into complete silence, but that was what his silence said. What was it he had postponed ? What was it he wanted still to postpone ? She grew a little scared while they strolled together and while she thought. The indication, all indirect, was too vague to be flagrant, but it was as if somehow he were feeling differently. Fleda Vetch didn't suspect him at first of feeling differently to *her*, but only of feeling differently to Mona ; yet she was not unconscious that this latter difference would have had something to do with his being on the grass there beside her. She had read in novels about gentlemen who on the eve of marriage, winding up the past, had surrendered themselves for the occasion to the influence of a former tie ; and there was something in Owen's behaviour now, something in his very face, that suggested a resemblance to one of those gentlemen. But whom and what, in that case, would Fleda herself resemble ? She wasn't a former tie, she wasn't any tie at all ; she was only a deep little person for whom happiness was a kind of pearl-diving plunge. Happiness was down at the very bottom of all that had lately occurred ; for all that had lately occurred was that Owen Gereth had come and gone at Poynton. That was the small sum of her experience, and what it had made for her was her own affair, quite consistent with her not having dreamed it had made a relation—at least what *she* called one—for Owen. The old relation, at any rate, was with Mona—Mona whom he had known so very much longer.

They walked far, to the south-west corner of the great Gardens, where, by the old round pond and the old red palace, when she had put out her hand to him in farewell, declaring that from the gate she must positively take a conveyance, it seemed suddenly to rise between them that this was a real separation. She was on his mother's side, she belonged to his mother's life, and his mother, in the future, would never, never come to Poynton. After what had passed she wouldn't even be at his wedding, and it was not possible now that Mr. Gereth should mention that ceremony to the girl, much less express a wish that the girl should be present at it. Mona, from decorum and with reference less to the bridegroom than to the bridegroom's mother, would of course not invite any such creature as Miss Vetch. Everything therefore was ended ; they would go their different ways ; it was the last time they should stand face to face. They looked at each other with the fuller sense of it and, on Owen's part, with an expression of dumb trouble, the intensification of his frequent appeal to any interlocutor to add the right thing to what he said. It struck Fleda at this moment that the right thing might easily be the wrong. At any rate he only said : " I want you to understand, you know—I want you to understand."

What did he want her to understand ? He seemed unable to bring it out, and this understanding was moreover exactly what she wished not to arrive at. Bewildered as she was she had already taken in as much as she should know what to do with ; the blood also was rushing into her face. He liked her—it was stupefying—more than he really ought : that was what was the matter with him and what he desired her to swallow ; so that she was suddenly as frightened as some thoughtless girl who finds herself the object of an overture from a married man.

" Good-bye, Mr. Gereth—I *must* get on ! " she declared with a cheerfulness that she felt to be an unnatural grimace. She broke away from him sharply, smiling, backing across the grass and then turning altogether and moving as fast as she could. " Good-bye, good-bye ! " she threw off again as she went, wondering if he would overtake her before she reached the gate ; conscious with a red disgust that her movement was almost a run ; conscious too of the very confused handsome face with which he would look after her. She felt as if she had answered a kindness with a great flouncing snub, but in any case she had got away—though the distance to the gate, her ugly gallop down the Broad Walk, every graceless jerk of which hurt her, seemed endless. She signed from afar to a cab on the stand in the

Kensington Road and scrambled into it, glad of the encompassment of the four-wheeler that had officiously obeyed her summons and that, at the end of twenty yards, when she had violently pulled up a glass, permitted her to feel herself all wretchedly ready to burst into tears.

VII

As soon as her sister had been married she went down to Mrs. Gereth at Ricks—a promise to this effect having been promptly exacted and given ; and her inner vision was much more fixed on the alterations there, complete now as she understood, than on the success of her plotting and pinching for Maggie's happiness. Her imagination, in the interval, had indeed had plenty to do and numerous scenes to visit ; for when on the summons just mentioned it had taken a flight from West Kensington to Ricks, it had hung but an hour over the terrace of painted pots and then yielded to a current of the upper air that swept it straight off to Poynton and to Waterbath. Not a sound had reached her of any supreme clash, and Mrs. Gereth had communicated next to nothing ; giving out that, as was easily conceivable, she was too busy, too bitter and too tired for vain civilities. All she had written was that she had got the new place well in hand and that Fleda would be surprised at the way it was turning out. Everything was even yet upside down ; nevertheless, in the sense of having passed the threshold of Poynton for the last time, the amputation, as she called it, had been performed. Her leg had come off—she had now begun to stump along with the lovely wooden substitute ; she would stump for life, and what her young friend was to come and admire was the beauty of her movement and the noise she made about the house. The reserve of Poynton, as well as that of Waterbath, had been matched by the austerity of Fleda's own secret, under the discipline of which she had repeated to herself a hundred times a day that she rejoiced in cares so heavy as to exclude all thought of it. She had lavished herself, in act, on Maggie and the curate, and had opposed to her father's selfishness a heavenly patience. The young couple wondered why they had waited so long, since everything seemed after all so easy. She had thought of everything, even to how the " quietness " of the wedding should be relieved by champagne and her father—very firmly—kept brilliant on a single bottle. Fleda knew, in short, and liked the knowledge, that for several weeks she had appeared exemplary in every relation of life.

She had been perfectly prepared to be surprised at Ricks, for Mrs. Gereth was a wonder-working wizard, with a command, when all was said, of good material ; but the impression in wait for her on the threshold made her catch her breath and falter. Dusk had fallen when she arrived, and in the plain square hall, one of the few good features, the glow of a Venetian lamp just showed on either wall,. in perfect proportion, a small but splendid tapestry. This instant perception that the place had been dressed at the expense of Poynton was a shock : it was as if she had abruptly seen herself in the light of an accomplice. The next moment, folded in Mrs. Gereth's arms, her eyes were diverted ; but she had already had, in a flash the vision of great gaps in the other house. The two tapestries, not the biggest pieces but those most splendidly toned by time, had been on the whole its most uplifted pride. When she could really see again she was on a sofa in the drawing-room, staring with intensity at an object soon distinct as the great Italian cabinet that had been in the red saloon. All without looking she was sure the room was occupied by just such other objects, stuffed with as many as it could hold of the trophies of her friend's struggle. By this time the very fingers of her glove, resting on the seat of the sofa, had thrilled at the touch of an old velvet brocade, a wondrous texture she could recognise, would have recognised among a thousand, without dropping her eyes on it. They stuck to the cabinet with dissimulated dread while she painfully asked herself if she should notice it, notice everything, or just pretend not to be affected. How could she pretend not to be affected with the very pendants of the lustres tinkling at her and with Mrs. Gereth, beside her, staring at her even as she herself stared at the cabinet and hunching up the back of Atlas under his globe ? She was appalled at this image of what Mrs. Gereth had on her shoulders. That lady was waiting and watching her, bracing herself and preparing the same face of confession and defiance she had shown at Poynton the day she had been surprised in the corridor. It was farcical not to speak ; and yet to exclaim, to participate, would give one a bad sense of being mixed up with a theft. This ugly word sounded, for herself, in Fleda's silence, and the very violence of it jarred her into a scared glance, as of a creature detected, to right and left. But what again the full picture most showed her was the far-away empty sockets, a scandal of nakedness between high bleak walls. She at last uttered something formal and incoherent—she didn't know what : it had no relation to either house. Then she felt all her friend's weight, as it were, once more on her arm. " I've arranged a charming room for you—it's really lovely. You'll be very happy there." This was spoken with extraordinary sweetness and with a smile that meant : " Oh I know what you're thinking ; but what does it matter when you're so loyally on my side ? " It had come indeed to a question of " sides," Fleda thought, for the whole place was in battle array. In the soft lamplight, with one fine feature after another looming up into sombre richness, it defied her not to pronounce it a triumph of taste. Her passion for beauty leaped back into life ; and was not what now most appealed to it a certain gorgeous audacity ? Mrs. Gereth's high hand was, as mere great effect, the climax of the impression.

" It's too wonderful what you've done with the house ! "—the visitor met her friend's eyes. They lighted up with joy, that friend herself was so pleased with what she had done. This was not at all, in its accidental air of enthusiasm, what Fleda wanted to have said : it offered her as stupidly announcing from the first minute on whose side she was. Such was clearly the way Mrs. Gereth took it ; she threw herself upon the delightful girl and tenderly embraced her again ; so that Fleda soon went on with a studied difference and a cooler inspection. " Why you brought away absolutely everything ! "

" Oh no, not everything. I saw how little I could get into this scrap of a house. I only brought away what I required."

Fleda had got up ; she took a turn round the room. " You ' required ' the very best pieces—the *morceaux de musée*, the individual gems ! "

" I certainly didn't want the rubbish, if that's what you mean." Mrs. Gereth, on the sofa, followed the direction of her companion's eyes ; with the light of her satisfaction still in her face she slowly rubbed her large handsome hands. Wherever she was she was herself the great piece in the gallery. It was the first Fleda had heard of there being " rubbish " at Poynton, but she didn't for the moment take up this false plea ; she only, from where she stood in the room, called out, one after the other, as if she had had a list before her, the items that in the great house had been scattered and that now, if they had a fault, were too much like a minuet danced on a hearth-rug. She knew them each by every inch of their surface and every charm of their character—knew them by the personal name their distinctive sign or story had given them ; and a second time she felt how, against her intention, this uttered knowledge struck her hostess as so much free approval. Mrs. Gereth was never indifferent to approval, and there was nothing she could so love you for as for doing justice to her deep morality. There was a particular gleam in her eyes when Fleda exclaimed at last, dazzled by the display, " And even the Maltese cross ! " That description, though technically incorrect, had always been applied at Poynton to a small but marvellous crucifix of ivory, a masterpiece of delicacy, of expression and of the great Spanish period, the existence and precarious accessibility of which she had heard of at Malta, years before, by an odd and romantic chance —a clue followed through mazes of secrecy till the treasure was at last unearthed.

" ' Even ' the Maltese cross ? " Mrs. Gereth rose as she sharply echoed the words. " My dear child, you don't suppose I'd have sacrificed *that* ! For what in the world would you have taken me ? "

" A *bibelot* the more or less," Fleda said, " could have made little difference in this grand general view of you. I take you simply for the greatest of all conjurors. You've operated with a quickness—and with a quietness ! " Her voice just trembled as she spoke, for the plain meaning of her words was that what her friend had achieved belonged to the class of operations essentially involving the protection of darkness. Fleda felt she really could say nothing at

all if she couldn't say she took in the risks heroically run, all the danger surmounted. She completed her thought by a resolute and perfectly candid question. "How in the world did you get off with them ? "

Mrs. Gereth confessed to the fact of great evasions with a cynicism that surprised her. " By calculating, by choosing my time. I *was* quiet and I *was* quick. I manœuvred, prepared my ground ; then at the last I rushed !" Fleda drew a long breath : she saw in the poor woman something much better than sophistical ease, a crude elation that was a comparatively simple state to deal with. Her elation, it was true, was not so much from what she had done as from the way she had done it—by as brilliant a stroke as any commemorated in the annals of punished crime. " I succeeded because I had thought it all out and left nothing to chance. The whole business was organised in advance, so that the mere carrying it into effect took but a few hours. It was largely a matter of money : oh I was horribly extravagant—I had to turn on so many people. But they were all to be had—a little army of workers, the packers, the porters, the helpers of every sort, the men with the mighty vans. It was a question of arranging in Tottenham Court Road and of paying the price. I haven't paid it yet ; there'll be a horrid bill ; but at least the thing's done ! Expedition pure and simple was the essence of the bargain. ' I can give you two days,' I said ; ' I can't give you another second.' They undertook the job, and the two days saw them through. The people came down on a Tuesday morning ; they were off on the Thursday. I admit that some of them worked all Wednesday night. I had thought it all out ; I stood over them ; I showed them how. Yes, I coaxed them, I made love to them. Oh I was inspired—they found me wonderful. I neither ate nor slept, but I was as calm as I am now. I didn't know what was in me ; it was worth finding out. I'm very remarkable, my dear : I lifted tons with my own arms. I'm tired, very, very tired ; but there's neither a scratch nor a nick, there isn't a teacup missing." Magnificent both in her exhaustion and in her triumph she sank on the sofa again, the sweep of her eyes a rich synthesis and the restless friction of her hands a clear betrayal. "Upon my word," she laughed, "they really look better here ! "

Fleda had listened in awe. "And no one at Poynton said anything ? There was no alarm ? "

"What alarm should there have been ? Owen left me almost defiantly alone. I had taken a special time I had reason to believe safe from a descent." Fleda had another wonder, which she hesitated to express : it would scarcely do to ask if such a heroine hadn't stood in fear of her servants. She knew more-over some of the secrets of the heroine's humorous household rule, all made up of shocks to shyness and provocations to curiosity—a diplomacy so artful that several of the maids quite yearned to accom-pany her to Ricks. Mrs. Gereth, reading sharply the whole of her visitor's thought, caught it up with fine frankness. "You mean that I was watched—that he had his myrmidons, pledged to wire him if they should see what I was ' up to ' ? Precisely. I know the three persons you have in mind : I had them in mind myself. Well, I took a line with them—I settled them."

Fleda had had no one in particular in mind and had never believed in the myrmidons ; but the tone in which Mrs. Gereth spoke added to her suspense. "What did you do to them ? "

"I took hold of them hard—I put them in the forefront. I made them work."

" To move the furniture ? "

" To help, and to help so as to please me. That was the way to take them : it was what they had least expected. I marched up to them and looked each straight in the eye, giving him the chance to choose if he'd gratify me or gratify my son. He gratified *me*. They were too stupid ! "

She massed herself more and more as an immoral woman, but Fleda had to recognise that another person too would have been stupid and another person too would have gratified her. " And when did all this take place ? "

" Only last week ; it seems a hundred years. We've worked here as fast as we worked there, but I'm not settled yet : you'll see in the rest of the house. However, the worst's over."

" Do you really think so ? " Fleda presently inquired. " I mean does he after the fact, as it were, accept it ? "

" Owen—what I've done ? I haven't the least idea," said Mrs. Gereth.

" Does Mona ? "

" You mean that she'll be the soul of the row ? "

" I hardly see Mona as the ' soul ' of anything," the girl replied. " But have they made no sound ? Have you heard nothing at all ? "

" Not a whisper, not a step, in all the eight days. Perhaps they don't know. Perhaps they're crouching for a leap."

" But wouldn't they have gone down as soon as you left ? "

" They may not have known of my leaving." Fleda wondered afresh ; it struck her as scarcely supposable that some sign shouldn't have flashed from Poynton to London. If the storm was taking this term of silence to gather, even in Mona's breast, it would probably discharge itself in some thunderburst. The great hush of every one concerned was strange; but when she pressed Mrs. Gereth for the sense of it that lady only replied with her brave irony: " Oh I took their breath away ! " She had no illusions, however ; she was still prepared to fight. What indeed was her spoliation of Poynton but the first engagement of a campaign ?

All this was exciting, but Fleda's spirit dropped, at bedtime, in the quarter embellished for her particular pleasure, where she found several of the objects that in her earlier room she had most admired. These had been re-enforced by other pieces from other rooms, so that the quiet air of it was a harmony without a break, the finished picture of a maiden's bower. It was the sweetest Louis Seize, all assorted and combined—old, chastened, figured, faded France. Fleda was impressed anew with her friend's genius for composition. She could say to herself that no girl in England, that night, went to rest with so picked a guard ; but there was no joy for her in her privilege, no sleep even for the tired hours that made the place, in the embers of the fire and the winter dawn, look grey, somehow, and loveless. She couldn't care for such things when they came to her in such ways ; there was a wrong about them all that turned them to ugliness. In the watches of the night she saw Poynton dishonoured ; she had cherished it as a happy whole, she reasoned, and the parts of it now around her seemed to suffer like chopped limbs. To lie there in the stillness was partly to listen for some soft low plaint from them. Before going to bed she had walked about with Mrs. Gereth and seen at whose expense the whole house had been furnished. At poor Owen's from top to bottom—there wasn't a chair he hadn't sat upon. The maiden-aunt had been exterminated—no trace of her to tell her tale. Fleda tried to think of some of the things at Poynton still unappropriated, but her memory was a blank about them, and in the effort to focus the old combinations she saw again nothing but gaps and scars, a vacancy that gathered at moments into something worse. This concrete image was her greatest trouble, for it was Owen Gereth's face, his sad, strange eyes, fixed upon her now as they had never been. They stared at her out of the darkness and their expression was more than she could bear : it seemed to say that he was in pain and that it was somehow her fault. He had looked to her to help him, yet this was what her help had been. He had done her the honour to ask her to exert herself in his interest, confiding to her a task of difficulty but of the highest delicacy. Hadn't that been exactly the sort of service she longed to render him ? Well, her way of rendering it had been simply to betray him and hand him over to his enemy. Shame, pity, resentment oppressed her in turn ; in the last of these feelings the others were soon submerged. Mrs. Gereth had imprisoned her in that torment of taste, but it was clear to her for an hour at least that she might hate Mrs. Gereth.

Something else, however, when morning came, was even more intensely definite : the most odious thing in the world for her would be ever again to meet Owen. She took on the spot a resolve to neglect no precaution that could lead to her going through life without that calamity. After this, while she dressed, she took still another. Her position had become in a few hours intolerably false ; in as few more hours as possible she would therefore put an end to it. The way to put an end would be to let her friend know that, to her great regret, she couldn't be with her now, couldn't cleave to her to the point that everything about them so plainly urged. She dressed with a sort of violence, a symbol of the manner in which this purpose had been precipitated.

The more they parted company the less likely she was to come across Owen ; for Owen would be drawn closer to his mother now by the very necessity of bringing her down. Fleda, in the inconsequence of distress, wished to have nothing to do with her fall ; she had had too much to do with everything. She was well aware of the importance, before breakfast and in view of any light they might shed on the question of motive, of not suffering her invidious expression of a difference to be accompanied by the traces of tears ; but it none the less came to pass, down- stairs, that after she had subtly put her back to the window to make a mystery of the state of her eyes she stupidly let a rich sob escape her before she could properly meet the consequences of being asked if she wasn't delighted with her room. This accident struck her on the spot as so grave that she felt the only refuge to be instant hypocrisy, some graceful impulse that would charge her emotion to the quickened sense of her friend's generosity—a demon- stration entailing a flutter round the table and a renewed embrace, yet not so successfully improvised but that Fleda fancied Mrs. Gereth to have been only half-reassured. She had been startled at any rate and might remain suspicious : this reflexion inter- posed by the time, after breakfast, our young woman had recovered sufficiently to say what was in her heart. She accordingly didn't say it that morning at all. She had absurdly veered about ; she had encountered the shock of the fear that Mrs. Gereth, with sharpened eyes, might wonder why the deuce (she often wondered in that phrase) she had grown so warm about Owen's rights. She would doubtless at a pinch be able to defend them on abstract grounds, but that would involve a discussion, and the idea of a discussion made her nervous for her secret. Until in some way Poynton should return the blow and give her

a cue she must keep nervousness down ; and she
called herself a fool for having forgotten, however
briefly, that her one safety was in silence.

Directly after luncheon her friend took her into
the garden for a glimpse of the revolution—or at least,
said the mistress of Ricks, of the great row—that had
been decreed there ; but the ladies had scarcely
placed themselves for this view before the younger
one found herself embracing a prospect that opened
in quite another quarter. Her attention was called
to it, oddly, by the streamers of the parlour-maid's
cap, which, flying straight behind the neat young
woman who unexpectedly burst from the house and
showed a long red face as she ambled over the grass,
seemed to articulate in their flutter the name that
Fleda lived at present only to catch. "Poynton
—Poynton ! " said the morsels of muslin ; so that the
parlour-maid became on the instant an actress in
the drama, and Fleda, assuming pusillanimously that
she herself was only a spectator, looked across the
footlights at the exponent of the principal part. The
manner in which this artist returned the look showed
her as equally preoccupied. Both were haunted alike
by possibilities, but the apprehension of neither, before
the announcement was made, had taken the form
of the arrival at Ricks, in the flesh, of Mrs. Gereth's
victim. When the messenger informed them that
Mr. Gereth was in the drawing-room the blank
" Oh ! " emitted by Fleda was quite as precipitate
as the sound on her hostess's lips, besides being, as
she felt, much less pertinent. " I thought it would
be somebody," that lady afterwards said ; " but I
expected on the whole a solicitor's clerk." Fleda
didn't mention that she herself had expected on the
whole a brace of constables. She wondered at Mrs.
Gereth's question to the parlour-maid.

" For whom did he ask ? "

" Why for *you* of course, dearest friend ! " Fleda interjected, falling instinctively into the address that embodied the intensest pressure.   She wanted to put Mrs. Gereth between her and her danger.

" He asked for Miss Vetch, mum," the girl replied with a face that brought startlingly to Fleda's ear the muffled chorus of the kitchen.

" Quite proper," said Mrs. Gereth austerely.   Then to Fleda : " Please go to him."

" But what to do ? "

" What you always do — see what he wants." Mrs. Gereth dismissed the maid. " Tell him Miss Vetch will come."   Fleda saw that nothing was in the mother's imagination at this moment but the desire not to meet her son.   She had completely broken with him and there was little in what had just happened to repair the rupture.   It would now take more to do so than his presenting himself un-invited at her door.   " He's right in asking for you —he's aware that you're still our communicator ; nothing has occurred to alter that.   To what he wishes to transmit through you I'm ready, as I've been ready before, to listen.   As far as *I'm* concerned, if I couldn't meet him a month ago how am I to meet him to-day ?   If he has come to say ' My dear mother, you're here, in the hovel into which I've flung you, with consolations that give me pleasure,' I'll listen to him ; but on no other footing.   That's what you're to ascertain, please.   You'll oblige me as you've obliged me before.   There ! "   Mrs. Gereth turned her back and with a fine imitation of superiority began to redress the miseries immediately before her. Fleda meanwhile hesitated, lingered for some minutes where she had been left, feeling secretly that her fate still had her in hand.   It had put her face to face with Owen Gereth and evidently meant to keep her so. She was reminded afresh of two things : one of which was that, though she judged her friend's rigour, she had never really had the story of the scene enacted in the great awe-stricken house between the intimate adversaries weeks before—the day the elder took to her bed in her overthrow. The other was that at Ricks as at Poynton it was before all things her own place to accept thankfully a usefulness not, she must remember, universally acknowledged. What determined her at the last, while Mrs. Gereth disappeared in the shrubbery, was that, though at a distance from the house and with the drawing-room turned the other way, she could absolutely see the young man alone there with the sources of his pain. She saw his simple stare at his tapestries, heard his heavy tread on his carpets and the hard breath of his sense of unfairness. At this she went to him fast.

VIII

" I ASKED for you," he said when she stood there,
" because I heard from the flyman who drove me from
the station to the inn that he had brought you here
yesterday. We had some talk—he mentioned it."

" You didn't know I was here ? "

" No. I knew only you had had in London all
you told me that day to do ; and it was Mona's idea
that after your sister's marriage you were staying on
with your father. So I thought you were with him
still."

" I am," Fleda replied, idealising a little the fact.
" I'm here only for a moment. But do you mean,"
she went on, " that if you had known I was with your
mother you wouldn't have come down ? "

The way Owen hung fire at this question made it
sound more playful than she had intended. She had
in fact no consciousness of any intention but to confine
herself rigidly to her function. She could already
see that in whatever he had now braced himself for
she was an element he had not reckoned with. His
preparation had been of a different sort—the sort
congruous with his having been careful to go first
and lunch solidly at the inn. He had not been forced
to ask for her, but she became aware in his presence
of a particular desire to make him feel that no harm
could really come to him. She might upset him, as
people called it, but she should take no advantage of

having done so. She had never seen a person with whom she wished more to be light and easy, to be exceptionally human. The account he presently gave of the matter was that he indeed wouldn't have come if he had known she was on the spot ; because then, didn't she see ? he could have written to her. He would have had her there to let fly at his mother.

" That would have saved me—well, it would have saved me a lot. Of course I'd rather see you than her," he somewhat awkwardly added. " When the fellow spoke of you I assure you I quite jumped at you. In fact I've no real desire to see Mummy at all. If she thinks I *like* it——!" He sighed disgustedly. " I only came down because it seemed better than any other way. I didn't want her to be able to say I hadn't been all right. I daresay you know she has taken everything ; or if not quite everything at least a lot more than one ever dreamed. You can see for yourself—she has got half the place down. She has got them crammed—you can see for yourself ! " He had his old trick of artless repetition, his helpless iteration of the obvious ; but he was sensibly different for Fleda, if only by the difference of his clear face mottled over and almost disfigured by little points of pain. He might have been a fine young man with a bad toothache, with the first even of his life. What ailed him above all, she felt, was that trouble was new to him. He had never known a difficulty ; he had taken all his fences, his world wholly the world of the personally possible, rounded indeed by a grey suburb into which he had never had occasion to stray. In this vulgar and ill-lighted region he had evidently now lost himself. " We left it quite to her honour, you know," he said ruefully.

" Perhaps you've a right to say you left it a little to mine." Mixed up with the spoils there, rising before him as if she were in a manner their keeper, she felt she must absolutely dissociate herself. Mrs. Gereth had made it impossible to do anything but give her away. " I can only tell you that on my side I left it to her. I never dreamed either that she would pick out so many things."

" And you don't really think it's fair, do you ? You *don't* ! " He spoke very quickly ; he really seemed to plead.

Fleda just faltered. " I think she has gone too far." Then she added : " I shall immediately tell her I've said that to you."

He appeared puzzled by this statement, but he presently rejoined : " You haven't then said to her what you think ? "

" Not yet ; remember that I got here only last night." She struck herself as ignobly weak. " I had had no idea what she was doing. I was taken completely by surprise. She managed it wonderfully."

" It's the sharpest thing I ever saw in *my* life ! " They looked at each other with intelligence, in appreciation of the sharpness, and Owen quickly broke into a loud laugh. The laugh was in itself natural, but the occasion of it strange ; and stranger still to Fleda, so that she too almost laughed, the inconsequent charity with which he added : " Poor dear old Mummy ! That's one of the reasons I asked for you," he went on—" to see if you'd back her up."

Whatever he said or did she somehow liked him the better for it. " How can I back her up, Mr. Gereth, when I think, as I tell you, that she has made a great mistake ? "

" A great mistake ! That's all right." He spoke —it wasn't clear to her why—as if this attestation had been a great point gained.

" Of course there are many things she hasn't taken," Fleda continued.

" Oh yes, a lot of things. But you wouldn't know the place, all the same." He looked about the room with his discoloured, swindled face, which deepened Fleda's compassion for him, conjuring away any smile at so candid an image of the dupe. " You'd know this one soon enough, wouldn't you ? These are just the things she ought to have left. Is the whole house full of them ? "

" The whole house," said Fleda uncompromisingly. She thought of her lovely room.

" I never knew how much I cared for them. They're awfully valuable, aren't they ? " Owen's manner mystified her ; she was conscious of a return of the agitation he had produced in her on that last bewildering day, and she reminded herself that, now she was warned, it would be inexcusable of her to allow him to justify the fear that had dropped on her. " Mother thinks I never took any notice, but I assure you I was awfully proud of everything. Upon my honour I *was* proud, Miss Vetch."

There was an oddity in his helplessness ; he appeared to wish to persuade her and to satisfy himself that she sincerely felt how worthy he really was to treat what had happened as an injury. She could only exclaim almost as helplessly as himself : " Of course you did justice ! It's all most painful. I shall instantly let your mother know," she again declared, " the way I've spoken of her to you." She clung to that idea as to the sign of her straightness.

" You'll tell her what you think she ought to do ? " he asked with some eagerness.

" What she ought to do ? "

" *Don't* you think it—I mean that she ought to give them up ? "

" To give them up ? " Fleda cast about her again.

" To send them back—to keep it quiet." The girl had not felt the impulse to ask him to sit down among the monuments of his wrong, so that, nervously, awkwardly, he fidgeted over the room with his hands in his pockets and an effect of returning a little into possession through the formulation of his view. " To have them packed and despatched again, since she knows so well how. She does it beautifully "—he looked close at two or three precious pieces. " What's sauce for the goose is sauce for the gander ! "

He had laughed at his way of putting it, but Fleda remained grave. " Is that what you came to say to her ? "

" Not exactly those words. But I did come to say "—he stammered, then brought it out—" I did come to say we must have them right back."

" And did you think your mother would see you ? "

" I wasn't sure, but I thought it right to try—to put it to her kindly, don't you see ? If she won't see me then she has herself to thank. The only other way would have been to set the lawyers at her."

" I'm glad you didn't do that."

" I'm dashed if I want to ! " Owen honestly responded. " But what's a fellow to do if she won't meet a fellow ? "

" What do you call meeting a fellow ? " Fleda asked with a smile.

" Why letting *me* tell her a dozen things she can have."

This was a transaction that Fleda had after a moment to give up trying to represent to herself. " If she won't do that——? " she went on.

" I'll leave it all to my solicitor. *He* won't let her off, by Jove. I know the fellow ! "

" That's horrible ! " said Fleda, looking at him in woe.

" It's utterly beastly."

His want of logic as well as his vehemence startled her ; and with her eyes still on his she considered before asking him the question these things suggested. At the last she asked it. " Is Mona very angry ? "

" Oh dear yes ! " said Owen.

She had noted that he wouldn't speak of Mona without her beginning. After waiting fruitlessly now for him to say more she continued : " She has been there again ? She has seen the state of the house ? "

" Oh dear yes ! " he repeated.

Fleda disliked to appear not to take account of his brevity, but it was just because she was struck by it that she felt the pressure of the desire to know more. What it suggested was simply what her intelligence supplied, for he was incapable of any art of insinuation. Wasn't it at all events the rule of communication with him for her to say on his behalf what he couldn't say ? This truth was present to the girl as she inquired if Mona greatly resented what Mrs. Gereth had done. He satisfied her promptly ; he was standing before the fire, his back to it, his long legs apart, his hands, behind him, rather violently jiggling his gloves. " She hates it awfully. In fact she refuses to put up with it at all. Don't you see ? —she saw the place with all the things."

" So that of course she misses them."

" Misses them—rather ! She was awfully sweet on them." Fleda remembered how sweet Mona had been, and reflected that if that was the sort of plea he had prepared it was indeed as well he shouldn't see his mother. This was not all she wanted to know, but it came over her that it was all she needed. " You see it puts me in the position of not carrying out what I promised," Owen said. " As she says herself "—he hung fire an instant—" it's just as if I had obtained her under false pretences." Just before, when he spoke with more drollery than he knew, it had left Fleda serious ; but now his own clear gravity had the effect of exciting her mirth. She laughed out, and he looked surprised, but went on : " She regards it as a regular sell."

Fleda was silent ; yet finally, as he added nothing, she exclaimed : " Of course it makes a great differ-ence ! " She knew all she needed, but none the less she risked after another pause an interrogative remark. " I forgot when it is your marriage takes place ? "

He came away from the fire and, apparently at a loss where to turn, ended by directing himself to one of the windows. " It's a little uncertain. The date isn't quite fixed."

" Oh I thought I remembered that at Poynton you had told me a day and that it was near at hand."

" I daresay I did ; it was for the nineteenth. But we've altered that—she wants to shift it." He looked out of the window ; then he said : " In fact it won't come off till Mummy has come round."

" Come round ? "

" Put the place as it was." In his off-hand way he added : " You know what I mean ! "

He spoke not impatiently, but with a kind of intimate familiarity, the mildness of which made her feel a pang for having forced him to tell her what was embarrassing to him, what was even humiliating. Yes indeed, she knew all she needed : all she needed was that Mona had proved apt at putting down that wonderful patent-leather foot. Her type was mis-leading only to the superficial, and no one in the world was less superficial than Fleda. She had guessed the truth at Waterbath and had suffered from it at Poynton ; at Ricks the only thing she could do was to accept it with the dumb exaltation that she felt rising. Mona had been prompt with her exercise of the member in question, for it might be called prompt to do that sort of thing before marriage. That she had indeed been premature who might say

save those who should have read the matter in the
full light of results ? Neither at Waterbath nor at
Poynton had even Fleda's thoroughness discovered
all there was—or rather all there wasn't—in Owen
Gereth. " Of course it makes all the difference ! "
she said in answer to his last words. She pursued
the next moment : " What you wish me to say from
you then to your mother is that you demand immediate and practically complete restitution ? "

" Yes, please. It's tremendously good of you."

" Very well then. Will you wait ? "

" For Mummy's answer ? " Owen stared and
looked perplexed ; he was more and more fevered
with so much vivid expression of his case. " Don't
you think that if I'm here she may hate it worse—
suppose I may want to make her reply bang off ? "

Fleda weighed it. " You don't then ? "

" I want to take her in the right way, don't you
know ?—treat her as if I gave her more than just an
hour or two."

" I see," said Fleda. " Then if you don't wait—
good-bye."

This again seemed not what he wanted. " Must
you do it bang off ? "

" I'm only thinking she'll be impatient—I mean,
you know, to learn what will have passed between
us."

" I see," said Owen, looking at his gloves. " I
can give her a day or two, you know. Of course I
didn't come down to sleep," he went on. " The inn
seems a beastly hole. I know all about the trains—
having no idea you were here." Almost as soon as
his entertainer he was struck with the absence of the
visible, in this, as between effect and cause. " I
mean because in that case I should have felt I could
stop over. I should have felt I could talk with you
a blessed sight longer than with Mummy."

" We've already talked a long time," smiled Fleda.

" Awfully, haven't we ? " He spoke with the stupidity she didn't object to. Inarticulate as he was he had more to say ; he lingered perhaps because vaguely aware of the want of sincerity in her encouragement to him to go. " There's one thing, please," he mentioned, as if there might be a great many others too. " Please don't say anything about Mona."

She didn't understand. " About Mona ? "

" About it being *her* that thinks she has gone too far." This was still slightly obscure, but now Fleda understood. " It mustn't seem to come from *her* at all, don't you know ? That would only make Mummy worse."

Fleda knew exactly how much worse, but felt a delicacy about explicitly assenting : she was already immersed moreover in the deep consideration of what might make " Mummy " better. She couldn't see as yet at all, could only clutch at the hope of some inspiration after he should go. Oh there was a remedy, to be sure, but it was out of the question ; in spite of which, in the strong light of Owen's troubled presence, of his anxious face and restless step, it hung there before her for some minutes. She guessed that, remarkably, beneath the decent rigour of his errand, the poor young man, for reasons, for weariness, for disgust, would have been ready not to insist. His fitness to fight his mother had left him—he wasn't in fighting trim. He had no natural avidity and even no special wrath ; he had none that had not been taught him, and it was his doing his best to learn the lesson that had made him so sick. He had his delicacies, but he hid them away like presents before Christmas. He was hollow, perfunctory, pathetic ; he had been girded by another hand. That hand had naturally been Mona's, and it was heavy even now on his strong, broad back. Why then had he originally rejoiced so in its touch ? Fleda dashed aside this question, for it had nothing to do with her problem. Her problem was to help him to live as a gentleman and carry through what he had undertaken ; her problem was to reinstate him in his rights. It was quite irrelevant that Mona had no intelligence of what she had lost—quite irrelevant that she was moved not by the privation but by the insult. She had every reason to be moved, though she was so much more movable, in the vindictive way at any rate, than one might have supposed—assuredly more than Owen himself had imagined.

"Certainly I shall not mention Mona," Fleda said, " and there won't be the slightest necessity for it. The wrong's quite sufficiently yours, and the demand you make perfectly justified by it."

" I can't tell you what it is to me to feel you on my side ! " Owen exclaimed.

" Up to this time," said Fleda after a pause, " your mother has had no doubt of my being on hers."

" Then of course she won't like your changing."

" I daresay she won't like it at all."

" Do you mean to say you'll have a regular kick-up with her ? "

" I don't exactly know what you mean by a regular kick-up. We shall naturally have a great deal of discussion—if she consents to discuss at all. That's why you must decidedly give her two or three days."

" I see you think she *may* refuse to discuss at all," said Owen.

" I'm only trying to be prepared for the worst. You must remember that to have to withdraw from the ground she has taken, to make a public surrender of what she had publicly appropriated, will go uncommonly hard with her pride."

Owen considered ; his face seemed to broaden, but not into a smile. " I suppose she's tremendously proud, isn't she ? " This might have been the first time it had occurred to him.

" You know better than I," said Fleda, speaking with high extravagance.

" I don't know anything in the world half so well as you. If I were as clever as you I might hope to get round her." Owen waited for more thought ; then he went on : " In fact I don't quite see what even you can say or do that will really fetch her."

" Neither do I, as yet. I must think—I must pray ! " the girl pursued, smiling. " I can only say to you that I'll try. I *want* to try, you know—I want to help you." He stood looking at her so long on this that she added with much distinctness : " So you must leave me, please, quite alone with her. You must go straight back."

" Back to the inn ? "

" Oh no, back to town. I'll write to you to-morrow."

He turned about vaguely for his hat. " There's the chance of course that she may be afraid."

" Afraid you mean of the legal steps you may take ? "

" I've got a perfect case—I could have her up. The Brigstocks say it's simply stealing."

" I can easily fancy what the Brigstocks say ! " Fleda permitted herself to remark without solemnity.

" It's none of their business, is it ? " was Owen's unexpected rejoinder. Fleda had already noted that no one so slow could ever have had such quick transitions.

She showed her amusement. " They've a much better right to say it's none of mine."

" Well, at any rate, you don't call her names."

Fleda wondered if Mona did ; and this made it all the finer of her to exclaim in a moment : " You don't know what I shall call her if she holds out ! "

Owen gave her a gloomy glance ; then he blew a speck off the crown of his hat. " But if you do have a set-to with her ? "

He paused so long for a reply that Fleda said : " I don't think I know what you mean by a set-to."

" Well, if she calls *you* names."

" I don't think she'll do that."

" What I mean to say is if she's angry at your backing me up — what will you do then ? She can't possibly like it, you know."

" She may very well not like it ; but everything depends. I must see what I shall do. You mustn't worry about me."

She spoke with decision, but Owen seemed still unsatisfied. " You won't go away, I hope ? "

" Go away ? "

" If she does take it ill of you."

Fleda moved to the door and opened it. " I'm not prepared to say. You must have patience and see."

" Of course I must," said Owen—" of course, of course." But he took no more advantage of the open door than to say : " You want me to be off, and I'm off in a minute. Only before I go please answer me a question. If you *should* leave my mother where would you go ? "

She blinked a little at the immensity of it. " I haven't the least idea."

" I suppose you'd go back to London."

" I haven't the least idea," Fleda repeated.

" You don't — a — live anywhere in particular, do you ? " the young man went on. He looked conscious as soon as he had spoken ; she could see that he felt himself to have alluded more grossly than he meant to the circumstance of her having, if one were plain about it, no home of her own. He had meant it as an allusion of a highly considerate sort to all she would sacrifice in the case of a quarrel with his mother ; but there was indeed no graceful way of touching on that. One just couldn't be plain about it.

Fleda, wound up as she was, shrank from any treatment at all of the matter ; she simply neglected his question. " I *won't* leave your mother," she said instead. " I'll produce an effect on her. I'll convince her absolutely."

" I believe you will if you look at her like that ! "

She was wound up to such a height that there might well be a light in her pale, fine little face—a light that, while for all return at first she simply shone back at him, was intensely reflected in his own. " I'll make her see it, I'll make her see it ! "—she rang out like a silver bell. She had at that moment a perfect faith she should succeed ; but it passed into something else when, the next instant, she became aware that Owen, quickly getting between her and the door she had opened, was sharply closing it, as might be said, in her face. He had done this before she could stop him, and he stood there with his hand on the knob and smiled at her strangely. Clearer than he could have spoken it was the sense of those seconds of silence.

" When I got into this I didn't know you, and now that I know you how can I tell you the difference ? And *she's* so different, so ugly and vulgar, in the light of this squabble. No, like *you* I've never known one. It's another thing, it's a new thing altogether. Listen to me a little : can't something be done ? " It was what had been in the air in those moments at Kensington, and it only wanted words to be a committed act. The more reason, to the girl's excited mind, why it shouldn't have words ; her one thought was not to hear, to keep the act uncommitted. She would do this if she had to be horrid.

"Please let me out, Mr. Gereth," she said; on which he opened the door with a debate so very brief that in thinking of these things afterwards—for she was to think of them for ever—she wondered in what tone she must have spoken. They went into the hall, where she came upon the parlour-maid, of whom she asked if Mrs. Gereth had come in.

"No, miss; and I think she has left the garden. She has gone up the back road." In other words they had the whole place to themselves. It would have been a pleasure, in a different mood, to converse with that parlour-maid.

"Please open the house-door," said Fleda.

Owen, as if in quest of his umbrella, looked vaguely about the hall—looked even wistfully up the staircase—while the neat young woman complied with Fleda's request. Owen's eyes then wandered out of the framed aperture. "I think it's awfully nice here," he struck off. "I assure you I could do with it myself."

"I should think you might, with half your things here! It's Poynton itself—almost. Good-bye, Mr. Gereth," Fleda added. Her intention had naturally been that the neat young woman, releasing the guest, should remain to close the door on his departure. That functionary, however, had acutely vanished behind a swinging screen of green baize garnished with brass nails, a horror Mrs. Gereth had not yet had time to abolish. Fleda put out her hand, but Owen turned away—he couldn't find his umbrella. She passed into the open air—she was determined to get him out; and in a moment he joined her in the little plastered portico which had small resemblance to any feature of Poynton. It was, as Mrs. Gereth had said, the portico of a house in Brompton.

"Oh I don't mean with all the things here," he

explained in regard to the opinion he had just expressed. " I mean I could put up with it just as it was ; it had a lot of good things, don't you think ? I mean if everything was back at Poynton, if everything was all right." But the high flight of this idea showed somehow the broken wing. Fleda didn't understand his explanation unless it had reference to another and more wonderful exchange — the restoration to the great house not only of its tables and chairs but of its alienated mistress. This would imply the installation of his own life at Ricks, and obviously that of another person. Such another person could scarcely be Mona Brigstock. He put out his hand now ; and once more she heard his unsounded words. " With everything patched up at the other place I could live here with *you*. Don't you see what I mean ? "

She saw perfectly and, with a face in which she yet flattered herself that nothing of her vision appeared, simply gave him her hand. " Good-bye, good-bye."

He held her very firmly, keeping her even after the effort she made for release—an effort not repeated, as she felt it best not to show she was flurried. That solution—of her living with him at Ricks— disposed of him beautifully and disposed not less so of herself ; it disposed admirably too of Mrs. Gereth. Fleda could only vainly wonder how it provided for poor Mona. While he looked at her, grasping her still, she felt that now indeed she was paying for his mother's extravagance at Poynton—the vividness of that lady's public plea that little Fleda Vetch was the person to ensure the general peace. It was to this vividness poor Owen had come back, and if Mrs. Gereth had had more discretion little Fleda Vetch wouldn't have been in a predicament. She saw that Owen had now his sharpest necessity of speech, and so long as he didn't let go her hand she could only submit to him. Her defence would be perhaps to look blank and hard; so she looked as blank and as hard as she could, with the reward of an immediate sense that this was not a bit what he wanted. It even made him flounder as for sudden compunction, some recall to duty and to honour. Yet he none the less brought out: "There's one thing I daresay I ought to tell you, if you're going so kindly to act for me; though of course you'll see for yourself it's a thing it won't do to tell *her*." What was it? He made her wait again, and while she waited, under firm coercion, she had the extraordinary impression that his simplicity was in eclipse. His natural honesty was like the scent of a flower, and she felt at this moment as if her nose had been brushed by the bloom without the odour. The allusion was undoubtedly to his mother; and was not what he meant about the matter in question the opposite of what he said— that it just *would* do to tell her? It would have been the first time he had intended the opposite of what he said, and there was certainly an interest in the example as well as a challenge to suspense in the ambiguity. "It's just that I understand from Mona, you know," he stammered; "it's just that she has made no bones about bringing home to me——!" He tried to laugh and in the effort faltered again.

"About bringing home to you?"—Fleda encouraged him.

He was sensible of it, he surmounted his difficulty. "Why, that if I don't get the things back—every blessed one of them except a few *she*'ll pick out— she won't have anything more to say to me."

Fleda after an instant encouraged him again. "To say to you?"

"Why she simply won't have me, don't you see?"

Owen's legs, not to mention his voice, had wavered

while he spoke, and she felt his possession of her hand loosen so that she was free again. Her stare of perception broke into a lively laugh. " Oh you're all right, for you *will* get them. You will ; you're quite safe ; don't worry ! " She fell back into the house with her hand on the door. " Good-bye, good-bye." She repeated it several times, laughing bravely, quite waving him away and, as he didn'. move and save that he was on the other side of it, closing the door in his face quite as he had closed that of the drawing-room in hers. Never had a face, never at least had such a handsome one, been presented so straight to that offence. She even held the door a minute lest he should try to come in again. At last as she heard nothing she made a dash for the stairs and ran up.

IX

In knowing a while before all she needed she had been far from knowing as much as that ; so that once above, where, in her room, with her sense of danger and trouble, the age of Louis Seize suddenly struck her as wanting in taste and point, she felt she now for the first time knew her temptation. Owen had put it before her with an art beyond his own dream. Mona would cast him off if he didn't proceed to extremities — if his negotiation with his mother should fail he would be completely free. That negotiation depended on a young lady to whom he had pressingly suggested the condition of his freedom ; and as if to aggravate the young lady's predicament designing fate had sent Mrs. Gereth, as the parlour-maid said, " up the back road." This would give the young lady the more time to make up her mind that nothing should come of the negotiation. There would be different ways of putting the question to Mrs. Gereth, and Fleda might profitably devote the moments before her return to a selection of the way that would most surely be tantamount to failure. This selection indeed required no great adroitness ; it was so conspicuous that failure would be the reward of an effective introduction of Mona. If that ab-horred name should be properly invoked Mrs. Gereth would resist to the death, and before envenomed resistance Owen would certainly retire. His retirement would be into single life, and Fleda reflected that he had now gone away conscious of having practically told her so. She could only say as she waited for the back road to disgorge that she hoped it was a consciousness he enjoyed. There was something *she* enjoyed, but that was a very different matter. To know she had become to him an object of desire gave her wings that she felt herself flutter in the air : it was like the rush of a flood into her own accumulations. These stored depths had been fathomless and still, but now, for half an hour, in the empty house, they spread till they overflowed. He seemed to have made it right for her to confess to herself her secret. Strange then there should be for him in return nothing that such a confession could make right ! How could it make right his giving up Mona for another woman ? His position was a sorry appeal to Fleda to legitimate that. But he didn't believe it himself, he had none of the courage of his perversity. She could easily see how wrong everything must be when a man so made to be manly was wanting in courage. She had upset him, yes, and he had spoken out from the force of the jar of finding her there. He had upset her too, goodness knew, but she was one of those who could pick themselves up. She had the real advantage, she considered, of having kept him from seeing she had been overthrown.

She had moreover at present completely recovered her feet, though there was in the intensity of the effort required for this a vibration that throbbed away into an immense allowance for the young man. How could she after all know what, in the disturbance wrought by his mother, Mona's relations with him might have become ? If he had been able to keep his wits, such as they were, more about him he would probably have felt—as sharply as she felt on his behalf — that so long as those relations were not

371

ended he had no right to say even the little he had
said. He had no right to appear to wish to draw in
another girl to help him to run away. If he was in a
plight he must get out of the plight himself, he must
get out of it first, and anything he should have to say
to any one else must be deferred and detached. She
herself at any rate—it was her own case that emerged
—couldn't dream of assisting him save in the sense
of their common honour. She could never be the girl
to be drawn in ; she could never lift her finger against
Mona. There was something in her that would make
it a shame to her for ever to have owed her happiness
to an interference. It would seem intolerably vulgar
to her to have " ousted " the daughter of the Brigstocks ; and merely to have abstained even wouldn't
sufficiently assure her she had been straight. Nothing
was really straight but to justify her little pensioned
presence by her use ; and now, won over as she was
to heroism, she could see her use only as some high
and delicate deed. She couldn't in short do anything at all unless she could do it with a degree of
pride, and there would be nothing to be proud of in
having arranged for poor Owen to get off easily.
Nobody had a right to get off easily from pledges so
deep and sacred. How could Fleda doubt they had
been tremendous when she knew so well what any
pledge of her own would be ? If Mona was so formed
that she could hold such vows light this was Mona's
particular affair. To have loved Owen apparently,
and yet to have loved him only so much, only to the
extent of a few tables and chairs, was not a thing
she could so much as try to grasp. Of a different manner of loving she was herself ready to give an instance,
an instance of which the beauty indeed would not be
generally known. It would not perhaps if revealed
be generally understood, inasmuch as the effect of the
special pressure she proposed to exercise would be,

should success attend it, to keep him tied to an affection that had died a sudden and violent death. Even in the ardour of her meditation Fleda remained in sight of the truth that it would be an odd result of her magnanimity to prevent her friend's shaking off a woman he disliked. If he didn't dislike Mona what was the matter with him ? And if he did, Fleda asked, what was the matter with her own silly self ?

Our young lady met this branch of the temptation it pleased her frankly to recognise by declaring that to encourage any such cruelty would be tortuous and base. She had nothing to do with his dislikes ; she had only to do with his good nature and his good name. She had joy of him just as he was, but it was of these things she had the greatest. The worst aversion and the liveliest reaction wouldn't alter the fact —since one was facing facts—that but the other day his strong arms must have clasped a remarkably handsome girl as close as she had permitted. Fleda's emotion at this time was a wondrous mixture, in which Mona's permissions and Mona's beauty figured powerfully as aids to reflexion. She herself had no beauty, and *her* permissions were the stony stares she had just practised in the drawing-room—a consciousness of a kind appreciably to add to the strange sense of triumph that made her generous. We may not perhaps too much diminish the merit of that generosity if we mention that it could take the flight we are considering just because really, with the telescope of her long thought, Fleda saw what might bring her out of the wood. Mona herself would bring her out ; at the least Mona possibly might. Deep down plunged the idea that even should she achieve what she had promised Owen there was still the contingency of Mona's independent action. She might by that time, under stress of temper or of whatever it was that was now moving her, have said or done the things there is no patching up. If the rupture should come from Waterbath they might all be happy yet. This was a calculation that Fleda wouldn't have committed to paper, but it affected the total of her sentiments. She was meanwhile so remarkably constituted that while she refused to profit by Owen's mistake, even while she judged it and hastened to cover it up, she could drink a sweetness from it that consorted little with her wishing it mightn't have been made. There was no harm done, because he had instinctively known, poor dear, with whom to make it, and it was a compensation for seeing him worried that he hadn't made it with some horrid mean girl who would immediately have dished him by making a still bigger one. Their protected error (for she indulged a fancy that it was hers too) was like some dangerous, lovely, living thing that she had caught and could keep—keep vivid and helpless in' the cage of her own passion and look at and talk to all day long. She had got it well locked up there by the time that from an upper window she saw Mrs. Gereth again in the garden. At this she went down to meet her.

X

FLEDA's line had been taken, her word was quite
ready : on the terrace of the painted pots she broke
out before her benefactress could put a question.
" His errand was perfectly simple : he came to demand that you shall pack everything straight up
again and send it back as fast as the railway will
carry it."

The back road had apparently been fatiguing to
Mrs. Gereth ; she rose there rather white and wan
with her walk. A certain sharp thinness was in her
ejaculation of " Oh ! " — after which she glanced
about her for a place to sit down. The movement
was a criticism of the order of events that offered
such a piece of news to a lady coming in tired ; but
Fleda could see that in turning over the possibilities
this particular peril was the one that during the last
hour her friend had turned up oftenest. At the end
of the short grey day, which had been moist and mild,
the sun was out ; the terrace looked to the south, and
a bench, formed as to legs and arms of iron representing knotted boughs, stood against the warmest wall
of the house. The mistress of Ricks sank upon it and
presented to her companion the handsome face she
had composed to hear everything. Strangely enough
it was just this fine vessel of her attention that made
the girl most nervous about what she must drop in.
" Quite a ' demand,' dear, is it ? " asked Mrs. Gereth,
drawing in her cloak.

" Oh that's what I should call it ! "— Fleda laughed to her own surprise.

" I mean with the threat of enforcement and that sort of thing."

" Distinctly with the threat of enforcement — of what would be called, I suppose, coercion."

" What sort of coercion ? " said Mrs. Gereth.

" Why legal, don't you know ?— what he calls setting the lawyers at you."

" Is that what he calls it ? " She seemed to speak with disinterested curiosity.

" That's what he calls it," said Fleda.

Mrs. Gereth considered an instant. " Oh the lawyers ! " she exclaimed lightly. Seated there almost cosily in the reddening winter sunset, only with her shoulders raised a little and her mantle tightened as if from a slight chill, she had never yet looked to Fleda so much in possession nor so far from meeting unsuspectedness halfway. " Is he going to send them down here ? "

" I daresay he thinks it may come to that."

" The lawyers can scarcely do the packing," Mrs. Gereth playfully remarked.

" I suppose he means them—in the first place at least—to try to talk you over."

" In the first place, eh ? And what does he mean in the second ? "

Fleda debated ; she hadn't foreseen that so simple an inquiry could disconcert her. " I'm afraid I don't know."

" Didn't you ask ? " Mrs. Gereth spoke as if she might have said, " What then were you doing all the while ? "

" I didn't ask very much," said her companion. " He has been gone some time. The great thing seemed to be to understand clearly that he wouldn't be content with anything less than what he mentioned."

" My just giving everything back ? "

" Your just giving everything back."

" Well, darling, what did you tell him ? " Mrs. Gereth blandly proceeded.

Fleda faltered again, wincing at the term of endearment, at what the words took for granted, charged with the confidence she had now committed herself to betray. " I told him I'd tell you ! " She smiled, but felt her smile too poor a thing and even that Mrs. Gereth had begun to look at her with some fixedness.

" Did he seem very angry ? "

" He seemed very sad. He takes it very hard," Fleda added.

" And how does *she* take it ? "

" Ah that—that I felt a delicacy about asking."

" So you didn't get it out of him ? " The words had the note of surprise.

Fleda was embarrassed ; she had not made up her mind definitely to lie. " I didn't think you'd care." That small untruth she would risk.

" Well — I don't ! " Mrs. Gereth declared ; and Fleda felt less guilty to hear her, for the words were as far from the purpose as her own. " Didn't you say anything in return ? " the elder woman continued.

" Do you mean in the way of justifying you ? "

" I didn't mean to trouble you to do that. My justification," said Mrs. Gereth, sitting there warmly and, in the lucidity of her thought, which nevertheless hung back a little, dropping her eyes on the gravel —" my justification was all the past. My justification was the cruelty——" But at this, with a short sharp gesture, she checked herself. " It's too good of me to talk—now." She produced these sentences with a cold patience, as if addressing Fleda in the girl's virtual and actual character of Owen's representative.

Our young lady crept to and fro before the bench, combating the sense that it was occupied by a judge, looking at her boot-toes, reminding herself in doing so of Mona, and lightly crunching the pebbles as she walked. She moved about because she was afraid, putting off from moment to moment the exercise of the courage she had been sure she possessed. That courage would all come to her if she could only be equally sure that what she should be called upon to do for Owen would be to suffer. She had wondered, while Mrs. Gereth spoke, how that lady would describe her justification. She had described it as if to be irreproachably fair, give her adversary the benefit of every doubt and then dismiss the question for ever. " Of course," Mrs. Gereth went on, " if we didn't succeed in showing him at Poynton the ground we took it's simply that he shuts his eyes. What I supposed was that you would have given him your opinion that if I was the woman so signally to assert myself I'm also the woman to rest on it unshakably enough."

Fleda stopped in front of her hostess. " I gave him my opinion that you're very logical, very obstinate and very proud."

" Quite right, my dear : I'm a rank bigot—about that sort of thing ! " Mrs. Gereth jerked her head at the contents of the house. " I've never denied it. I'd kidnap — to save them, to convert them — the children of heretics. When I know I'm right I go to the stake. Oh he may burn me alive ! " she cried with a happy face. " Did he abuse me ? " she then demanded.

Fleda had remained there, gathering in her purpose. " How little you know him ! "

Mrs. Gereth stared, then broke into a laugh that her companion had not expected. " Ah my dear, certainly not so well as you ! " The girl, at this, turned away again—she felt she looked too conscious ; and she was aware that during a pause Mrs. Gereth's eyes watched her as she went. She faced about afresh to meet them, but what she met was a question that re-enforced them. " Why had you a ' delicacy ' as to speaking of Mona ? "

She stopped again before the bench, and an inspiration came to her. " I should think *you* would know," she said with proper dignity.

Blankness was for a moment on Mrs. Gereth's brow ; then light broke — she visibly remembered the scene in the breakfast-room after Mona's night at Poynton. " Because I contrasted you—told him *you* were the one ? " Her eyes looked deep. " You were—you are still ! "

Fleda gave a bold dramatic laugh. " Thank you, my love—with all the best things at Ricks ! "

Mrs. Gereth considered, trying to penetrate, as it seemed ; but at last she brought out roundly : " For you, you know, I'd send them back ! "

The girl's heart gave a tremendous bound ; the right way dawned upon her in a flash. Obscurity indeed the next moment engulfed this course, but for a few thrilled seconds she had understood. To send the things back " for her " meant of course to send them back if there were even a dim chance that she might become mistress of them. Fleda's palpitation was not allayed as she asked herself what portent Mrs. Gereth had suddenly descried of such a chance : the light could be there but by a sudden suspicion of her secret. This suspicion in turn was a tolerably straight consequence of that implied view of the propriety of surrender from which she was well aware she could say nothing to dissociate herself. What she first felt was that if she wished to rescue the spoils she wished also to rescue her secret. So she looked as innocent as she could and said as quickly as she might : " For me ?   Why in the world for me ? "

" Because you're so awfully keen."

" Am I ?   Do I strike you so ?   You know I hate him," Fleda went on.

She had the sense for a while of Mrs. Gereth's regarding her with the detachment of some stern clever stranger.   " Then what's the matter with you ? Why do you want me to give in ? "

Fleda hesitated ; she felt herself reddening.   " I've only said your son wants it.   I haven't said *I* do."

" Then say it and have done with it ! "

This was more peremptory than any word her friend, though often speaking in her presence with much point, had ever yet deliberately addressed her. It affected her like the crack of a whip, but she confined herself with an effort to taking it as a reminder that she must keep her head.   " I know he has his engagement to carry out."

" His engagement to marry ?   Why, it's just that engagement we loathe ! "

" Why should *I* loathe it ? " Fleda asked with a strained smile.   Then before Mrs. Gereth could reply she pursued : " I'm thinking of his general under-taking — to give her the house as she originally saw it."

" To give her the house ! "—Mrs. Gereth brought up the words from the depth of the unspeakable. The effect was like the moan of an autumn wind, and she turned as pale as if she had heard of the landing, there on her coast, of a foreign army.

" I'm thinking," Fleda continued, " of the simple question of his keeping faith on an important clause of his contract : it doesn't matter whether with a stupid person or with a monster of cleverness. I'm thinking of his honour and his good name."

" The honour and good name of a man you hate ? "

" Certainly," the girl resolutely answered. " I don't see why you should talk as if one had a petty mind. You don't think so. It's not on that assumption you've ever dealt with me. I can do your son justice—as he put his case to me."

" Ah then he did put his case to you ! " Mrs. Gereth cried with an accent of triumph. " You seemed to speak just now as if really nothing of any consequence had passed between you."

" Something always passes when one has a little imagination," our young lady declared.

" I take it you don't mean that Owen has any ! " Mrs. Gereth answered with her large laugh.

Fleda had a pause. " No, I don't mean that Owen has any," she returned at last.

" Why is it you hate him so ? " her hostess abruptly put to her.

" Should I love him for all he has made you suffer ? "

Mrs. Gereth slowly rose at this and, coming over the walk, took her young friend to her breast and kissed her. She then passed into one of Fleda's an arm perversely and imperiously sociable. " Let us move a little," she said, holding her close and giving a slight shiver. They strolled along the terrace and she brought out another question. " He *was* eloquent then, poor dear—he poured forth the story of his wrongs ? "

Fleda smiled down at her companion, who, cloaked and perceptibly bowed, leaned on her heavily and gave her an odd unwonted sense of age and cunning. She took refuge in an evasion. " He couldn't tell me anything I didn't know pretty well already."

" It's very true you know everything. No, dear, you haven't a petty mind ; you've a lovely imagination and you're the nicest creature in the world. If you were inane, like most girls—like every one in fact—I'd have insulted you, I'd have outraged you, and then you'd have fled from me in terror. No, now that I think of it," Mrs. Gereth went on, " you wouldn't have fled from me : nothing, on the contrary, would have made you budge. You'd have cuddled into your warm corner, but you'd have been wounded and weeping and martyrised, and have taken every opportunity to tell people I'm a brute—as indeed I should have been ! " They went to and fro, and she wouldn't allow Fleda, who laughed and protested, to attenuate with any light civility this spirited picture. She praised her cleverness and her patience ; then she said it was getting cold and dark and they must go in to tea. She delayed quitting the place, however, and reverted instead to Owen's ultimatum, about which she asked another question or two ; in particular whether it had struck Fleda that he really believed she'd give way.

" I think he really believes that if I try hard enough I can make you." After uttering which words our young woman stopped short and emulated the embrace she had received a few moments before.

" And you've promised to try : I see. You didn't tell me that either," Mrs. Gereth added as they moved. " But you're rascal enough for anything ! " While Fleda was occupied in thinking in what terms she could explain why she had indeed been rascal enough for the reticence thus denounced, her companion broke out with a question somewhat irrelevant and even in form somewhat profane. " Why the devil, at any rate, doesn't it come off ? "

Fleda hesitated. " You mean their marriage ? "

" Of course I mean their marriage ! "

She thought again. " I haven't the least idea."

" You didn't ask him ? "

" Oh how in the world can you fancy ? " She spoke in a shocked tone.

" Fancy your putting a question so indelicate ?
I should have put it—I mean in your place ; but
I'm quite coarse, thank God ! " Fleda felt privately
that she herself was coarse, or at any rate would
presently have to be ; and Mrs. Gereth, with a purpose
that struck her as increasing, continued : " What
then *was* the day to be ? Wasn't it just one of
these ? "

" I'm sure I don't remember."

It was part of the great rupture and an effect of
Mrs. Gereth's character that up to this moment she
had been completely and haughtily indifferent to
that detail. Now, however, she had a visible reason
for being sure. She bethought herself and she broke
out : " Isn't the day past ? " Then stopping short
she added : " Upon my word they must have put it
off ! " As Fleda made no answer to this she became
insistent. " *Have* they put it off ? "

" I haven't the least idea," said the girl.

Her hostess was again looking at her hard.
" Didn't he tell you—didn't he say anything about
it ? "

Fleda meanwhile had hád time to make her
reflexions, which were moreover the continued throb
of those that had occupied the interval between
Owen's departure and his mother's return. If she
should now repeat his words this wouldn't at all play
the game of her definite vow ; it would only play the
game of her little gagged and blinded desire. She
could calculate well enough the result of telling Mrs.
Gereth, how she had had it from Owen's troubled lips
that Mona was only waiting for the restitution and
would do nothing without it. The thing was to obtain
the restitution without imparting that knowledge.
The only way also not to impart it was not to tell any
truth at all about it ; and the only way to meet this
last condition was to reply to her companion as she

presently did. " He told me nothing whatever. He didn't touch on the subject."

" Not in any way ? "

" Not in any way."

Mrs. Gereth watched her and considered. " You haven't the notion they're waiting for the things ? "

" How should I have ? I'm not in their counsels."

" I dare say they are—or that Mona is." Mrs. Gereth weighed it again ; she had a bright idea. " If I don't give in I'll be hanged if she'll not break off."

" She'll never, never break off," said Fleda.

" Are you sure ? "

" I can't be sure, but it's my belief."

" Derived from *him* ? "

The girl hung fire a few seconds. " Derived from him."

Mrs. Gereth gave her a long last look, then turned abruptly away. " It's an awful bore you didn't really get it out of him ! Well, come to tea," she added rather dryly, passing straight into the house.

XI

THE sense of her dryness, which was ominous of a
complication, made Fleda, before complying, linger
a little on the terrace : she felt the need moreover of
taking breath after such a flight into the cold air of
denial. When at last she rejoined Mrs. Gereth she
found her erect before the drawing-room fire. Their
tea had been set out in the same quarter, and the
mistress of the house, for whom the preparation of it
was generally a high and undelegated function, pre-
served a posture to which the hissing urn made no
appeal. This omission was such a further sign of
something to come that to disguise her apprehension
Fleda straightway and without apology took the duty
in hand ; only however to be promptly reminded that
she was performing it confusedly and not counting
the journeys of the little silver shovel she emptied
into the pot. "Not *five*, my dear—the usual three,"
said her hostess with the same irony ; watching her
then in silence while she clumsily corrected her mistake. The tea took some minutes to draw, and Mrs.
Gereth availed herself of them suddenly to exclaim :
" You haven't yet told me, you know, how it is you
propose to ' make ' me ! "

" Give everything back ? " Fleda looked into the
pot again and uttered her question with a briskness
that she felt to be a trifle overdone. " Why, by
putting the question well before you ; by being so

385

eloquent that I shall persuade you, shall act on you ;
by making you sorry for having gone so far," she said
boldly. " By simply and earnestly asking it of you,
in short ; and by reminding you at the same time that
it's the first thing I ever have so asked. Oh you've
done things for me—endless and beautiful things," she
exclaimed ; " but you've done them all from your own
generous impulse—I've never so much as hinted to
you to lend me a postage-stamp."

" Give me a cup of tea," said Mrs. Gereth. A
moment later, taking the cup, she replied : " No,
you've never asked me for a postage-stamp."

" That gives me a pull ! " Fleda returned with
briskness.

" Puts you in the situation of expecting I shall do
this thing just simply to oblige you ? "

Well, the girl took it so. " You said a while ago
that for me you *would* do it."

" For you, but not for your eloquence. Do you
understand what I mean by the difference ? " Mrs.
Gereth asked as she stood stirring her tea.

Fleda, to postpone answering, looked round, while
she drank it, at the beautiful room. " I don't in the
least like, you know, your having brought away so
much. It was a great shock to me, on my arrival
here, to find how you had plunged."

" Give me some more tea," said Mrs. Gereth ; and
there was a moment's silence as Fleda poured out
another cup. " If you were shocked, my dear, I'm
bound to say you concealed your shock."

" I know I did. I was afraid to show it."

Mrs. Gereth drank off her second cup. " And
you're not afraid now ? "

" No, I'm not afraid now."

" What has made the difference ? "

" I've pulled myself together." Fleda paused ;
then she added : " And I've seen Mr. Owen."

" You've seen Mr. Owen "— Mrs. Gereth concurred. She put down her cup and sank into a chair
in which she leaned back, resting her head and
gazing at her young friend. " Yes, I did tell you a
while ago that for you I'd do it. But you haven't
told me yet what you'll do in return."

Fleda cast about. " Anything in the wide world
you may require."

" Oh ' anything ' is nothing at all ! That's too
easily said." Mrs. Gereth, reclining more completely,
closed her eyes with an air of disgust, an air indeed
of yielding to drowsiness.

Fleda looked at her quiet face, which the appearance of oblivious sleep always made particularly
handsome ; she noted how much the ordeal of the
last few weeks had added to its indications of age.
" Well then, try me with something. What is it you
demand ? "

At this, opening her eyes, Mrs. Gereth sprang
straight up. " Get him away from her ! "

Fleda marvelled : her companion had in an instant
become young again. " Away from Mona ? How in
the world—— ? "

" By not looking like a fool ! " cried Mrs. Gereth
very sharply. She kissed her, however, on the spot,
to make up for this roughness, and with an officious
hand took off the hat which, on coming into the
house, our young lady had not removed. She applied a friendly touch to the girl's hair and gave a
business-like pull to her jacket. " I say don't look
like an idiot, because you happen not to be one—
not the least bit. *I'm* idiotic ; I've been so, I've
just discovered, ever since our first days together.
I've been a precious donkey. But that's another
affair."

Fleda, as if she humbly assented, went through
no form of controverting this ; she simply stood

passive to her friend's sudden invocation of her personal charms. " How can I get him away from her ? " she presently demanded.

" By letting yourself go."

" By letting myself go ? " She spoke mechanically, still more like an idiot, and felt as if her face flamed out the insincerity of her question. It was vividly back again, the vision of the real way to act on Mrs. Gereth. This lady's movements were now rapid ; she turned off from her as quickly as she had seized her, and Fleda sat down to steady herself for full responsibility.

Her hostess, without taking up her appeal, gave a violent poke at the fire and again dealt with her. " You've done two things then to-day — haven't you ? — that you've never done before. One has been asking me the service or favour or concession —whatever you call it—that you just mentioned ; the other has been telling me (certainly too for the first time !) an immense little fib."

" An immense little fib ? " Fleda felt weak ; she was glad of the support of her seat.

" An immense big one then ! " Mrs. Gereth said sharply. " You don't in the least ' hate ' Owen, my darling. You care for him very much. In fact, my own, you're in love with him—there ! Don't tell me any more lies ! " she cried with a voice and a face under which Fleda recognised that there was nothing but to hold one's self and bear up. When once the truth was out it was out, and she could see more and more every instant that it offered the only way. She accepted therefore what had to come ; she leaned back her head and closed her eyes as her companion had done just before. She would have covered her face with her hands but for the still greater shame. " Oh you're a wonder, a wonder," said Mrs. Gereth ; " you're magnificent, and I was right, as soon as I saw you, to pick you out and trust you!" Fleda closed her eyes tighter at this last word, but her friend kept it up. "I never dreamed of it till a while ago—when, after he had come and gone, we were face to face. Then something stuck out of you; it strongly impressed me, and I didn't know at first quite what to make of it. It was that you had just been with him and that you were not natural. Not natural to *me*," she added with a smile. "I sat forward, I promise you, and all that this might mean was to dawn upon me when you said you had asked nothing about Mona. It put me on the scent, but I didn't show you, did I? I felt it was *in* you, deep down, and that I must draw it out. Well, I *have* drawn it, and it's a blessing. Yesterday, when you shed tears at breakfast, I was awfully puzzled. What has been the matter with you all the while? Why Fleda, it isn't a crime, don't you know that?" cried the delighted amazing woman. "When I was a girl I was always in love, and not always with such nice people as Owen. I didn't behave so well as you; compared with you I think I must have been odious. But if you're proud and reserved it's your own affair; I'm proud too, though I'm not reserved — that's what spoils it. I'm stupid above all—that's what I am; so dense I really blush for it. However, no one but you could have deceived me. If I trusted you moreover it was exactly to be cleverer than myself. You must be so now more than ever.!" Suddenly Fleda felt her hands grasped: Mrs. Gereth had plumped down at her feet and was leaning on her knees. "Save him—save him: you *can*!" she passionately pleaded. "How could you not like him when he's such a dear? He *is* a dear, darling; there's no harm in my own boy! You can do what you will with him —you know you can! What else does he give us all this time for? Get him away from her: it's as if he

389

entreated you, poor wretch ! Don't abandon him to such a fate, and I'll never abandon *you*. Think of him with that creature, that family, that future ! If you'll take him I'll give up everything. There, it's a solemn promise, the most sacred of my life. Get the better of her and he shall have every stick I grabbed. Give me your word and I'll accept it. I'll write for the packers to-night ! "

Fleda, before this, had fallen forward on her companion's neck, and the two women, clinging together, had got up while the younger wailed on the other's bosom. " You smooth it down because you see more in it than there can ever be ; but after my hideous double game how will you be able to believe in me again ? "

" I see in it simply what *must* be, if you've a single spark of pity. Where on earth was the double game when you've behaved like such a saint ? You've been beautiful, you've been exquisite, and all our trouble's over."

Fleda, drying her eyes, shook her head ever so sadly. " No, Mrs. Gereth, it isn't over. I can't do what you ask—I can't meet your condition."

Mrs. Gereth stared ; the cloud again darkened her face. " Why, in the name of goodness, when you adore him ? I know what you see in him," she declared in another tone. " You're quite right ! "

Fleda gave a faint stubborn smile. " He cares for her too much."

" Then why doesn't he marry her ? He's giving you an extraordinary chance."

" He doesn't dream I've ever thought of him," said Fleda. " Why should he if you didn't ? "

" It wasn't with me you were in love, my duck." Then Mrs. Gereth added : " I'll go and tell him."

" If you do any such thing you shall never see me again—absolutely, literally never ! "

Mrs. Gereth looked hard at her young friend, betraying how she saw she must believe her. " Then you're perverse, you're wicked. Will you swear he doesn't know ? "

" Of course he doesn't know ! " cried Fleda indignantly.

Her benefactress was silent a little. " And that he has no feeling on *his* side ? "

" For me ? " Fleda stared. " Before he has even married her ? "

Mrs. Gereth gave a sharp laugh at this. " He ought at least to appreciate your wit. Oh my dear, you *are* a treasure ! Doesn't he appreciate anything ? Has he given you absolutely no symptom—not looked a look, not breathed a sigh ? "

" The case," said Fleda coldly, " is as I've had the honour to state it."

" Then he's as big a donkey as his mother ! But you know you've got to account for their delay," Mrs. Gereth remarked.

" Why have I got to ? " Fleda asked after a moment.

" Because you were closeted with him here so long. You can't pretend at present, you know, not to have any art."

The girl debated ; she was conscious that she must choose between two risks. She had had a secret and the secret was spoiled. Owen had one, ripe but from yesterday, still unbruised, and the greater risk now was that his mother should lay her formidable hand upon it. All Fleda's tenderness for him moved her to protect it ; so she faced the smaller peril. " Their delay," she brought herself to reply, " may perhaps be Mona's doing. I mean because he has lost her the things."

Mrs. Gereth jumped at this. " So that she'll break altogether if I keep them ? "

Fleda winced. " I've told you what I believe about

391

that. She'll make scenes and conditions ; she'll worry him. But she'll hold him fast ; she'll never let him go."

Mrs. Gereth turned it over. " Well, I'll keep them to try her," she finally pronounced ; at which Fleda felt quite sick, as for having given everything and got nothing.

XII

"I must in common decency let him know I've talked of the matter with you," she said to her hostess that evening. "What answer do you wish me to write him?"

"Write him that you must see him again," said Mrs. Gereth.

Fleda looked very blank. "What on earth am I to see him for?"

"For anything you like!"

The girl would have been struck with the levity of this had she not already, in an hour, felt the extent of the change suddenly wrought in her commerce with her friend—wrought above all, to that friend's view, in her relation to the great issue. The effect of all that had followed Owen's visit was to make this relation the very key of the crisis. Pressed upon her, goodness knew, the crisis had been, but it now put forth big encircling arms—arms that squeezed till they hurt and she must cry out. It was as if everything at Ricks had been poured into a common receptacle, a public ferment of emotion and zeal, out of which it was ladled up, with a splash, to be tasted and talked about; everything at least but the one little treasure of knowledge that she kept back. She ought to have liked this, she reflected, because it meant sympathy, meant a closer union with the source of so much in her life that had been beautiful and renovating; but there were fine instincts in her that stood off. She had had—and it was not merely at this time — to recognise that there were things for which Mrs. Gereth's famous *flair* was not so happy as for bargains and " marks." It wouldn't be happy now as to the best action on the knowledge she had just gained ; yet as from this moment they were still more intimately together, so a person deeply in her debt would simply have to stand and meet what was to come. There were ways in which she could sharply incommode such a person, and not only with the best conscience in the world but with a high brutality of good intentions. One of the straightest of these strokes, Fleda saw, would be the dance of delight over the mystery she, terrible woman, had profaned ; the loud lawful tactless joy of the explorer leaping upon the strand. Like any other lucky discoverer she would take possession of the fortunate island. She was nothing if not practical : almost the only thing she took account of in her young friend's soft secret was the excellent use she could make of it— a use so much to her taste that she refused to feel a hindrance in the quality of the material. Fleda put into Mrs. Gereth's answer to her question a good deal more meaning than it would have occurred to her a few hours before that she was prepared to put, but she had on the spot a foreboding that even so broad a hint would live to be bettered.

" Do you suggest I shall propose to him to come down here again ? " she soon proceeded.

" Dear no. Say you'll go up to town and meet him." It *was* bettered, the broad hint ; and Fleda felt this to be still more the case when, returning to the subject before they went to bed, her companion said : " I make him over to you wholly, you know— to do what you like with. Deal with him in your own clever way—I ask no questions. All I ask is that you put it through."

" That's charming," Fleda replied, " but it doesn't tell me a bit, you'll be so good as to consider, in what terms to write to him. It's not an answer from you to the message I was to give you."

" The answer to his message is perfectly distinct. He shall have everything in the place the minute he'll say he'll marry you."

" You really pretend," Fleda asked, " to think me capable of transmitting him that news ? "

" What else can I really pretend — when you threaten so to cast me off if I speak the word myself ? "

" Oh if *you* speak the word——! " the girl murmured very gravely ; yet happy at least to know that in this direction Mrs. Gereth confessed herself warned and helpless. Then she added : " How can I go on living with you on a footing of which I so deeply disapprove ? Thinking as I do that you've despoiled him far more than is just or merciful—for if I expected you to take something I didn't in the least expect you to take everything—how can I stay here without a sense that I'm backing you up in your cruelty and participating in your ill-gotten gains ? " Fleda was determined that if she had the chill of her exposed and investigated state she should also have the convenience of it, and that if Mrs. Gereth popped in and out of the chamber of her soul she would at least return the freedom. " I shall quite hate, you know, in a day or two, every object that surrounds you— become blind to all the beauty and rarity that I formerly delighted in. Don't think me harsh ; there's no use in my not being frank now. If I leave you everything's at an end."

Mrs. Gereth, however, was imperturbable : Fleda had to recognise that her advantage had become too real. " It's too beautiful, the way you care for him ; it's music in my ears. Nothing else but such a passion could make you say such things ; that's the way I should have been too, my dear. Why didn't you tell me sooner ? I'd have gone right in for you; I never would have moved a candlestick. Don't stay with me if it torments you : don't, if it costs you so much, be where you see all the plunder. Go up to town—go back for a little to your father's. It need be only for a little ; two or three weeks will make us all right. Your father will take you and be glad, if you'll only make him understand what it's a question of—of your getting yourself off his hands for ever. *I'll* make him understand, you know, if you feel shy. I'd take you up myself, I'd go with you to spare your being bored : we'd put up at an hotel and we might amuse ourselves a bit. We haven't had much innocent pleasure since we met, have we ? But of course that wouldn't suit our book. I should be a bugaboo to Owen—I should be fatally in the way. Your chance is there— your chance is to be alone. For God's sake use it to the right end. If you're in want of money I've a little I can give you. But I ask no questions—not a question as small as your shoe ! "

She asked no questions, but she took the most extraordinary things for granted : Fleda felt this still more at the end of a couple of days. On the second of these our young lady wrote to Owen : her emotion had to a certain degree cleared itself — there was something she could briefly say. If she had given everything to Mrs. Gereth and as yet got nothing, so she had on the other hand quickly reacted—it took but a night—against the discouragement of her first check. Her desire to serve him was too passionate, the sense that he counted upon her too sweet : these things caught her up again and gave her a new patience and a new subtlety. It shouldn't really be for nothing she had given so much ; deep within her burned again the resolve to get something back. So what she wrote to Owen was simply that she had had a great scene with his mother, but that he must be patient and give her time. It was difficult, as they both had expected, but she was working her hardest for him. She had made an impression—she would do everything to follow it up. Meanwhile he must keep intensely quiet and take no other steps ; he must only trust her and pray for her and believe in her perfect loyalty. She made no allusion whatever to Mona's attitude, nor to his not being, as regarded that young lady, master of the situation ; but she said in a post-script, referring to his mother, " Of course she wonders a good deal why your marriage doesn't take place." After the letter had gone she regretted having used the word " loyalty " ; there were two or three vaguer terms she might as well have employed. The answer she immediately received from Owen was a little note the deficiencies of which she met by describing it to herself as pathetically simple, but which, to prove that Mrs. Gereth might ask as many questions as she liked, she at once made his mother read. He had no art with his pen, he had not even a good hand, and his letter, a short profession of friendly confidence, was couched but in a few familiar and colourless words of acknowledgment and assent. The gist of it was that he would certainly, since Miss Vetch recommended it, not hurry mamma too much. He wouldn't for the present cause her to be approached by any one else, but would nevertheless continue to hope she'd see she must really come round. " Of course, you know," he added, " she can't keep me waiting indefinitely. Please give her my love and tell her that. If it can be done peaceably I know you're just the one to do it."

Fleda had awaited his rejoinder in deep suspense ; such was her imagination of the possibility of his having, as she tacitly phrased it, let himself go on paper that when it arrived she was at first almost afraid to open it. There was indeed a distinct danger, for if he should take it into his head to write her love-letters the whole chance of aiding him would drop : she should have to return them, she should have to decline all further communication with him ; it would be the end alike of dreams and of realities. This imagination of Fleda's was a faculty that easily embraced all the heights and depths and extremities of things ; that made a single mouthful in particular of any tragic or desperate necessity. She was perhaps at first just a trifle disappointed not to find in the risky note some syllable that strayed from the text ; but the next moment she had risen to a point of view from which it presented itself as a production almost inspired in its simplicity. It was simple even for Owen, and she wondered what had given him the cue to be more so than usual. Then she admirably saw how natures that are right just do the things that are right. He wasn't clever — his manner of writing showed it ; but the cleverest man in England couldn't have had more the instinct that in the conditions was the supremely happy one, the instinct of giving her something that would do beautifully to be shown to Mrs. Gereth. This was deep divination, for naturally he couldn't know the line Mrs. Gereth was taking. It was furthermore explained—and that was the most touching part of all—by his wish that she herself should notice how awfully well he was behaving. His very bareness called her attention to his virtue, and these were the exact fruits of her beautiful and terrible admonition. He was cleaving to Mona ; he was doing his duty ; he was making tremendously sure he should be without reproach.

If Fleda handed her friend the letter as a triumphant gage of the innocence of the young man's heart her elation lived but a moment after Mrs. Gereth had pounced on the tell-tale spot in it. " Why in the world then does he still not breathe a breath about the day, the *day*, the DAY ? " She repeated the word with a crescendo of superior acuteness ; she proclaimed that nothing could be more marked than its absence—an absence that simply spoke volumes. What did it prove in fine but that she was producing the effect she had toiled for—that she had settled or was rapidly settling Mona ?

Such a challenge Fleda was obliged in some manner to take up. " You may be settling Mona," she returned with a smile, " but I can hardly regard it as sufficient evidence that you're settling Mona's lover."

" Why not, with such a studied omission on his part to gloss over in any manner the painful tension existing between them — the painful tension that, under Providence, I've been the means of bringing about ? He gives you by his silence clear notice that his marriage is practically off."

" He speaks to me of the only thing that concerns me. He gives me clear notice that he abates not one jot of his demand."

" Well then let him take the only way to get it satisfied ! "

Fleda had no need to ask again what such a way might be, nor was the ground supplied her cut away by the almost irritating confidence with which Mrs. Gereth could make her own arguments wait on her own wishes. These days, which dragged their length into a strange uncomfortable fortnight, had already borne more testimony to that element than all the other time the conspirators had lived through. Our young woman had been at first far from measuring the extent of an element that Owen himself would probably have described as her companion's " cheek." She lived now in a kind of bath of boldness, felt as if a fierce light poured in upon her from windows

opened wide ; and the singular part of the ordeal was
that she couldn't protest against it fully without
incurring even to her own mind some reproach of
ingratitude, some charge of smallness. If Mrs.
Gereth's apparent determination to hustle her into
Owen's arms was accompanied with an air of holding
her dignity rather cheap, this was after all only as a
consequence of her being held in respect to some
other attributes rather dear. It was a new version
of the old story of being kicked upstairs. The wonderful woman was the same woman who, in the summer,
at Poynton, had been so puzzled to conceive why
a good-natured girl shouldn't have contributed more
to the personal rout of the Brigstocks — shouldn't
have been grateful even for the handsome published
puff of Fleda Vetch. Only her passion was keener
now and her scruple more absent ; the prolonged
contest made a demand on her, and her pugnacity
had become one with her constant habit of using
such weapons as she could pick up. She had no
imagination about anybody's life save on the side
she bumped against. Fleda was quite aware that she
would have otherwise been a rare creature, but a
rare creature was originally just what she had struck
her as being. Mrs. Gereth had really no perception of
anybody's nature — had only one question about
persons : were they clever or stupid ? To be clever
meant to know the " marks." Fleda knew them by
direct inspiration, and a warm recognition of this had
been her friend's tribute to her character. The girl
now had hours of sombre hope she might never see
anything " good " again : that kind of experience was
clearly so broken a reed, so fallible a source of peace.
One would be more at peace in some vulgar little
place that should owe its *cachet* to a Universal Pro-
vider. There were nice strong simplifying horrors in
West Kensington ; it was as if they beckoned her and

wooed her back to them. She had a relaxed recollection of Waterbath ; and of her reasons for staying on at Ricks the force was rapidly ebbing. One of these was her pledge to Owen—her vow to press his mother close ; the other was the fact that of the two discomforts, that of being prodded by Mrs. Gereth and that of appearing to run after somebody else, the former remained for a while the more endurable.

As the days passed, however, it became plainer that her only chance of success would be in lending herself to this low appearance. Then moreover, at last, her nerves settling the question, the choice was simply imposed by the violence done her taste—done whatever was left of that high principle, at least, after the free and reckless satisfaction, for months, of great drafts and appeals. It was all very well to try to evade discussion : Owen Gereth was looking to her for a struggle, and it wasn't a bit of a struggle to be disgusted and dumb. She was on too strange a footing—that of having presented an ultimatum and having had it torn up in her face. In such a case as that the envoy always departed ; he never sat gaping and dawdling before the city. Mrs. Gereth every morning looked publicly into *The Morning Post*, the only newspaper she received ; and every morning she treated the blankness of that journal as fresh evidence that everything was " off." What did the *Post* exist for but to tell you your children were wretchedly married ?—so that if such a fount of misery was dry what could you do but infer that for once you had miraculously escaped ? She almost taunted Fleda with supineness in not getting something out of somebody — in the same breath indeed in which she drenched her with a kind of appreciation more onerous to the girl than blame. Mrs. Gereth herself had of course washed her hands of the matter ; but Fleda knew people who knew

Mona and would be sure to be in her confidence—
inconceivable people who admired her and had the
" entrée " of Waterbath.   What was the use therefore
of being the most natural and the easiest of letter-
writers, if no sort of side-light—in some pretext for
correspondence—was, by a brilliant creature, to be
got out of such barbarians ?   Fleda was not only
a brilliant creature, but she heard herself commended
in these days for attractions new and strange : she
figured suddenly in the queer conversations of Ricks
as a distinguished, almost as a dangerous, beauty.
That retouching of her hair and dress in which her
friend had impulsively indulged on a first glimpse
of her secret was by implication very frequently
repeated.   She had the impression not only of being
advertised and offered, but of being counselled, enlightened, initiated in ways she scarcely understood—
arts obscure even to a poor girl who had had, in good
society and motherless poverty, to look straight at
realities and fill out blanks.

These arts, when Mrs. Gereth's spirits were high,
were handled with a brave and cynical humour with
which Fleda's fancy could keep no step : they left
our young lady wondering what on earth her companion wanted her to do.   " I want you to cut in ! "
—that was Mrs. Gereth's familiar and comprehensive
phrase for the course she prescribed.   She challenged
again and again Fleda's picture, as she called it (though
the sketch was too slight to deserve the name), of the
indifference to which a prior attachment had committed the proprietor of Poynton.   " Do you mean
to say that, Mona or no Mona, he could see you that
way, day after day, and not have the ordinary feelings
of a man ?   Don't you know a little more, you absurd
affected thing, what men *are*, the brutes ? "   This
was the sort of interrogation to which Fleda was
fitfully and irrelevantly treated.   She had grown

almost used to the refrain. "Do you mean to say that when, the other day, one had quite made you over to him, the great gawk, and he was, on this very spot, utterly alone with you——?" The poor girl at this point never left any doubt of what she meant to say; but Mrs. Gereth could be trusted to break out in another place and at another time. At last Fleda wrote to her father that he must take her in a little, take her in while she looked about; and when, to her companion's delight, she returned to London that lady went with her to the station and wafted her on her way. *The Morning Post* had been delivered as they left the house, and Mrs. Gereth had brought it with her for the traveller, who never spent a penny on a newspaper. On the platform, however, when this young person was ticketed, labelled and seated, she opened it at the window of the carriage, exclaiming as usual, after looking into it a moment, " Nothing, nothing, nothing : don't tell *me* ! " Every day that there was nothing was a nail in the coffin of the marriage. An instant later the train was off, but, moving quickly beside it, while Fleda leaned inscrutably forth, Mrs. Gereth grasped her friend's hand and looked up with wonderful eyes. " Only let yourself go, darling—only let yourself go ! "

XIII

THAT she desired to ask no prudish questions Mrs.
Gereth conscientiously proved by closing her lips
tight after Fleda had gone to London.   No letter
from Ricks arrived at West Kensington, and Fleda,
with nothing to communicate that could be to the
taste of either party, forbore to open a correspondence.
If her heart had been less heavy she might have been
amused to feel how much free rope this reticence of
Ricks seemed to signify to her she could take.   She
had at all events no good news for her friend save in
the sense that her silence was not bad news.   She was
not yet in a position to write that she had " cut in " ;
but neither, on the other hand, had she gathered
material for announcing that Mona was undissever-
able from her prey.   She had made no use of the pen
so glorified by Mrs. Gereth to wake up the echoes of
Waterbath ; she had sedulously abstained from in-
quiring what in any quarter, far or near, was said or
suggested or supposed.   She only spent a matutinal
penny on *The Morning Post* ; she only saw on each
occasion that that inspired sheet had as little to say
about the imminence as about the collapse of certain
nuptials.   It was at the same time obvious that Mrs.
Gereth triumphed on these occasions much more
than she trembled, and that with a few such triumphs
repeated she should cease to tremble at all.   What
came out most, however, was that she had had a rare

preconception of the circumstances that would have ministered, had Fleda been disposed, to the girl's cutting in. It was brought home to Fleda that these circumstances would have particularly favoured intervention ; she was promptly forced to do them a secret justice. One of the effects of her intimacy with Mrs. Gereth was that she had quite lost all sense of intimacy with any one else. The lady of Ricks had made a desert round her, possessing and absorbing her so utterly that other partakers had fallen away. Hadn't she been admonished, months before, that people considered they had lost her and were reconciled on the whole to the privation ? Her present position in the great unconscious town showed distinctly for obscure : she regarded it at any rate with eyes suspicious of that lesson. She neither wrote notes nor received them ; she indulged in no reminders nor knocked at any doors ; she wandered vaguely in the western wilderness or cultivated shy forms of that " household art " for which she had had a respect before tasting the bitter tree of knowledge. Her only plan was to be as quiet as a mouse, and when she failed in the attempt to lose herself in the flat suburb she resembled — or thought she did — a lonely fly crawling over a dusty chart.

How had Mrs. Gereth known in advance that if she had chosen to be " vile " (that was what Fleda called it) everything would happen to help her ?— especially the way her poor father doddered after breakfast off to his club, giving the impression of seventy when he was really fifty-seven and leaving her richly alone for the day. He came back about midnight, looking at her very hard and not risking long words — only making her feel by inimitable touches that the presence of his family compelled him to alter all his hours. She had in their common sitting-room the company of the objects he was fond of saying he had collected — objects, shabby and battered, of a sort that appealed little to his daughter : old brandy-flasks and match-boxes, old calendars and hand-books, intermixed with an assortment of penwipers and ash-trays, a harvest gathered in from penny bazaars. He was blandly unconscious of that side of Fleda's nature which had endeared her to Mrs. Gereth, and she had often heard him wish to goodness there was something intelligible she cared for. Why didn't she try collecting something ?—it didn't matter what. She would find it gave an interest to life—there was no end to the little curiosities one could easily pick up. He was conscious of having a taste for fine things which his children had unfortunately not inherited. This indicated the limits of their acquaintance with him — limits which, as Fleda was now sharply aware, could only leave him to wonder what the mischief she was there for. As she herself echoed this question to the letter she was not in a position to clear up the mystery. She couldn't have given a name to her business nor have explained it save by saying that she had had to get away from Ricks. It was intensely provisional, but what was to come next ? Nothing could come next but a deeper anxiety. She had neither a home nor an outlook—nothing in all the wide world but a feeling of suspense. It was, morally speaking, like figuring in society with a wardrobe of one garment.

Of course she had her duty—her duty to Owen —a definite undertaking, re-affirmed, after his visit to Ricks, under her hand and seal ; but no sense of possession was attached to that, only a horrible sense of privation. She had quite moved from under Mrs. Gereth's wide wing ; and now that she was really among the penwipers and ash-trays she was swept, at the thought of all the beauty she had forsworn, by short wild gusts of despair. If her friend should really keep the spoils she would never return to her. If that friend should on the other hand part with them what on earth would there be to return to ? The chill struck deep as Fleda thought of the mistress of Ricks also reduced, in vulgar parlance, to what she had on her back : there was nothing to which she could compare such an image but her idea of Marie Antoinette in the Conciergerie, or perhaps the vision of some tropical bird, the creature of hot, dense forests, dropped on a frozen moor to pick up a living. The mind's eye could indeed see Mrs. Gereth only in her thick, coloured air ; it took all the light of her treasures to make her concrete and distinct. She loomed for a moment, in any mere house of compartments and angles, gaunt and unnatural ; then she vanished as if she had suddenly sunk into a quicksand. Fleda lost herself in the rich fancy of how, if *she* were mistress of Poynton, a whole province, as an abode, should be assigned there to the great queen-mother. She would have returned from her campaign with her baggage-train and her loot, and the palace would unbar its shutters and the morning flash back from its halls. In the event of a surrender the poor woman would never again be able to begin to collect : she was now too old and too moneyless, and times were altered and good things impossibly dear. A surrender, furthermore, to any daughter-in law save an oddity like Mona needn't at all be an abdication in fact ; any other fairly nice girl whom Owen should have taken it into his head to marry would have been positively glad to have, for the museum, a custodian equal to a walking catalogue, a custodian versed beyond any one anywhere in the mysteries of ministration to rare pieces. A fairly nice girl would somehow be away a good deal and would at such times count it a blessing to feel Mrs. Gereth at her post.

Fleda had from the first days fully recognised that, quite apart from any question of letting Owen know where she was, it would be a charity to give him some sign : it would be weak, it would be ugly to be diverted from this kindness by the fact that Mrs. Gereth had attached a tinkling bell to it. A frank relation with him was only superficially discredited : she ought for his own sake to send him a word of cheer. So she repeatedly reasoned, but as repeatedly delaying performance : if her general plan had been to be as still as a mouse an interview like the interview at Ricks would be an odd contribution to that ideal. Therefore with a confused preference of practice to theory she let the days go by; she judged nothing so imperative as the gain of precious time. She shouldn't be able to stay with her father for ever, but she might now reap the benefit of having married her sister—Maggie's union had been built up round a small spare room. Concealed in this retreat she might try to paint again, and abetted by the grateful Maggie—for Maggie at least was grateful—she might try to dispose of her work. She had not indeed struggled with a brush since her visit to Waterbath, where the sight of the family splotches had put her immensely on her guard. Poynton, moreover, had been an impossible place for producing ; no art more active than a Buddhistic contemplation could lift its head there. It had stripped its mistress clean of all feeble accomplishments ; she sometimes unrolled, her needles and silks, her gold and silver folded in it, a big, brave, flowery square of ancient unfinished " work " ; but her hand had sooner been imbrued with blood than with ink or with water-colour. Close to Fleda's present abode was the little shop of a man who mounted and framed pictures and desolately dealt in artists' materials. She sometimes paused before it to look at a couple of shy experiments for which its dull window constituted publicity ; small studies placed there on sale and full of warning to a young lady without fortune and without talent. Some such young lady had brought them forth in sorrow ; some such young lady, to see if they had been snapped up, had passed and re-passed as helplessly as she herself was doing. They never had been, they never would be snapped up ; yet they were quite above the actual attainment of some other young ladies. It was a matter of discipline with Fleda to take an occasional lesson from them; besides which when she now quitted the house she had to look for reasons after she was out. The only place to find them was in the shop-windows. They likened her to a servant-girl taking her " afternoon," but that didn't signify : perhaps some day she would resemble such a person still more closely. This continued a fortnight, at the end of which the feeling was suddenly dissipated. She had stopped as usual in the presence of the little pictures and then, as she turned away, had found herself face to face with Owen Gereth.

At the sight of him two fresh waves passed quickly across her heart, one at the heels of the other. The first was an instant perception that their meeting was not an accident ; the second a consciousness as prompt that the best place for it was the street. She knew before he told her that he had been to see her, and the next thing she knew was that he had had information from his mother. Her mind grasped these things while he said with a smile : " I saw only your back, but I knew like a shot. I was over the way. I've been at your house."

" How came you to know my house ? " Fleda asked.

" I like that ! " he laughed. " How came you not to let me know you were there ? "

Fleda, at this, thought it best also to laugh. " Since I didn't let you know why did you come ? "

" Oh I say ! " cried Owen. " Don't add insult to

injury. Why in the world didn't you let me know ?
I came because I want awfully to see you." He
rather floundered, then added : " I got the tip from
mother. She has written to me—fancy ! "

They still stood where they had met. Fleda's instinct was to keep him there ; the more that she could
already see him take for granted they would immediately proceed together to her door. He rose before
her with a different air : he looked less ruffled and
bruised than he had done at Ricks ; he showed a
recovered freshness. Perhaps, however, this was
only because she had scarcely seen him at all till now
in London form, as he would have called it —
" turned out " as he was turned out in town. In the
country, heated with the chase and splashed with the
mire, he had always much reminded her of a picturesque peasant in national costume. This costume,
as Owen wore it, varied from day to day ; it was as
copious as the wardrobe of an actor ; but it never
failed of suggestions of the earth and the weather,
the hedges and ditches, the beasts and birds. There
had been days when he struck her as all potent nature
in one pair of boots. It didn't make him now another
person that he was delicately dressed, shining and
splendid, that he had a higher hat and light gloves
with black seams and an umbrella as fine as a lance ;
but it made him, she soon decided, really handsomer,
and this in turn gave him — for she never could
think of him, or indeed of some other things, without
the aid of his vocabulary—a tremendous pull. Yes,
that was for the moment, as he looked at her, the
great fact of their situation—his pull was tremendous. She tried to keep the acknowledgment of it
from trembling in her voice as she said to him with
more surprise than she really felt : " You've then
reopened relations with her ? "

" It's she who has reopened them with me. I got

her letter this morning. She told me you were here and that she wished me to know it. She didn't say much; she just gave me your address. I wrote her back, you know, ' Thanks no end. Shall go to-day.' So we *are* in correspondence again, aren't we? She means of course that you've something to tell me from her, hey? But if you have why haven't you let a fellow know?" He waited for no answer to this, he had so much to say. "At your house, just now, they told me how long you've been here. Haven't you known all the while that I'm counting the hours? I left a word for you—that I would be back at six; but I'm awfully glad to have caught you so much sooner. You don't mean to say you're not going home!" he exclaimed in dismay. "The young woman there told me you went out early."

"I've been out a very short time," said Fleda, who had hung back with the general purpose of making things difficult for him. The street would make them difficult; she could trust the street. She reflected in time, however, that to betray she was afraid to admit him would give him more a feeling of facility than of anything else. She moved on with him after a moment, letting him direct their course to her door, which was only round a corner; she considered as they went that it mightn't prove such a stroke to have been in London so long and yet not have called him. She desired he should feel she was perfectly simple with him, and there was no simplicity in that. None the less, on the steps of the house, though she had a key, she rang the bell; and while they waited together and she averted her face she looked straight into the depths of what Mrs. Gereth had meant by giving him the "tip." This had been perfidious, had been monstrous of Mrs. Gereth, and Fleda wondered if her letter had contained only what Owen repeated.

XIV

WHEN they had passed together into her father's little place and, among the brandy-flasks and pen-wipers, still more disconcerted and divided, the girl—to do something, though it would make him stay—had ordered tea, he put the letter before her quite as if he had guessed her thought. " She's still a bit nasty—fancy ! " He handed her the scrap of a note he had pulled out of his pocket and from its envelope. " Fleda Vetch," it ran, " is at West Kensington—10 Raphael Road. Go to see her and try, for God's sake, to cultivate a glimmer of intelligence." When, handing it back to him, she took in his face she saw how his heightened colour was the effect of watching her read such an allusion to his want of wit. Fleda knew what it was an allusion to, and his pathetic air of having received this buffet, tall and fine and kind as he stood there, made her conscious of not quite concealing her knowledge. For a minute she was kept mute by an angered sense of the trick thus played her. It was a trick because she considered there had been a covenant ; and the trick consisted of Mrs. Gereth's having broken the spirit of their agreement while conforming in a fashion to the letter. Under the girl's menace of a complete rupture she had been afraid to make of her secret the use she itched to make ; but in the course of these days of separation she had gathered pluck to hazard an indirect betrayal. Fleda measured her hesitations and the impulse she had finally obeyed, which the continued procrastination of Waterbath had encouraged, had at last made irresistible. If in her high-handed manner of playing their game she had not named the thing hidden she had named the hiding-place. It was over the sense of this wrong that Fleda's lips closed tight : she was afraid of aggravating her case by some sound that would quicken her visitor's attention. A strong effort, however, helped her to avoid the danger ; with her constant idea of keeping cool and repressing a visible flutter she found herself able to choose her words. Meanwhile he had exclaimed with his uncomfortable laugh : " That's a good one for me, Miss Vetch, isn't it ? "

" Of course you know by this time that your mother's very direct," said Fleda.

" I think I can understand well enough when I know what's to be understood," the young man returned. " But I hope you won't mind my saying that you've kept me pretty well in the dark about that. I've been waiting, waiting, waiting—so much has depended on your news. If you've been working for me I'm afraid it has been a thankless job. Can't she say what she'll do, one way or the other ? I can't tell in the least where I am, you know. I haven't really learnt from you, since I saw you there, where *she* is. You wrote me to be patient, and I should like to know what else I've been. But I'm afraid you don't quite realise what I'm to be patient *with*. At Waterbath, don't you know ? I've simply to account and answer, piece by piece, for my damned property. Mona glowers at me and waits, and I, hang it, I glower at *you* and do the same." Fleda had gathered fuller confidence as he continued ; so plain was it that she had succeeded in not dropping into his mind the spark that might produce the glimmer his mother had tried to rub up. But even her small safety gave a start when after an appealing pause he went on : " I hope, you know, that all this time you're not keeping anything back from me."

In the full face of what she was keeping back such a hope could only make her wince ; but she was prompt with her explanations in proportion as she felt they failed to meet him. The smutty maid came in with tea-things, and Fleda, moving several objects, eagerly accepted the diversion of arranging a place for them on one of the tables. " I've been trying to break your mother down because it has seemed there may be some chance of it. That's why I've let you go on expecting it. She's too proud to veer round all at once, but I think I speak correctly in saying I've made an impression."

In spite of ordering tea she had not invited him to sit down ; she herself made a point of standing. He hovered by the window that looked into Raphael Road ; she kept at the other side of the room ; the stunted slavey, gazing wide-eyed at the beautiful gentleman and either stupidly or cunningly bringing but one thing at a time, came and went between the tea-tray and the open door.

" You pegged at her so hard ? " Owen asked.

" I explained to her fully your position and put before her much more strongly than she liked what seemed to me her absolute duty."

He waited a little. " And having done that you came away ? "

She felt the full need of giving a reason for her movement, but at first only said with cheerful frankness : " I came away."

Her companion again seemed to search her. " I thought you had gone to her for several months."

" Well," Fleda replied, " I couldn't stay. I didn't like it. I didn't like it at all—I couldn't bear it," she went on. " In the midst of those trophies of Poynton, living with them, touching them, using them, I felt as if backing her up. As I wasn't a bit of an accomplice, as I hate what she has done, I didn't want to be, even to the extent of the mere look of it—what is it you call such people ?—an accessory after the fact." There was something she kept back so rigidly that the joy of uttering the rest was double. She yielded to the sharp need of giving him all the other truth. There was a matter as to which she had deceived him, and there was a matter as to which she had deceived Mrs. Gereth, but her lack of pleasure in deception as such came home to her now. She busied herself with the tea and, to extend the occupation, cleared the table still more, spreading out the coarse cups and saucers and the vulgar little plates. She was aware she produced more confusion than symmetry, but she was also aware she was violently nervous. Owen tried to help her with something : this made indeed for disorder. " My reason for not writing to you," she pursued, " was simply that I was hoping to hear more from Ricks. I've waited from day to day for that."

" But you've heard nothing ? "

" Not a word."

" Then what I understand," said Owen, " is that practically you and Mummy have quarrelled. And you've done it—I mean you personally—for *me*."

" Oh no, we haven't quarrelled a bit ! " Then with a smile : " We've only diverged."

" You've diverged uncommonly far ! "— Owen laughed pleasantly back. Fleda, with her hideous crockery and her father's collections, could conceive that these objects, to her visitor's perception even more strongly than to her own, measured the length of the swing from Poynton and Ricks ; she couldn't forget either that her high standards must figure vividly enough even to Owen's simplicity to make him reflect that West Kensington was a tremendous fall. If she had fallen it was because she had acted for him. She was all the more content he should thus see she *had* acted, as the cost of it, in his eyes, was none of her own showing. " What seems to have happened," he said, " is that you've had a row with her and yet not moved her ! "

She felt her way ; she was full of the impression that, notwithstanding her scant help, he saw his course clearer than he had seen it at Ricks. He might mean many things, and what if the many should mean in their turn only one ? " The difficulty is, you understand, that she doesn't really see into your situation." She had a pause. " She doesn't make out why your marriage hasn't yet taken place."

Owen stared. " " Why, for the reason I told you : that Mona won't take another step till mother has given full satisfaction. Everything must be there, every blessed ' stolen ' thing. You see everything *was* there the day of that fatal visit."

" Yes, that's what I understood from you at Ricks," said Fleda ; " but I haven't repeated it to your mother." She had hated at Ricks to talk with him about Mona, but now that scruple was swept away. If he could speak of Mona's visit as fatal she need at least not pretend not to notice it. It made all the difference that she had tried to assist him and had failed : to give him any faith in her service she must give him all her reasons but one. She must give him, in other words, with a corresponding omission, all Mrs. Gereth's. " You can easily see that, as she dislikes your marriage, anything that may seem to make it less certain works in her favour. Without my telling her, she has suspicions and views that are simply suggested by your delay. Therefore it didn't seem to me right to make them worse. By

holding off long enough she thinks she may put an
end to your engagement. If Mona's waiting she
believes she may at last tire Mona out." This, in
all conscience, Fleda felt to be lucid enough.

So the young man, following her attentively, appeared equally to feel. " So far as that goes," he
promptly declared, " she *has* at last tired Mona out."
He uttered the words with a strange approach to
hilarity.

Fleda's surprise at this aberration left her a moment
looking at him. " Do you mean your marriage is off ? "

He answered with the oddest gay pessimism.
" God knows, Miss Vetch, where or when or what
my marriage is ! If it isn't ' off ' it certainly, at the
point things have reached, isn't *on*. I haven't seen
Mona for ten days, and for a week I haven't heard
from her. She used to write me every week, don't
you know ? She won't budge from Waterbath and
I haven't budged from town." Then he put it plain.
" If she does break will mother come round ? "

Fleda, at this, felt her heroism meet its real test
—felt that in telling him the truth she should effectively raise a hand to push his impediment out of
the way. Was the knowledge that such a motion
would probably dispose for ever of Mona capable
of yielding to the conception of still giving her every
chance she was entitled to ? That conception was
heroic, but at the same moment it reminded our
young woman of the place it had held in her plan
she was also reminded of the not less urgent claim
of the truth. Ah the truth—there was a limit to
the impunity with which one could juggle with that
value, which in itself never shifted. Wasn't what
she had most to remember the fact that Owen had
a right to his property, and that he had also her
vow to stand by him in the recovery of it ? How
did she stand by him if she hid from him the only

process of recovery of which she was quite sure ?
For an instant that seemed to her the fullest of her
life she debated. " Yes," she said at last, " if your
marriage really drops she'll give up everything she
has taken."

" That's just what makes Mona hesitate ! " Owen
honestly stated. " I mean the idea that I shall get
back the things only if she gives me up."

Fleda thought an instant. " You mean makes her
hesitate to keep you—not hesitate to renounce you ? "

He looked a trifle befogged. " She doesn't see
the use of hanging on, as I haven't even yet put the
matter into legal hands. She's awfully keen about
that, and awfully disgusted that I don't. She says
it's the only real way and she thinks I'm afraid to
take it. She has given me time and then has given
me again more. She says I give Mummy too much.
She says I'm a muff to go pottering on. That's why
she's drawing off so hard, don't you see ? "

" I don't see very clearly. Of course you must give
her what you offered her ; of course you must keep
your word. There must be no mistake about *that* ! "
the girl declared.

His bewilderment visibly increased. " You think
then, as she does, that I *must* send down the police ? "

The mixture of reluctance and dependence in this
made her feel how much she was failing him : she
had the sense of " breaking " too. " No, no, not
yet ! " she said, though she had really no other and
no better course to prescribe. " Doesn't it occur to
you," she asked in a moment, " that if Mona is, as
you say, drawing away, she may have in doing so a
very high motive ? She knows the immense value of
all the objects detained by your mother, and to restore
the spoils of Poynton she's ready—is that it ?—to
make a sacrifice. The sacrifice is that of an engagement she had entered upon with joy."

He had been blank a moment before, but he followed this argument with success—a success so immediate that it enabled him to produce with decision : " Ah she's not that sort ! She wants them herself," he added ; " she wants to feel they're hers ; she doesn't care whether I have them or not. And if she can't get them she doesn't want *me*. If she can't get them she doesn't want anything at all."

This was categoric : Fleda drank it in. " She takes such an interest in them ? "

" So it appears."

" So much that they're *all*, in the whole business, and that she can let everything else absolutely depend upon them ? "

Owen weighed it as if he felt the responsibility of his answer ; but that answer nevertheless came, and, as Fleda could see, out of a wealth of memory. " She never wanted them particularly till they seemed to be in danger. Now she has an idea about them, and when she gets hold of an idea—oh dear me ! " He broke off, pausing and looking away as with a sense of the futility of expression : it was the first time she had heard him explain a matter so pointedly or embark at all on a generalisation. It was striking, it was touching to her, as he faltered, that he appeared but half capable of floating his generalisation to the end. The girl, however, was so far competent to fill up his blank as that she had divined on the occasion of Mona's visit to Poynton what would happen in case of the accident at which he glanced. She had there with her own eyes seen Owen's betrothed get hold of an idea. " I say, you know, *do* give me some tea ! " he went on irrelevantly and familiarly.

Her profuse preparations had all this time had no sequel, and with a laugh that she felt to be awkward she hastily prepared his draught. " It's sure to be horrid," she said ; " we don't have at all good things." She offered him also bread and butter, of which he partook, holding his cup and saucer in his other hand and moving slowly about the room. She poured herself a cup, but not to take it ; after which, without wanting it, she began to eat a small stale biscuit. She was struck with the extinction of the unwillingness she had felt at Ricks to contribute to the bandying between them of poor Mona's name ; and under this influence she presently resumed : " Am I to understand that she engaged herself to marry you without caring for you ? "

He looked into Raphael Road. " She *did* care for me awfully. But she can't stand the strain."

" The strain of what ? "

" Why of the whole wretched thing."

" The whole thing has indeed been wretched, and I can easily conceive its effect on her," Fleda sagaciously said.

Her visitor turned sharp round. " You *can* ? " There was a light in his strong stare. " You can understand its spoiling her temper and making her come down on *me* ? She behaves as if I were of no use to her at all ! "

Fleda wondered even to extravagance. " She's rankling under the sense of her wrong."

" Well, was it I, pray, who perpetrated the wrong ? Ain't I doing what I can to get the thing arranged ? "

The ring of his question made his anger at Mona almost resemble for a minute an anger at Fleda ; and this resemblance in turn caused our young lady to observe how it became him to speak, as he did for the first time in her hearing, with that degree of heat, and to use, for the first time too, such a term as " perpetrated." In addition his challenge rendered still more vivid to her the mere flimsiness of her own aid. "Yes, you've been perfect," she said. "You've had a most difficult part. You've had to show tact and patience as well as firmness with your mother, and you've strikingly shown them. It's I who, quite unintentionally, have deceived you. I haven't helped you at all to your remedy."

"Well, you wouldn't at all events have ceased to like me, would you?" Owen demanded. It evidently mattered to him to know if she really justified Mona. "I mean of course if you *had* liked me—liked me as *she* liked me," he explained.

Fleda looked this appeal in the face only long enough to recognise that in her embarrassment she must take instant refuge in a higher one. "I can answer that better if I know how kind to her you've been. *Have* you been kind to her?" she asked as simply as she could.

"Why rather, Miss Vetch! I've done every blessed thing she has ever wished," he protested. "I rushed down to Ricks, as you saw, with fire and sword, and the day after that I went to see her at Waterbath." At this point he checked himself, though it was just the point at which her interest deepened. A different look had come into his face as he put down his empty teacup. "But why should I tell you such things for any good it does me? I gather you've no suggestion to make me now except that I shall request my solicitor to act. *Shall* I request him to act?"

Fleda scarce caught his words: something new had suddenly come into her mind. "When you went to Waterbath after seeing me," she asked, "did you tell her all about that?"

Owen looked conscious. "All about it?"

"That you had had a long talk with me without seeing your mother at all?"

"Oh yes, I told her exactly, and that you had been

421

most awfully kind and that I had placed the whole thing in your hands."

Fleda gazed as at the scene he reported. " Perhaps that displeased her," she at last suggested.

" It displeased her fearfully." He brought it out with a rush.

" Fearfully ? " broke from the girl. Somehow, at the word, she was startled.

" She wanted to know what right you had to meddle. She said you weren't honest."

" Oh ! " Fleda cried with a long wail. Then she controlled herself. " I see."

" She abused you and I defended you. She de- nounced you——"

She checked him with a gesture. " Don't tell me what she did ! " She had coloured up to her eyes, where, as with the effect of a blow in the face, she quickly felt the tears gathering. It was a sudden drop in her great flight, a shock to her attempt to watch over Mona's interests. While she had been straining her very soul in this attempt the subject of her magnanimity had been practically pronouncing her vile. She took it all in, however, and after an instant was able to speak with a smile. She wouldn't have been surprised to learn indeed that her smile was queer. " You spoke a while ago of your mother's and my quarrelling about you. It's much more true that you and Mona have quarrelled about *me*."

The proposition was fairly simple, but he seemed for an instant to have to walk round it. " What I mean to say is, don't you know, that Mona, if you don't mind my saying so, has taken into her head to be jealous."

" I see," said Fleda. " Well, I daresay our con- ferences have looked very odd."

" They've looked very beautiful and they've *been*

very beautiful. Oh I've told her the sort you are ! " the young man pursued.

" That of course hasn't made her love me better."

" No, nor love me,"—he jumped at it now. " Of course, you know, she *says*—so far as that goes—that she loves me."

" And do you say you love her ? "

" I say nothing else—I say it all the while. I said it the other day about ninety times." Fleda made no immediate rejoinder to this, and before she could choose one he repeated his question of a moment before. " *Am* I to tell my solicitor to act ? "

She had at that moment turned away from this solution, precisely because she saw in it the great chance for herself. If she should determine him to adopt it she might put out her hand and take him. It would shut in Mrs. Gereth's face the open door of surrender : she would flare up and fight, flying the flag of a passionate, an heroic defence. The case would obviously go against her, but the proceedings would last longer than Mona's patience or Owen's propriety. With a formal rupture he would be at large ; and she had only to tighten her fingers round the string that would raise the curtain on that scene. " You tell me you ' say ' you love her, but is there nothing more in it than your saying so ? You wouldn't say so, would you, if it's not true ? What in the world has become in so short a time of the affection that led to your engagement ? "

" The deuce knows what has become of it, Miss Vetch ! " Owen cried. " It seemed all to go to pot as this horrid struggle came on." He was close to her now and, with his face lighted again by the relief of it, he looked all his helpless history into her eyes. " As I saw you and noticed you more, as I knew you better and better, I felt less and less —I couldn't help it—about anything or any one else.

I wished I had known you sooner—I knew I should have liked you better than any one in the world. But it wasn't you who made the difference," he eagerly continued, " and I was awfully determined to stick to Mona to the death. It was she herself who made it, upon my soul, by the state she got into, the way she sulked, the way she took things and the way she let me have it ! She destroyed our prospects and our happiness—upon my honour she destroyed them. She made just the same smash of them as if she had kicked over that tea-table. She wanted to know all the while what was passing between us, between you and me ; and she wouldn't take my solemn assurance that nothing was passing but what might have directly passed between me and old Mummy. She said a pretty girl like you was a nice old Mummy for me, and, if you'll believe it, she never called you anything else but that. I'll be hanged if I haven't been good, haven't I ? I haven't breathed a breath of any sort to you, have I ? You'd have been down on me hard if I had, wouldn't you ? You're down on me pretty hard as it is, I think, aren't you ? But I don't care what you say now, or what Mona says either, or a single rap what any one says : she has given me at last by her confounded behaviour a right to speak out, to utter the way I feel about it. The way I feel about it, don't you know ? is that it had all better come to an end. You ask me if I don't love her, and I suppose it's natural enough you should. But you ask it at the very moment I'm half-mad to say to you that there's only one person on the whole earth I *really* love, and that that person ——" Here he pulled up short, and Fleda wondered if it were from the effect of his perceiving, through the closed door, the sound of steps and voices on the landing of the stairs. She had caught this sound herself with surprise and a vague uneasiness : it was not

THE SPOILS OF POYNTON

an hour at which her father ever came in, and there
was no present reason why she should have a visitor.
She had a fear which after a few seconds deepened :
a visitor was at hand ; the visitor would be simply
Mrs. Gereth. That lady wished for a near view of the
consequence of her note to Owen. Fleda straightened
herself with the instant thought that if this was what
Mrs. Gereth desired Mrs. Gereth should have it in
a form not to be mistaken. Owen's pause was the
matter of a moment, but during that moment our
young couple stood with their eyes holding each other's
eyes and their ears catching the suggestion, still
through the door, of a murmured conference in the
hall. Fleda had begun to move to cut it short when
Owen stopped her with a grasp of her arm. " You're
surely able to guess," he said with his voice down
and her arm pressed as she had never known such a
tone or such a pressure—" you're surely able to guess
the one person on earth I love ? "

The handle of the door turned and she had only
time to jerk at him : " Your mother ! "

But as the door opened the smutty maid, edging
in, announced " Mrs. Brigstock ! "

XV

Mrs. Brigstock, in the doorway, stood looking from one of the occupants of the room to the other ; then they saw her eyes attach themselves to a small object that had lain hitherto unnoticed on the carpet. This was the biscuit of which, on giving Owen his tea, Fleda had taken a perfunctory nibble : she had immediately laid it on the table, and that subsequently, in some precipitate movement, she should have brushed it off was doubtless a sign of the agitation that possessed her. For Mrs. Brigstock there was apparently more in it than met the eye. Owen at any rate picked it up, and Fleda felt as if he were removing the traces of some scene that the newspapers would have characterised as lively. Mrs. Brigstock clearly took in also the sprawling tea-things and the marks as of a high tide in the full faces of her young friends. These elements made the little place a vivid picture of intimacy. A minute was filled by Fleda's relief at finding her visitor not to be Mrs. Gereth, and a longer space by the later sense of what was really more compromising in the case presented. It dimly occurred to her that the lady of Ricks had also written to Waterbath. Not only had Mrs. Brigstock never paid her a call, but Fleda would have been unable to figure her so employed. A year before the girl had spent a day under her roof, but never feeling that Mrs. Brigstock regarded this as constituting a bond. She

426

had never stayed in any house but Poynton in which the imagination of a bond, on one side or the other, prevailed. After the first astonishment she dashed gaily at her guest, emphasising her welcome and wondering how her whereabouts had become known at Waterbath. Hadn't Mrs. Brigstock quitted that residence for the very purpose of laying her hand on the associate of Mrs. Gereth's misconduct ? The spirit in which this hand was to be laid our young woman was yet to ascertain ; but she was a person who could think ten thoughts at once—a circumstance which, even putting her present plight at its worst, gave her a great advantage over a person who required easy conditions for dealing even with one. The very vibration of the air, however, told her that whatever Mrs. Brigstock's sense might originally have been it was now sharply affected by the sight of Owen. He was essentially a surprise : she had reckoned with everything that concerned him but his personal presence. With that, in awkward silence, she had begun to deal, as Fleda could see, while she effected with friendly aid an embarrassed transit to the sofa. Owen would be useless, would be deplorable : this aspect of the case Fleda had taken in as well. Another aspect was that he would admire her, adore her, exactly in proportion as she herself should rise gracefully superior. Fleda felt for the first time free to let herself " go," as Mrs. Gereth had said, and she was full of the sense that to " go " meant now to aim straight at the effect of moving Owen to rapture at her simplicity and tact. It was her impression that he had no positive dislike of Mona's mother ; but she couldn't entertain that notion without a glimpse of the implication that he had a positive dislike of Mrs. Brigstock's daughter. Mona's mother declined tea, declined a better seat, declined a cushion, declined to remove her boa : Fleda guessed that she had not come on purpose to be dry, but that the voice of the invaded room had itself given her the hint.

"I just came on the mere chance," she said. "Mona found yesterday somewhere the card of invitation to your sister's marriage that you sent us, or your father sent us, some time ago. We couldn't be present—it was impossible; but as it had this address on it I said to myself that I might find you here."

"I'm very glad to be at home," Fleda responded.

"Yes, that doesn't happen very often, does it?" Mrs. Brigstock looked round afresh at Fleda's home.

"Oh I came back a while ago from Ricks. I shall be here now till I don't know when."

"We thought it very likely you'd have come back. We knew of course of your having been at Ricks. If I didn't find you I thought I might perhaps find Mr. Vetch," Mrs. Brigstock went on.

"I'm sorry he's out. He's always out—all day long."

Mrs. Brigstock's round eyes grew rounder. "All day long?"

"All day long," Fleda smiled.

"Leaving you quite to yourself?"

"A good deal to myself, but a little, to-day, as you see, to Mr. Gereth"—and the girl looked at Owen to draw him into their sociability. For Mrs. Brigstock he had immediately sat down; but the movement had not corrected the sombre stiffness possessing him at sight of her. Before he found a response to the appeal addressed to him Fleda turned again to her other visitor. "Is there any purpose for which you would like my father to call on you?"

Mrs. Brigstock received this question as if it were not to be unguardedly answered; upon which Owen intervened with pale irrelevance. "I wrote to Mona this morning of Miss Vetch's being in town ; but of course the letter hadn't arrived when you left home."

" No, it hadn't arrived. I came up for the night —I've several matters to attend to." Then looking with an intention of fixedness from one of her companions to the other, " I'm afraid I've interrupted your conversation," Mrs. Brigstock said. She spoke without effectual point, had the air of merely announcing the fact. Fleda had not yet been confronted with the question of the sort of person Mrs. Brigstock was ; she had only been confronted with the question of the sort of person Mrs. Gereth scorned her for being. She was really somehow no sort of person at all, and it came home to Fleda that if Mrs. Gereth could see her at this moment she would scorn her more than ever. She had a face of which it was impossible to say anything but that it was pink, and a mind it would be possible to describe only had one been able to mark it in a similar fashion. As nature had made this organ neither green nor blue nor yellow there was nothing to know it by : it strayed and bleated like an unbranded sheep. Fleda felt for it at this moment much of the kindness of compassion, since Mrs. Brigstock had brought it with her to do something for her that she regarded as delicate. Fleda was quite prepared to assist its use might she only divine what it wanted to do. What she divined however, more and more, was that it wanted to do something different from what it had wanted to do in leaving Waterbath. There was still nothing to enlighten her more specifically in the way her visitor continued : " You must be very much taken up. I believe you quite espouse his dreadful quarrel."

Fleda gained time by a vague echo. " His dreadful quarrel ? "

" About the contents of the house. Aren't you looking after them for him ? "

" She knows how awfully kind you've been to me,"
Owen explained to their young friend. He showed
such discomfiture that he really gave away their
situation; and Fleda found herself divided between
the hope that he would take leave and the wish that
he should see the whole of what the occasion might
enable her to bring to pass for him.

She addressed herself to Mrs. Brigstock. " Mrs.
Gereth, at Ricks the other day, asked me particularly
to see him for her."

" And did she ask you also particularly to see him
here in town ? " Mrs. Brigstock's hideous bonnet
seemed to argue for the unsophisticated truth ; and
it was on Fleda's lips to reply that such had indeed
been Mrs. Gereth's request. But she checked herself, and before she could say anything else Owen
had taken up the question.

" I made a point of letting Mona know that I
should be here, don't you see ? That's exactly what
I wrote her this morning."

" She would have had little doubt you'd be here
if you had a chance," Mrs. Brigstock returned. " If
your letter had arrived it might have prepared me
for finding you here at tea. In that case I certainly
wouldn't have come."

" I'm glad then it didn't arrive. Shouldn't you
like him to leave us ? " Fleda asked.

Mrs. Brigstock looked at Owen and considered :
nothing showed in her face but that it turned a deeper
pink. " I should like him to come with *me*." There
was no menace in her tone, but she evidently knew
what she wanted. As Owen made no response to this
Fleda glanced at him to invite him to assent ; then for
fear he wouldn't, and thus would make his case
worse, she took upon herself to express for him all
such readiness. She had no sooner spoken than she
felt in the words a bad effect of intimacy : she had

answered for him as if she had been his wife. Mrs. Brigstock continued to regard him without passion and spoke only to Fleda. " I've not seen him for a long time—I've particular things to say to him."

" So have I things to say to you, Mrs. Brigstock," Owen interjected. With this he took up his hat as for prompt departure.

The other visitor meanwhile kept at their hostess. " What's Mrs. Gereth going to do ? "

" Is that what you came to ask me ? " Fleda demanded.

" That and several other things."

" Then you had much better let Mr. Gereth go, and stay by yourself and make me a pleasant visit. You can talk with him when you like, but it's the first time you've been to see me."

This appeal had evidently a certain effect ; Mrs. Brigstock visibly wavered. " I can't talk with him whenever I like," she returned ; " he hasn't been near us since I don't know when. But there are things that have brought me here."

" They can't be things of any importance," Owen, to Fleda's surprise, suddenly asserted. He had not at first taken up Mrs. Brigstock's expression of a wish to carry him off : Fleda could see the instinct at the bottom of this to be that of standing by her, of seeming not to abandon her. But abruptly, all his soreness working within him, it had struck him he should abandon her still more if he should leave her to be dealt with by the messenger from Waterbath. " You must allow me to say, you know, Mrs. Brigstock, that I don't think you should come down on Miss Vetch about anything. It's very good of her to take the smallest interest in us and our horrid vulgar little squabble. If you want to talk about it talk about it with *me*." He was flushed with the idea of protecting Fleda, of exhibiting his consideration for her. " I

431

don't like you cross-questioning her, don't you see ? She's as straight as a die : *I'll* tell you all about her ! " he declared with a reckless laugh. " Please come off with me and let her alone."

Mrs. Brigstock, at this, became vivid at once ; Fleda thought her look extraordinary. She stood straight up—a queer distinction in her whole person and in everything of her face but her mouth, which she gathered into a small, tight orifice. The girl was painfully divided ; her joy was deep within, but it was more relevant to the situation that she shouldn't appear to associate herself with the tone of familiarity in which Owen addressed a lady who had been, and was perhaps still, about to become his mother-in-law. She laid on Mrs. Brigstock's arm a repressive, persuasive hand. Mrs. Brigstock, however, had already exclaimed on her having so wonderful a defender. " He speaks, upon my word, as if I had come here to be rude to you ! "

At this, grasping her hard, Fleda laughed ; then she achieved the exploit of delicately kissing her. " I'm not in the least afraid to be alone with you or of your tearing me to pieces. I'll answer any question that you can possibly dream of putting to me."

" I'm the proper person to answer Mrs. Brigstock's questions," Owen broke in again, " and I'm not a bit less ready to meet them than you are." He was firmer than she had ever seen him ; it was as if she hadn't dreamed he could be so firm.

" But she'll only have been here a few minutes. What sort of a visit is that ? " Fleda cried.

" It has lasted long enough for my purpose," Mrs. Brigstock judiciously declared. " There was something I wanted to know, but I think I know it now."

" Anything you don't know I daresay I can tell you ! " Owen observed as he impatiently smoothed his hat with the cuff of his coat.

Fleda by this time desired immensely to keep his companion, but she saw she could do so only at the cost of provoking on his part a further exhibition of the sheltering attitude which he exaggerated precisely because it was the first thing, since he had begun to " like " her, that he had been able frankly to do for her. It was not to her advantage that Mrs. Brigstock should be more struck than she already was with that benevolence. " There may be things you know that I don't," she presently said to her all reasonably and brightly. " But I've a sort of sense that you're labouring under some great mistake."

Mrs. Brigstock, at this, looked into her eyes more deeply and yearningly than she had supposed Mrs. Brigstock could look : it was the flicker of a mild, muddled willingness to give her a chance. Owen, however, quickly spoiled everything. " Nothing's more probable than that Mrs. Brigstock is doing what you say ; but there's no one in the world to whom you owe an explanation. I may owe somebody one —I daresay I do. But not you—no ! "

" But what if there's one that it's no difficulty at all for me to give ? " Fleda sweetly argued. " I'm sure that's the only one Mrs. Brigstock came to ask, if she came to ask any at all."

Again the good lady looked hard at her young friend. " I came, I believe, Fleda, just—you know— to plead with you."

Fleda, with her lighted face, hesitated a moment. " As if I were one of those bad women in a play ? "

The remark was disastrous : Mrs. Brigstock, on whom the grace of it was lost, evidently thought it singularly free. She turned away as from a presence that had really defined itself as objectionable, and the girl had a vain sense that her good humour, in which there was an idea, was taken for impertinence, or at least for levity. Her allusion was improper even if she herself wasn't. Mrs. Brigstock's emotion simplified : it came to the same thing. " I'm quite ready," that lady said to Owen rather grandly and woundedly. " I do want to speak to you very much."

" I'm completely at your service." Owen held out his hand to Fleda. " Good-bye, Miss Vetch. I hope to see you again to-morrow." He opened the door for Mrs. Brigstock, who passed before Miss Vetch with an oblique, averted salutation. Owen and Fleda, while he stood at the door, then faced each other darkly and without speaking. Their eyes met once more for a long moment, and she was conscious there was something in hers that the darkness didn't quench, that he had never seen before and that he was perhaps never to see again. He stayed long enough to take it—to take it with a sombre stare that just showed the dawn of wonder ; then he followed Mrs. Brigstock out of the house.

XVI

He had uttered the hope that he should see her the
next day, but Fleda could easily reflect that he
wouldn't see her if she were not there to be seen. If
there was a thing in the world she desired at that
moment it was that the next day should have no
point of resemblance with the day that had just
elapsed. She accordingly rose to the conception of an
absence : she would go immediately down to Maggie.
She ran out that evening and telegraphed to her sister,
and in the morning she quitted London by an early
train. She required for this step no reason but the
sense of necessity. It was a strong personal need ;
she wished to interpose something, and there was
nothing she could interpose but distance, but time.
If Mrs. Brigstock had to deal with Owen she would
allow Mrs. Brigstock the chance. To be there, to be
in the midst of it, was the reverse of what she craved :
she had already been more in the midst of it than had
ever entered into her plan. At any rate she had
renounced her plan ; she had no plan now but the plan
of separation. This was to abandon Owen, to give
up the fine office of helping him back to his own ; but
when she had undertaken that office she had not foreseen that Mrs. Gereth would defeat it by a manœuvre
so remarkably simple. The scene at her father's
rooms had extinguished all offices, and the scene at
her father's rooms was of Mrs. Gereth's producing.

Owen must at all events now act for himself : he had
obligations to meet, he had satisfactions to give, and
Fleda fairly ached with the wish he might be equal
to them. She never knew the extent of her tenderness
for him till she became conscious of the present
force of her desire that he should be superior, be
perhaps even sublime. She obscurely made out that
superiority, that sublimity mightn't after all be fatal.
She closed her eyes and lived for a day or two in the
mere beauty of confidence. It was with her on the
short journey ; it was with her at Maggie's ; it
glorified the mean little house in the stupid little town.
Owen had grown larger to her : he would do, like a
man, whatever he should have to do. He wouldn't
be weak — not as she was : she herself was weak
exceedingly.

Arranging her few possessions in Maggie's fewer
receptacles she caught a glimpse of the bright side
of the fact that her old things were not such a problem as Mrs. Gereth's. Picking her way with Maggie
through the local puddles, diving with her into
smelly cottages and supporting her, at smellier shops,
in firmness over the weight of joints and the taste of
cheese, it was still her own secret that was universally
interwoven. In the puddles, the cottages, the shops
she was comfortably alone with it ; that comfort prevailed even while, at the evening meal, her brother-
in-law invited her attention to a diagram, drawn with
a fork on too soiled a tablecloth, of the scandalous
drains of the Convalescent Home. To be alone with
it she had come away from Ricks, and now she knew
that to be alone with it she had come away from
London. This advantage was of course menaced,
though not immediately destroyed, by the arrival
on the second day of the note she had been sure she
should receive from Owen. He had gone to West
Kensington and found her flown, but he had got her

address from the little maid and then hurried to a
club and written to her. " Why have you left me
just when I want you most ? " he demanded. The
next words, it was true, were more reassuring on the
question of his steadiness. " I don't know what your
reason may be," they went on, " nor why you've not
left a line for me ; but I don't think you can feel that
I did anything yesterday that it wasn't right for me
to do. As regards Mrs. Brigstock certainly I just
felt what was right and I did it. She had no business
whatever to attack you that way, and I should have
been ashamed if I had left her there to worry you.
I won't have you worried by any one. No one shall
be disagreeable to you but me. I didn't mean to be
so yesterday, and I don't to-day ; but I'm perfectly
free now to want you, and I want you much more
than you've allowed me to explain. You'll see how
right I am if you'll let me come to you. Don't be
afraid—I'll not hurt you nor trouble you. I give you
my honour I'll not hurt any one. Only I *must* see
you about what I had to say to Mrs. B. She was
nastier than I thought she could be, but I'm behaving
like an angel. I assure you I'm all right—that's
exactly what I want you to see. You owe me something, you know, for what you said you would do
and haven't done ; what your departure without a
word gives me to understand—doesn't it ?—that you
definitely can't do. Don't simply forsake me. See
me if you only see me once. I shan't wait for any
leave, I shall come down to-morrow. I've been looking into trains and find there's something that will
bring me just after lunch and something very good
for getting me back. I won't stop long. For God's
sake be there."

This communication arrived in the morning, but
Fleda would still have time to wire a protest. She
debated on that alternative ; then she read the note

over and found in one phrase an exact statement of her duty. Owen's simplicity had so expressed it that her subtlety had nothing to answer. She owed him something for her obvious failure—what she owed him was to receive him. If indeed she had known he would make this attempt she might have been held to have gained nothing by flight. Well, she had gained what she had gained—she had gained the interval. She had no compunction for the greater trouble she should give the young man ; it was now doubtless right he should have as much trouble as possible. Maggie, who thought she was in her confidence, yet was immensely not, had reproached her for having quitted Mrs. Gereth, and Maggie was just in this proportion gratified to hear of the visitor with whom, early in the afternoon, Fleda would have to ask to be left alone. Maggie liked to see far, and now she could sit upstairs and rake the whole future. She had known that, as she familiarly said, there was something the matter with Fleda, and the value of that knowledge was augmented by the fact that there was apparently also something the matter with Mr. Gereth.

Fleda, downstairs, learned soon enough what this was. It was simply that, as he insisted afresh the moment he stood before her, he was now all right. When she asked him what he meant by that term he replied that he meant he could practically regard himself henceforth as a free man : he had had at West Kensington, as soon as they got into the street, such a beastly horrid scene with Mrs. Brigstock.

" I knew what she wanted to say to me : that's why I was determined to get her off. I knew I shouldn't like it, but I was perfectly prepared," said Owen. " She brought it out as soon as we got round the corner. She asked me point-blank if I was in love with you."

THE SPOILS OF POYNTON

"And what did you say to that?"

"That it was none of her business."

"Ah," said Fleda, "I'm not so sure!"

"Well, *I* am, and I'm the person most concerned.
Of course I didn't use just those words: I was perfectly civil, quite as civil as she. But I told her I
didn't consider she had a right to put me any such
question. I said I wasn't sure that even Mona had,
with the extraordinary line, you know—I mean that
she knew—Mona had taken. At any rate the whole
thing, the way *I* put it, was between Mona and me;
and between Mona and me, if she didn't mind, it
would just have to remain."

Fleda waited for more. "All that didn't answer
her question."

"Then you think I ought to have told her?"

Again our young lady reflected. "I think I'm
rather glad you didn't."

"I knew what I was about," said Owen. "It
didn't strike me she had the least right to come down
on us that way and try to overhaul us."

Fleda looked very grave, weighing the whole
matter. "I daresay that when she started, when
she arrived, she didn't mean to 'come down.'"

"What then did she mean to do?"

"What she said to me just before she went: she
meant to plead with me."

"Oh, I heard her—rather!" said Owen. "But
plead with you for what?"

"For you, of course—to entreat me to give you
up. She thinks me awfully designing—that I've
taken some sort of possession of you."

Owen stared. "You haven't lifted a finger! It's
I who have taken possession."

"Very true, you've done it all yourself." Fleda
spoke gravely and gently, without a breath of
coquetry. "But those are shades between which

439

she's probably not obliged to distinguish. It's enough for her that we're repulsively intimate."

" I am, but you're not ! " Owen exclaimed.

Fleda gave a dim smile. " You make me at least feel that I'm learning to know you very well when I hear you say such a thing as that. Mrs. Brigstock came to get round me, to supplicate me," she went on ; " but to find you there looking so much at home, paying me a friendly call and shoving the tea-things about — that was too much for her patience. She doesn't know, you see, that I'm after all a decent girl. She simply made up her mind on the spot that I'm a very bad case."

" I couldn't stand the way she treated you, and that was what I had to say to her," Owen returned.

" She's simple and slow, but she's not a fool : I think she treated me on the whole very well." Fleda remembered how Mrs. Gereth had treated Mona when the Brigstocks came down to Poynton.

Owen evidently thought her painfully perverse. " It was you who carried it off ; you behaved like a brick. And so did I, I consider. If you only knew the difficulty I had ! I told her you were the noblest and straightest of women."

" That can hardly have removed her impression that there are things I put you up to."

" It didn't," Owen replied with candour. " She said our relation, yours and mine, isn't innocent."

" What did she mean by that ? "

" As you may suppose, I put it to her straight. Do you know what she had the cheek to tell me ? " Owen asked. " She didn't better it much. She said she meant that it's jolly unnatural."

Fleda considered afresh. " Well, it is ! " she brought out at last.

" Then, upon my honour, it's only you who make it so ! " Her perversity was distinctly too much for him. " I mean you make it so by the way you keep me off."

" Have I kept you off to-day ? " Fleda sadly shook her head, raising her arms a little and dropping them.

Her gesture of resignation gave him a pretext for catching at her hand, but before he could take it she had put it behind her. They had been seated together on Maggie's single sofa, and her movement brought her to her feet while Owen, looking at her reproachfully, leaned back in discouragement. " What good does it do me to be here when I find you only a stone ? "

She met his eyes with all the tenderness she had not yet uttered, and she had not known till this moment how great was the accumulation. " Perhaps, after all," she risked, " there may be even in a stone still some little help for you."

He sat there a minute staring at her. " Ah you're beautiful, more beautiful than any one," he broke out, " but I'll be hanged if I can ever understand you ! On Tuesday, at your father's, you were beautiful—as beautiful, just before I left, as you are at this instant. But the next day, when I went back, I found it had apparently meant nothing ; and now again that you let me come here and you shine at me like an angel, it doesn't bring you an inch nearer to saying what I want you to say." He remained a moment longer in the same position, then jerked himself up. " What I want you to say is that you like me—what I want you to say is that you pity me." He sprang up and came to her. " What I want you to say is that you'll *save* me ! "

Fleda cast about. " Why do you need saving when you announced to me just now that you're a free man ? "

He too hesitated, but he was not checked. " It's

just for the reason that I'm free. Don't you know what I mean, Miss Vetch ? I want you to marry me."

Miss Vetch, at this, put out her hand in charity; she held his own, which quickly grasped it a moment, and if he had described her as shining at him it may be assumed that she shone all the more in her deep still smile. " Let me know what you mean by your ' freedom ' first," she said. " I gather that Mrs. Brigstock was not wholly satisfied with the way you disposed of her question."

" I daresay she wasn't. But the less she's satisfied the more I'm free."

" What bearing have *her* feelings, pray ? " Fleda asked.

" Why, Mona's much worse than her mother, you know. She wants much more to give me up."

" Then why doesn't she do it ? "

" She will, as soon as her mother gets home and tells her."

" Tells her what ? " Fleda went on.

" Why, that I'm in love with *you* ! "

Fleda debated. " Are you so very sure she will ? "

" Certainly I'm sure, with all the evidence I already have. That will finish her ! " Owen declared.

This made his companion thoughtful again. " Can you take such pleasure in her being ' finished '— a poor girl you've once loved ? "

He waited long enough to take in the question ; then with a serenity startling even to her knowledge of his nature, " I don't think I can have *really* loved her, you know," he pronounced.

She broke into a laugh that gave him a surprise as visible as the emotion it represented. " Then how am I to know you ' really ' love—anybody else ? "

" Oh I'll show you that ! " said Owen.

" I must take it on trust," the girl pursued. " And what if Mona doesn't give you up ? " she added.

He was baffled but a few seconds ; he had thought of everything. " Why, that's just where you come in."

" To save you ? I see. You mean I must get rid of her for you." His blankness showed for a little that he felt the chill of her cold logic, but as she waited for his rejoinder she knew to which of them it cost most. He gasped a minute, and that gave her time to say : " You see, Mr. Owen how impossible it is to talk of such things yet ! "

Like lightning he had grasped her arm. " You mean you *will* talk of them ? " Then as he began to take the flood of assent from her eyes : " You *will* listen to me ? Oh you dear, you dear—when, when ? "

" Ah when it isn't mere misery ! " The words had broken from her in a sudden loud cry, and what next happened was that the very sound of her pain upset her. She heard her own true note ; she turned short away from him ; in a moment she had burst into sobs ; in another his arms were round her ; the next she had let herself go so far that even Mrs. Gereth might have seen it. He clasped her, and she gave herself — she poured out her tears on his breast. Something prisoned and pent throbbed and gushed ; something deep and sweet surged up — something that came from far within and far off, that had begun with the sight of him in his indifference and had never had rest since then. The surrender was short, but the relief was long : she felt his warm lips on her face and his arms tighten with his full divination. What she did, what she *had* done, she scarcely knew : she only was aware, as she broke from him again, of what had taken place on his own amazed part. What had taken place was that, with the click of a spring, he saw. He had cleared the high wall at a bound ; they were together without a veil. She had not a shred of a secret left ; it was as if a whirlwind had come and gone, laying low the great false front she had built up stone by stone. The strangest thing of all was the momentary sense of desolation.

" Ah all the while you *cared* ? " Owen read the truth with a wonder so great that it was visibly almost a sadness, a terror caused by his sudden perception of where the impossibility was not. That treacherously placed it perhaps elsewhere.

" I cared, I cared, I cared ! "—she wailed it as to confess a misdeed. " How couldn't I care ? But you mustn't, you must never, never ask ! It isn't for us to talk about," she protested. " Don't speak of it, don't speak ! "

It was easy indeed not to speak when the difficulty was to find words. He clasped his hands before her as he might have clasped them at an altar ; his pressed palms shook together while he held his breath and while she stilled herself in the effort to come round again to the real and the thinkable. He assisted this effort, soothing her into a seat with a touch as anxious as if she had been truly something sacred. She sank into a chair and he dropped before her on his knees ; she fell back with closed eyes and he buried his face in her lap. There was no way to thank her but this act of prostration, which lasted, in silence, till she laid consenting hands on him, touched his head and stroked it, let her close possession of it teach him his long blindness. He made the whole fall, as she yet felt it, seem only his—made her, when she rose again, raise him at last, softly, as if from the abasement of it. If in each other's eyes now, however, they saw the truth, this truth, to Fleda, looked harder even than before — all the harder that when, at the very moment she recognised

444

it, he murmured to her ecstatically, in fresh possession of her hands, which he drew up to his breast,
holding them tight there with both his own : " I'm
saved, I'm saved—I *am* ! I'm ready for anything.
I have your word. Come ! " he cried, as if from the
sight of a response slower than he needed and in the
tone he so often had of a great boy at a great game.

She had once more disengaged herself with the
private vow that he shouldn't yet touch her again.
It was all too horribly soon—her sense of this had
come straight back. " We mustn't talk, we mustn't
talk ; we must wait ! "—she had to make that clear.
" I don't know what you mean by your freedom ; I
don't see it, I don't feel it. Where is it yet, where,
your freedom ? If it's real there's plenty of time,
and if it isn't there's more than enough. I hate
myself," she insisted, " for having anything to say
about her : it's like waiting for dead men's shoes !
What business is it of mine what she does ? She has
her own trouble and her own plan. It's too hideous
to watch her so and count on her ! "

Owen's face, at this, showed a reviving dread, the
fear of some darksome process of her mind. " If you
speak for yourself I can understand. But why is it
hideous for me ? "

" Oh I mean for myself ! " Fleda quickly cried.
" *I* watch her, *I* count on her : how can I do anything else ? If I count on her to let me definitely
know how we stand I do nothing in life but what
she herself has led straight up to. I never thought
of asking you to ' get rid of her ' for me, and I never
would have spoken to you if I hadn't held that I *am*
rid of her, that she has backed out of the whole thing.
Didn't she do so from the moment she began to put
it off ? I had already applied for the licence ; the
very invitations were half-addressed. Who but she,
all of a sudden, required an unnatural wait ? It was

445

none of *my* doing ; I had never dreamed of anything
but coming up to the scratch." Owen grew more
and more lucid and more confident of the effect of
his lucidity. " She called it ' taking a stand '—taking
it to see what mother would do. I told her mother
would do what I'd make her do ; and to that she
replied that she'd like to see me make her first. I
said I'd arrange that everything should be all right,
and she said she really preferred to arrange it herself.
It was a flat refusal to trust me in the smallest degree.
Why then had she pretended so tremendously to care
for me ? And of course at present," said Owen,
" she trusts me, if possible, still less."

Fleda paid this statement the homage of a minute's
muteness. " As to that, naturally, she has reason."

" Why on earth has she reason ? " Then as his
companion, moving away, simply threw up her hands,
" I never looked at you—not to call looking—till
she had regularly driven me to it," he went on. " I
know what I'm about. I do assure you I'm all
right ! "

" You're not all right—you're all wrong ! " Fleda
cried in sudden despair. " You mustn't stay here,
you mustn't ! " she repeated in still greater anxiety.
" You make me say dreadful things, and I feel as if I
made *you* say them." But before he could reply she
took it up in another tone. " Why in the world, if
everything had changed, didn't you break off ? "

" I—— ? " The words moved him to visible stupefaction. " Can you ask me that when I only wanted
to please you ? Didn't you seem to show me, in your
wonderful way, that that was exactly how ? If I
didn't break off it was just on purpose to leave it to
Mona. If I didn't break off it was just so that there
shouldn't be a thing to be said against me."

The instant after her challenge she had faced
him again in self-reproof. " There *isn't* a thing to

be said against you, and I don't know what folly
you make me talk ! You *have* pleased me, and you've
been right and good, and it's the only comfort, and
you must go. Everything must come from Mona,
and if it doesn't come we've said entirely too much.
You must leave me alone—for ever."

" For ever ? " Owen gasped.

" I mean unless everything's different."

" Everything *is* different when I know you ! "

Fleda winced at his knowledge ; she made a wild
gesture which seemed to whirl it out of the room.
The mere allusion was like another attack from him.
" You don't know me—you don't—and you must go
and wait ! You mustn't break down at this point."

He looked about him and took up his hat : it was
as if in spite of frustration he had got the essence
of what he wanted and could afford to agree with her
to the extent of keeping up the forms. He covered
her with his fine simple smile, but made no other
approach. " Oh I'm so awfully happy ! " he cried.

She hung back now ; she would only be impeccable
even though she should have to be sententious.
" You'll be happy if you're perfect ! " she risked.

He laughed out at this, and she wondered if, with
a new-born acuteness, he saw the absurdity of her
speech and that no one was happy just because no
one could be what she so easily prescribed. " I don't
pretend to be perfect, but I shall find a letter to-
night ! "

" So much the better, if it's the kind of one you
desire." That was the most she could say, and
having made it sound as dry as possible she lapsed
into a silence so pointed as to deprive him of all pretext for not leaving her. Still, nevertheless, he stood
there, playing with his hat and filling the long pause
with a strained and unsatisfied smile. He wished
to obey her thoroughly, to appear not to presume

on any advantage he had won from her; but there was clearly something he longed for besides. While he showed this by hanging on she thought of two other things. One of these was that the look of him after all failed to bear out his description of his bliss. As for the other, it had no sooner come into her head than she found it seated, in spite of her resolution, on her lips. It took the form of an inconsequent question. "When did you say Mrs. Brigstock was to have gone back?"

Owen stared. "To Waterbath? She was to have spent the night in town, don't you know? But when she left me after our talk I said to myself that she'd take an evening train. I know I made her want to get home."

"Where did you separate?" Fleda asked.

"At the West Kensington Station—she was going to Victoria. I had walked with her there, and our talk was all on the way."

Fleda turned it over. "If she did go back that night you'd have heard.from Waterbath by this time."

"I don't know," said Owen. "I thought I might hear this morning."

"She can't have gone back," Fleda declared. "Mona would have written on the spot."

"Oh yes, she *will* have written bang off!" he cheerfully conceded.

She thought again. "So that even in the event of her mother's not having got home till the morning you'd have had your letter at the latest to-day. You see she has had plenty of time."

Owen took it in; then "Oh she's all right!" he laughed. "I go by Mrs. Brigstock's certain effect on her—the effect of the temper the old lady showed when we parted. Do you know what she asked me?" he sociably continued. "She asked me in a kind of nasty manner if I supposed you 'really' cared anything about me. Of course I told her I supposed you didn't—not a solitary rap. How could I ever suppose you did—with your extraordinary ways? It doesn't matter. I could see she thought I lied."

"You should have told her, you know, that I had seen you in town only that one time," Fleda said.

"By Jove, I did—for *you*! It was only for you."

Something in this touched the girl so that for a moment she couldn't trust herself to speak. "You're an honest man," she said at last. She had gone to the door and opened it. "Good-bye."

Even yet, however, he hung back. "But say there's no letter——" he anxiously began. He began, but there he left it.

"You mean even if she doesn't let you off? Ah you ask me too much!" Fleda spoke from the tiny hall, where she had taken refuge between the old barometer and the old mackintosh. "There are things too utterly for yourselves alone. How can I tell? What do I know? Good-bye, good-bye! If she doesn't let you off it will be because she *is* attached to you."

"She's not, she's not: there's nothing in it! Doesn't a fellow know?—except with *you*!" Owen ruefully added. With this he came out of the room, lowering his voice to secret supplication, pleading with her really to meet him on the ground of the negation of Mona. It was this betrayal of his need of support and sanction that made her retreat, harden herself in the effort to save what might remain of all she had given, given probably for nothing. The very vision of him as he thus morally clung to her was the vision of a weakness somewhere at the core of his bloom, a blessed manly weakness which, had she only the valid right, it would be all easy and sweet to take care of. She faintly sickened, however, with the sense that there was as yet no valid right poor

Owen could give. " You can take it from my honour, you know," he painfully brought out, " that she quite loathes me."

Fleda had stood clutching the knob of Maggie's little painted stair-rail ; she took, on the stairs, a step backward. " Why then doesn't she prove it in the only clear way ? "

" She *has* proved it. Will you believe it if you see the letter ? "

" I don't want to see any letter," said Fleda. " You'll miss your train."

Facing him, waving him away, she had taken another upward step ; but he sprang to the side of the stairs, and brought his hand, above the banister, down hard on her wrist. " Do you mean to tell me that I must marry a woman I hate ? "

From her step she looked down into his raised face. " Ah you see it's not true that you're free ! " She seemed almost to exult. " It's not true, it's not true ! "

He only, at this, like a buffeting swimmer, gave a shake of his head and repeated his question : " Do you mean to tell me I must marry such a woman ? "

Fleda gasped too ; he held her fast. " No. Anything's better than that."

" Then in God's name what must I do ? "

" You must settle that with Mona. You mustn't break faith. Anything's better than that. You must at any rate be utterly sure. She must love you—how can she help it ? *I* wouldn't give you up ! " said Fleda. She spoke in broken bits, panting out her words. " The great thing is to keep faith. Where's a man if he doesn't ? If he doesn't he may be so cruel. So cruel, so cruel, so cruel ! " Fleda repeated. " I couldn't have a hand in that, you know : that's my position—that's mine. You offered her marriage. It's a tremendous thing for her." Then looking at him another moment, "*I* wouldn't give you up!" she said again. He still had hold of her arm; she took in his blank dread. With a quick dip of her face she reached his hand with her lips, pressing them to the back of it with a force that doubled the force of her words. "Never, never, never!" she cried; and before he could succeed in seizing her she had turned and, flashing up the stairs, got away from him even faster than she had got away at Ricks.

XVII

TEN days after his visit she received a communication
from Mrs. Gereth—a telegram of eight words, exclusive
of signature and date. " Come up immediately
and stay with me here "—it was characteristically
sharp, as Maggie said ; but, as Maggie added, it was
also characteristically kind. " Here " was an hotel
in London, and Maggie had embraced a condition of
life which already began to produce in her some
yearning for hotels in London. She would have
responded on the spot and was surprised that her
sister seemed to wait. Fleda's demur, which lasted
but an hour, was expressed in that young lady's own
mind by the reflexion that in obeying her friend's
call she shouldn't know what she should be " in for."
Her friend's call, however, was but another name
for her friend's need, and Mrs. Gereth's bounty had
laid her under obligations more marked than any
hindrance. In the event—that is at the end of her
hour—she testified to her gratitude by taking the
train and to her mistrust by leaving her luggage.
She went as if going up for the day. In the train,
however, she had another thoughtful hour, during
which it was her mistrust that mainly deepened.
She felt as if for ten days she had sat in darkness
and looked to the east for a dawn that had not
glimmered. Her mind had lately been less occupied
with Mrs. Gereth ; it had been so exceptionally

452

occupied with Mona. If the sequel was to justify
Owen's prevision of Mrs. Brigstock's action on her
daughter this action was at the end of a week still
thoroughly obscure. The stillness all round had been
exactly what Fleda desired, but it gave her for a time
a deep sense of failure, the sense of a sudden drop
from a height at which she had had all things beneath
her. She had nothing beneath her now ; she herself
was at the bottom of the heap. No sign had reached
her from Owen — poor Owen who had clearly no
news to give about his precious letter from Waterbath. If Mrs. Brigstock had hurried back to obtain
that this letter should be written Mrs. Brigstock
might then have spared herself so great an inconvenience. Owen had been silent for the best of all
reasons—the reason that he had had nothing in life
to say. If the letter had not been written he would
simply have had to introduce some large qualification into his account of his freedom. He had left his
young friend under her refusal to listen to him till
he should be able, on the contrary, to extend that
picture ; and his present submission was all in keeping with the rigid honesty that his young friend had
prescribed.

It was this that formed the element through which
Mona loomed large ; Fleda had enough imagination,
a fine enough feeling for life, to be impressed with
such an image of successful immobility. The massive
maiden at Waterbath *was* successful from the moment
she could entertain her resentments as if they had
been poor relations who needn't put her to expense.
She was a magnificent dead weight ; there was
something positive and portentous in her quietude.
" What game are they all playing ? " poor Fleda
could only ask ; for she had an intimate conviction
that Owen was now under the roof of his betrothed.
That was stupefying if he really hated his betrothed ;

and if he didn't really hate her what had brought him to Raphael Road and to Maggie's ? Fleda had no real light, but she felt that to account for the absence of any sequel to their last meeting would take a supposition of the full sacrifice to charity that she had held up before him. If he had gone to Waterbath it had been simply because he had had to go. She had as good as told him he would have to go ; that this was an inevitable incident of his keeping perfect faith—faith so literal that the smallest subterfuge would always be a reproach to him. When she tried to remember that it was for herself he was taking his risk she felt how weak a way that was of expressing Mona's supremacy. There would be no need of keeping him up if there was nothing to keep him up to. Her eyes grew wan as she discerned in the impenetrable air that Mona's thick outline never wavered an inch. She wondered fitfully what Mrs. Gereth had by this time made of it, and reflected with a strange elation that the sand on which the mistress of Ricks had built a momentary triumph was quaking beneath the surface. As *The Morning Post* still held its peace she would be of course more confident ; but the hour was at hand at which Owen would have absolutely to do either one thing or the other. To keep perfect faith was to inform against his mother, and to hear the police at her door would be Mrs. Gereth's awakening. How much she was beguiled Fleda could see from her having been for a whole month quite as deep and dark as Mona. She had left her young friend alone because of the certitude, cultivated at Ricks, that Owen had done the opposite. He had done the opposite indeed, but much good had that brought forth ! To have sent for her now, Fleda felt, was from this point of view wholly natural : she had sent for her to show at last how largely she had scored. If, however, Owen was really at Waterbath the refutation of that boast would be easy even to a primitive critic.

Fleda found Mrs. Gereth in modest apartments and with an air of fatigue in her distinguished face, a sign, as she privately remarked, of the strain of that effort to be discreet of which she herself had been having the benefit. It was a constant feature of their relation that this lady could make Fleda blench a little, and that the effect proceeded from the intense pressure of her confidence. If the confidence had been heavy even when the girl, in the early flush of devotion, had been able to feel herself yield most, it drew her heart into her mouth now that she had reserves and conditions, now that she couldn't simplify with the same bold hand as her protectress. In the very brightening of the tired look and at the moment of their embrace Fleda felt on her shoulders the return of the load ; whereupon her spirit quailed as she asked herself what she had brought up from her trusted seclusion to support it. Mrs. Gereth's free manner always made a joke of weakness, and there was in such a welcome a richness, a kind of familiar nobleness, that suggested shame to a harried conscience. Something had happened, she could see, and she could also see, in the bravery that seemed to announce it had changed everything, a formidable assumption that what had happened was what a healthy young woman must like. The absence of luggage had made this young woman feel meagre even before her companion, taking in the bareness at a second glance, exclaimed upon it and roundly rebuked her. Of course she had expected her to stay.

Fleda thought best to show bravery too and to show it from the first. "What you expected, dear Mrs. Gereth, is exactly what I came up to ascertain. It struck me as right to do that first. Right, I mean, to ascertain without making preparations."

" Then you'll be so good as to make them on the spot ! " Mrs. Gereth was most emphatic. " You're going abroad with me."

Fleda wondered, but she also smiled. " To-night —to-morrow ? "

" In as few days as possible. That's all that's left for me now." Fleda's heart, at this, gave a bound ; she wondered to what particular difference in Mrs. Gereth's situation as last known to her it referred. " I've made my plan," her friend continued : " I go at least for a year. We shall go straight to Florence ; we can manage there. I of course don't look to you, however," she added, " to stay with me all that time. That will require to be settled. Owen will have to join us as soon as possible ; he may not be quite ready to get off with us. But I'm convinced it's quite the right thing to go. It will make a good change. It will put in a decent interval."

Fleda listened ; she was deeply mystified. " How kind you are to me ! " she presently said. The picture suggested so many questions that she scarce knew which to ask first. She took one at a venture. " You really have it from Mr. Gereth that he'll give us his company ? "

If Mr. Gereth's mother smiled in response to this Fleda knew that her smile was a tacit criticism of such a mode of dealing with her son. Fleda habitually spoke of him as Mr. Owen, and it was a part of her present system to appear to have relinquished that right. Mrs. Gereth's manner confirmed a certain betrayal of her pretending to more than she felt ; her very first words had conveyed it, and it reminded Fleda of the conscious courage with which, weeks before, the lady had met her visitor's first startled stare at the clustered spoils of Poynton. It was her practice to take immensely for granted whatever she wished. " Oh if you'll answer for him it will do quite as well ! " With this answer she put her hands on the girl's shoulders and held them at arm's length, as to shake them a little, while in the depths of her shining eyes Fleda saw something obscure and unquiet. " You bad false thing, why didn't you tell me ? " Her tone softened her harshness, and her visitor had never had such a sense of her indulgence. Mrs. Gereth could show patience ; it was a part of the general bribe, but it was also like the presentation of a heavy bill before which Fleda could only fumble in a penniless pocket. " You must perfectly have known at Ricks, and yet you practically denied it. That's why I call you bad and false ! " It was apparently also why she again almost roughly kissed her.

" I think that before I satisfy you I had better know what you're talking about," Fleda said.

Mrs. Gereth looked at her with a slight increase of hardness. " You've done everything you need for modesty, my dear ! If he's sick with love of you, you haven't had to wait for me to inform you."

Fleda knew herself turn pale. " Has he informed *you*, dear Mrs. Gereth ? "

Dear Mrs. Gereth smiled sweetly. " How could he when our situation is such that he communicates with me only through you and that you're so tortuous you conceal everything ? "

" Didn't he answer the note in which you let him know I was in town ? " Fleda asked.

" He answered it sufficiently by rushing off on the spot to see you."

Mrs. Gereth met this allusion with a prompt firmness that made almost insolently light of any ground of complaint, and Fleda's own sense of responsibility was now so vivid that all resentments comparatively shrank. She had no heart to produce a grievance ; she could only, left as she was with the little mystery on her hands, produce after a moment a question.

" How then do you come to know that your son has ever thought——? "

" That he would give his ears to get you ? " Mrs. Gereth broke in. " I had a visit from Mrs. Brigstock."

Fleda opened her eyes. " She went down to Ricks ? "

" The day after she had found Owen at your feet. She knows everything."

Fleda shook her head sadly : she was more startled than she cared to show. This odd journey of Mrs. Brigstock's, which, with a simplicity equal for once to Owen's, she had not divined, now struck her as at bottom of the hush of the last ten days. " There are things she doesn't know ! " she presently returned.

" She knows he'd do anything to marry you."

" He hasn't told her so," Fleda said.

" No, but he has told *you*. That's better still ! " laughed Mrs. Gereth. " My dear child," she went on with an air that affected the girl as a blind profanity, " don't try to make yourself out better than you are. *I* know what you are — I haven't lived with you so much for nothing. You're not quite a saint in heaven yet. Lord, what a creature you'd have thought me in my good time ! But you do like it fortunately, you idiot. You're pale with your passion, you sweet thing. That's exactly what I wanted to see. I can't for the life of me think where the shame comes in." Then with a finer significance, a look that seemed to Fleda strange, she added : " It's all right."

" I've seen him but twice," said Fleda.

" But twice ? " Mrs. Gereth still smiled.

" On the occasion, at papa's, that Mrs. Brigstock told you of, and one day, since then, down at Maggie's."

" Well, those things are between yourselves, and

you seem to me both poor creatures at best." She spoke with a rich humour which made her attitude indeed a complacency. " I don't know what you've got in your veins. You absurdly exaggerate the difficulties. But enough's as good as a feast, and when once I get you abroad together—— ! " Mrs. Gereth checked herself as from excess of meaning ; what might happen when she should get them abroad together was to be gathered only from the way she slowly rubbed her hands.

The gesture, however, made the promise so definite that for a moment her companion was almost beguiled. Yet there was still nothing to account for the wealth of her certitude : the visit of the lady of Waterbath appeared but half to explain it. " Is it permitted to be surprised," Fleda deferentially asked, " at Mrs. Brigstock's thinking it would help her to see you ? "

" It's never permitted to be surprised at the aberrations of born fools," said Mrs. Gereth. " If a cow should try to calculate, that's the kind of happy thought she'd have. Mrs. Brigstock came down to plead with me."

Fleda mused a moment. " That's what she came to do with *me*," she then honestly returned. " But what did she expect to get of you—with your opposition so marked from the first ? "

" She didn't know I want *you*, my dear. It's a wonder, with all my violence — the gross publicity I've given my desires. But she's as stupid as an owl —she doesn't feel your charm."

Fleda felt herself flush slightly, and her amusement at this was ineffective. " Did you tell her all about my charm ? Did you make her understand you want me ? "

" For what do you take me ? I wasn't such a booby."

" So as not to aggravate Mona ? " Fleda suggested.

" So as not to aggravate Mona, naturally. We've had a narrow course to steer, but thank God we're at last in the open ! "

" What do you call the open, Mrs. Gereth ? " Fleda demanded. Then as that lady faltered : " Do you know where Mr. Owen is to-day ? "

His mother stared. " Do you mean he's at Waterbath ? Well, that's your own affair. I can bear it if *you* can."

" Wherever he is I can bear it," Fleda said. " But I haven't the least idea where he is."

" Then you ought to be ashamed of yourself ! " her friend broke out with a change of note that showed how deep a passion underlay everything she had said. The poor woman, catching her hand, however, the next moment, as if to retract something of this harshness, spoke more patiently. " Don't you understand, Fleda, how immensely, how devotedly I've trusted you ! " Her tone was indeed a supplication.

Fleda was infinitely shaken ; she couldn't immediately speak. " Yes, I understand. Did she go to you to complain of me ? "

" She came to see what she could do. She had been tremendously upset the day before by what had taken place at your father's, and she had posted down to Ricks on the inspiration of the moment. She hadn't meant it on leaving home ; it was the sight of you closeted there with Owen that had suddenly determined her. The whole story, she said, was written in your two faces : she spoke as if she had never seen such an exhibition. Owen was on the brink, but there might still be time to save him, and it was with this idea she had bearded me in my den. ' What won't a mother do, you know ? '—that was

one of the things she said. What wouldn't a mother
do indeed? I thought I had sufficiently shown her
what! She tried to break me down by an appeal
to my good nature, as she called it, and from the
moment she opened on *you*, from the moment she
denounced Owen's falsity, I was as good-natured as
she could wish. I understood it as a plea for mere
mercy — because you and he between you were
killing her child. Of course I was delighted that
Mona should be killed, but I was studiously kind
to Mrs. Brigstock. At the same time I was honest, I
didn't pretend to anything I couldn't feel. I asked
her why the marriage hadn't taken place months
ago, when Owen was perfectly ready ; and I showed
her how completely that fatuous mistake on Mona's
part cleared his responsibility. It was she who had
killed *him*—it was she who had destroyed his affection, his illusions. Did she want him now when he
was estranged, when he was disgusted, when he had
a sore grievance ? She reminded me that Mona had
a sore grievance too, but admitted she hadn't come
to me to speak of that. What she had come for was
not to get the old things back, but simply to get
Owen. What she wanted was that I would, in simple
pity, see fair play. Owen had been awfully bedevilled—she didn't call it that, she called it ' mis-
led ' ; but it was simply you who had bedevilled
him. He would be all right still if I would only see
you well out of the way. She asked me point-blank
if it was possible I could want him to marry you."

Fleda had listened in unbearable pain and growing
terror, as if her companion, stone by stone, were
piling some fatal mass upon her breast. She had the
sense of being buried alive, smothered in the mere
expansion of another will ; and now there was but
one gap left to the air. A single word, she felt, might
close it, and with the question that came to her lips

as Mrs. Gereth paused she seemed to herself to ask, in cold dread, for her doom. " What did you say to that ? " she gasped.

" I was embarrassed, for I saw my danger—the danger of her going home and saying to Mona that I was backing you up. It had been a bliss to learn that Owen had really turned to you, but my joy didn't put me off my guard. I reflected intensely a few seconds ; then I saw my issue."

" Your issue ? " Fleda echoed.

" I remembered how you had tied my hands about saying a word to Owen."

Fleda wondered. " And did you remember the little letter that, with your hands tied, you still succeeded in writing him ? "

" Perfectly ; my little letter was a model of reticence. What I remembered was all that in those few words I forbade myself to say. I had been an angel of delicacy—I had effaced myself like a saint. It wasn't for me to have done all that and then figure to such a woman as having done the opposite. Besides, it was none of her business."

" Is that what you said to her ? " the girl asked.

" I said to her that her question revealed a total misconception of the nature of my present relations with my son. I said to her that I had no relations with him at all and that nothing had passed between us for months. I said to her that my hands were spotlessly clean of any attempt to make up to you. I said to her that I had taken from Poynton what I had a right to take, but had done nothing else in the world. I was determined that since I had bitten my tongue off to oblige you I would at least have the righteousness that my sacrifice gave me."

" And was Mrs. Brigstock satisfied with your answer ? "

" She was visibly relieved."

"It was fortunate for you," said Fleda, "that she's apparently not aware of the manner in which, almost under her nose, you advertised me to him at Poynton."

Mrs. Gereth appeared to recall that scene ; she smiled with a serenity remarkably effective as showing how cheerfully used she had grown to invidious allusions to it. "How should she be aware of it ? "

"She would if Owen had described your outbreak to Mona."

"Yes, but he didn't describe it. All his instinct was to conceal it from Mona. He wasn't conscious, but he was already in love with you ! " Mrs. Gereth declared.

Fleda shook her head wearily. "No—I was only in love with *him* ! "

Here was a faint illumination with which Mrs. Gereth instantly mingled her fire. "You dear old wretch ! " she exclaimed ; and she again, with ferocity, embraced her young friend.

Fleda submitted like a sick animal : she would submit to everything now. "Then what further passed ? "

"Only that she left me thinking she had got something."

"And what had she got ? "

"Nothing but her luncheon. But *I* got everything ! "

"Everything ? " Fleda quavered.

Mrs. Gereth, struck apparently by something in her tone, looked at her from a tremendous height. "Don't fail me now ! "

It sounded so like a menace that, with a full divination at last, the poor girl fell weakly into a chair. "What on earth have you done ? "

Mrs. Gereth stood there in all the glory of a great stroke. "I've settled you." She filled the room, to Fleda's scared vision, with the glare of her magnificence. " I've sent everything back."

" Everything ? " Fleda wailed.

" To the smallest snuff-box. The last load went yesterday. The same people did it. Poor little Ricks is empty." Then as if, for a crowning splendour, to check all deprecation, " They're yours, you goose ! " the wonderful woman concluded, holding up her handsome head and rubbing her white hands. But there were tears none the less in her deep eyes.

XVIII

FLEDA was slow to take in the announcement, but
when she had done so she felt it to be more than
her cup of bitterness would hold. Her bitterness
was her anxiety, the taste of which suddenly sickened
her. What had she on the spot become but a dire
traitress to her friend ? The treachery increased with
the view of the friend's motive, a motive splendid as
a tribute to her value. Mrs. Gereth had wished to
make sure of her and had reasoned that there would
be no such way as by a large appeal to her honour.
If it be true, as men have declared, that the sense of
honour is weak in women, some of the bearings of
this stroke might have thrown a light on the question. What was now at all events put before Fleda
was that she had been made sure of, since the greatness of the surrender imposed an obligation as great.
There was an expression she had heard used by
young men with whom she danced : the only word
to fit Mrs. Gereth's intention was that Mrs. Gereth
had designed to " fetch " her. It was a calculated,
it was a crushing bribe ; it looked her in the eyes
and said awfully : " That's what I do for you ! "
What Fleda was to do in return required no pointing
out. The sense at present of how little she had done
it made her almost cry out with pain ; but her first
endeavour in face of the fact was to keep such a cry
from reaching her companion. How little she had

done it Mrs. Gereth didn't yet know, and possibly there would be still some way of turning round before the discovery. On her own side too Fleda had almost made one : she had known she was wanted, but she had not after all conceived how magnificently much. She had been treated by her friend's act as a conscious prize, but her value consisted all in the power the act itself imputed to her. As high bold diplomacy it dazzled and carried her off her feet. She admired the noble risk of it, a risk Mrs. Gereth had faced for the utterly poor creature the girl now felt herself. The change it instantly wrought in her was moreover extraordinary : it transformed at a touch her feeling on the subject of concessions. A few weeks earlier she had jumped at the duty of pleading for them, practically quarrelling with the lady of Ricks for her refusal to restore what she had taken. She had been sore with the wrong to Owen, she had bled with the wounds of Poynton ; now, however, as she heard of the replenishment of the void that had so haunted her she came as near sounding an alarm as if from the deck of a ship she had seen a person she loved jump into the sea. Mrs. Gereth had become in a flash the victim ; poor little Ricks had yielded up its treasure in a night. If Fleda's present view of the " spoils " had taken precipitate form the form would have been a frantic command. It was indeed for mere want of breath she didn't shout " Oh stop them — it's no use ; bring them back — it's too late ! " And what most kept her breathless was her companion's very grandeur. Fleda distinguished as never before the purity of the passion concerned ; it made Mrs. Gereth august and almost sublime. It was absolutely unselfish— she cared nothing for mere possession. She thought solely and incorruptibly of what was best for the objects themselves ; she had surrendered them to the

presumptive care of the one person of her acquaintance who felt about them as she felt herself and whose
long lease of the future would be the nearest approach
that could be compassed to committing them to a
museum. Now it was indeed that Fleda knew what
rested on her ; now it was also that she measured
as for the first time her friend's notion of the natural
influence of a grand " haul." Mrs. Gereth had risen
to the idea of blowing away the last doubt of what her
young charge would gain, of making good still more
than she was obliged to make it the promise of weeks
before. It was one thing for the girl to have learnt
that in a certain event restitution would be made ;
it was another for her to see the condition, with a
noble trust, treated in advance as performed, and to
know she should have only to open a door to find
every old piece in every old corner. To have played
such a card would be thus, for so grand a gambler,
practically to have won the game. Fleda had certainly
to recognise that, so far as the theory of the matter
went, the game had been won. Oh she had been
made sure of !

She couldn't, however, succeed for so very many
minutes in putting off her exposure. " Why didn't
you wait, dearest ? Ah why didn't you wait ? "—
if that inconsequent appeal kept rising to her lips
to be cut short before it was spoken, this was only
because at first the humility of gratitude helped her
to gain time, enabled her to present herself very
honestly as too overcome to be clear. She kissed
her companion's hands, she did homage at her feet,
she murmured soft snatches of praise, and yet in the
midst of it all was conscious that what she really
showed most was the dark despair at her heart. She
saw the poor woman's glimpse of this strange reserve
suddenly widen, heard the quick chill of her voice
pierce through the false courage of endearments.

" Do you mean to tell me at such an hour as this that you've really lost him ? "

The tone of the question made the idea a possibility for which Fleda had nothing from this moment but terror. " I don't know, Mrs. Gereth ; how can I say ? " she asked. " I've not seen him for so long ; as I told you just now, I don't even know where he is. That's by no fault of his," she hurried on : " he would have been with me every day if I had consented. But I made him understand, the last time, that I'll receive him again only when he's able to show me his release as quite signed and sealed. Oh he can't yet, don't you see ?—and that's why he hasn't been back. It's far better than his coming only that we should both be miserable. When he does come he'll be in a better position. He'll be tremendously moved by the wonderful thing you've done. I know you wish me to feel you've done it as much for me as for Owen, but your having done it for me is just what will delight him most ! When he hears of it," said Fleda in panting optimism, " when he hears of it——! " There indeed, regretting her advance and failing of every confidence, she quite broke down. She was wholly powerless to say what Owen would do when he heard of it. " I don't know what he won't make of you and how he won't hug you ! " she had to content herself with meanly declaring. She had drawn her terrible dupe and judge to a sofa with a vague instinct of pacifying her and still, after all, gaining time ; but it was a position in which that extraordinary character, portentously patient again during this demonstration, looked far from inviting a " hug." Fleda found herself tricking out the situation with artificial flowers, trying to talk even herself into the fancy that Owen, whose name she now made simple and sweet, might come in upon them at any moment. She felt an immense need to be understood and justified ; she abjectly averted her face from all she might have to be forgiven. She pressed on her hostess's arm as if to keep her quiet till she should really know, and then, after a minute, she poured out the clear essence of what in happier days had been her " secret." " You mustn't think I don't adore him when I've told him so to his face. I love him so that I'd die for him—I love him so that it's horrible. Don't look at me therefore as if I hadn't been kind, as if I hadn't been as tender as if he were dying and my tenderness were what would save him. Look at me as if you believe me, as if you feel what I've been through. Darling Mrs. Gereth, I could kiss the ground he walks on. I haven't a rag of pride ; I used to have, but it's gone. I used to have a secret, but every one knows it now, and any one who looks at me can say, I think, what's the matter with me. It's not so very fine, my secret, and the less one really says about it the better ; but I want you to have it from me because I was stiff before. I want you to see for yourself that I've been brought as low as a girl can very well be. It serves me right," Fleda laughed, " if I was ever proud and horrid to you ! I don't know what you wanted me, in those days at Ricks, to do, but I don't think you can have wanted much more than what I've done. The other day at Maggie's I did things that made me afterwards think of you ! I don't know what girls may do ; but if he doesn't know that there isn't an inch of me that isn't his—— ! " Fleda sighed as if she couldn't express it ; she piled it up, as she would have said ; holding Mrs. Gereth with dilated eyes she seemed to sound her for the effect of these professions. " It's idiotic," she wearily smiled ; " it's so strange that I'm almost angry for it, and the strangest part of all is that it isn't even happiness. It's anguish—it was from the first ; from the first there was a bitter-

THE SPOILS OF POYNTON

ness and a dread. But I owe you every word of the
truth. You don't do him justice either ; he's a dear,
I assure you he's a dear : I'd trust him to the last
breath. I don't think you really know him. He's
ever so much cleverer than he makes any show of ;
he's remarkable in his own shy way. You told me at
Ricks that you wanted me to let myself go, and I've
' gone ' quite far enough to discover as much as that,
as well as all sorts of other delightful things about
him. You'll tell me I make myself out worse than I
am," said the girl, feeling more and more in her companion's attitude a quality that treated her speech
as a desperate rigmarole and even perhaps as a piece
of cold immodesty. She wanted to make herself out
" bad "—it was a part of her justification ; but it
suddenly occurred to her that such a picture of her
extravagance imputed a want of gallantry to the
young man. " I don't care for anything you think,"
she declared, " because Owen, don't you know ? sees
me as I am. He's so kind that it makes up for everything ! "

This attempt at gaiety was futile ; the silence with
which for a minute her great swindled benefactress
greeted her troubled plea brought home to her afresh
that she was on the bare defensive. " Is it a part of
his kindness never to come near you ? " Mrs. Gereth
inquired at last. " Is it a part of his kindness to leave
you without an inkling of where he is ? " She rose
again from where Fleda had kept her down ; she
seemed to tower there in the majesty of her gathered
wrong. " Is it a part of his kindness that after I've
toiled as I've done for six days, and with my own
weak hands, which I haven't spared, to denude myself, in your interest, to that point that I've nothing
left, as I may say, but what I have on my back—is
it a part of his kindness that you're not even able to
produce him for me ? "

There was a high contempt in this which was for
Owen quite as much, and in the light of which Fleda
felt that her effort at plausibility had been mere
grovelling. She rose from the sofa with an humiliated
sense of rising from ineffectual knees. That discom-
fort, however, lived but an instant : it was swept
away in a rush of loyalty to the absent. She herself
could bear his mother's scorn, but to avert it from
all *his* decency she broke out with a quickness that
was like the raising of an arm. " Don't blame him—
don't blame him : he'd do anything on earth for me !
It was I," said Fleda eagerly, " who sent him back to
her. I made him go, I pushed him out of the house.
I declined to have anything to say to him except on
another footing."

Mrs. Gereth stared as at some gross material
ravage. " Another footing ? What other footing ? "

" The one I've already made so clear to you : my
having it from her in black and white, as you may say,
that she freely gives him up."

" Then you think he lies when he tells you he has
recovered his liberty ? "

Fleda failed of presence of mind a moment ; after
which she exclaimed with a certain hard pride : " He's
enough in love with me for anything ! "

" For anything apparently save to act like a man
and impose his reason and his will on your incredible
folly. For anything save to put an end, as any man
worthy of the name would have put it, to your
systematic, to your idiotic perversity. What are you,
after all, my dear, I should like to know, that a gentleman who offers you what Owen offers should have
to meet such wonderful exactions, to take such
extraordinary precautions about your sweet little
scruples ? " Her resentment rose to a high insolence
which Fleda took full in the face and which, for the
moment at least, had the horrible force to present to

her vengefully a showy side of the truth. It gave her a blinding glimpse of lost alternatives. "I don't know what to think of him," Mrs. Gereth went on; "I don't know what to call him: I'm so ashamed of him that I can scarcely speak of him even to *you*. But indeed I'm so ashamed of you both together that I scarcely know in common decency where to look." She paused to give Fleda the full benefit of this harsh statement; then she exclaimed with the very best of her coarseness: "Any one but a jackass would have tucked you under his arm and marched you off to the Registrar!"

Fleda wondered; with her free imagination she could wonder even while her cheek stung from a slap. "To the Registrar?"

"That would have been the sane sound immediate course to adopt. With a grain of gumption you'd both instantly have felt it. *I* should have found a way to take you, you know, if I had been what Owen's supposed to be. *I* should have got the business over first—then the rest could come when you liked! Good God, girl, your place was to stand before me as a woman honestly married. One doesn't know what one has hold of in touching you, and you must excuse my saying that you're literally unpleasant to me to meet as you are. Then at least we could have talked, and Owen, if he had the ghost of a sense of humour, could have snapped his fingers at your refinements."

This stirring speech affected our young lady as if it had been the shake of a tambourine borne toward her from a gipsy dance: her head seemed to go round and she felt a sudden passion in her feet. The thrill, however, was but meagrely expressed in the flatness with which she heard herself presently say: "I'll go to the Registrar now."

"Now?" Magnificent was the sound Mrs. Gereth

threw into this monosyllable. "And pray who's to take you?" Fleda gave a colourless smile, and her companion continued: "Do you literally mean that you can't put your hand upon him?" Fleda's sick grimace appeared to irritate her; she made a short imperious gesture. "Find him for me, you fool—*find* him for me!"

"What do you want of him," Fleda dismally asked —"feeling as you do to both of us?"

"Never mind how I feel, and never mind what I say when I'm furious!" Mrs. Gereth still more incisively added. "Of course I cling to you, you wretches, or I shouldn't suffer as I do. What I want of him is to see that he takes you; what I want of him is to go with you myself to the place." She looked round the room as if, in feverish haste, for a mantle to catch up; she bustled to the window as if to spy out a cab: she would allow half an hour for the job. Already in her bonnet, she had snatched from the sofa a garment for the street: she jerked it on as she came back. "Find him, find him," she repeated; "come straight out with me to try at least and get *at* him!"

"How can I get *at* him? He'll come when he's ready," our young woman quavered.

Mrs. Gereth turned on her sharply. "Ready for what? Ready to see me ruined without a reason or a reward?"

Fleda could at first say nothing; the worst of it all was the something still unspoken between them. Neither of them dared utter it, but the influence of it was in the girl's tone when she returned at last with great gentleness: "Don't be cruel to me—I'm very unhappy." The words produced a visible impression on Mrs. Gereth, who held her face averted and sent off through the window a gaze that kept pace with the long caravan of her treasures. Fleda knew she was watching it wind up the avenue of Poynton—Fleda participated indeed fully in the vision ; so that after a little the most consoling thing seemed to her to add : " I don't see why in the world you take so for granted that he's, as you say, ' lost.' "

Mrs. Gereth continued to stare out of the window, and her stillness denoted some success in controlling herself. " If he's not lost why are you unhappy ? "

" I'm unhappy because I torment you and you don't understand me."

" No, Fleda, I don't understand you," said Mrs. Gereth, finally facing her again. " I don't understand you at all, and it's as if you and Owen were of quite another race and another flesh. You make me feel very old-fashioned and simple and bad. But you must take me as I am, since you take so much else *with* me ! " She spoke now with the drop of her resentment, with a dry and weary calm. " It would have been better for me if I had never known you," she pursued, " and certainly better if I hadn't taken such an extraordinary fancy to you. But that too was inevitable : everything, I suppose, is inevitable. It was all my own doing—you didn't run after me : I pounced on you and caught you up. You're a stiff little beggar, in spite of your pretty manners : yes, you're hideously misleading. I hope you feel how handsome it is of me to recognise the independence of your character. It was your clever sympathy that did it—your beautiful feeling for those accursed vanities. You were sharper about them than any one I had ever known, and that was a thing I simply couldn't resist. Well," the poor lady concluded after a pause, " you see where it has landed us ! "

" If you'll go for him yourself I'll wait here," said Fleda.

Mrs. Gereth, holding her mantle together, appeared for a while to consider. " To his club, do you mean ? "

" Isn't it there, when he's in town, that he has a room ? He has at present no other London address," Fleda said. " It's there one writes to him."

" How do *I* know, with my wretched relations with him ? " Mrs. Gereth cried.

" Mine have not been quite so bad as that," Fleda desperately smiled. Then she added : " His silence, *her* silence, our hearing nothing at all—what are these but the very things on which, at Poynton and at Ricks, you rested your assurance that everything is at an end between them ? "

Mrs. Gereth looked dark and void. " Yes, but I hadn't heard from you then that you could invent nothing better than, as you call it, to send him back to her."

" Ah but on the other hand "—the girl sprung to this—" you've learned from them what you didn't know, you've learned by Mrs. Brigstock's visit that he cares for me." She found herself in the position of availing herself of optimistic arguments that she formerly had repudiated ; her refutation of her companion had completely changed its ground. A fever of ingenuity had started to burn in her, though she was painfully conscious, on behalf of her success, that it was visible as fever. She could herself see the reflexion of it gleam in her critic's sombre eyes.

" You plunge me in stupefaction," that personage answered, " and at the same time you terrify me. Your account of Owen's inconceivable, and yet I don't know what to hold on by. He cares for you, it does appear, and yet in the same breath you tell me that nothing is more possible than that he's spending these days at Waterbath. Pardon me if I'm so dull as not to see my way in such darkness. If he's at Waterbath he doesn't care for you. If he cares for you he's not at Waterbath."

" Then where is he ? " poor Fleda helplessly wailed.

She caught herself up, however ; she would do her best to be brave and clear. Before Mrs. Gereth could reply, with due obviousness, that this was a question for her not to ask but to answer, she found an air of assurance to say : " You simplify far too much. You always did and you always will. The tangle of life is much more intricate than you've ever, I think, felt it to be. You slash into it," cried Fleda finely, " with a great pair of shears ; you nip at it as if you were one of the Fates ! If Owen's at Waterbath he's there to wind everything up."

His mother shook her head with slow austerity. " You don't believe a word you're saying. I've frightened you, as you've frightened me : you're whistling in the dark to keep up our courage. I do simplify, doubtless, if to simplify is to fail to comprehend the inanity of a passion that bewilders a young blockhead with bugaboo barriers, with hideous and monstrous sacrifices. I can only repeat that you're beyond me. Your perversity's a thing to howl over. However," the poor woman continued with a break in her voice, a long hesitation and then the dry triumph of her will, " I'll never mention it to you again ! Owen I can just make out ; for Owen *is* a blockhead. Owen's a blockhead," she repeated with a quiet tragic finality, looking straight into Fleda's eyes. " I don't know why you dress up so the fact that he's disgustingly weak."

Fleda at last, before her companion's, lowered her look. " Because I love him. It's because he's weak that he needs me," she added.

" That was why his father, whom he exactly resembles, needed *me*. And I didn't fail his father," said Mrs. Gereth. She gave her visitor a moment to appreciate the remark ; after which she pursued : " Mona Brigstock isn't weak. She's stronger than you ! "

"I never thought she was weak," Fleda answered. She looked vaguely round the room with a new purpose : she had lost sight of her umbrella.

"I did tell you to let yourself go, but it's clear enough that you really haven't," Mrs. Gereth declared. "If Mona has got him——"

Fleda had accomplished her search ; her hostess paused. "If Mona has got him ? " the girl panted, tightening the umbrella.

"Well," said Mrs. Gereth profoundly, "it will be clear enough that Mona *has*."

"Has let herself go ? "

"Has let herself go." Mrs. Gereth spoke as if she meant it to the fullest extent of her cynicism and saw it in every detail.

Fleda felt the tone and finished her preparation ; then she went and opened the door. "We'll look for him together," she said to her friend, who stood a moment taking in her face. "They may know something about him at the Colonel's."

"We'll go there." Mrs. Gereth had picked up her gloves and her purse. "But the first thing," she went on, "will be to wire to Poynton."

"Why not to Waterbath at once ? " Fleda asked.

Her companion wondered. "In *your* name ? "

"In my name. I noticed a place at the corner."

While Fleda held the door open Mrs. Gereth drew on her gloves. "Forgive me," she presently said. "Kiss me," she added.

Fleda, on the threshold, kissed her. Then they both went out.

477

XIX

In the place at the corner, on the chance of its saving time, Fleda wrote her telegram—wrote it in silence under Mrs. Gereth's eye and then in silence handed it to her. "I send this to Waterbath, on the possibility of your being there, to ask you to come to me." Mrs. Gereth held it a moment, read it more than once; then keeping it, and with her eyes on her companion, seemed to consider. There was the dawn of a kindness in her look; Fleda measured in it, as the reward of complete submission, a slight relaxation of her rigour.

"Wouldn't it perhaps after all be better," she asked, "before doing this, to see if we can make his whereabouts certain?"

"Why so? It will be always so much done," said Fleda. "Though I'm poor," she added with a smile, "I don't mind the shilling."

"The shilling's *my* shilling," said Mrs. Gereth.

Fleda stayed her hand. "No, no—I'm superstitious. To succeed it must be all me!"

"Well, if that will make it succeed!" Mrs. Gereth took back her shilling, but she still kept the telegram. "As he's most probably not there——"

"If he shouldn't be there," Fleda interrupted, "there will be no harm done."

"If he 'shouldn't be' there!" Mrs. Gereth ejaculated. "Heaven help us, how you assume it!"

478

" I'm only prepared for the worst. The Brigstocks
will simply send any telegram on."

" Where will they send it ? "

" Presumably to Poynton."

" They'll read it first," said Mrs. Gereth. " Yes,
Mona will. She'll open it under the pretext of having
it repeated, and then will probably do nothing. She'll
keep it as a proof of your immodesty."

" What of that ? " asked Fleda.

" You don't mind her seeing it ? "

Rather musingly and absently she shook her head.
" I don't mind anything."

" Well then, that's all right," said Mrs. Gereth as
wanting only to feel she had been irreproachably
considerate. After this she was gentler still, yet had
another point to clear up. " Why have you given, for
a reply, your sister's address ? "

" Because if he does come to me he must come to
me there. If that telegram goes," said Fleda, " I
return to Maggie's to-night."

Her friend seemed to wonder at this. " You won't
receive him here with me ? "

" No, I won't receive him here with you. Only
where I received him last—only there again." As to
this Fleda was firm.

But Mrs. Gereth had obviously now had some
practice in following queer movements prompted
by queer feelings. She resigned herself, though she
fingered the paper a moment longer. She appeared
to hesitate, then brought out : " You couldn't then,
if I release you, make your message a little stronger ? "

Fleda gave her a faint smile. " He'll come if he
can."

She met fully what this conveyed ; with decision
she pushed in the telegram. But she laid her hand
quickly on another form and with still greater decision wrote another message. " This from *me*,"

she said to Fleda when she had finished : " to catch him possibly at Poynton. Will you read it ? "

Fleda turned away. " Thank you."

" It's stronger than yours."

" I don't care "—and the girl moved to the door. Mrs. Gereth, having paid for the second missive, rejoined her, and they drove together to Owen's club, where the elder lady alone got out. Fleda, from the hansom, watched through the glass doors her brief conversation with the hall-porter and then met in silence her return with the news that he had not seen Owen for a fortnight and was keeping his letters till called for. These had been the last orders ; there were a dozen letters lying there. He had no more information to give, but they would see what they could find at Colonel Gereth's. To any connexion with this inquiry, however, Fleda now roused herself to object, and her friend had indeed to recognise that on second thoughts it couldn't be quite to the taste of either of them to advertise in the remoter reaches of the family that they had forfeited the confidence of the master of Poynton. The letters lying at the club proved effectively that he was not in London, and this was the question that immediately concerned them. Nothing could concern them further till the answers to their telegrams should have had time to arrive. Mrs. Gereth had got back into the cab, and, still at the door of the club, they sat staring at their need of patience. Fleda's eyes rested, in the great hard street, on passing figures that struck her as puppets pulled by strings. After a little the driver challenged them through the hole in the top. " Anywhere in particular, ladies ? "

Fleda decided. " Drive to Euston, please."

" You won't wait for what we may hear ? " Mrs. Gereth asked.

" Whatever we hear I must go." As the cab went

on she added : " But I needn't drag *you* to the station."

Mrs. Gereth had a pause ; then " Nonsense ! " she sharply replied.

In spite of this sharpness they were now almost equally and almost tremulously mild ; though their mildness took mainly the form of an inevitable sense of nothing left to say. It was the unsaid that occupied them—the thing that for more than an hour they had been going round and round without naming it. Much too early for Fleda's train, they encountered at the station a long half-hour to wait. Fleda made no further allusion to Mrs. Gereth's leaving her ; their dumbness, with the elapsing minutes, grew to be in itself a reconstituted bond. They slowly paced the great grey platform, and presently Mrs. Gereth took the girl's arm and leaned on it with a hard demand for support. It seemed to Fleda not difficult for each to know of what the other was thinking—to know indeed that they had in common two alternating visions, one of which at moments brought them as by a common impulse to a pause. This was the one that was fixed ; the other filled at times the whole space and then was shouldered away. Owen and Mona glared together out of the gloom and disappeared, but the replenishment of Poynton made a shining steady light. The old splendour was there again, the old things were in their places. Our friends looked at them with an equal yearning ; face to face on the platform, they counted them in each other's eyes. Fleda had come back to them by a road as strange as the road they themselves had followed. The wonder of their great journeys, the prodigy of this second one, was the question that made her occasionally stop. Several times she uttered it, asked how this and that difficulty had been met. Mrs. Gereth replied with pale lucidity

—was naturally the person most familiar with the truth that what she undertook was always somehow achieved. To do it was to do it—she had more than one kind of magnificence. She confessed there, audaciously enough, to a sort of arrogance of energy, and Fleda, going on again, her appeal more than answered and her arm rendering service, flushed in her diminished identity with the sense that such a woman was great.

" You do mean literally everything, to the last little miniature on the last little screen ? "

" I mean literally everything.   Go over them with the catalogue ! "

Fleda went over them while they walked again ; she had no need of the catalogue.   At last she spoke once more.   " Even the Maltese cross ? "

" Even the Maltese cross.   Why not that as well as everything else ?—especially as I remembered how you like it."

Finally, after an interval, the girl exclaimed : " But the mere fatigue of it, the exhaustion of such a feat !   I drag you to and fro here while you must be ready to drop."

" I'm very, very tired."   Mrs. Gereth's slow head-shake was tragic.   " I couldn't do it again."

" I doubt if they'd bear it again ! "

" That's another matter : they'd bear it if *I* could. There won't have been, this time either, a shake or a scratch.   But I'm too tired—I very nearly don't care."

" You must sit down then till I go," said Fleda. " We must find a bench."

" No.   I'm tired of *them* : I'm not tired of you. This is the way for you to feel most how much I rest on you."   Fleda had a compunction, wondering as they continued to stroll whether it was right after all to leave her.   She believed, however, that if the flame might for the moment burn low it was far from dying out ; an impression presently confirmed by the way Mrs. Gereth went on : " But one's fatigue's nothing. The idea under which one worked kept one up. For you I *could*—I can still. Nothing will have mattered if *she's* not there."

There was a question that this imposed, but Fleda at first found no voice to utter it : it was the thing that between them, since her arrival, had been so consciously and vividly unsaid. Finally she was able to breathe : " And if she *is* there—if she's there already ? "

Mrs. Gereth's rejoinder too hung back ; then when it came—from sad eyes as well as from lips barely moved—it was unexpectedly merciful. " It will be very hard." That was all now, and it was poignantly simple. The train Fleda was to take had drawn up ; the girl kissed her as if in farewell. Mrs. Gereth submitted, then after a little brought out : " If we *have* lost—— ! "

" If we have lost ? " Fleda repeated as she paused again.

" You'll all the same come abroad with me ? "

" It will seem very strange to me if you want me. But whatever you ask, whatever you need, that I will now always do."

" I shall need your company," said Mrs. Gereth. Fleda wondered an instant if this were not practically a demand for penal submission—for a surrender that, in its complete humility, would be a long expiation. But there was none of the latent chill of the vindictive in the sequel. " We can always, as time goes on, talk of them together."

" Of the spoils—— ? " Fleda had selected a third-class compartment : she stood a moment looking into it and at a fat woman with a basket who had already taken possession. " Always ? " she said, turning again to her friend. " Never ! " she exclaimed. She got into the carriage and two men with bags and boxes immediately followed, blocking up door and window so long that when she was able to look out again Mrs. Gereth had gone.

XX

THERE came to her at her sister's no telegram in answer to her own : the rest of that day and the whole of the next elapsed without a word either from Owen or from his mother. She was free, however, to her infinite relief, from any direct dealing with suspense, and conscious, to her surprise, of nothing that could show her, or could show Maggie and her brother-in-law, that she was excited. Her excitement was composed of pulses as swift and fine as the revolutions of a spinning top : she supposed she was going round, but went round so fast that she couldn't even feel herself move. Her trouble occupied some quarter of her soul that had closed its doors for the day and shut out even her own sense of it ; she might perhaps have heard something if she had pressed her ear to a partition. Instead of that she sat with her patience in a cold still chamber from which she could look out in quite another direction. This was to have achieved an equilibrium to which she couldn't have given a name : indifference, resignation, despair were the terms of a forgotten tongue. The time even seemed not long, for what were the stages of the journey but the very items of Mrs. Gereth's surrender ? The detail of that performance, which filled the scene, was what Fleda had now before her eyes. The part of her loss that she could think of was the reconstituted splendour of Poynton. It was the beauty she was most touched by that, in tons, she had lost—the beauty that, charged upon big wagons, had safely crept to its home. But the loss was a gain to memory and love ; it was to her too at last that, in condonation of her treachery, the spoils had crept back. She greeted them with open arms ; she thought of them hour after hour ; they made a company with which solitude was warm and a picture that, at this crisis, overlaid poor Maggie's scant mahogany. It was really her obliterated passion that had revived, and with it an immense assent to Mrs. Gereth's early judgement of her. She equally, she felt, was of the religion, and like any other of the passionately pious she could worship now even in the desert. Yes, it was all for *her* ; far round as she had gone she had been strong enough : her love had gathered them in. She wanted indeed no catalogue to count them over ; the array of them, miles away, was complete ; each piece, in its turn, was perfect to her ; she could have drawn up a catalogue from memory. Thus again she lived with them, and she thought of them without a question of any personal right. That they might have been, that they might still be hers, that they were perhaps already another's, were ideas that had too little to say to her. They were nobody's at all— too proud, unlike base animals and humans, to be reducible to anything so narrow. It was Poynton that was theirs ; they had simply recovered their own. The joy of that for them was the source of the strange peace that had descended like a charm.

It was broken on the third day by a telegram from Mrs. Gereth. "Shall be with you at 11.30—don't meet me at station." Fleda turned this over ; she was sufficiently expert not to disobey the injunction. She had only an hour to take in its meaning, but that hour was longer than all the previous time. If Maggie had studied her convenience the day Owen came, Maggie was also at the present juncture a miracle of refinement. Increasingly and resentfully mystified, in spite of all reassurance, by the impression that Fleda suffered much more than she gained from the grandeur of the Gereths, she had it at heart to exemplify the perhaps truer distinction of nature that characterised the house of Vetch. She was not, like poor Fleda, at every one's beck, and the announced visitor was to see no more of her than what the arrangement of luncheon might tantalisingly show. Maggie described herself to her sister as intending for a just provocation even the agreement she had had with her husband that he also should keep away. Fleda accordingly awaited alone the subject of so many manœuvres—a period that was slightly prolonged even after the drawing-room door, at 11.30, was thrown open. Mrs. Gereth stood there with a face that spoke plain, but no sound fell from her till the withdrawal of the maid, whose attention had immediately attached itself to the rearrangement of a window-blind and who seemed, while she bustled at it, to contribute to the pregnant silence ; before the duration of which, however, she retreated with a sudden stare.

" He has done it," said Mrs. Gereth, turning her eyes avoidingly but not unperceivingly about her and in spite of herself dropping an opinion upon the few objects in the room. Fleda, on her side, in her silence observed how characteristically she looked at Maggie's possessions before looking at Maggie's sister. The girl understood and at first had nothing to say ; she was still dumb while their guest selected, after dryly balancing, a seat less distasteful than the one that happened to be nearest. On the sofa near the window the poor woman finally showed what the two last days had done for the age of her face. Her eyes at last met Fleda's. " It's the end."

" They're married ? "

" They're married."

Fleda came to the sofa in obedience to the impulse
to sit down by her ; then paused before her while
Mrs. Gereth turned up a dead grey mask. A tired
old woman sat there with empty hands in her lap.
" I've heard nothing," said Fleda. " No answer
came."

" That's the only answer. It's the answer to everything." So Fleda saw ; for a minute she looked over
her companion's head and far away. " He wasn't at
Waterbath. Mrs. Brigstock must have read your
telegram and kept it. But mine, the one to Poynton,
brought something. ' We are here—what do you
want ? ' " Mrs. Gereth stopped as if with a failure
of voice ; on which Fleda sank upon the sofa and
made a movement to take her hand. It met no
response ; there could be no attenuation. Fleda
waited ; they sat facing each other like strangers. " I
wanted to go down," Mrs. Gereth presently continued.
" Well, I went."

All the girl's effort tended for the time to a single
aim—that of taking the thing with outward detachment, speaking of it as having happened to Owen
and to his mother and not in any degree to herself.
Something at least of this was in the encouraging
way she said : " Yesterday morning ? "

" Yesterday morning. I saw him."

Fleda hesitated. " Did you see *her* ? "

" Thank God, no ! "

Fleda laid on her arm a hand of vague comfort, of
which Mrs. Gereth took no notice. " You've been
capable, just to tell me, of this wretched journey—
of this consideration that I don't deserve ? "

" We're together, we're together," said Mrs.
Gereth. She looked helpless as she sat there, her
eyes, unseeingly enough now, on a tall Dutch clock,

old but rather poor, that Maggie had had as a wedding-gift and that eked out the bareness of the room.

To Fleda, in the face of the event, it appeared that this was exactly what they were not : the last inch of common ground, the ground of their past inter-course, had fallen from under them. Yet what was still there was the grand style of her companion's treatment of her. Mrs. Gereth couldn't stand upon small questions, couldn't in conduct make small differences. " You're magnificent ! " her young friend exclaimed. " There's an extraordinary greatness in your generosity."

" We're together, we're together," Mrs. Gereth lifelessly repeated. " That's all we *are* now ; it's all we have." The words brought to Fleda a sudden vision of the empty little house at Ricks ; such a vision might also have been what her companion found in the face of the stopped Dutch clock. Yet with this it was clear she would still show no bitter-ness : she had done with that, had given the last drop to those horrible hours in London. No passion even was left her, and her forbearance only added to the force with which she represented the final vanity of everything.

Fleda was so far from a wish to triumph that she was absolutely ashamed of having anything to say for herself ; but there was one thing, all the same, that not to say was impossible. " That he has done it, that he couldn't *not* do it, shows how right I was." It settled for ever her attitude, and she spoke as if for her own mind ; then after a little she added very gently, for Mrs. Gereth's : " That's to say it shows he was bound to her by an obligation that, however much he may have wanted to, he couldn't in any sort of honour break."

Blanched and bleak, Mrs. Gereth looked at her. " What sort of an obligation do you call that ? No such obligation exists for an hour between any man and any woman who have hatred on one side. He had ended by hating her, and he hates her now more than ever."

" Did he tell you so ? " Fleda asked.

" No. He told me nothing but the great gawk of a fact. I saw him but for three minutes." She was silent again, and Fleda, as before some lurid image of this interview, sat without speaking. " Do you wish to appear as if you don't care ? " Mrs. Gereth presently demanded.

" I'm trying not to think of myself."

" Then if you're thinking of Owen how can you *bear* to think ? "

Sadly and submissively Fleda shook her head ; the slow tears had come into her eyes. " I can't. I don't understand—I don't understand ! " she broke out.

" *I* do then." Mrs. Gereth looked hard at the floor. " There was no obligation at the time you saw him last—when you sent him, hating her as he did, back to her."

" If he went," Fleda asked, " doesn't that exactly prove that he recognised one ? "

" He recognised rot ! You know what *I* think of him." Fleda knew ; she had no wish to provoke a fresh statement. Mrs. Gereth made one—it was her sole faint flicker of passion—to the extent of declaring that he was too abjectly weak to deserve the name of a man. For all Fleda cared !—it was his weakness she loved in him. " He took strange ways of pleasing you ! " her friend went on. " There was no obligation till suddenly, the other day, the situation changed."

Fleda wondered. " Suddenly—— ? "

" It came to Mona's knowledge—I can't tell you how, but it came—that the things I was sending back had begun to arrive at Poynton. I had sent them for you, but it was *her* I touched." Mrs. Gereth paused ; Fleda was too absorbed in her explanation to do anything but take blankly the full cold breath of this. " They were there, and that determined her."

" Determined her to what ? "

" To act, to take means."

" To take means ? " Fleda repeated.

" I can't tell you what they were, but they were powerful. She knew how," said Mrs. Gereth.

Fleda received with the same stoicism the quiet immensity of this allusion to the person who had *not* known how. But it made her think a little, and the thought found utterance, with unconscious irony, in the simple interrogation : " Mona ? "

" Why not ? She's a brute."

" But if he knew that so well, what chance was there in it for her ? "

" How can I tell you ? How can I talk of such horrors ? I can only give you, of the situation, what I see. He knew it, yes. But as she couldn't make him forget it she tried to make him like it. She tried and she succeeded : that's what she did. She's after all so much less of a fool than he. And what *else* had he originally liked ? " Mrs. Gereth shrugged her shoulders. " She did what you wouldn't ! " Fleda's face had grown dark with her wonder at the sense of this, but her friend's empty hands offered no balm to the pain in it. " It was that if it was anything. Nothing else meets the misery of it. Then there was quick work. Before he could turn round he was married."

Fleda, as if she had been holding her breath, gave the sigh of a listening child. " At that place you spoke of in town ? "

" At a Registry-office—like a pair of low atheists."

491

The girl considered. " What do people say of that ? I mean the ' world.' "

" Nothing, because nobody knows. They're to be married on the seventeenth at Waterbath church. If anything else comes out everybody's a little prepared. It will pass for some stroke of diplomacy, some move in the game, some outwitting of *me*. It's known there has been a great row with me."

Fleda was mystified. " People surely know at Poynton," she objected, " if, as you say, she's there."

" She was there, day before yesterday, only for a few hours. She met him in London and went down to see the things."

Fleda remembered that she had seen them only once. " Did *you* see them ? " she then ventured to ask.

" Everything."

" Are they right ? "

" Quite right. There's nothing like them," said Mrs. Gereth. At this her companion took up one of her hands again and kissed it as she had done in London. " Mona went back that night ; she was not there yesterday. Owen stayed on," she added.

Fleda stared. " Then she's not to live there ? "

" Rather ! But not till after the public marriage." Mrs. Gereth seemed to muse ; then she brought out : " She'll live there alone."

" Alone ? "

" She'll have it to herself."

" He won't live with her ? "

" Never ! But she's none the less his wife, and you're not," said Mrs. Gereth, getting up. " Our only chance is the chance she may die."

Fleda appeared to measure it : she appreciated her visitor's magnanimous use of the plural. " Mona won't die," she replied.

" Well, *I* shall, thank God ! Till then "—and with

this, for the first time, Mrs. Gereth put out her hand
—" don't desert me."

Fleda took her hand, clasping it for a renewal of
engagements already taken. She said nothing, but
her silence committed her as solemnly as the vow
of a nun. The next moment something occurred to
her. " I mustn't put myself in your son's way, you
know."

Mrs. Gereth gave a laugh of bitterness. " You're
prodigious ! But how shall you possibly be more
out of it ? Owen and I——" She didn't finish her
sentence.

" That's your great feeling about him," Fleda
said ; " but how, after what has happened, can it be
his about you ? "

Mrs. Gereth waited. " How do you know what
has happened ? You don't know what I said to
him."

" Yesterday ? "

" Yesterday."

They looked at each other with a long deep gaze.
Then, as Mrs. Gereth seemed again about to speak,
the girl, closing her eyes, made a gesture of strong
prohibition. " Don't tell me ! "

" Merciful powers, how you worship him ! " Mrs.
Gereth wonderingly moaned. It was for Fleda the
shake that made the cup overflow. She had a pause,
that of the child who takes time to know that he
responds to an accident with pain ; then, dropping
again on the sofa, she broke into tears. They were
beyond control, they came in long sobs, which for a
moment her friend, almost with an air of indifference, stood hearing and watching. At last Mrs.
Gereth too sank down again. Mrs. Gereth soundlessly wearily wept.

XXI

" It looks just like Waterbath ; but, after all, we bore
that together " : these words formed part of a letter
in which, before the seventeenth, Mrs. Gereth, writing from disfigured Ricks, named to Fleda the day
on which she would be expected to arrive there on
a second visit. " I shan't for a long time to come,"
the missive continued, " be able to receive any one
who may *like* it, who would try to smooth it down,
and me with it ; but there are always things you
and I can comfortably hate together, for you're the
only person who comfortably understands. You
don't understand quite everything, but of all my
acquaintance you're far away the least stupid. For
action you're no good at all ; but action's over, for
me, for ever, and you'll have the great merit of
knowing when I'm brutally silent what I shall be
thinking about. Without setting myself up for
your equal I daresay I shall also know what are
your own thoughts. Moreover, with nothing else
but my four walls, you'll at any rate be a bit of
furniture. For that, a little, you know, I've always
taken you—quite one of my best finds. So come
if possible on the fifteenth."

The position of a scrap of furniture was one that
Fleda could conscientiously accept, and she by no
means insisted on so high a place in the list. This
communication made her easier, if only by its ac-

knowledgment that her friend had something left: it
still implied recognition of the principle of property.
Something to hate, and to hate " comfortably," was
at least not the utter destitution to which, after their
last interview, she had helplessly seemed to see the
ex-mistress of Poynton go forth. She remembered
indeed that in the state in which they first saw it she
herself had " liked " the blest refuge of Ricks ; and
she now wondered if the tact for which she was commended had then operated to make her keep her
kindness out of sight. She was at present ashamed of
such obliquity and made up her mind that if this
happy impression, quenched in the translated spoils,
should revive on the spot, she would utter it to her
companion without reserve. Yes, she was capable
of as much " action " as that : all the more that the
spirit of her hostess seemed for the time at least
wholly to have failed. The mother's three minutes
with the son had been a blow to all talk of travel,
and after her woeful hour at Maggie's she had, like
some great moaning wounded bird, made her way
with wings of anguish back to the nest she knew
she should find empty. Fleda, on that dire day,
could neither keep her nor give her up ; she had
pressingly offered to return with her, but Mrs.
Gereth, in spite of the theory that their common
grief was a bond, had even declined all escort to
the station, conscious apparently of something abject
in her collapse and almost fiercely eager, as with
a personal shame, to be unwatched. All she had
said to Fleda was that she would go back to Ricks
that night, and the girl had lived for days after with
a dreadful image of her position and her misery there.
She had had a vision of her now lying prone on some
unmade bed, now pacing a bare floor as a lioness
deprived of her cubs. There had been moments
when her mind's ear was strained to listen for some

sound of grief wild enough to be wafted from afar. But the first sound, at the end of a week, had been a note announcing, without reflexions, that the plan of going abroad had been abandoned. " It has come to me indirectly, but with much appearance of truth, that *they* are going—for an indefinite time. That quite settles it ; I shall stay where I am, and as soon as I've turned round again I shall look for you." The second letter had come a week later, and on the fifteenth Fleda was on her way to Ricks.

Her arrival took the form of a surprise very nearly as violent as that of the other time. The elements were different, but the effect, like the other, arrested her on the threshold : she stood there stupefied and delighted at the magic of a passion of which such a picture represented the low-water mark. Wound up but sincere, and passing quickly from room to room, Fleda broke out before she even sat down. " If you turn me out of the house for it, my dear, there isn't a woman in England for whom it wouldn't be a privilege to live here." Mrs. Gereth was as honestly bewildered as she had of old been falsely calm. She looked about at the few sticks that, as she afterwards phrased it, she had gathered in, and then hard at her guest, as to protect herself against a joke all too cruel. The girl's heart gave a leap, for this stare was the sign of an opportunity. Mrs. Gereth was all unwitting ; she didn't in the least know what she had done. Therefore as Fleda could tell her, Fleda suddenly became the one who knew most. That counted for the moment as a splendid position ; it almost made all the difference. Yet what contradicted it was the vivid presence of the artist's idea. " Where on earth did you put your hand on such beautiful things ? "

" Beautiful things ? " Mrs. Gereth turned again to the little worn bleached stuffs and the sweet spindle-legs. "They're the wretched things that were here—that stupid starved old woman's."

"The maiden-aunt's, the nicest, the dearest old woman that ever lived? I thought you had got rid of the maiden-aunt."

"She was stored in an empty barn—stuck away for a sale; a matter that, fortunately, I've had neither time nor freedom of mind to arrange. I've simply, in my extremity, fished her out again."

"You've simply, in your extremity, made a delight of her." Fleda took the highest line and the upper hand, and as Mrs. Gereth, challenging her cheerfulness, turned again a lustreless eye over the contents of the place, she broke into a rapture that was unforced, yet that she was conscious of an advantage in being able to feel. She moved, as she had done on the previous occasion, from one piece to another, with looks of recognition and hands that lightly lingered, but she was as feverishly jubilant now as she had of old been anxious and mute. "Ah the little melancholy tender tell-tale things: how can they *not* speak to you and find a way to your heart? It's not the great chorus of Poynton; but you're not, I'm sure, either so proud or so broken as to be reached by nothing but that. This is a voice so gentle, so human, so feminine—a faint far-away voice with the little quaver of a heart-break. You've listened to it unawares; for the arrangement and effect of everything — when I compare them with what we found the first day we came down— shows, even if mechanically and disdainfully exercised, your admirable, your infallible hand. It's your extraordinary genius; you make things 'compose' in spite of yourself. You've only to be a day or two in a place with four sticks for something to come of it!"

"Then if anything has come of it here, it has

come precisely of just four. That's literally, by the inventory, all there are ! " said Mrs. Gereth.

" If there were more there would be too many to convey the impression in which half the beauty resides — the impression somehow of something dreamed and missed, something reduced, relinquished, resigned : the poetry, as it were, of something sensibly *gone*." Fleda ingeniously and triumphantly worked it out. " Ah, there's something here that will never be in the inventory ! "

" Does it happen to be in your power to give it a name ? " Mrs. Gereth's face showed the dim dawn of an amusement at finding herself seated at the feet of her pupil.

" I can give it a dozen. It's a kind of fourth dimension. It's a presence, a perfume, a touch. It's a soul, a story, a life. There's ever so much more here than you and I. We're in fact just three ! "

" Oh if you count the ghosts—— ! "

" Of course I count the ghosts, confound you ! It seems to me ghosts count double—for what they were and for what they are. Somehow there were no ghosts at Poynton," Fleda went on. " That was the only fault."

Mrs. Gereth, considering, appeared to fall in with this fine humour. " Poynton was too splendidly happy."

" Poynton was too splendidly happy," Fleda promptly echoed.

" But it's cured of that now," her companion added.

" Yes, henceforth there'll be a ghost or two."

Mrs. Gereth thought again : she found her young friend suggestive. " Only *she* won't see them."

" No, ' she ' won't see them." Then Fleda said : " What I mean is, for this dear one of ours, that if she had (as I *know* she did ; it's in the very touch of the air !) a great accepted pain——"

She had paused an instant, and Mrs. Gereth took her up. " Well, if she had ? "

Fleda still hung fire. " Why, it was worse than yours."

Mrs. Gereth debated. " Very likely." Then she too hesitated. " The question is if it was worse than yours."

" Mine ? " Fleda looked vague.

" Precisely. Yours."

At this our young lady smiled. " Yes, because it was a disappointment. She ha¹ been so sure."

" I see. And you were never sure."

" Never. Besides, I'm happy," said Fleda.

Mrs. Gereth met her eyes a while. " Goose ! " she quietly remarked as she turned away. There was a curtness in it ; nevertheless it represented a considerable part of the basis of their new life.

On the eighteenth *The Morning Post* had at last its clear message, a brief account of the marriage, from the residence of the bride's mother, of Mr. Owen Gereth of Poynton Park to Miss Mona Brigstock of Waterbath. There were two ecclesiastics and six bridesmaids and, as Mrs. Gereth subsequently said, a hundred frumps, as well as a special train from town : the scale of the affair sufficiently showed that the preparations had been in hand for some time back. The happy pair were described as having taken their departure for Mr. Gereth's own seat, famous for its unique collection of artistic curiosities. The newspaper and letters, the fruits of the first London post, had been brought to the mistress of Ricks in the garden ; and she lingered there alone a long time after receiving them. Fleda kept at a distance ; she knew what must have happened, for from one of the windows she saw her rigid in a chair, her eyes strange and fixed, the newspaper open on the ground and the letters untouched in her lap. Before the morning's end she had disappeared and the rest of that day remained in her room : it recalled to Fleda, who had picked up the newspaper, the day, months before, on which Owen had come down to Poynton to make his engagement known. The hush of the house at least was the same, and the girl's own waiting, her soft wandering, through the hours : there was a difference indeed sufficiently great and of which her companion's absence might in some degree have represented a considerate recognition. That was at any rate the meaning Fleda, devoutly glad to be alone, attached to her opportunity. Mrs. Gereth's sole allusion the next day to the subject of their thoughts has already been mentioned : it was a dazzled glance at the fact that Mona's quiet pace had really never slackened.

Fleda fully assented. " I said of our disembodied friend here that she had suffered in proportion as she had been sure. But that's not always a source of suffering. It's Mona who must have been sure ! "

" She was sure of *you* ! " Mrs. Gereth returned. But this didn't diminish the satisfaction taken by Fleda in showing how serenely and lucidly she herself could talk.

XXII

HER relation with her wonderful friend had however in becoming a new one begun to shape itself
almost wholly on breaches and omissions. Something had dropped out altogether, and the question
between them, which time would answer, was whether
the change had made them strangers or yokefellows.
It was as if at last, for better or worse, they were, in
a clearer cruder air, really to know each other. Fleda
wondered how Mrs. Gereth had escaped hating her :
there were hours when it seemed that such a feat
might leave after all a scant margin for future accidents. The thing indeed that now came out in its
simplicity was that even in her shrunken state the
lady of Ricks was larger than her wrongs. As for
the girl herself, she had made up her mind that her
feelings had no connexion with the case. It was her
claim that they had never yet emerged from the
seclusion into which, after her friend's visit to her at
her sister's, we saw them precipitately retire : if she
should suddenly meet them in straggling procession
on the road it would be time enough to deal with
them. They were all bundled there together, likes
with dislikes and memories with fears ; and she had
for not thinking of them the excellent reason that
she was too occupied with the actual. The actual
was not that Owen Gereth had seen his necessity
where she had pointed it out ; it was that his mother's

bare spaces demanded all the tapestry the recipient of her bounty could furnish. There were moments during the month that followed when Mrs. Gereth struck her as still older and feebler and as likely to become quite easily amused.

At the end of it, one day, the London paper had another piece of news : " Mr. and Mrs. Owen Gereth, who arrived in town last week, proceed this morning to Paris." They exchanged no word about it till the evening, and none indeed would then have been uttered had not the mistress of Ricks irrelevantly broken out : " I daresay you wonder why I declared the other day with such assurance that he wouldn't live with her. He apparently *is* living with her."

" Surely it's the only proper thing for him to do."

" They're beyond me—I give it up," said Mrs. Gereth.

" I don't give it up—I never did," Fleda returned.

" Then what do you make of his aversion to her ? "

" Oh she has dispelled it."

Mrs. Gereth said nothing for a minute. " You're prodigious in your choice of terms ! " she then simply ejaculated.

But Fleda went luminously on ; she once more enjoyed her great command of her subject. " I think that when you came to see me at Maggie's you saw too many things, you had too many ideas."

" You had none at all," said Mrs. Gereth. " You were completely bewildered."

" Yes, I didn't quite understand—but I think I understand now. The case is simple and logical enough. She's a person who's upset by failure and who blooms and expands with success. There was something she had set her heart upon, set her teeth about—the house exactly as she had seen it."

" She never saw it at all, she never looked at it ! " cried Mrs. Gereth.

" She doesn't look with her eyes ; she looks with her ears. In her own way she had taken it in ; she knew, she felt when it had been touched. That probably made her take an attitude that was extremely disagreeable. But the attitude lasted only while the reason for it lasted."

" Go on—I can bear it now," said Mrs. Gereth. Her companion had just perceptibly paused.

" I know you can, or I shouldn't dream of speaking. When the pressure was removed she came up again. From the moment the house was once more what it had to be her natural charm reasserted itself."

" Her natural charm ! "—Mrs. Gereth could barely articulate.

" It's very great ; everybody thinks so ; there must be something in it. It operated as it had operated before. There's no need of imagining anything very monstrous. Her restored good humour, her splendid beauty and Mr. Owen's impressibility and generosity sufficiently cover the ground. His great bright sun came out ! "

" And his great bright passion for another person went in. Your explanation would doubtless be perfect if he didn't love you."

Fleda was silent a little. " What do you know about his ' loving ' me ? "

" I know what Mrs. Brigstock herself told me."

" You never in your life took her word for any other matter."

" Then won't yours do ? " Mrs. Gereth demanded. " Haven't I had it from your own mouth that he cares for you ? "

Fleda turned pale, but she faced her companion and smiled. " You confound, Mrs. Gereth. You mix things up. You've only had it from my own mouth that I care for *him* ! "

It was doubtless in contradictious allusion to this

(which at the time had made her simply drop her head as in a strange vain reverie) that Mrs. Gereth said, a day or two later to her inmate : " Don't think I shall be a bit affected if I'm here to see it when he comes again to make up to you."

" He won't do that," the girl replied. Then she added, smiling : " But if he should be guilty of such bad taste it wouldn't be nice of you not to be disgusted."

" I'm not talking of disgust ; I'm talking of its opposite," said Mrs. Gereth : " of any reviving pleasure one might feel in such an exhibition. I shall feel none at all. You may personally take it as you like ; but what conceivable good will it do ? "

Fleda wondered. " To me, do you mean ? "

" Deuce take you, no ! To what we don't, you now, by your wish, ever talk about."

" The spoils ? " Fleda considered again. " It will do no good of any sort to anything or any one. That's another question I'd rather we shouldn't discuss, please," she gently added.

Mrs. Gereth shrugged her shoulders. " It certainly isn't worth it ! "

Something in her manner prompted her companion, with a certain inconsequence, to speak again. " That was partly why I came back to you, you know —that there should be the less possibility of anything painful."

" Painful ? " Mrs. Gereth stared. " What pain can I ever feel again ? "

" I meant painful to myself," Fleda, with a slight impatience, explained.

" Oh I see." Her friend was silent a minute. " You use sometimes such odd expressions. Well, I shall last a little, but I shan't last for ever."

" You'll last quite as long—— " But she suddenly dropped.

Mrs. Gereth took her up with a cold smile that seemed the warning of experience against hyperbole. " As long as what, please ? "

The girl thought an instant ; then met the difficulty by adopting, as an amendment, the same tone. " As any danger of the ridiculous."

That did for the time, and she had moreover, as the months went on, the protection of suspended allusions. This protection was marked when, in the following November, she received a letter directed in a hand a quick glance at which sufficed to make her hesitate to open it. She said nothing then or afterwards ; but she opened it, for reasons that had come to her, on the morrow. It consisted of a page and a half from Owen Gereth, dated from Florence, but with no other preliminary. She knew that during the summer he had returned to England with his wife and that after a couple of months they had again gone abroad. She also knew, without communication, that Mrs. Gereth, round whom Ricks had grown submissively and indescribably sweet, had her own view of her daughter-in-law's share in this second migration. It was a piece of calculated insolence— a stroke odiously directed at showing whom it might concern that now she had Poynton fast she was perfectly indifferent to living there. *The Morning Post*, at Ricks, had again been a resource : it was stated in that journal that Mr. and Mrs. Owen Gereth proposed spending the winter in India. There was a person to whom it was clear she led her wretched husband by the nose. Such was the light in which the contemporary scene was offered to Fleda until, in her own room, late at night, she broke the seal of her letter.

" I want you inexpressibly to have as a remembrance something of mine—something of real value. Something from Poynton is what I mean and what

I should prefer. You know everything there, and far
better than I what's best and what isn't. There
are a lot of differences, but aren't some of the smaller
things the most remarkable? I mean for judges,
and for what they'd bring. What I want you to take
from me, and to choose for yourself, is the thing in
the whole house that's most beautiful and precious.
I mean the ' gem of the collection,' don't you know?
If it happens to be of such a sort that you can take
immediate possession of it—carry it right away
with you—so much the better. You're to have it
on the spot, whatever it is. I humbly entreat of you
to go down there and see. The people have complete
instructions: they'll act for you in every possible
way and put the whole place at your service. There's
a thing mamma used to call the Maltese cross and
that I think I've heard her say is very wonderful.
Is *that* the gem of the collection? Perhaps you'd
take it or anything equally convenient. Only I do
want you awfully to let it be the very pick of the place.
Let me feel that I can trust you for this. You won't
refuse if you'll simply think a little what it must be
that makes me ask."

Fleda read that last sentence over more times
even than the rest: she was baffled—she couldn't
think at all of what in particular made him ask. This
was indeed because it might be one of so many things.
She returned for the present no answer; she merely,
little by little, fashioned for herself the form that her
answer should eventually wear. There was only one
form that was possible—the form of doing, at her
time, what he wished. She would go down to Poynton as a pilgrim might go to a shrine, and as to this
she must look out for her chance. She lived with her
letter, before any chance came, a month, and even
after a month it had mysteries for her that she couldn't
meet. What did it mean what did it represent, to

what did it correspond in his imagination or his soul ?
What was behind it, what was before it, what was,
in the deepest depth, within it ? She said to herself
that with these questions she was under no obligation to deal. There was an answer to them that, for
practical purposes, would do as well as another : he
had found in his marriage a happiness so much
greater than, in the distress of his dilemma, he had
been able to take heart to believe, that he now felt
he owed her a token of gratitude for having kept
him in the straight path. That explanation, I say,
she could throw off ; but no explanation in the least
mattered : what determined her was the simple
strength of her impulse to respond. The passion for
which what had happened had made no difference,
the passion that had taken this into account before
as well as after, found here an issue that there was
nothing whatever to choke. It found even a relief
to which her imagination immensely contributed.
Would she act upon his offer ? She would act with
secret rapture. To have as her own something splendid that he had given her, of which the gift had been
his signed desire, would be a greater joy than the
greatest she had believed to be left her, and she felt
that till the sense of this came home she had even
herself not known what burned in her successful
stillness. It was an hour to dream of and watch for ;
to be patient was to draw out the sweetness. She
was capable of feeling it as an hour of triumph, the
triumph of everything in her recent life that had not
held up its head. She moved there in thought—
in the great rooms she knew ; she should be able to
say to herself that, for once at least, her possession
was as complete as that of either of the others whom
it had filled only with bitterness. And a thousand
times yes—her choice should know no scruple : the
thing she should go down to take would be up to the

height of her privilege. The whole place was in her eyes, and she spent for weeks her private hours in a luxury of comparison and debate. It should be one of the smallest things because it should be one she could have close to her ; and it should be one of the finest because it was in the finest he saw his symbol. She said to herself that of what it would symbolise she was content to know nothing more than just what her having it would tell her. At bottom she inclined to the Maltese cross—with the added reason that he had named it. But she would look again and judge afresh ; she would on the spot so handle and ponder that there shouldn't be the shade of a mistake.

Before Christmas she had a natural opportunity to go to London : there was her periodical call on her father to pay as well as a promise to Maggie to redeem. She spent her first night in West Kensington, with the idea of carrying out on the morrow the purpose that had most of a motive. Her father's affection was not inquisitive, but when she mentioned to him that she had business in the country that would oblige her to catch an early train he deprecated her excursion in view of the menace of the weather. It was spoiling for a storm : all the signs of a winter gale were in the air. She replied that she would see what the morning might bring ; and it brought in fact what seemed in London an amendment. She was to go to Maggie the next day, and now that she started her eagerness had become suddenly a pain. She pictured her return that evening with her trophy under her cloak ; so that after looking, from the door-step, up and down the dark street, she decided with a new nervousness and sallied forth to the nearest place of access to the " Underground." The December dawn was dolorous, but there was neither rain nor snow ; it was not even cold, and the atmosphere of West Kensington, purified by the wind, was like a dirty old coat that had been bettered by a dirty old brush. At the end of almost an hour, in the larger station, she had taken her place in a third-class compartment; the prospect before her was the run of eighty minutes to Poynton. The train was a fast one, and she was familiar with the moderate measure of the walk to the park from the spot at which it would drop her.

Once in the country indeed she saw that her father was right: the breath of December was abroad with a force from which the London labyrinth had protected her. The green fields were black, the sky was all alive with the wind; she had, in her anxious sense of the elements, her wonder at what might happen, a reminder of the surmises, in the old days of going to the Continent, that used to worry her on the way, at night, to the horrid cheap crossings by long sea. Something, in a dire degree at this last hour, had begun to press on her heart: it was the sudden imagination of a disaster, or at least of a check, before her errand was achieved. When she said to herself that something might happen she wanted to go faster than the train. But nothing could happen save a dismayed discovery that, by some altogether unlikely chance, the master and mistress of the house had already come back. In that case she must have had a warning, and the fear was but the excess of her hope. It was every one's being exactly where every one was that lent the quality to her visit. Beyond lands and seas and alienated for ever, they in their different ways gave her the impression to take as she had never taken it. At last it was already there, though the darkness of the day had deepened; they had whizzed past Chater—Chater which was the station before the right one. Off in that quarter was an air of wild rain, but there shimmered straight across it a brightness that was the colour of the great interior she had been haunting. That vision settled before her—in the house the house was all ; and as the train drew up she rose, in her mean compartment, quite proudly erect with the thought that all for Fleda Vetch then the house was standing there.

But with the opening of the door she encountered a shock, though for an instant she couldn't have named it : the next moment she saw it was given her by the face of the man advancing to let her out, an old lame porter of the station who had been there in Mrs. Gereth's time and who now recognised her. He looked up at her so hard that she took an alarm and before alighting broke out to him : " They've come back ? " She had a confused absurd sense that even he would know that in this case she mustn't be there. He hesitated, and in a few seconds her alarm had completely changed its ground : it seemed to leap, with her quick jump from the carriage, to the ground that was that of his stare at her. " Smoke ? " She was on the platform with her frightened sniff ; it had taken her a minute to become aware of an extra-ordinary smell. The air was full of it, and there were already heads at the windows of the train, looking out at something she couldn't see. Some one, the only other passenger, had got out of another carriage, and the old porter hobbled off to close his door. The smoke was in her eyes, but she saw the station-master, from the end of the platform, identify her too and come straight at her. He brought her a finer shade of surprise than the porter, and while he was coming she heard a voice at a window of the train say that something was " a good bit off—a mile from the town." That was just what Poynton was. Then her heart stood still at the white wonder in the station-master's face.

" You've come down to it, miss, already ? "

At this she knew. " Poynton's on fire ? "

" Gone, miss—with this awful gale. You weren't wired ? Look out ! " he cried in the next breath, seizing her ; the train was going on, and she had given a lurch that almost made it catch her as it passed. When it had drawn away she became more conscious of the pervading smoke, which the wind seemed to hurl in her face.

" *Gone ?* " She was in the man's hands ; she clung to him.

" Burning still, miss. Ain't it quite too dreadful ? Took early this morning—the whole place is up there."

In her bewildered horror she tried to think. " Have they come back ? "

" Back ? They'll be there all day ! "

" Not Mr. Gereth, I mean—nor his wife ? "

" Nor his mother, miss—not a soul of *them* back. A pack o' servants in charge—not the old lady's lot, eh ? A nice job for caretakers ! Some rotten chimley or one of them portable lamps set down in the wrong place. What has done it is this cruel, cruel night." Then as a great wave of smoke half-choked them he drew her with force to the little waiting-room. " Awkward for you, miss—I see ! "

She felt sick ; she sank upon a seat, staring up at him. " Do you mean that great house is *lost* ? "

" It was near it, I was told, an hour ago—the fury of the flames had got such a start. I was there myself at six, the very first I heard of it. They were fighting it then, but you couldn't quite say they had got it down."

Fleda jerked herself up. " Were they saving the things ? "

" That's just where it was, miss—to get *at* the blessed things. And the want of right help—it maddened me to stand and see 'em muff it. This ain't a place, like, for anything organised. They don't come up to a *reel* emergency."

She passed out of the door that opened toward the village, and met a great acrid gust. She heard a far-off windy roar which, in her dismay, she took for that of flames a mile away, and which, the first instant, acted upon her as a wild solicitation. " I must go there." She had scarcely spoken before the same omen had changed into an appalling check.

Her vivid friend, moreover, had got before her ; he clearly suffered from the nature of the control he had to exercise. " Don't do that, miss—you won't care for it at all." Then as she waveringly stood her ground : " It's not a place for a young lady, nor, if you'll believe me, a sight for them as are in any way affected."

Fleda by this time knew in what way she was affected : she became limp and weak again ; she felt herself give everything up. Mixed with the horror, with the kindness of the station-master, with the smell of cinders and the riot of sound was the raw bitterness of a hope that she might never again in life have to give up so much at such short notice. She heard herself repeat mechanically, yet as if asking it for the first time : " Poynton's *gone* ? "

The man faltered. " What can you call it, miss, if it ain't really saved ? "

A minute later she had returned with him to the waiting-room, where, in the thick swim of things, she saw something like the disc of a clock. " Is there an up-train ? "

" In seven minutes."

She came out on the platform : everywhere she met the smoke. She covered her face with her hands. " I'll go back."

This book designed by
William B. Taylor
is a production of
Heron Books, London

Published by Heron Books, London
By arrangement with Macmillan & Co

Printed and bound by Hazell Watson & Viney Ltd,
Aylesbury, Bucks

Printed and bound in England